Mayne Reid

The Star of Empire

A romance

Mayne Reid

The Star of Empire
A romance

ISBN/EAN: 9783337245566

Printed in Europe, USA, Canada, Australia, Japan

Cover: Foto ©Andreas Hilbeck / pixelio.de

More available books at **www.hansebooks.com**

THE STAR OF EMPIRE

THE STAR OF EMPIRE

A Romance

BY

CAPT. MAYNE REID

AUTHOR OF "THE PIERCED HEART,"
ETC. ETC.

"Westward the course of empire takes its way."—
BISHOP BERKELEY.

LONDON:

JOHN AND ROBERT MAXWELL

MILTON HOUSE, 14 & 15, SHOE LANE, FLEET STREET,
AND
35, ST. BRIDE STREET, LUDGATE CIRCUS, E.C.

CONTENTS

THE

STAR OF EMPIRE

———•◦•———

CHAPTER I.

THE HALF-BROTHERS

In a wood, within ten miles of Windsor, two youths are
seen, gun in hand, in pursuit of game. A brace of
thorough-bred setters, guarding the cover in front, and a
well-equipped keeper, walking obsequiously in the rear,
preclude any suspicion of poaching; though the personal
appearance of the young sportsmen needs no such testimony.

The wood is only an extensive pheasant-cover, and their
father is its owner. They are the sons of General Harding,
an old Indian officer; who, with a hundred thousand
pounds, garnered during twenty years' active service in
the East, has purchased an estate in the pleasant shire of
Bucks, in the hope of restoring healthy action to a liver
impaired upon the hot plains of Hindostan.

A fine old Elizabethan mansion, of red brick, now and
then visible through the openings of the cover, told that
the General had laid out his *lacs* with considerable taste,
while five hundred acres of finely timbered park, a " home
farm," and half a dozen others rented out—to say nothing
of the wood-covers and cottage tenements—proved that
the *ci-devant* soldier had not carefully collected a hundred

thousand pounds in India to be carelessly squandered in England.

The two young sportsmen, already introduced as his sons, are his only sons—in short, the only members of his family, with the exception of a maiden sister, who, being sixty years old, and otherwise extremely uninteresting, will not conspicuously figure in this, our narrative.

Looking at the two youths, as they step through the pheasant-cover, you perceive there is but slight difference in their size. There is in their age, and still more in their personal appearance. Both are what is usually termed dark, but there is a difference in the degree. He who is the elder, and who bears the baptismal name "Nigel," has a complexion almost olive, with straight black hair that under the sunlight exhibits a purplish iridescence.

Henry, the younger, with fair skin and ruddier cheek, has hair of an auburn brown, drooping adown his neck, like clusters of Spanish chestnuts.

So great is their dissimilarity in personal appearance, that a stranger would scarce believe the two young sportsmen to be brothers.

Nor are they so in the exact signification of the word. Both can call General Harding father; but if the word "mother" be mentioned, their thoughts would be directed to two different personages no longer on the earth. Nigel's should stray back to Hyderabad, to a tomb in the environs of that ancient city; Henry's to a grave of later date in the quiet precinct of an English country churchyard.

The explanation is easy; General Harding is not the only man, soldier or civilian, who has twice submitted his neck to the matrimonial yoke; though few have ever wedded two wives so different in character. Physically, mentally, morally, the Hindoo lady of Hyderabad was as unlike her Saxon successor as India is to England.

Looking at Nigel Harding and his half-brother, Henry, one could not help perceiving that the dissimilarity had been transmitted from mothers to sons, without any great distraction caused by the blood of a common father. An incident occurring in the cover gives evidence of this.

Though especially a pheasant preserve, the young sportsmen are not in pursuit of the bird with strong whirring wings. The setters search for smaller game. It is mid-winter. A week ago, the youths might have been seen, capped and gowned, loitering along the aisles of Oriel College, Oxford. Now home for the holidays, what better than beating the home-covers? The frost-bound earth forbids indulgence in the grand chase; but it gives rare sport by driving the snipe and woodcock—both migratory birds among the Chilterns—to the open waters of the running rivulet.

Up the banks of one—a brook that, defying the frost, gurgles musically among the trees—the young sportsmen are directing their search. This, with the spaniels, tells that woodcock is their game. There are two dogs, a white and a black, both of pure breed, but not equally well trained. The black sets steady as a rock; the white quarters more wildly, runs rash, and has twice flushed the game without setting it.

The white dog belongs to Nigel—the black to his half-brother.

A third time the spaniel shows his imperfect training by flushing a cock before the interposing boughs will allow a fair shot.

The blood sprung from Hyderabad can stand it no longer. It is hot even under the shadows of a winter wood in the Chilterns.

"I'll teach the cur a lesson!" cries Nigel, leaning his gun against a tree, and drawing a clasp-knife. "What you should have taught him long ago, Doggy Dick, if you'd half done your duty."

"Lor, Muster Nigel," replies the gamekeeper, to whom the apostrophe has been addressed, "I've whipped the animal till my arms ached. 'Tain't no use. The steady ain't in him."

"I'll put it into him then!" cries the young Anglo-Indian, striding, knife in hand, towards the spaniel; "see if I don't."

"Stay, Nigel!" interposed Henry; "you are surely not going to do the dog an injury."

"And what to you, if I am? He is *mine*, not *yours*."

" Only, that I should think it very cruel of you. The fault may not be his, poor dumb brute. As you say, it. may be Dick who is to blame, for not properly training him."

" Thank'ee, Muster Henry ! 'Bleeged to yer for yer compliment. In coorse it be all my doin'; tho' not much thank for doin' my best. Howsoever, I'm obleeged to ye, Muster Henry."

Doggy Dick, who, though young, is neither graceful nor good-looking, accompanies his rejoinder with a glance that bespeaks a mind still more ungraceful than his person.

" Bother your talk—both !" vociferates the impatient Nigel. " I'm going to chastise the cur, as he deserves, and not as you may like it, Master Harry. I want a twig for him."

The twig, when cut from its parent stem, turns out to be a stick three-quarters of an inch in diameter.

With this, the peccant spaniel is brutally belaboured, till the woods for a mile around re-echoed its howlings.

Henry begs of his brother to desist.

In vain ; Nigel continues the cudgelling.

" Gi'e it him !" cries the unfeeling keeper—" do the beggar good !"

" You Dick ! I shall report you to my father."

An angry exclamation from the half-brother, and a sullen scowl from the savage in gaiters, is the only notice taken of Henry's threat. Nigel, irritated by it, only strikes more spitefully.

" Shame, Nigel ! Shame ! You've beaten the poor brute enough—more than enough. Have done !"

" Not till I've given him a mark to remember me !"

" What are going to do to him? What more?" hurriedly asks Henry, seeing that Nigel has flung away the stick, and stands threateningly with his knife. Surely you don't intend——"

" To split his ear ! That is what I intend doing."

" For shame ! You shall not !"

" Shall not ? But I shall, and will."

" You shall split my hand first !" cries the humane youth, flinging himself on his knees, and with both hands covering the head of the spaniel.

" Hands off, Henry ! The dog is my own : I shall do what I please to him. Hands off, I say ! "

" I won't ! "

" Then take the consequences."

With his left hand Nigel clutches at the animal's ear, at the same time lunging out recklessly with the knife-blade.

Blood spurts up into the faces of both, and falls in crimson spray over the flax-like coat of the spaniel. It is not the blood of Nigel's dog, but his brother—the little finger of whose left hand shows a deep, longitudinal cut from knuckle to nail.

" You see what you've got by your interference !" cries Nigel, without the slightest show of regret. " Next time you'll keep your claws out of harm's way."

The unfeeling observation, more than the hurt received, at length stirs the Saxon blood of the younger brother.

" Coward !" he cries. " Throw your knife away, and stand up. Though you *are* three years older than I, I don't fear you. You shall pay for this."

Nigel, maddened by the challenge from one whom he had hitherto controlled, drops the knife; and the half-brothers close in a fisticuff, with anger as intense as if no kindred blood ran in their veins.

As already stated, there is but slight difference in their size—Nigel the taller, Henry of stouter build. But in this sort of encounter the Saxon sinews soon show their superiority over the more flaccid frame of the Anglo-Indian; and in ten minutes' time the latter appears but too well pleased when the keeper interferes to prevent his further punishment.

Had it gone the other way, Doggy Dick would have allowed the combat to continue.

There is no thought of further sport for that day. The woodcocks are permitted to remain unflushed in their shrubby cover.

Henry, binding up his wounded hand in a kerchief, strides direct homeward, followed by the black setter.

Nigel skulks a little behind, with Doggy Dick by his side, and the blood-besprinkled spaniel at his heels.

*   *   *   *   *

General Harding is astonished at the early return of the sportsmen. Is the stream frozen up, and the woodcocks gone to more open quarters?

The stained kerchief comes under his eye, and the split finger requires explanation. So, too, a purple ring around the eye of his eldest born! The truth has to be told, each giving his version.

The younger brother is at a disadvantage : for the testimony is two to one—the keeper declaring against him. For all that, truth triumphs in the mind of the astute old soldier, and although both his sons are severely reprimanded, Nigel receives the heaviest half of the censure.

It is a sad day's sport for all—the black setter alone excepted.

Doggy Dick does not escape unscathed. Ere parting from the presence of the General, the license is taken from his pocket; the velveteen shooting-jacket stripped from his shoulders; and he receives his discharge, with a caution never to show himself again in the Beechwood preserves, under the penalty of being treated as a poacher!

CHAPTER II.

DOGGY DICK

DOGGY DICK, on being discharged by General Harding, in a short time succeeded in obtaining another and similar situation. It was on an estate bordering that of the General's, whose covers came within a field or two of meeting with those of his neighbour. This gentleman was a City magnate—by name, Whibley; who, having accumulated a fortune by sharp trading on the Stock Exchange, had purchased the estate in question, and commenced playing squire on an extensive scale.

Between the old officer and the new-comer there was no cordiality; on the contrary, some coolness. General Harding had an instinctive contempt for the vulgar ostentation usually exhibited by these social *parvenus;* who must needs ride to the parish church in a carriage and pair, though his residence be but three hundred yards from the churchyard gate!

Of this class was the gentleman in question.

In addition to the dissimilarity of tastes between a retired officer and retired stockbroker, a dispute had early occurred between them about rights of game belonging to a strip of waste that stretched triangularly along their respective estates.

It was a trifling affair, but well calculated to increase their mutual coolness; which at length ended in a hostility —silent, but understood. To this, perhaps, more than any professional merit, was Doggy Dick indebted for his promotion to be head-keeper of the Whibley preserves; just the course which a *parvenu* would take for the satisfaction of his spite.

In that same year, when the shooting season came

round, the young Hardings discovered a scarcity of game in their father's preserves. The General did not often go gunning himself, and would not have noticed this falling off. Neither, perhaps, would Nigel; but Henry, who was passionately fond of field sports, at once perceived that there was a thinner stock of pheasants than in the preceding season. All the more surprising to him, because it was a good year for game generally, and pheasants in particular. The Whibley covers were swarming with them; and they were reported plentiful in the country around!

At first it became a question whether General Harding's gamekeeper had attended to his trust. No poaching had been reported, except some trifling cases of boys who had been detected stealing eggs in the hatching season. But this had not occurred on a scale sufficient to account for the scarcity.

Besides, the new gamekeeper was reported one of the best; had been provided with a full set of watchers; while, on the Whibley side, there was a staff equally strong, with Doggy Dick at their head.

While reflecting on this, it occurred to Mr. Henry Harding that something might have been done to attract the pheasants across to the Whibley covers. Perhaps a better lay of feed had been there provided for them?

He knew that neither Doggy Dick nor his master owed any goodwill toward him or his father; and a trick of this kind would be compatible with the character of the stockbroker.

Still there was nothing in it beyond a certain discourtesy; and it only made it necessary that some steps should be taken to create a counter-attraction for the game.

Patches of buckwheat were sown here and there, and other favourite pheasants' food was liberally laid through the covers.

In the following season the result was the same, or worse—the strong, whirring wing was sparingly heard among the Harding preserves. Even partridges had become scarce in the swedes and stubble; while on the Whibley estate both were in abundance.

The General's gamekeeper, when taken to task, admitted that during the breeding season he had found several pheasants' nests rifled of their eggs. He could not account for it. There was no one ever seen in the covers, except occasionally the keepers from the neighbouring estate. But, of course, they would not do such a thing as steal eggs.

"Indeed," thought Henry Harding, "I'm not so sure of that. On the contrary, it appears to me the only way to account for our scarcity of game."

He communicated these thoughts to his father; and Whibley's keepers were forbidden the range. It was deemed discourteous, and widened the breach between the soldier and retired stockbroker.

Another breeding season came round, and the young Hardings were at home for the Easter holidays. It was at this time of the year that the chief damage appeared to have been done.

No amount of winter poaching can cause such havoc in a preserve as that arising from the destruction or abstraction of the eggs. A farmer's boy may do greater damage in one day than the most incorrigible gang of poachers in a month; with all their nets, traps, guns, and other appliances to boot.

Knowing this, the Harding covers were this year still more carefully watched—additional men being employed. A goodly number of nests was noted, and a better September expected.

But although the future seemed fair, Henry Harding was not satisfied with the past. He chafed at his disappointment on the two preceding seasons, and was determined on discovering the cause. For this purpose he adopted an expedient.

On a certain day a holiday was given to the keepers on the Harding estate, which included the watchers as well. It was fixed for the date of some races, held about ten miles off. The General's drag was granted for taking them to the race-course. The holiday was promised a week in advance, so that the fact might become known to the keepers of the adjoining estate.

The race day came; the drag rattled off, loaded with half

a score of men in coats of velveteen. They were the keepers and watchers. For that day the Harding preserves were left to take care of themselves—a fine opportunity for poachers !

So a stranger might have thought; but not so Henry Harding.

Shortly before the drag drove off, he was seen to enter the covers, cane in hand, and take his way toward their further side—where they were bounded by the estate of the stockbroker. He walked quietly, almost stealthily, through the copses. A poacher could not have proceeded with greater caution.

Between the two preserves there was a strip of common land—the waste already alluded to as having caused contention. Near its edge stood an ancient elm, swathed in ivy. In its first fork, amidst the green festoons, Henry Harding ensconced himself, took a cigar out of his case, lit it, and commenced smoking.

The position he had chosen was excellent for his purpose. On one side it commanded a view of the waste. No one could cross from Whibley to Harding without being seen. On the other, it overlooked a broad expanse of the Harding covers—known to be a favourite haunt of the pheasants, and one of their noted places of nesting.

The watcher kept his perch for a considerable time, without discovering anything to reward him for his vigilance. He smoked one cigar, then another, and was half-way through the third.

His patience was becoming exhausted—to say nothing of the irksomeness of his seat on the corrugated elm. He began to think that his suspicions—hitherto directed against Doggy Dick—were without foundation. He even reasoned about their injustice. After all, Doggy might not be so bad as he had deemed him.

Speak of the fiend, and he is near. Think of him, and he is not far off. So was it in the case of Doggy Dick. As the stump of the third cigar was burned within an inch of his teeth, Whibley's head-keeper hove in sight.

He was first seen standing upon the edge of the Whibley cover, his ill-favoured face protruding stealthily through the screen of " withies."

In this position he stood for some time, reconnoitring the ground. Then, stepping out, silent and cat-like, he made his way across the neutral territory, and plunged into the Harding preserves.

Henry scanned him with the eye of a lynx, or detective. There was now the prospect of something to reward him for his long watching and the strain of sitting upon the elm.

As was expected, Doggy took his way across the open expanse, where several nests had been " noted." He still kept to his cat-like tread, crouching, and looking suspiciously around him.

This did not hinder him from flushing a pheasant. One rose with a sonorous whirr ; while another went fluttering along the sward, as if both its wings had been broken.

The hen looked as if Doggy might have covered her with his hat, or killed her with a stick.

He did not attempt to do either ; but bending over the forsaken nest, he took out the eggs, and carefully deposited them in his game-bag.

Out of the same bag he took something which Henry saw him scatter over the ground in the neighbourhood of the nest.

This done, he walked on in search of another.

" Come," thought Henry, " one brood is enough to be sacrificed in this sort of way—enough for my purpose."

Throwing away the stump of his cigar, he dropped down from the tree, and rushed after the nest-robber.

Doggy saw him, and attempted to escape to the Whibley covers. But before he could cross the fence, the fingers of his pursuer were tightly grappled upon the collar of his velveteen coat ; and he came to the ground, crashing the eggs in his game-bag. This was turned inside out, until the spilled yelks and shattered shells gave proof of the plunder he had committed.

Henry Harding was at this time a strapping youth, with strength and spirit inherited from his soldier father. Moreover, he was acting with right on his side.

The keeper had neither his weight nor his inches, and was further enfeebled by his sense of wrongdoing. Under

these circumstances, he saw the absurdity of making resistance.

He made none ; but permitted the irate youth to cudgel
him with his malacca cane, until every bone in his body
seemed about to be shattered like the egg-shells emptied
out of his game-bag.

"Now, you thief!" cried young Harding, when his
passion was at length spent, "you can go back to Mr.
Whibley's covers, and hatch whatever plot may suit you
and your snob of a master, but no more of my pheasants'
eggs."

Doggy did not dare to make reply, lest it should tempt a
fresh application of the malacca. Clambering over the
fence, he hobbled back across the common, and hid himself among the hazels of the Whibley preserves.

Turning toward the plundered nest, Henry Harding
examined the ground in its proximity. He discovered a
scattering of buckwheat, that had been steeped in some
sweet-smelling liquid. It was the same he had seen Doggy
distribute over the sward.

He collected a quantity of it in his kerchief, and carried
it home.

On analysis it proved to be poison.

Though there was no trial instituted, the story, with all
its details, soon became known in the neighbourhood.
Doggy Dick knew better than to bring an action for assault ;
and the Hardings were satisfied with the punishment that
had been already administered to him.

As for the retired stockbroker, he had no alternative
but to discharge his peccant gamekeeper ; who from that
time became notorious as the most adroit poacher in the
parish.

The submissiveness with which he had received the castigation administered by Henry Harding, seemed afterward
to have been a source of regret to him ; for in future en-
counters with gamekeepers, he had proved himself a desperate and dangerous assailant—so dangerous, that in a
conflict with one of General Harding's watchers, occurring
about a year afterward, he inflicted a severe wound upon
the man, resulting in his death.

He saved his neck by making his escape out of the country; and though traced to Boulogne, and thence to Marseilles—in the company of some jockeys, who were taking English horses to Italy—he finally eluded justice by hiding himself in some corner of that classic land—then covered by a network of petty States—not only obstructive to justice, but corrupt in its administration.

CHAPTER III.

THREE years had elapsed, and the half-brothers were again home from college.

They had both stepped beyond the boundaries of boyhood. Nigel was of age, and Henry full-grown.

Nigel had become known for sedateness of conduct, economy in expenditure, and close application to his studies.

Henry, on the other hand, had won a very different character. If not considered an absolute scapegrace, he was looked upon as a young gentleman of somewhat loose habits ; hating books, loving all sorts of jollity, and scorning economy, as if it were the curse of life.

In reality, Nigel was only restrained by an astute, secretive, and selfish nature ; while Henry, with a heart of more generous inclinings, gave way to the seductions of pleasure, with a freedom that might be tempered by time.

The General, however satisfied with the conduct of his elder son, was not pleased with the proclivities of the younger ; more especially, as his heart, like Jacob's, had a yearning for his latest born.

Although struggling against any preference, he could not help thinking at times how much happier it would have made him, if Henry would but imitate the conduct of Nigel—even though their *rôles* should be reversed. But it seemed as if this desire was not to be gratified. During their sojourn within college walls, the rumours of many *diableries*, of which his younger son had been the hero, were scarce compensated by the reports of scholastic triumphs on the part of the elder.

It is true that Nigel himself had been habitually the herald to proclaim these mingled insinuations and successes, for Henry was but an indifferent correspondent. His letters, when they did come, were but too confirmatory of the contents of those written by his brother—being generally solicitations for a little more cash.

The *ci-devant* soldier—himself generous to a fault—had never failed to forward the cheque; caring less for the money than the way in which it was being spent.

The education of the Harding youths was now considered complete. They were enjoying that pleasant interval of idleness, when the chrysalis of the school is about to burst forth into a butterfly, and wing its way through the world.

If the old rancour existed, it showed no outward sign. A stranger would have seen nothing between the half-brothers beyond a fair fraternal friendship.

Henry was frank and outspoken: Nigel, reserved and taciturn; but this was their natural disposition, and no one remarked upon it. In all matters of parental respect, the elder brother was the more noticed. He was implicit in his obedience to the wishes of his father; while Henry, on the other hand, was prone to neglect this duty; though only in matters of minor consequence, such as keeping late hours, lavish expenditure, and the like. But by such acts the father's heart was often sorely grieved—his affection terribly tested.

At length came a cause that tried the temper of the half-brothers toward one another; one before which the strongest fraternal affection has oft changed into bitter hostility. It was love. Both fell in love—and with the same woman—Belle Mainwaring.

Miss Belle Mainwaring was a young lady whose fair face and fascinating manners might have turned wiser heads than those of the two ex-collegians. She was older than either; but if not in its first blush, she was still in the bloom of her beauty. Like her baptismal name, she was a belle in her own corner of the county, which was that inhabited by the Hardings.

She was the daughter of an Indian officer—a poor colonel, who, less fortunate than the General, had left his bones in the Punjaub, and his widow just sufficient to maintain her in a simple cottage residence that stood outside and not far from the palings of Beechwood Park.

It was a dangerous proximity for two youths just entering on manhood, and with very little business before them beyond making love, and afterward settling down with a wife. Both would be amply provided for without troubling their heads about a profession.

The paternal estate, under the hammer, would any day have realized a clear hundred thousand ; and he who can't live upon half of this is not likely to increase it by a calling.

That the property would be equally divided there was no reason to doubt. There was no entail, and General Harding was not the man from whom an act of partiality might be expected.

The old soldier was not without traits of eccentricity—not exactly crotchets or caprices, but a certain dogmatism of design, and an unwillingness to be thwarted in his ways—derived, no doubt, from his long exercise of military authority. This, however, was not likely to influence him in matters of a paternal character ; and unless some terrible provocation should arise, his sons, at his death, would, no doubt, have an equal share in the gainings of his life.

So thought the social circle in which the Hardings moved, or such part of it as took so much interest in their movements. With this fair presumption of being provided for, what could the young Hardings do but look out for something to love ; and, in looking out, upon whom should the eyes of both become fixed but on Belle Mainwaring ?

They did, with all the ardent admiration of youth ; and as she returned their respective glances with that speaking reciprocity which only a coquette can give, both fell in love with her.

The inspiration came on the same day, the same hour, perhaps on the same instant. It was at a grand archery fête, given by the General himself, to which Miss Mainwaring and her mother had been invited. The archer god was also present at the entertainment, and pierced the hearts of General Harding's two sons with a single arrow.

There was a remarkable difference in their way of showing it. To Miss Mainwaring Henry was all assiduity, lavish of little attentions—ran to recover her arrows, handed her the bow, held her sunshade while she bent it, and stood ready to fling himself at her feet. Nigel, on the other hand, held himself aloof, affected indifference to her presence, tried to pique her by showing partiality to others, with many like manœuvres suggested by a calculating and crafty spirit.

In one thing the elder brother succeeded: in concealing his new-sprung passion from the spectators.

The younger was not so fortunate. Before the archery fête broke up every guest upon the ground could tell that at least one arrow had been shot home to the mark; and that mark the heart of Henry Harding.

CHAPTER IV

A COQUETTE

I HAVE often wondered what the world would be without woman; whether if it were without her, man would care longer to live in it, or whether he would then find it just the place he has been all his life longing for, and would wish never to leave it. I have wondered and pondered upon this point, until speculation became lost in obscurity. It is perhaps the most interesting philosophical question of our existence—its most important—and yet no philosopher, as far as I know, has given a satisfactory answer to it.

I am aware of the two theories that have been propounded—to one another opposite as are the poles.

One makes woman the sole object of our existence—her smile its only blessing. For her we work and watch, we dig and delve, we fight and write, we talk and strive. Without her we would do none of these things; in short, do nothing, since there would be no motive for doing.

"What then?" say the advocates of this theory; "would existence be tolerable without a motive? Would it be possible?"

For our part we can only give the interrogative answer of the phlegmatic Spaniard, " *Quien sabe?*"—no answer at all.

The other theory is, that woman, instead of being life's object and blessing, is but its distraction and curse. The supporters of this hypothesis make no pretence to gallantry, but simply point to experience. Without her, say they, the world would be happy, and with her, they triumphantly add, what is it?

Perhaps the only way to reconcile the two theories, is to steer midway between them; to regard both as wrong, and both as right; to hold woman in this world as being alike a blessing and a bane; or rather that there are two sorts of women in it: one born to bless—the other to curse —mankind!

It grieves me to class Belle Mainwaring with the latter —for she was beautiful, and might have belonged to the former. I knew her myself—if not well, at least sufficiently to give her correct classification. Perhaps I, too, might have fallen under her fascinations, had I not discovered that they were false, and this saved me.

I made my discovery just in time, though by accident. It was in a ball-room. Belle liked dancing—as do most young ladies of the attractive kind; and there were but few balls in the county, public or private, civilian or military, where you might not meet her.

I met her at the hunt ball of B——. It was the first time I had seen her. I was introduced by one of the stewards, who chanced to have an impediment in his speech. It was of the nasal kind, caused by a split lip. In pronouncing the word "captain," the first syllable came out sounding as "count." There was then a break, and the second "ain" might have been taken or *mis*-taken for the prefix "Von." My Christian and baptismal names slurred together, as they were by the stammering steward, might have passed muster as Germanic; at all events, for some time afterward—before I could find an opportunity to rectify the error—I was honoured by Miss Mainwaring with a title that did not belong to me.

I was further honoured by having it inscribed upon her dancing card—much oftener than I, in my humility, had any right to expect. We danced several measures together, round and square. I was pleased, flattered—something more—charmed and delighted. Who would not, at being so signalized by one of the belles of the ball-room?—and she *was* one.

I began to fancy that it was all up with me, that I had found not only an agreeable partner for the night, but for life. I was all the better satisfied to see scowling faces around me, and hear whispered insinuations, that I was having more than my share of this charming creature. It was the pleasantest hunt ball I had ever attended.

So far up to a certain hour. Then things became less agreeable. I had deposited my partner on a couch, alongside a stately dame, introduced to me as her mother. I saw that this lady did not take kindly to me; but, on the contrary, sat stiff, frigid, and uncommunicative. Failing to thaw her, I made my bow and sauntered off among the crowd, promising to return to Miss Mainwaring for still another dance, for which I had succeeded in engaging her.

Not being able to find distraction away from her, I soon returned and sat down on a chair close to the couch occupied by mother and daughter.

As they were engaged in a close conversation, neither of them saw me, and, of course, I did not intrude. But, as their voices were above a whisper, I could not help hearing them, and the mention of my own name made it difficult for me to withdraw.

" A count ! " said the mother; " you are beside yourself, my child "

" But Mr. Southwick introduced him to me as such; and he has all the air of it."

All the air of it—I liked that.

" Count Fiddlestrings ! Mr. Southwick is a fool and an ass ! He's only a paltry captain—on half-pay at that—without the shadow of an expectation. Lady C—— has been telling me all about him."

" Indeed ! "

I thought there was a sigh ; but I could not be sure of it. I should have liked it very much; but then what came after should have rendered me indifferent to it.

" And you've engaged yourself to him for another dance, while young Lord Poltover has been twice here to ask for you—absolutely on his knees for me to intercede for him ! "

" What's to be done ? "

" Done ! throw him over. Tell him you forgot that you had a previous engagement with Lord P——."

" Very well, mamma; if you say so, I'll do that. I'm so sorry it should have happened."

There was no sigh this time—else I might have held my

peace and stolen quietly away. But I found that I could not retreat without being discovered. In fact, I was at that moment discovered ; and I determined on making a clean breast of it.

"I should be sorry, Miss Mainwaring," said I, addressing myself directly to the daughter, and without heeding the confusion of either herself or her mother, "sorry to stand in the way of a previous engagement, and rather than Lord Poltover should get on his knees for the third time, I beg to release you from that made with a ' paltry captain.' "

With a bow which I supposed suitable to the circumstances, I parted from the Mainwarings, and did my best to get rid of my chagrin by dancing with any girl who would accept for her partner a captain on half-pay.

Fortunately, before the ball was over, I found one who caused me to forget my *contretemps* with Miss Belle Mainwaring.

I often met this lady afterward; but never spoke to her, except by that silent speech of the eyes that may say a good deal.

CHAPTER V

TWO STRINGS TO THE BOW

It might have been well for young Henry Harding, and perhaps his brother Nigel too, in their first essay at love-making with Miss Mainwaring, had they met with a similar mischance to that which had befallen me, and taken it in the same spirit.

As it was, they were either more or less fortunate. Neither was a half-pay captain without expectations, and, instead of a discouragement almost amounting to dismissal, for a long time both were permitted to bask in the smiles of the beautiful Belle.

There was a marked difference in the way the two brothers respectively pressed their suit. Henry essayed to carry Belle Mainwaring's heart by storm. Nigel, as his nature dictated, preferred making approach by sap and trenching. The former made love with the boldness of the lion ; the latter with the insidious stealth of the tiger. When Henry believed himself successful, he made no attempt to conceal his gratification. When the chances seemed to go against him, with equal openness did he exhibit his chagrin.

The reverse with Nigel when fortune appeared to smile upon his suit : he showed no sign of being conscious of it. He appeared alike impassible under her frown.

So little demonstrative was he in his affection for Miss Mainwaring, there were few believed in it ; though among this few was the lady herself.

From what I could learn, and sometimes by the evidence of my own eyes, she played her cards to perfection, her mother acting as *croupier* to the game.

It was not long before she knew that she had choice

between the two, though it was some time before she declared it. Now one appeared to be the favourite—anon the other; until the most intimate of her associates were puzzled as to her partiality, or whether she even cared for either.

It was at least a question; for the beautiful Belle did not restrict herself to receiving only the admiration of the half-brothers Harding. There were other young gentlemen in the neighbourhood who, at balls and archery gatherings, were favoured with an occasional smile, and Miss Mainwaring's heart was considered still doubtful in its inclinings.

There was a time, however, when it was supposed to have declared itself. At all events, there was a reason for its doing so. An incident occurred in the hunting-field which should have entitled Henry Harding to the hand of Belle Mainwaring—that is, supposing it to be true that the brave deserve the fair.

It was an incident so rare as to be worth recording, irrespective of its bearing upon our tale.

The hunt was with the staghounds, and the "meet" had taken place close to a pond of considerable size, upon one of the open commons not rare among the Chiltern Hills.

As the stag bounded away from the cart, his eye had caught the gleam of water, and in his hour of distress he remembered it.

Being a lazy brute, he did not run far, but, guided by instinct, soon turned back toward the pond.

He arrived at it before the carriages that had come to the meet had cleared away from the ground. Among them was the pony phaeton that contained Mrs. Mainwaring and her daughter Belle, the latter looking as roseate on that crisp winter morning as if her cheeks had taken their colour from the scarlet coats of the hunters around her.

The *atelage* to which she belonged was drawn up close to the edge of the pond, parallel with its bank.

The stag, on returning, shaved close past the pony's nose, and plunged into the water. The consequence was that the latter became alarmed even to frenzy, and instead of turning toward the road, it wheeled round in the opposite direction, and rushed into the pond after the stag—dragging the phaeton along with it.

It did not stop till the water was up over the steps of the carriage, and the ladies' feet were immersed in the chilly flood. But then the stag had stopped, too—at bay—and, believing the "trap" to be its cruel pursuer, the bayed animal turned and charged upon pony, carriage, and contents.

The pony was knocked down in the traces, and then came the boy in buttons, who was perched conspicuously on the seat behind. On the antlers of the enraged animal he was hoisted skyward, and fell with a plunge into the water.

Next came the turn of the two ladies, or would have come, had relief not been near. The smock-frocks had gone away from the ground, following the chase; and it was not they who rushed to the rescue. Nor was it Nigel Harding, who was first by the edge of the pond, having got there through being last in the field. But there stayed he, sitting irresolute in his saddle; and Belle Mainwaring might have had a stag's horn through her heart, but that his brother had galloped up nearly at the same time. He, instead of reining up by the water's edge, dashed on through it, till his horse stood by the side of the carriage. Next moment he sprung out of the saddle, and took the stag by the horns.

The struggle that ensued might have ended ill for him; but by this time a smock-frock, in the shape of a hedger, up to his armpits in the water, drew his chopper across the throat of the stag, and the conflict came to an end.

The pony, but slightly injured, was got upon its feet; the page, half drowned, was hoisted back to his pinnacle; and the carriage, with its frightened occupants, conducted safely to the shore.

Everybody left the ground with the belief that Miss Belle Mainwaring would at some day not far distant become Mrs. Henry Harding. More especially did the chaw-bacons believe it, and were delighted with the idea; for with them, as is generally the case, the younger brother was the favourite.

CHAPTER VI.

At Beechwood Park there was comfort of every kind; but not that perfect tranquillity which its owner had counted upon when retiring to this fair residence to pass the remainder of his days.

With his property all was well. Since his purchase of the estate—like other lands around—it had nearly doubled in value; and so far as fortune was concerned, there was no source of uneasiness.

But there was from something else—something dearer to him than his houses and lands. It arose from the conduct of his two sons. Notwithstanding their apparent cordiality in his presence, on both sides assumed, their father had found reasons for believing there was no fraternal affection, but instead a tacit enmity between them. Though this was more openly exhibited on the part of the younger, it was deep-rooted in the heart of his first-born. Henry, of a generous, forgiving nature, could at any time during college days have been induced to forego it, had his brother met him but half-way in any measure of reconciliation. But this Nigel never desired to do. And the early estrangement had now deepened into hostility—the cause, of course, being Belle Mainwaring.

It was a long time before the General knew of this dangerous cloud that was looming up on the horizon of his tranquil life. He had taken it for granted that his sons, like most of the young men so circumstanced, before thinking of marriage, would want to see something of the world. It did not occur to him that to the eyes of an ardent youth, beautiful Miss Mainwaring was a world in

herself; after seeing which, all earth besides might present
but a dull, prosaic aspect.

It was not this, however, that at first troubled the spirit
of the retired officer ; but only the behaviour of his boys.
With Nigel's he was contented enough.   Than this, nothing could be more satisfactory, except in the estrangement toward his brother, and the occasional exhibition of
ill-feeling which the father could not fail to perceive. , It
was Henry's conduct that formed the chief source of his
anxiety; his extravagant habits; his proneness to dissipation ;
and, in one or two instances, his positive disobedience of
paternal orders ; which, though only in some trivial
matters of expenditure, had been exaggerated, by the
secret side representations of his elder brother, into matters
of momentous importance.

The counsels of the General, not having been seriously
taken to heart, soon became chidings, and these in their
turn, being alike unheeded, assumed the form of threats
and hints about disinheritance.

Henry, who now deemed himself a man, met such re-
minders with a spirit of independence, that only irritated
his father to a still greater degree.

In this unhappy way were things going on, when the
General was made aware of a matter more affecting the
future welfare of his son than all the dissipations and disobedience of which he had yet been guilty.   It was his
partiality for Miss Mainwaring.   Of Nigel's inclining
toward the same quarter he knew nothing; nor, indeed,
did others ; though almost everybody in the neighbourhood had long been aware of her conquest over
Henry.

It was shortly after the incident at the stag-hunt that
the General became apprised of it.   That affair had led
him to reflect; and, although proud of the gallantry his
son had displayed, the old soldier saw in it a danger far
greater than that of the struggle through which he had so
conspicuously passed.

He was led to make inquiries, which resulted in a discovery giving him the greatest uneasiness.

It arose from the fact that he knew the antecedents of

Mrs. Mainwaring. He had known both her husband and herself in India; and this knowledge, so far from inspiring him with respect for the relict of his late brother officer, had impressed him with a very opposite opinion. With the character of the daughter he was, of course, less acquainted. The latter had grown up during a long period of separation; but from what he had seen and heard of her, since his arrival in England—from what he was every day seeing and hearing—he had come to the conclusion that it was a case of "like mother, like daughter."

And, if so, it would not suit his views that she should become daughter-in-law to him.

The thought filled him with serious alarm; and he at once set about concocting some scheme to counteract the danger.

How was he to proceed? Deny his son the privilege of associating with the Mainwarings? Lay an embargo on his visits to the villa-cottage of the widow, which he now learned had been of late suspiciously frequent?

It was a question whether his commands would be submitted to; and this thought still further irritated him.

Over the widow herself he had no authority in any way. Though her cottage stood close to his park, it was not his property; her landlord was a lawyer of little respect in the neighbourhood; and it would have served no purpose, even could he have given her notice to quit.

Things had already gone too far for such strategy as that.

And as for the damsel herself, she was not going to hide her beautiful face from the gaze of his son solely to accommodate him. It might not appear any more in his own dining or drawing room. But there were scores of other places where it could be seen in all its bewitching beauty—in the church, on the hunting-field, in the ball-room; and every day along the green lanes that encompassed Beechwood Park, smiling coquettishly under the turned-up rim of a prettily trimmed hat.

The old soldier was too skilled a tactician to believe that

any benefit could be obtained from an attack so open to repulses—and these, of the most humiliating character. Some stratagem must be resorted to ; and to the conception of this he determined to devote all the energies of his nature.

He had already, in his mind, the glimmering of a scheme that promised success ; and this imparted a ray of comfort that kept him from going quite out of his senses.

CHAPTER VII.

PLOTTERS FOR FORTUNE

THE stag-hunt, at which Henry Harding had exhibited such gallant courage, had been the very last of the hunting season; and, soon after, spring stole over the shire of Bucks, clothing its beechen forests and grassy glades in a new livery of the gayest green. The crake had come into the cornfield; the cuckoo winged her way across the common, uttering her soft monotonous notes; and the nightingale had once more taken possession of the coppice, from whence, through the livelong night, pealed forth its incomparable song. It was the month of May, that sweet season when all Nature seems to submit itself to the tender inclinings of love; when not only the shy birds of the air, but the chased creatures of the earth—alike tamed and emboldened by its influence—stray beyond the safety of their coverts in pursuit of those pleasures at other seasons denied them.

Whether the love-month has any influence on the passions of the human species is a disputed question. Perhaps, in man's primitive state, such may have been the case, and Nature's suggestiveness may have extended also to him; but at whatever season affection may spring up between two young hearts, surely this is the time of the year Nature has designed it should reach maturity.

It seemed so in the case of Henry Harding. In the month of May, his passion for Belle Mainwaring had reached the point that should end in a declaration; and upon this he determined.

With the outside world it was still a question whether the passion was reciprocal, though it was generally thought that the coquette had been at length captured, and by

Henry Harding. The eligibility of the match favoured this view of the case, though not more than the personal appearance of the man.

At this time the younger son of General Harding was just entering upon manhood, and possessed a face and figure alike manly and graceful. The only blemish that could be brought against him was of a moral nature, as already mentioned ; a proneness to dissipation. But time might remedy this ; and even as things stood, it did not so materially damage him in the eyes of his lady acquaintances—more than one of whom would have been willing to take Miss Mainwaring's chances.

The light in which Belle regarded him may be best learned from a conversation which, about this time, took place over the breakfast-table in her mother's cottage—the speakers being her mother and herself.

" And you would marry him ? " interrogated Mrs. Mainwaring after some remark that had introduced the name of Henry Harding.

" I would, mamma, and, with your leave, will."

" What about *his* leave ? "

" Ha—ha," laughed Belle, with a confident air. " I think I may count upon that. He has as good as given it."

" Already ! But has he really declared himself—in words, I mean ? "

" Not exactly in words. But, dear ma, since I suppose you will insist upon knowing my secrets, before giving your consent, I may as well tell you at once. He will declare himself soon—this very day, if I am not astray in my chronology."

" What reason have you for thinking so ? "

" Only his having hinted at having—something important to say to me—time fixed for a call he is to make this afternoon. What else could it be ? "

Mrs. Mainwaring made no reply ; but sat thoughtful, as if not altogether pleased with the communication her daughter had made.

" I hope, *cher* mamma, you are contented ? "

" With what, my child ? "

" With—with—well, to have Henry Harding for your son-in-law. Does it satisfy you ? "

" My dearest child," answered the Indian officer's widow, with that cautious air peculiar to her country—she was Scotch—"it is a serious question, this, very serious, and requires careful consideration. You know how very straitened are our circumstances ; how your poor dear father left little to support us—having but little to leave?"

" I should think I do know," peevishly interposed Belle. " Twice turning my ball-dresses, and then dyeing them into wearing silks, has taught me all that. But what has it to do with my marrying Henry Harding ? All the more reason why I should. He, at all events, is not likely to be troubled with straitened circumstances."

" I am not so sure of it, my child."

" Ah ! you know something about his expectations, then ? —something you have not told me ? Is it so, mamma ? "

" I know very little. I wish it were otherwise, and I could be sure."

" But his father is rich. There are but the two sons ; and you have already told me that the estate is not entailed, or whatever you call it, and that he can divide it equally between them. Half would satisfy me."

" And me too, child ; if we were sure of half. But there lies the difficulty. It is the fact of the estate not being entailed that makes it. Were that done, there would be none."

" Then I could marry Henry ? "

" No—Nigel."

" Oh, mamma ! what do you mean ? "

" The estate would then be Nigel's by the simple law of entail. As it is now, it is all uncertain how they will inherit. It will depend on the will. It may go by a caprice of their father—and I know General Harding well enough to believe him capable of such caprice."

In her turn Belle became silent and thoughtful.

"There is reason to fear," continued the match-making, perhaps match-spoiling, mother, " that the General may disinherit Henry altogether, or, at most, leave him only a maintenance. He is certainly very much dissatisfied with his conduct, and for a long time has been vainly endeavouring to change it. I won't say the young man is loose in his habits. If he were, I would not hear of him for your husband. No, my child ; poor as we are, it needn't come to that."

As the widow said this, she looked half interrogatively toward her daughter, who replied with a smile of assenting significance.

" Henry Harding," continued the cautious mother, " is too generous—too profuse in his expenditures."

"But, mamma, would not marriage cure him of that ? He would then have me to think of, and would take better care of his money."

" True—true—supposing him to be possessed of it. But therein lies the doubt—the difficulty, I may call it— about your accepting him."

" But I love him. I do indeed."

" I am sorry for that, my child. You should have been more cautious—until better assured about his circumstances. You must leave it to time. You will, if you love me."

" And if, as I have told you—this afternoon—what answer ? "

" Evasive, my dear. Nothing easier. You have me to fall back upon. You are my only child. My consent will be necessary. Come, Belle ! you need no instructions from me. You will lose nothing by a little procrastination. You have nothing to fear from it, and everything to gain. Without it, you may become the wife of one poorer than ever your father was; and instead of having to turn your silk dresses, you may have none to turn. Be prudent, therefore, in the step you are about to take."

Belle only answered with a sigh ; but it was neither so sad nor deep as to cause any apprehension to her counsellor; while the sly look that accompanied it told that she had determined upon *prudence*.

CHAPTER VIII.

FATHER AND SON

GENERAL HARDING was accustomed to spend much time in his studio, or library, it might be called : since it contained a goodly number of books.

They were mostly volumes that related to Oriental subjects—more especially works upon India and its campaigns ; but there were also many devoted to science and natural history ; while scattered here and there upon tables were odd numbers of the " Oriental Magazine," the " Transactions of the Asiatic Society," and the " Calcutta Englishman."

There were also large pamphlets, in blue parliamentary covers, that related only to the affairs of the Hon. E.I.C.

In poring over these volumes, the retired *militaire* was accustomed to pass much of his time. The subjects, with the descriptions attached, recalled scenes in his past life, the souvenirs of which gave him pleasure ; enabling him to while away many an hour that, amidst the seclusion of the Chiltern Hills, might have otherwise hung heavily on his hands.

Each new book about India was sure to find its way into the General's library ; and though never a very keen sportsman, he could enjoy the descriptions of hunting scenes to be found in the pages of " Markham " and the " Old Shikaree ; " since, in these, there is something to interest, not only the sportsman, but the student of Nature.

On a certain morning he had entered his studio ; but with no intention of devoting himself to the tranquil study of his books.

On the contrary, he did not even seat himself ; but

commenced pacing the floor with a quick step and clouded front that denoted some agitation of mind.

Every now and then he would stop, strike his clenched hand against his forehead, mutter a few words to himself, and then stride on again !

Among his mutterings could be distinguished some words that guided to the subject of his thoughts, and the names " Nigel " and " Henry " constantly occurring, told that both his sons had a share in his cogitations—though chiefly the latter, whose name was most frequently pronounced.

" This boy Henry has half driven me mad with his wild ways. And now, worse than all—his affair with this girl! From what I've heard, there can be no doubt that she's entangled him—no doubt of its having become serious. It won't do—must be broken off, cost what it will. She's not the stuff to make an honest man's wife out of.

" I'd care less if it were Nigel, But no, she won't do for either—for no son of mine. I knew her mother too well. Poor Mainwaring ! Many a dog's day he spent with her in India. Like mother, like daughter.

" By Heaven ! it won't do; and I shall put a stop to it !

" I think I know how," continued he, reflectively. " If he's mad, she isn't ; and therein I may find my means for saving the poor lad from the worst of all misfortunes, a wicked wife."

The General made several turns in silence, as if maturing some plan.

" Yes ; that's the way to save him ! " he at length joyfully exclaimed, " perhaps the only way. And there's no time to be lost about it. While I'm thinking he may be acting—may have gone too far for me to get him out of the scrape. I shall see him at once ; see and question him."

The General stooped over the table ; pressed upon a spring bell, and then resumed his pacing.

The bell brought the butler, a portly individual ; who, so far as could be judged by his get-up, was quite as respectable as the old officer himself.

" Williams ! "

" General ? "

" My son Henry—find out if he's upon the premises."

" He is on the premises, General. He's down at the stables. Groom says he's going to mount the brown filly."

" The brown filly! Why, she's never been ridden before."

" She never has, General. I think it very dangerous, but that's just what Master Henry likes. I spoke to persuade him against it; but, then, Master Nigel told me to mind my own business."

" Send quick to the stable! Tell him I forbid it. Tell him, moreover, to come to me. Haste, Williams, haste ! "

" Ever running into danger, as if he loved it," said the General, continuing his soliloquy, " so like I once was myself. The brown filly! Ah! I wish that was all. The Mainwaring damsel's worse danger than that."

At this moment the peccant Henry made his appearance, breeched, booted, and spurred, as if for the hunting-field.

" Did you send for me, father ? "

" Of course I did. You were going to mount the brown filly ? "

" I am going. Have you any objection to my doing so ? "

" Do you want your neck broken ? "

" Ha, ha, ha! There's not much fear of that. I think you make light of my horsemanship, papa ? "

" You carry too much confidence, sir—far too much. You mount a vicious mare without consulting me. You do other and more important things without consulting me. I intend putting a stop to it."

" What other things do you refer to, papa ? "

" Many other things. You spend money foolishly— like a madman ! And, like a maniac, you are now rushing upon a danger of a still graver kind—upon destruction, sir—rank, absolute destruction ! "

" Of what are you speaking, father ? Do you mean by mounting the filly ? "

" The filly—no, sir, not the filly. You may back her,

and break your neck for aught I care. I'm speaking of a woman."

The word woman caused the youth to turn pale. He had thought that, to his father at least, his love for Miss Mainwaring was still a secret. No other woman could be meant.

"I do not understand you, papa," was his evasive response.

"But you do, sir, perfectly. If I gave the name of this woman you wouldn't be any the wiser than you are now—you know it too well. I'll tell you, for all that. I refer to Miss Belle Mainwaring."

Henry made no reply, but stood blushing in the presence of his parent.

"And now, sir; about this woman, I have only six words to say : *you must give her up*——"

" Father ! "

"I won't listen to any of your love-sick appeals. Don't repeat them. They'll only be wasted on me. I repeat, you must give Belle Mainwaring up ; at once, absolutely, and for ever ! "

"Father," said the youth, in a firm voice, in his breast love pleading for justice, "you ask me to do what is not in my power. I acknowledge that between myself and Miss Mainwaring there is something more than the affection of friendship. It has gone further than mere feeling. There have been words—I may say promises—between us. To break them requires the consent of both parties ; and for me to do so, without first consulting her, would be a cruel injustice, to which I cannot lend myself. No, father, not even with the alternative of incurring your displeasure."

General Harding stood for a moment silent—pretending to reflect, but furtively contemplating his son. A superficial observer could have seen only anger at this filial defiance, where one skilled in physiognomy might have detected something like admiration mingling with the sentiment. If there was such, however, in his heart, his speech did not show it.

"Enough, sir ! You have made up your mind to disobey me!—very well! Understand, then, what this disobedience will cost you. I suppose you know the meaning of an entailed estate?"

The General paused, as if for an answer.

"I know nothing about it, papa; something connected with a will, I believe."

"The very reverse. An entailed estate has nothing to do with a will. Now, my estate is *not* entailed, and *is* connected with one. It is about this will I am going to talk to you. I can make one, giving my property to whomsoever I please—either to your brother Nigel or yourself. Marry Miss Mainwaring, and it shall be Nigel's; still to you I shall leave just enough to carry you out of the country—just one thousand pounds sterling. Now, sir, you hear what I have said?"

"I hear it, father, and with sorrow. I shall be sorry to lose the inheritance I had reason to expect, but far more your esteem. Both, however, must be parted with, if there be no other consideration for my retaining them. Whether I am to marry Miss Mainwaring or not, must depend upon Miss Mainwaring herself. I think, father, you understand me?"

"Too well, sir—too well; and I answer by telling you that I have passed my word, and it shall be kept. You may go and mount the filly, and thank God that she don't do with your neck what you are likely to do with your father's heart—break it. Begone, sir!"

Without saying a word, Henry walked out of the room, slowly and sadly.

"The image of his mother! Who could not help liking the lad, in spite of his rebellious spirit and—with all his wasteful habits? Damme! it won't do to have such a noble heart sacrificed upon a worthless jade of a woman! He must be saved!"

Once more the General pressed upon the spring bell—this time more violently than before.

It brought the butler back in double-quick time.

"Williams!'"

"General?"

"My carriage—soon as the horses can be put to."

Williams disappeared to cause execution of the order.

A few more turns to and fro across the Turkey carpet, a few muttered soliloquies, and the carriage wheels grated upon the gravel outside.

Williams helped the General to his hat and gloves, saw him down the stairs, handed him into the carriage, and watched it rolling away, just as Henry, on the back of the brown filly, was fighting her across the greensward of the park, endeavouring to keep her head in the opposite direction.

CHAPTER IX.

THE CHECKMATE

Mr. WOOLET sat in his office, which was separated from that of his solitary clerk by a thick wall and a narrow doorway between.

But there was another wall of slighter dimensions, inclosing Mr. Woolet's room, and partitioning off a kind of cupboard inclosure, into which, when Mr. Woolet required it, said clerk could introduce himself; and then standing cat-like and silent, hear what passed between his employer and any client whose conversation it was deemed necessary to make a note of.

After this it is scarce necessary to add that Mr. Woolet was an attorney, and though the scene of his practice was a quiet country town in the quiet shire of Bucks, it was carried on with as much sharpness and trickery as if it lay among the low courts surrounding Newgate, or the slums of Clerkenwell.

The great City does not monopolize the plant called pettifogging. It thrives equally as strong in the county town. Even the village knows it to its cost; and the poor cottager, in his leaky shed at three shillings a week, is too often encompassed by its toils.

Of such small fish Mr. Woolet had hooked his hundreds, and had prospered by their capture to the keeping of a carriage and pair.

But as yet none of the big ones had entered his net, the largest being the widow Mainwaring, who had been caught while taking from him a lease of her cottage.

The carriage, therefore, had been long kept to no purpose, or less than none; since, not being in accord with his position, it only brought him ridicule.

This, however, could not last for ever. The gentry could not always hold out against such a glittering attraction. Some swell must in time stand in need of Mr. Woolet's peculiar services, and enable him to achieve the much wished-for position.

And so it seemed to turn out, as one day a carriage much grander than Mr. Woolet's own, with a coachman nearly a quarter of a ton in weight, and a powdered footman beside him, drove through the street of the little town in which Mr. Woolet lived, and pulled up opposite his office.

Perhaps the lawyer was never more delighted in his life than when his clerk protruded his phiz inside the office door, and announced in *sotto voce* the arrival of General Harding.

In a moment after, the same individual ushered the General into his presence.

A masonic sign communicated to the clerk caused his disappearance, and the instant after that pale-faced familiar was skulking like a ghoul inside the cupboard inclosure.

" General Harding, I believe ? " said the obsequious attorney, bowing to the lowest button of his visitor's surtout.

" Yes," bluffly responded the old soldier. " That is my name. Yours is——"

" Woolet, General ; E. Woolet, at your service."

" Well, I want some service from you—if you're not otherwise engaged."

" Any engagement, General, must stand aside for you. Whàt can I do to oblige you ? "

" To oblige me, nothing. I want your services as an attorney. You are one, I believe ? "

" My name is in the law list, General. You can see it here."

Mr. Woolet took up a small volume, and was handing it to the General.

" Never mind about the list," bluntly interrupted the soldier. " I see it on your sign. That's enough for me. What I'm in search of is an attorney who can make a will. I suppose you can do that ? "

"Well, General, although I cannot boast of my professional abilities, I think I can arrange the making of a will."

"Enough said. Sit down, and get about it."

Considering that he kept a carriage himself, Mr. Woolet might have felt a little offended by this brusque behaviour on the part of his new client. It was the first time he had ever been so treated in his own office; but then it was the first time he had ever had a client of such a class, and he knew better than to show feeling under the infliction.

Without saying another word, he sat down before his table—the General taking a seat on the opposite side—and waited for the latter to proceed.

"Write down as I dictate," said the General, without even prefixing the word "please."

The lawyer, still obsequious, signified assent—at the same time seizing a pen, and placing a sheet of blue foolscap before him.

"I hereby will and bequeath to my eldest son, Nigel Harding, all my real and personal estate, comprising my houses and lands, also my stock in Indian securities, excepting one thousand pounds to be sold out of the last, and paid over to my other and youngest son, Henry Harding, as his sole legacy left from my estate."

To this extent the lawyer finished the writing, and waited for his client to proceed.

"You have done, have you?" asked the General.

"So far as you've dictated, General, I have."

"Have you written down the date?"

"Not yet, General."

"Then put it in."

Woolet took up his pen and complied.

"Have you a witness at hand? If not, I can bring in my footman."

"You need not do that, General. My clerk will do for one witness."

"Oh! it wants two, does it?"

"That's the law, General; but I myself can be the second."

" All right then.　Let me sign."

And the General rose from his seat, and leaned over toward the table.

" But, General," interposed the lawyer, thinking the will a somewhat short one, " is this all?　You have two sons ? "

" Of course I have.　Haven't I said so in my will ? "

" But surely——"

" Surely what ? "

" You are not going to——"

" I am going to sign my will—if you will allow me.　If not, I must get it made elsewhere."

Mr. Woolet was too much a man of business to offer any further opposition.　It was no affair of his beyond the giving satisfaction to his new client; and to accomplish this he at once pushed the paper before the General, at the same time presenting him with the pen.

The General signed; the lawyer and his clerk—summoned from the cupboard—attested ; and the will was complete.

" Now make me a copy of it," demanded the General. " The original you may keep till called for."

The copy was made ; the General buttoned it up in the breast of his surtout ; and then, without even cautioning the lawyer to secrecy, stepped back into his carriage, and was soon rolling along the four miles of road lying between the village and his own park.

" There's something queer about all this," soliloquized the pettifogger, when left alone in his office.　" Queer he should come to me, instead of going to his own solicitor ; and queerer still, he should disinherit the younger son— or next thing to it.　His property cannot be worth less than a cool £100,000; and all to go to that half negro, while the other, as most people thought, would have a half share of it.　After all it's not so strange.　He's angry with the younger son ; and in making this will he comes to me, instead of going to Lawson, who he knows might say something to dissuade him from his purpose.　I have no doubt he will stick to it, unless the young scamp leaves off his idle ways.　General Harding is not a man to be trifled with, even by his own son. But whether this will is to remain good or not, it's my duty to make it known to a third party, who for certain reasons will be deeply interested in its contents; and who, whether she may ever be able to thank me for communicating them, will at all events keep the secret of my doing so. She shall hear of it within the hour. Mr. Roby ! ".

The pale face of the unarticled clerk appeared within the doorway—prompt as a stage spirit summoned through a trap.

" Tell my coachman to clap the horses into my carriage —quick as tinder."

The spirit disappeared without making reply, and just as his invoker had finished the folding of the lately attested will, and made a minute of what had transpired between him and the testator, carriage wheels were heard outside the door of the office.

In six seconds after Woolet was in his " trap," as he was used condescendingly to call it—and rattling along a country road, the same taken ten minutes before by the more ostentatious equipage of the retired Indian officer.

Although driving the same way, the destination of the two vehicles was different. The chariot was bound for Beechwood Park, the " trap " for a less pretentious residence outside its inclosure, occupied by the widow Mainwaring.

CHAPTER X.

THE BAIT TAKEN

THE relict of the late colonel who had left his bones in the Punjaub and his widow with only a slight maintenance, had still been left sufficient to maintain a " turn-out." True, it was but a pony and phaeton, but the pony was spirited, the phaeton a neat one, and, with the charming Belle in it, hat on head, whip and ribbons in hand, it might have been termed stylish. The appearance was improved by a boy in buttons, who sat upon the back seat, well trained to sustain the dignity of the situation.

This choice little tableau of country life might have been seen at the gate of Mrs. Mainwaring's villa at eleven o'clock of that same day on which the conversation already reported had passed between herself and her daughter in the breakfast-room. It was an early hour for a drive, but it was to be a drive upon business—with her lawyer. It was never accomplished, for just as the sprightly Belle had taken her seat in the phaeton, adjusted her drapery, and commenced " catching flies " with her whip, what should appear coming up the road, and at a spanking pace, but the two-horse trap of that lawyer himself, Mr. Woolet.

The trap was evidently *en route* for the residence where more than once it had discharged its owner upon matters of business. Its approach was a fortunate circumstance, so thought Mrs. Mainwaring, so thought her daughter, neither of whom on that particular day desired to drive to the town. It was not one that had been set apart for shopping ; more important matters were on the *tapis*, and these could be arranged with Mr. Woolet upon the spot.

The phaeton was at once abandoned, " Buttons " receiving orders to keep the pony by the gate, and the ladies, followed by the lawyer, returned into the cottage. The attorney was received in the drawing-room, but as the business could have nothing to do with the beautiful Belle, her presence was excused, and she sauntered out again, leaving her mother alone with Mr. Woolet.

Though there was still a certain obsequiousness about the lawyer's manner, it was very different from that he had exhibited when dealing with General Harding. There was a vast distinction between a live Indian General, possessed of a hundred thousand pounds, and a defunct colonel's widow, with scarce so many pence. Still Mrs. Mainwaring was a lady of acknowledged social position, with a daughter who might at no distant day have the control of a gentleman who had a hundred thousand pounds, and who might become a profitable client of whoever chanced at the time to be her mother's solicitor. Mr. Woolet was a sharp, far-seeing individual, and this forecast had not escaped him. If he showed himself more at ease in the presence of the colonel's widow than he had done in that of the General, it was simply because he recognised in the lady a nature more like his own—less scrupulous upon points either of honour or etiquette.

" Have you any business with me, Mr. Woolet ? " asked the lady, without making known the fact that she was about going on business to him.

" Well, Mrs. Mainwaring, scarce enough to make it worth while my calling upon you—at all events, interrupting your drive. What I have to say may be of no importance, but five minutes will suffice for saying it."

" Take what time you please, Mr. Woolet. Our drive had no object—a little shopping affair of my daughter's that can be disposed of any hour. Please be seated."

The attorney took a chair, Mrs. Mainwaring herself sunk into a couch.

" Something connected with the cottage ? " she continued in a tone of studied indifference. " I think the rent is paid up to——"

" Oh, nothing of that," interrupted the lawyer. " You are too punctual in your payments, Mrs. Mainwaring, to need reminding from me. I have come upon an affair that, indeed, now that I think of it, may look like interference on my part; but it is one that may be of importance, and studying your interest as my client, I deem it my duty, and I hope, if in error, you will not be offended by my apparent overzeal."

The widow opened her eyes, once beautiful enough, but now only expressive of surprise. The manner of the attorney, his tone of confidence—of an almost friendly assurance—led her to look for some pleasant revelation. What could it be?

"Overzeal on your part can never be offensive, Mr. Woolet—at least, not to me. Please let me know what you have to communicate. Whether it concern me or not, I promise you it shall have my full consideration, and such response as I can give."

"First, Mrs. Mainwaring, I must ask a question that from any other might be deemed impertinent; but you have done me the honour to trust me as your legal adviser, and that must be my excuse. There is a rumour abroad—indeed, I might say, something more than a rumour—that your daughter is about to be—to contract an alliance with one of the sons of General Harding. May I ask if this rumour has any truth in it?"

"Well, Mr. Woolet, to you I shall answer frankly that there is some truth in it."

"May I further ask which of the General's sons is to be the fortunate and, I may say, happy individual?"

"Really, Mr. Woolet! But why do you want to know that?"

"I have my reason, madam—a reason that also concerns you, if I am not mistaken."

"In what way?"

"By reading this you will learn."

A sheet of bluish foolscap, with the ink scarcely dried upon it, was spread out before the eyes of the widow. It was the will of General Harding.

She coloured while reading it. With all the coolness of Scotch blood—with all the steadiness of nerve produced by an eventful life—a long accompaniment of her husband's Indian campaigns—she could not conceal the emotion called forth by what she read upon this sheet of foolscap. It was like the echo of her own thoughts—a response to the reflections that scarce an hour before had been not only passing through her mind, but forming the subject of her conversation.

Adroitly as woman could—and Mrs. Mainwaring was not the most simple of her sex—she endeavoured to make light of the knowledge she thus obtained. She was only sorry that General Harding should so far forget his duties as a parent to make such a distinction between his two sons. Both were equally of his own blood, and though the younger might have been of better behaviour, still he was the younger, and time might cure him of those habits which appeared to have given offence to his father. For herself, Mrs. Mainwaring was very sorry indeed, and although it did not so essentially concern her, she could not do otherwise than thank Mr. Woolet for his disinterested kindness in letting her know the terms of this strange testament, and should always feel grateful to him for what he had done.

The last clause of her speech was delivered in a tone not to be mistaken by such an astute listener as was Mr. Woolet, and, at its conclusion, he folded up the will and prepared to take his departure. To repeat excuses and say that he had only done what he deemed his duty were empty words, and so understood by both.

A glass of sherry, with a biscuit, and the interview was ended. Mr. Woolet returned to his trap, and was soon rolling back to the town, while Buttons was commanded to return the pony to its stable.

The sauntering Belle was summoned back into the drawing-room.

"What did he want, mamma?" was her inquiry on entering. "Anything that concerns me?"

"I should think so. If you marry Henry Harding you will marry a pauper. I have seen the will. His father has disinherited him."

Miss Mainwaring sunk upon the sofa with a cry that told rather of disappointment than despair.

CHAPTER XI.

In the afternoon of that same day Miss Belle Mainwaring sat upon a sofa in a state of expectancy not easily described. It is all the more difficult from its being so rare—that is, the circumstances were under which she sat. She was in the position of a young lady who expects a proposal of marriage to be made to her, and who has already determined upon declining it. She was strong in this determination, though her strength came not from her own inclinations. She was but acting under the commands of her mother.

She was not without some trouble of spirit as to the course she was about to take. In reality, she loved the man she was going to reject—more than she imagined then —more than she knew until long afterward. Flirt as she had been, and still was, conqueress of many a heart, she was not without one herself. It might not be of the purest and truest; but, such as it was, Henry Harding appeared to have won it.

For all that he was not to wear it, unless it could be worn with all the adornments of wealth, and amidst the costliest luxuries of social life.

She now knew he could not do this; and though her heart might still be his, her hand must go to some other —to his brother Nigel, perhaps, she may have whispered to herself. She was a beautiful woman, Belle Mainwaring, tall, large, and exquisitely moulded—a figure that becomes the reclining attitude required by a couch, and as she so reclined upon ordinary occasions, the observer might well have been excused for admiring her.

On the day in question her attitude was different. It

was not easy, not well befitting her figure. She sat bolt
upright, now and then starting to her feet, pacing the
room in quick, hurried strides, stopping a moment by the
window, and scanning the road outside, and then returning
to the couch, and staying there for a short time, a prey to
unrest and anxiety.

At times she would sit reflecting on the answer she
should give—how it might be shaped so as to make it
least unpalatable to him who was to receive it. She had
no doubt about its bitterness, for she felt confident in
having the heart of the man about to offer her his hand.
She did not wish to unnecessarily give him pain, and she
studied the style of her intended refusal until she fancied
she had most cunningly arranged it. But then would
come a spasm of her own heart's pain, for to say " No,"
was costing it an effort, and at this the whole structure
would give way, leaving her answer unshaped as before.

Once she was on the point of changing her purpose, and,
prompted by the nobility of love, giving way to her better
nature. She would accept Henry Harding spite of his
adverse fortune—spite of the counsels of her mother.

But this noble resolve remained but a moment in her
mind. It passed like a flash of lightning, only showing
more distinctly the dark clouds that would surround such
a course. A husband disinherited, a thousand pounds
alone left him—it would scarce be enough to furnish the
feast and the trousseau she might expect upon the day of
her marriage! Preposterous! Her mother was in the
right, and she must yield to the maternal will.

There was another thought had kept her to this determination. She felt confident in her conquest ; and if at any
future time she might see fit to give way to her predilection,
it might still be possible to do so. General Harding might
repent the disinheritance of his youngest son, and revoke
the will he had made, perhaps in a moment of spite or
passion. Neither the lawyer who had made it, nor her
own mother, had any idea of the General doing so. It was
not in keeping with his character. But Belle believed
differently. She saw through the eyes of hope, lighted by
the light of love.

In such a frame of mind did Miss Mainwaring await the expected visit of Henry Harding; nor was there any change when the boy in buttons announced his arrival, and the moment after ushered him into the room. Perhaps, just at that moment, at sight of his handsome face and manly form, her heart may have faltered in its resolution. But only for an instant. A thought of his disinheritance, and it was again firm.

She was right as to the object of his coming. Indeed, he had all but declared it at their last interview—all but accomplished it. Words had already passed between them that might have been construed on his side to a proposal, on hers to an acceptance. He now came in all the confident expectation of formally closing the engagement by the terms of a betrothal.

Frank, loyal, and without thought of trick or deception, he at once declared his errand.

The answer went like an arrow through his heart, its poison but little subdued by the fact of its being conditional. The conditions were, "the consent of mamma."

Henry Harding could not understand this. She, the imperious Belle, who in his eyes seemed armed with all power and authority, to have her happiness dependent on the will of a mother, and that mother known to be at the same time selfish and capricious! It was a rebuff unexpected, and filled him with forebodings as to what might be the decision of Miss Mainwaring's mother. He was not one to bear the agony of doubt, and at once demanded to see her.

This demand was complied with, and in less than five minutes after, the couch, lately graced by the fair, frivolous daughter, was occupied by the staid, serious mother—the daughter absenting herself from the interview.

In the frigid face of the widow Henry Harding read his fate. His forebodings were confirmed. Mrs. Mainwaring was sensible of the honour he would have conferred by becoming her son-in-law, and deeply thankful for the offer; but the position in which she and her daughter were placed made such a union impossible. Mr. Harding must know that by the sudden death of her late dear husband she had been left in straitened circumstances—that Belle was therefore without fortune; and that as he, Mr. Harding, was in the same position, a union between the two would not only be impolitic, but absolute insanity. Though poor, her child had always been accustomed, if not to the luxuries, at least to the comforts, of a home. What would be her condition as the mother of a family, with a husband struggling to maintain them? Mrs. Mainwaring could not speculate on such a fate for her dear child; and although Mr. Harding was young, and had the world all before him, he had not been brought up to any profession promising a maintenance, nor yet to those habits likely to lead to it. For these reasons she, Mrs. Mainwaring, must firmly, but respectfully, decline the offered alliance.

Throughout the speech, which partook somewhat of the nature of a lecture, Henry Harding sat listening in silence, but with astonishment strongly depicted in his features. This had reached its climax long before the last sentence was delivered.

"Surely, madam," said he, giving vent to his surprise, "you can not mean this?"

"Mean what, Mr. Harding?"

"What you have said of my inability to support a— your daughter. I know nothing of the struggle you speak of. I admit I have no profession, but my expectations are not so poor as to make it necessary I should have one. Surely my father's estate is sufficient to provide against such a future as you allude to? And there are but two of us to share it!"

"If that be your belief, Mr. Harding," rejoined the widow, in the same cold, relentless tone in which she had all along been speaking, "I am sorry to be the first to disabuse you of it. The estate you speak of will not be so equally divided. Your share in it will be a legacy of a thousand pounds. Such a trifling sum would not go far toward the maintenance of an establishment!"

Henry Harding stayed not to answer the last remark, made half interrogatively. In those that preceded it he had heard enough to satisfy him that he had no longer any business in the drawing-room of Mrs. Mainwaring ; and hurriedly recovering hat and cane, he bade her an abrupt good morning.

He did not deign to address the same scant courtesy to her daughter. Between him and Belle Mainwaring was now opened a gulf so wide that it could never be bridged over, not even to save him from a broken heart.

As the rejected lover strode away from the cottage that contained what he late looked upon as his mistress, black clouds came rolling over the sky, as if to symbolize the black thoughts in his heart.

In all his youthful life it was the first great shock he had received—a shock both to soul and body, for in the announcement made by Mrs. Mainwaring there was a blow aimed at both. His love blighted, his fortune gone, both, as it were, in the same instant. But the bitterest reflection of all was that the love had gone with the fortune. The reverse he could have more calmly endured ; but to think that the love speeches that had been exchanged between him and Belle, the tender glances, and the soft secret pressure of hands that more than once had been mutually imparted—to think that all these had been false, heartless, and hollow, was enough to wound something more than the self-esteem of a nature open and noble as was his.

He could frame no excuse for her conduct. He tried, but without success. It was too clear the cause of her refusal, too clear were the conditions on which she would have accepted his love, and had led him to believe in its acceptance. It had been all pretence—the very essence of cunning and coquetry. It was over now, and with a bitter vow he resolved to expel her from his heart—from his thoughts, if that were possible. It was youth entering upon a hard struggle ; but to a nature like his, and under such temptation to continue it, there was a chance of success. The woman he had hitherto looked upon as the type of all that was innocent and angelic had proved herself not only capricious, but cunning, selfish, mean, less deserving of love than contempt. If he could but bear this impression upon his mind there would be a hope of his recovering the heart he had so inconsiderately sacrificed. He registered a mental vow to do this, and then turned his thoughts upon his father. Against him he was all anger. He had no doubt that the threat had been carried out—the will had been made that very morning. The minuteness of Mrs. Mainwaring's information—even to the exact amount of his own legacy—left him no room to question its correctness. How she had obtained it he neither knew nor cared. She was sharp-witted enough to have placed herself in communication with his father's solicitor, whom he supposed to have made the will; but he did not stay to speculate upon this. His thoughts were all turned upon the testator himself, who by that single stroke had deprived him at once of his love and his living.

In the agony of his soul he could not see how his father had befriended him—how he had saved him from a fate far worse than disinheritance. His contempt for the cruel coquette was not yet keen enough for the perception of that.

His father's threat had been only conditional. He might now return with a chance of the will being revoked. He might not be restored to full favour. There might be some punishment for his disobedience, as complete and defiant as if his suit had succeeded. But such a grand penalty would scarce be exacted. It was not compatible with the indulgence he had already experienced.

A meaner spirit would have reasoned thus. Nigel Harding would have done so, and returned to seek the favours he had forfeited.

Not so Henry. His pride had been touched—stung to the quick, and in the midst of his mortification, with his soul suffering from its thwarted passion, while pacing the path homeward to his father's mansion, he resolved that that mansion should know him no more.

And he kept his resolution. On reaching the park-gates, instead of entering, he walked on to the nearest inn, and thence took a fly to the nearest railway station.

In another hour he was in the midst of the metropolis, with a thought of never again beholding the green Chiltern Hills or the shire of Buckingham.

CHAPTER XII

On that same evening, as usual, there were four chairs placed at the dinner-table of General Harding. One was empty that was to have been occupied by his younger son.

" Where is he ? " asked the General, drawing the napkin across his breast.

Nigel knew not. Of course the old maid could not tell. With her the scapegrace was not a favourite, and she took no heed of his movements. The butler was questioned, but knew not where Master Henry had gone. Nigel could tell this : he had seen him take the path toward the cottage of the Mainwarings, and a frown darkened on his brow as he imparted the intelligence.

" He may have stayed for dinner," added the elder brother, " Mrs. Mainwaring makes him so welcome."

" She won't after a while," rejoined the General, with a smile that to some extent relieved the dark frown he, too, exhibited.

Nigel looked at his father, but forbore asking for an explanation. He seemed to divine something that gave him relief, for the cloud upon his brow became sensibly lighter.

Upon that subject the conversation dropped, nor would it have been resumed again during dinner, but, before the meal was ended, a communication came into the room through the medium of the butler. It was in the shape of a note, evidently scrawled in haste, and upon paper that could only have come from the escritoire of a cottage or a country inn. From the latter it had issued—the Hare and Hounds, a hostelry that stood not far from the gates of General Harding's park on the high-road to London. There was no post-mark, the letter having been hand-carried.

Hurried as was the scrawl of the superscription, the General recognised it as the handwriting of his son Henry.

The shadow returned to his countenance as he tore open the envelope. It grew darker as he deciphered the contents of the note enclosed therein. They were as follows :—

"FATHER,—I say 'father,' since I cannot dissimulate my real thoughts by prefixing the epithet ' dear'—when this reaches you I shall be on the road to London, and thence Heaven knows where, but never more to return to a house which by your own decreeing can no longer be a home to me. I could have borne my disinheritance, for perhaps I deserved it; but the consequences to which it has led are too cruel for me to think of it otherwise than with anger. But the deed is done, and let that be an end of it. I write to you now only to say that, as by the terms of your will, I may some day become the fortunate re-cipient of a thousand pounds, perhaps you will have no objections to pay it to me now, deducting, if you please, the usual interest, which I believe can be calculated according to the rules of the assurance societies. A thousand pounds at your death—which I hope may be far distant—would scarce be worth waiting for. Now it would serve my purpose, since I am determined to go abroad, and seek fortune under some more propitious sky than that which lowers over the Chiltern Hills. But if I do not find the sum at your London lawyer's within three days subject to my order, I shall make my way abroad all the same, and am not likely ever to ask for it again. So, father, you may choose in this matter whether to oblige me or not, and perhaps my kind brother Nigel, whose counsels you are so ready to take, may help you in deter-mining the choice.

"HENRY HARDING."

The General sprang from his chair long before he had finished reading the letter. He had read it by fits and starts, striding about the room, and, stamping his foot upon the floor till the glasses jingled upon the table.

"My Heavens!" he cried, "what is the meaning of this?"

"Of what, dear father?" asked the obsequious Nigel. "You have received some unpleasant news?"

"News!—news!—worse than news!"

"From whom, may I ask?"

"From Henry—the scamp!—the ungrateful—— Here, read this!" Nigel took the note and read.

"It is indeed an unpleasant communication—insulting, I should say. But what does it all mean? I am at a loss to understand it."

"No matter what it means. Enough for me to know that. Enough to think that he is gone. I know the boy well. He will keep his word. He's too like myself about that. Gone! O, God! gone!"

The General groaned as he traversed the Turkey carpet. The maiden aunt said nothing, but sat by the table quietly sipping her port and munching her walnuts. The storm went on.

"After all," put in Nigel with the pretence of tranquillizing it, "he means nothing with all this talk. He's young, foolish——"

"Means nothing!" roared the General, in a fresh burst of excitement. "Does it mean nothing to write such a letter as this, in which every word is a slight to my authority—a defiance?"

"That is true enough, and I know not what can have possessed him to speak as he has done. He's evidently angry about something—something I don't understand. But he'll get over it in time, though you may not so easily."

"Never! I will never forgive him. He has tried my temper too often; but this will be the last time. Disobedience such as his shall be overlooked no longer, to say nothing of the levity, the positive defiance, that accompanies it. By Heaven! he shall be punished for it!"

"In that regard," interposed the unctuous elder son, "since he has spoken of my giving you advice, it would be to leave him to himself—at least for a time. Perhaps after he has passed some months without the extravagant support you have hitherto so generously afforded him, he may feel less independent, and more prone to penitence. I think the thousand pounds he speaks of your having promised him, and which I know nothing about, should be kept——"

"He shan't have a shilling of it—not till my death."

"For your sake, my father, a long time I hope ; and for his, perhaps it may be all the better so."

"Better or worse, he shan't have a shilling of it—not a shilling. Let him starve till he comes to his senses."

"The best thing to bring him to his senses," chimed in Nigel; "and take my word for it, father, it will do that before long, you'll see."

This counsel seemed to tranquillize the excited spirit of the irate General at least for a time. He returned to the table and to his port, over which he sat alone, and to a much later hour than was his usual custom. The mellow wine may have made him more merciful ; but whether it was this or not, before going to bed he staggered to his studio, and wrote, in a somewhat unsteady hand, a letter to his London lawyer, directing the latter to pay to his son Henry on demand a cheque for the sum of £1,000.

He despatched the letter by a groom, to be in time for the morning post ; and all this he did with an air of caution, as if he intended to do good by stealth. But what appears caution to the mind of a man obfuscated with four bottles of port, may seem carelessness to those who are around him. There was one who looked upon it in this light. Nigel knew all about the writing of the letter, guessed its contents, and was privy to its despatch for the post. Outside the hall-door it was taken from the hands of the groom to whom it had been intrusted, and transferred to the hands of another individual who was said to be going past the village post-office. It was Master Nigel who caused the transferrence to be made. But from him the new messenger had received certain instructions, in consequence of which the letter never reached its destination.

CHAPTER XIII.

LONDON THUGS

On arriving in London Henry Harding put up at a West End hotel, which he had allowed his cabman to select, for he knew very little of London or its life. He had only paid two or three transient visits to it; and but few of his father's acquaintances resided in the metropolis. Upon these he did not think of calling. He supposed that the affair with his father might have transpired among them, perhaps his defeat by Belle Mainwaring; and he had resolved upon keeping out of sight to avoid the necessity of concealing his chagrin. Henry Harding had a proud spirit, and could neither have brooked ridicule nor accepted sympathy. For this reason, instead of hunting out any old college acquaintances he might have discovered in London, he rather avoided the chances of meeting them.

Besides the note written to his father he had addressed one to the footman, simply directing this individual to pack up his clothes, guns, canes, and other impedimenta, and send them on to Paddington Station "till called for." This was done; and the luggage in due time arrived at the hotel where he was staying. Some eight or ten pounds of loose money, that chanced to be in his pocket on leaving home, was all the cash he commanded; and this was out of his pocket before he had been half that number of days in London.

For the first time in his life he began to find what an inconvenient thing it is to be without cash—especially in the streets of a large city—though he yet only knew it as an inconvenience. He expected his father would accede to the request he had made, and send an order for the payment of the thousand pounds. To allow time for the transaction he kept away from the office of the solicitor for nearly a week. He then called to make the inquiry. It was simply whether any communication relating to him had been received from his father. In case there had been none, he did not wish the lawyer to be any wiser about the affair. None had been—not any. This was the answer given him.

In three days he called again and reiterated his former inquiry almost word for word. Almost word for word was the answer he had—not from the solicitor himself, but the head clerk of his office. General Harding had written no letter lately to Messrs. Lawson & Son (the name of the firm), either in reference to him or any other subject.

"He's not going to send it," bitterly soliloquized Henry as he left the solicitor's office. "I suppose I'm not punished enough, so he thinks, with my precious brother to back him. Well, he can keep it. I shall never ask another shilling from him if I should starve."

There is a sort of stern pleasure in this self-abnegation —at least during the early stages of its incipience. But it is a pleasure traceable rather to revenge than virtue, and often dies out before the passion that has given it birth.

With Henry Harding it was not so shortlived. His spirit had been sorely chafed by the treatment he had received, both from his sweetheart and his father. He could not separate them in his mind; and his resentment, directed against both, was strong enough to lead him to almost any resolution. He formed that of not going back to the office of the solicitor, and he kept it. It cost him a struggle to which, perhaps, a less proud spirit would have yielded, for he was soon suffering for want of cash. His spendthrift life had suddenly come to an end—since he had no means of continuing it; and he was forced to reflect on how he could find the means of a mere living. He had changed to a cheaper hotel, but even the accommodation of this would require to be paid for, so that his circumstances were approaching desperation. What was he to do? Enlist in the army? Offer himself aboard a merchant ship? Drive a cab? Carry a sandwich? Or sweep a crossing? None of these occupations were exactly to his

taste. Better than any or all of them, go abroad. There,
if it come to the worst, he could try one or the other.

But there were other chances to be found abroad; and
abroad he determined upon going. Fortunately, he had
sufficient left to carry him across the sea—even the great
Atlantic Ocean; for if his coin had been all spent, he had
still something in the shape of a valuable watch, pins,
and other *bijouterie*, that could be converted into currency.
These would yield enough to pay his passage to any
part of the New World—for he intended going to some
distant land—far away from his father and Belle Mainwaring.

He had converted his chattels into cash—a thing that
can be done in London in an incredibly short space of
time, if we are not particular about the price; he had
made a visit to the West India Docks for the purpose of
inspecting an advertised ship, and was returning home not
over-satisfied either with himself or his fortunes. The
berth offered him was shabby and not cheap, and he had
hesitated about accepting it. He had gone afterward to
Greenwich Park—the Elysian Fields of the humble excur-
sionist—and there, of course, partaken of tea and shrimps.
The hour was late as he dismounted from the knifeboard
of a Holborn 'bus, and turned down Little Queen Street
on the way to his quarters in Essex Street, Strand. He
had taken a Paddington 'bus as the only one plying westward at that hour.

As he stepped into the little street his eye fell upon an
oyster-shop, usually open to the latest hours of the night
and some of the earliest of the morning. Not satisfied
with the Greenwich diet of tea and shrimps—long since
digested—he entered the oyster-shop and gave an order
for a dozen of those luscious bivalves to be opened for
him. There was another guest standing before the bar—
a young man who had gone in before him, who had given a
similar order, and was already engaged in swallowing the
shell-fish.

With the appearance of this young man Henry Harding
was strangely impressed. He was handsome, of a complexion almost olive, dark curling hair, a full round eye,

and an aquiline nose—features that at once proclaimed him a foreigner. The few words to which he gave utterance confirmed it. They were spoken in very imperfect English, with an accent which appeared to be Italian. Notwithstanding a somewhat threadbare suit of clothes, his bearing told either of birth or breeding; in short, one could not have made much of a mistake in supposing him to have been brought up a gentleman.

If Henry Harding had been asked why the young man had interested him he perhaps could not have told. But it was his gentle air, coupled with garments that scarce corresponded, and, above all, the idea that he was looking upon a stranger in a strange land—alone, perhaps friendless—a foreshadowing of his own future. These were the thoughts passing through his mind, and at the moment made him look with a friendly eye upon his fellow oyster-eater before the bar.

He was in the mood to have addressed him, but a certain air of seriousness in the young man's countenance, coupled with the fact of his speaking English so imperfectly, with a fear that the intrusion might be mistaken, hindered the young ex-squire of the Chilterns from taking the liberty.

The other merely glanced at him, and noticing an aristocratic face, with a Bond Street style of dress, supposed, no doubt, that he was standing beside some " swell " who had just left one of the theatres close by. Such a character would be no company for him, and with this reflection he finished his oysters, paid for them over the counter, and passed out into the street.

The young Englishman saw him depart with a reflection just bordering upon pain. There was a face that had strangely interested him. It was not likely in the great world of London he would ever see it again. Besides, he would soon himself be beyond the confines of that world, still further lessening the chances of a re-encounter. With this thought he dismissed the stranger from his mind, paid the reckoning at the oyster-bar, and made a fresh start for his hostelry in the Strand.

He had cleared Little Queen Street, and entered the sister

street of similar name, but with melancholy thoughts, his mind being now absorbed with anxiety.

He had turned his face toward Lincoln's-Inn-Fields, as along the western edge of the square was his shortest route to Essex Street. The ponderous arch was before him, and he was proceeding quietly toward it, when under the long, low passage, dimly lit, he perceived what appeared to be the figures of three men. One of them was apparently tipsy, the other two taking care of him.

He didn't much relish squeezing past this group, but there was no help for it, and he kept on. When close up to them he saw that the drunken man was absolutely helpless, his legs refusing to do him the slightest service, and he was only prevented from sinking down on the pavement by the support of his companions, one on each side of him. They had halted under the shadow of the archway, and did not show any signs of moving onward. Perhaps they had had a long spell since leaving the " public," and wanted a little rest.

That was no business of Henry Harding's, and he was quite contented to pass on without interfering, the more so as the countenance of one of the two sober parties of the trio —turned for a moment toward him as he came up—clearly counselled the shunning of its owner. He was passing on, and had already got beyond the group, when curiosity prompted him to glance back. The face of a man so helplessly intoxicated as the one supported between the other two could not be other than a curious spectacle.

Henry Harding looked upon it. There was lamplight near by that enabled him to do so, and further to distinguish the countenance of the inebriate. It was not without an exclamation of surprise that he recognised features which had so strangely interested him—those of the stranger, late seen in the oyster-shop!

" What's this ? " he exclaimed, suddenly turning upon his heel and facing the trio—" this gentleman drunk ? "

" Drunk as Bacchis ! " answered one of the men. " We're tryin' to get 'im home, an' ha' been at it for the best part o' an hour."

" Indeed ! "

" Yis, sir. He's had a drap too much, as ye see. He's a friend of ours, and we don't want the perlice to take him to the station."

" Of course you don't!" said the young sprig of Beech-wood Park, now fully comprehending the case. "Well, that's kind of you both ; but as I am also a friend of this gentleman, you had better leave him in my charge, and save yourselves any further trouble. Do you agree to it?"

" Agree be blowed ! What do you mean ? "

" This ! " shouted Henry, who could no longer restrain his indignation. " This ! " he repeated, delivering a blow of his stout Buckinghamshire stick upon the head of one of the supporters : " And this ! " he cried thrice in rapid succession as the stick descended on the skull of the second scoundrel, and all three, garroters and garroted, sunk together upon the pavement.

By the merest accident in the world a policeman appeared upon the spot. In Lincoln's-Inn-Fields there are no area safes, and a great scarcity of rabbit-pie. As a consequence, the guardians of the night may be seen occasionally upon their beat ; and, as good luck would have it, one sauntering along Great Queen Street heard the scuffle under the arch, and hastened toward the spot.

He came up in time to assist Henry Harding in securing the two garroters, and stripping them of the spoils they had taken from the person of the stranger, of which they had already possessed themselves. All went together to the police station—the stranger by this time having partially recovered from his intoxication—of chloroform— whence, in a cab, he was taken by Henry Harding to his lodgings, and left there, with a promise on the part of his rescuer to return to him on the following day.

CHAPTER XIV

TURNED ARTIST

A SLIGHT incident—the dropping of a pin or the turning of a straw—may affect the whole current of a man's life. There may be a fixed fate, but if so, it often seems to be brought about, or depend upon, circumstances purely accidental. Had Henry Harding not gone home by Holborn Bars : had he not got down at the corner of Little Queen Street : had he not taken a fancy for shell-fish : had he not that day done a hundred other things, all of which may have indirectly conducted to the encounter above described —his whole after-life might have been as different from what is to chronicle, as if it were that of some other man.

In a week from that time he might have been on his way to the West Indies, or some part of the great American continent, perhaps never to come back ; whereas in a week from that time he was sitting in a studio, with a palette on his left thumb, a brush in his right hand, and an easel in front of him, while the classic blouse of brown holland and the embroidered cap told that he had turned artist.

The change in his life's programme can be easily explained. The gentleman whom he had rescued from the garroters had become his patron ; and listening to the counsels of the young Italian artist—for such was he—he had himself taken to painting as a means of procuring his livelihood. Nor was it such a despairing venture. He had already displayed taste in his school drawings ; and was, moreover, gifted with that aptitude for the art that usually leads to success. Almost from the first day spent in the studio, he was enabled to produce sketches that could be sold ; and these were followed by those " furniture pictures " which have given not only practice, but material support, to many an artist afterward eminent in the profession, and who, otherwise, might never have been heard of.

The young Italian painter—Luigi Torreani by name—was himself but a beginner, but with that talent both of conception and execution which distinguishes the country-men of Titian, he was rapidly rising in his profession. He had got beyond the point of painting for mere bread, and was receiving a price for his pictures that promised something more than a mere subsistence.

It was upon the strength of his own success that he had given counsel to his new acquaintance. He had done so, after ascertaining something of the situation and prospects of the strong gallant youth who had done him such an essential service. Henry at the time had told him but little of his antecedents. This was not needed to a mind generous as that of Luigi Torreani, and a spirit at the same time touched with a sense of gratitude. On discovering the young Englishman's project of self-banishment from his native land, he combated the idea with his counsel, and proposed in the event of his abandoning it, to instruct him in his own art. In fine, his proposal was accepted, and Henry Harding adopted the profession of painter.

From acquaintances thus strangely introduced to each other, the two young men, not greatly differing in years, became fast friends, sharing apartments, table, and studio together, and for many months the friendly association was continued. It was interrupted only by the advice of Luigi who, deeply interested in the success of his brother artist, became desirous that the latter should spend some time in Rome, to perfect himself by the contemplation of those classic forms still so plentiful in the ancient metro-polis of the world. For himself the young Italian needed no such suggestive models. A Roman by birth, he had commenced his studies in their midst, and had ended by transferring his practice to that modern metropolis where the painting of them was sure to be best paid for. The education of his pupil, therefore, was to be the reverse of his own. The young Englishman accepted the advice, less from any profound love of his art, or ambition to excel in it, than from a longing, such as most youths feel, to look upon Italy. Italy ! the classic land of our schoolboy exercises; the land of bright skies and soft summer scenes ; the land of Tasso, of Ariosto, of Byron, Boccaccio, and the Brigands! Who does not desire to behold such a land—classically poetical in its past, romantically picturesque in its present, and, it is hoped, to be free and prosperous in its future?

Henry Harding longed to look upon this land. And mingled with his longings was a hope he might there find Lethe, or at least some solace for a spirit still suffering sorely from the cruel treatment it had received—from a double disappointment in—its affection and its love.

So long as he remained in England, amid its sounds and scenes suggestive, these memories would for ever remain fresh. Perhaps in a foreign land, with strange objects under his eye, strange voices sounding in his ear, he might be enabled to realize the truth of the oft-quoted adage, " Absence conquers love."

CHAPTER XV.

ON the road to Rome leading out into the Campagna, a young man might have been seen wending his way toward the hill country where shoot down the spurs of the Apennines.

At a glance he was not an Italian. A fine open face, with cheeks of ruddy hue, curls caressing them of a rich auburn colour, but, above all, a frame of strong, almost herculean, build, borne forward by a free, unfettered step, pronounced him a son of the North —a Saxon.

A portfolio under his arm, a palette hooked upon his left thumb, some half-dozen camel-hair brushes carried in his hand, proclaimed his profession—a painter in 'search of a subject.

There was nothing in all this to attract the attention of those he met or passed upon the route; neither the personal appearance of the painter nor the paraphernalia that declared his calling. An artist on the roads around Rome is an entity that may be often encountered—though, perhaps, not so often as a bandit.

If any one took notice of the individual in question, it was merely to remark that he was a stranger—*un Inglese*—and perhaps wonder why he was trudging out towards the hills while he might be enjoying himself ten times better in the cabarets and inns of the Eternal City.

That the artist in question was *un Inglese* no one who saw him doubted; nor will the reader, when told that he was no other than Henry Harding.

Why he was upon a Roman instead of an English road is already known.

Flung upon his own resources in the great City of London—too proud to return to his father's home, stung by what he fancied to have been a refusal of his last request—he had, under the tutelage of his Italian friend, taken to painting as a regular profession.

He had not stained canvas without some success; enough to justify him in following the advice of Luigi Torreani, and completing his studies under the bright skies of Italy and amid the classic scenes of the seven-hilled city: Thither had he found his way, with no other support than the precarious earnings of his pencil—as might have been evidenced by his threadbare coat and chafed *chaussure,* as he trudged along the dusty road of the Romagna.

Whither was he going? He was far enough out to have almost lost sight of the Eternal City and those classic monuments that only give proofs of its decay. These, one would think, should have been the objects of his study— the subjects upon which to perfect it. And so they had been. He had painted them, one after another : portal and palace, sculptured figure and fresco, Capital and Coliseum, till his head was tired with such art delineation, and he was now on his way to the hills, to drink from the pure fountain of Nature, to fling rock and stream and tree upon the canvas under the light of an Italian sun and the canopy of an azure sky.

It was his first journey to the Campagna, and he was going without a guide—only inquiring now and then for Val-di-orno—a small mountain town lying near the Neapolitan frontier. To the "Sindico" of the place he carried a letter of introduction obtained from his son, who was the young Italian artist he had left behind him in London. But the chief object of this country excursion was to find some scene paintable, and worthy of being painted. He had not made many miles along his route before being tempted to stop, and tempted more than once. Every turn of the road presented him with a landscape, every peasant would have made a picture.

He resisted these allurements with the thought that these landscapes so nigh to the city might all have been sketched before, while the peasants could be caught at any time in the streets of Rome itself, and there painted in all their picturesqueness.

On towards some shaggy hills he saw looming out in the distance, and on he went, until near the close of the day he found himself toiling up a steep ravine, whose every turn gave him a tableau worthy of being transferred to canvas, and hung six feet high against the walls of the Royal Academy.

After a slight repast drawn from his wallet, and a smoke from his meerschaum pipe, he set about painting a scene which he at length selected. He fought against the fatigue of his journey, for the sake of catching a magnificent mellow sunset that had welcomed his approach to the place. He had no need to add to the " composition " of his picture. Rocks, trees, cliffs, torrents foaming over them, points of *chiaro* and *oscuro*, abruptly contrasted, all were under his eye.

If there was aught wanting to give life to the landscape, it was only a few figures—animal or human—and these would fill in with his fancy.

"Ah!" he reflected aloud, "just the scene for a band of brigands. I'd give something to have half a dozen of them in the foreground. I could then make a picture of these fantastic Turpins drawn from real life—a thing I take it has never been done before. That would be something to hang up in the Royal Academy—something worth wasting colour and canvas on. I'd give——"

"How much?" answered a voice that seemed to issue out of the rocks behind him. "How much would you give, Master Painter, for that ye speak o'? If you bid high enough, I daresay I mout find the means o' accommodatin' you."

Along with the voice came the footsteps of a man—not

in soft stealthy tread as of one approaching unawares, but
with a quick thump, as the man himself dropped down
from a rock to the little platform upon which the artist
had planted his " sticks."

The latter looked up—at first in surprise—then, rather
in pleased admiration. He was thinking only of his art;
and before him stood the very model of his imagination—
a man clad in a complete suit of plush and coloured velvet,
breeched, bandaged, and belted, with a plumed hat upon
his head, and a short carbine across his arms—in costume
and caparison the beau-ideal of a brigand ! Two things
alone hindered him from appearing the true heroic type
of stage representation—such as we are accustomed to see
in " Mazzaroni" and the " Devil's Brother." There was
a broad Saxon face, and a tongue unmistakably from the
shire of Somerset.

Both were so marked that but for the velveteen knee-
breeches, the waist-belt, the elaborately buttoned vest, and
the plumed hat upon his head, Henry Harding might have
thought himself at home, and in the presence of a man he
had met before.

Ere the young artist had sufficiently recovered from his
surprise to respond to the unexpressed salutation, the picturesque stranger continued—

" Want to paint brigands, do ye ? Well, there's a
chance for ye now. The band's close by, above a bit; I'll
call 'em down. Hey ! there, captain ! " changing his
English to Italian, " ye may come on. It's only one of
them poor devils o' daubers from the city. He wants to
take our likenesses. I s'pose you've no objection to his
doin' it ? "

Before the painter could make response, or remove his
paraphernalia out of the way, the ledge he had selected for
his " point of view " was crowded with figures—one and
all of them so picturesquely attired that had they stood in
the Corso, or elsewhere within police protection, he would
have been only too delighted to have painted them in the
most pre-Raphaelitish detail.

As it was, all thoughts of art were at once chased out of
his mind. He saw that he was encircled by banditti !

To attempt retreat was out of the question. They were above, below, on all sides of him. Even had he been swifter of foot than any of the gang, their carbines were slung handy—*en bandoliere;* and a volley from these would certainly have checked his course. There was no alternative but to resign himself to his fate.

CHAPTER XVI.

IF he who had surprised the painter at his task did not present the exact classic type of the stage bandit, there was one upon the ground who did. He stood a little in advance of the others, with that easy air that betokened authority. There was no mistaking this man's position. He was the chief.

His dress did not differ so materially from that of his followers in cut or fashion. It was but more costly in its material. Where their breeches were velveteen, his was of the finest silk velvet. Besides, there was a glitter about his arms, and a sparkle on the clasp that held the plume in his Calabrian hat, that bespoke real jewellery. His face, moreover, was not of the common cast. It was of the true Roman type, the nose and chin of exceeding prominence, with the broad oval jawbone, indicative of determination.

He might have been deemed handsome but for an expression of ferocity—animal, almost brutal—that gleamed and sparkled in his coal-black eyes.

If not handsome, he was sufficiently striking; and Henry Harding might have fancied himself confronted by the renowned "Fra Diavolo." Had he stepped from behind the proscenium of the scenic stage, or come bounding from a "back flat," the transpontine spectators would have hailed him as the hero they had come to the theatre to see.

For some seconds there was silence. The first spokesman had slunk into the rear of the band; and all stood waiting for the chief to commence speech or action.

The latter stood looking at the young artist—scanning him from head to foot. The scrutiny seemed to give him no great pleasure. There was not much booty to be expected in the pockets of such a threadbare coat, and a grin passed over his dark features as he pronounced, in contemptuous tone, the word :

" Artista ? "

" Si, signor," replied the artist, with as much *sang froid* as if he had been answering an ordinary question. " At your service, if you wish to sit or stand for your portrait."

" Portrait?   Bah !   What care I for your chalks and ochres, Signor Painter.   Better if you'd been a pedlar with a good fat pack.   That's the sort of toys for such as we.   You're from the Cittada?   What's brought you up here ? "

" My legs," replied the young Englishman, thinking that a bold front might be best under the circumstances.

" Cospetto !   I can tell that without asking.   Such boots as yours don't look much like the stirrup.   But come, declare yourself.   What have you got in your pockets?   A scudi or two, I suppose.   You're not so hard up as to be without that?   How much, signor ? "

" Three scudi."

" Hand them over."

" Here they are, you are welcome to them."

The brigand took the three coins with as much nonchalance as if he had been receiving them in liquidation for some service rendered.

" This all ? " he asked, again surveying the artist from head to foot.

" All I've got upon me."

" But you have more in the Cittada ? "

" A little more."

" How much ? "

" About four score scudi."

" Corpo di Bacco, a good sum.   Where is it lying ? "

" At my lodgings."

" Your landlord can lay hands upon it ? "

" He can, by breaking open my box."

" Good !   Now write out an order, giving him authority to break open the box, and send you the money.   Some paper, Giovanni! Your ink-horn, Giacomo! Here, Signor Artista, write!"

Seeing that it would be idle to make objection, the artist assented.

"Stay!" cried the brigand, arresting his pen, "you have something besides money at your lodgings? You Ingleses always carry about a stock of loose property. I include them in the requisition."

"There is not much to include. Another suit of clothes, but a trifle better than these you see on my back. A score or two of sketches—half-finished paintings—which you wouldn't value, even if the last touch had been given them."

"Ha, ha!" laughed the brigand, his comrades joining in the laugh. "You're a good judge of character, Signor Artista! You can keep your sketches, and your spare suit too; neither of which commodities would be likely to suit our market. Write then for the scudi!"

Again the artist was about to use the pen.

"Hold!" once more exclaimed the bandit. "You have friends in the Cittada. What a mistake I was making not to think of them! They can do something toward your ransom!"

"I have not a friend in Rome—at least not one who would pay five scudi to rescue me from a rope."

"Bah! you are jesting, signor!"

"I am speaking the simple truth."

"If that be so," said the brigand, who seemed to melt a little at mention of the rope. "If that be so," he added reflectingly, then—"Ah! we shall see. Hark you, Signor Painter, if what you say be true, you may sleep in your own lodgings to-night. If false, you will spend your night here in the hills, and perhaps minus your ears. You understand me?"

"It were dull of me not to do so."

"Buono—buono! And now one word of warning. Let there be no trickery in what you write—no deception in what you say. The messenger who carries your letter to the Cittada will learn all about you—even to the quality of your spare suit, and the value of your pictures. If you have friends he will find them out. If not, he will know

it. And by the Virgin! if it turns out that you are playing with us, your ears will answer for it."

" So be it. I accept the conditions."

" Enough! write on ! "

As dictated, the requisition was written. The sheet of
paper was folded, sealed with a piece of pitch, and directed
to the landlord of the lodgings in which the English artist
had set up his studio.

A man in the garb of a peasant of the Campagna was
selected from the band, and, charged with the strange
missive, at once despatched along the road that led toward
the Eternal City.

After kicking down the temporary easel which our
artist had erected, and pitching his slight sketch into the
torrent below, the brigands commenced their march up
the mountain—their captive keeping them company, with
no very pleasant anticipation of the hospitality that might
be in store for him.

CHAPTER XVII.

AN UNLUCKY RENCONTRE

You are surprised at the young Englishman taking things so coolly? To be captured by Italian bandits, famed for their ferocity, is not a trifling affair. And yet so Henry Harding seemed to consider it.

The explanation is simple, and easily intelligible. At any other period he might not only have chafed at his captivity, but felt fear for the consequences. Just then he was suffering from two other sorrows, that made this seem light—to be scarcely considered at all.

The disinheritance by his father was still fresh in his mind—still bitter; but far more bitter the rejection by his sweetheart.

Tortured by these cruel memories of the past, he recked less of what befell him either in the present or the future.

There was even a time when he would have courted such a distraction—during the first few weeks after his departure from home. Twelve months had since elapsed; and close application to his art had to some extent relieved him. Perhaps absence had done more than art—of which he was by no means passionately fond; for he was not one of the thorough enthusiasts who prate about the divine inspiration of painters. Chance alone had guided him to this profession, as the only means he could devise for earning his daily bread—chance, partly directed by taste, and partly by some previous study of his school-days.

So far it had served his purpose, and, enabling him to visit Rome, he had there imbibed a certain ambition to excel in it—enough to soften, though not obliterate, the memory of his misfortunes.

This was still keen enough to make him careless of what

might turn up—hence that strange demeanour in the presence of the bandits, at which you may have felt surprise.

Up the mountains they marched him by one of those execrable roads common in the Papal States, kept, no doubt, in better condition in the time of the Cæsars than to-day.

He speculated but little on where he was being taken. Of course to some forest lair—some mountain cavern, used as a bandit's den.

He was not without curiosity to see such a place ; and perhaps it was passing through his thoughts, that at some day he might avail himself of his present experience to paint a bivouac of brigands from real life.

He was no little surprised when a good-sized village came in sight; still more on seeing the bandits march boldly into it; and his surprise became astonishment when he saw them unsling their carbines, rest them against the walls of the houses, and make other preparations plainly denoting an intention there to pass the night.

The villagers appeared to have little fear of them. On the contrary, some of the men joined them in their wine-drinking; while some of the women rather encouraged than resented their rude sallies. Even the long-robed priest of the place passed to and fro through their midst, distributing crosses and benedictions, for all of which the brigands paid him in coin that had no doubt been taken from the pockets of some unfortunate traveller—perhaps of his own sacred cloth.

It was certainly a scene of sufficient originality to interest the eyes of a stranger—that stranger an artist—and the young Englishman, as he gazed upon it, for a time forgot that he was a captive.

Of this he was reminded as night drew near. Hitherto his captors had not even taken the precaution to tie him. His frank acceptance of the situation, with his apparent indifference to it, had led the chief to think lightly about his making an attempt to escape.

Besides, it would not so much matter. Before he could reach home, the sham peasant would have been to his lodgings and rifled the chest of its contents. The scudi would, at all events, be safe, and beyond these the brigand had formed no very sanguine expectations.

It was not likely there were rich friends, or any chance of a ransom. The well-worn wardrobe of. the painter spoke against such an hypothesis.

Rather in obedience to habit and usage than for any other reason did his captors determine to tie him up for the night, and just as the sun was sinking into the Tyrrhenian Sea two men were seen approaching the place where he had been left, provided with ropes for this purpose.

In one of these he recognised the man who had first saluted him on the platform. He had not forgotten the conversation that had passed between them, nor the tongue in which it had been carried on. That being English, the bandit must himself be an Englishman; as was also evident from his bright skin, hay-coloured hair, and broad bullish face, so unlike the sharp-featured, dark-visaged gentry who surrounded him.

Though at first no little astonished at encountering a countryman in such a place, and especially in such a showy guise—so different from the dull smock-frock the man had once evidently worn—he had ceased for a time to think of him.

Since their first meeting he had not come in contact with him. The fellow appeared to be among the least considered of the troop—only permitted prominence when called upon—and since the capture his services had not been required until now.

He appeared just such a man as one could scarcely see without thinking of rope; and armed with a coil of this he now approached to execute the order of the " captain."

So said he as he stopped in front of the prisoner, and commenced unreeving the cord.

It was the first time Henry Harding had been threatened with the degradation of being bound. To an Englishman there is something disagreeable in the very idea of it; but to a young gentleman late the presumed heir to £50,000, and who had never known a more irksome restriction than the statutes of Eton and Oxford, there was something repulsive in the prospect.

At first he indignantly refused to submit his wrists to being corded—protesting that there was no need for it. He had no intention of attempting to escape. He would stay with the brigands till morning, or the morning after that—any time till the messenger returned. Besides, they had promised him his liberty, on conditions that would be kept on his side, and he hoped on theirs.

His remonstrances were in vain.

" Dom conditions!" roughly replied the man, still occupied in uncoiling the rope. " We know nothin' 'bout them. Our business is to bind ye; them's the orders o' the captain."

And so saying, he proceeded to carry out "the orders o' the captain."

It looked hopeless enough; but still there might be a chance by appealing to the feelings of a countryman. The captive determined on making trial of it.

" You are an Englishman?" he said in his most conciliatory tone.

" I've been one," gruffly answered the bandit.

" I hope you still are."

" I'deed, do ye? What matters that?"

" I am one."

" Who the devil says you ain't' D'ye take me for a fool, not to see it in yer face, and hear it in the cursed lingo that I'd a hoped never to hear again?"

" Come, my good fellow! it's not often that an Englishman——"

" Stash yer palaver, dang ye! an' don't 'good fellow' me! Spread yer wrists now, an' get 'em ready for the rope. Just because you're English I'll tie 'em all the tighter—dang me if I don't '"

Perceiving that remonstrance was thrown away upon the renegade ruffian, and that resistance would only lead to ill-treatment, the young Englishman extended his hands to be tied.

The bandit seized hold of them by the wrists, and commenced twisting them so as to turn them back to back.

But the moment his eyes rested upon the left hand—upon the little finger with its red longitudinal scar—he dropped both as if they had been bars of hot iron, and started backward with a cry.

It was a cry that betokened recognition, mingled with a malignant joy.

The surprise which this occasioned to the captive was followed by another, arising from a different cause. He, too, had effected a recognition. In the brutal brigand before him he identified the gamekeeper, poacher, and murderer—Doggy Dick!

"Ho! ho!" cried Doggy Dick, dancing over the ground like one who had gone frantic from receiving news of some unexpected fortune—"ho! ho! you it be, Muster Henry Hardin'! Who would 'a expected to find you here, among the mountains o' Italy, i'stead o' the Chiltern Hills, where ye were so snug and comfotible? An' wi' such a poor coat upon yer back! Why, what ha' become o' the old General, an' the big property—the park, the farms, the woods, the covers, and the pheasants? Ah! the pheasants—you remember them, don't ye? And so do I, too—so do Doggy Dick—do an' will!"

As the renegade said this, a grin of diabolical significance made itself perceptible on his otherwise inexpressive features.

Henry Harding perceived it, but made no remark: he saw that words would be of no use.

"I dar' say Nigel, that sweet half-brother o' yours, has got 'em all—the park, and the farms, and the woods, and the covers, and the pheasants—ah! and I'd take my affidavy o' 't he's got that showy gal too you were so sweet upon, Muster Henry. She warn't likely to cotton to a man wi' such cloth on his back as you've got on yourn. Why, it look like it 'ad come out o' a pawnshop!"

By this time the blood of the Hardings had got up to boiling-point. Despite his stupidity, Doggy Dick perceived it. He saw that he had gone too far in his provocation, and regretted having done so before tying the hands of him provoked.

He would have retreated from the spot, but it was too

late. Before he could turn Henry Harding's left hand was upon his throat, the scarred finger pressing against his glottis; and with the right he received a blow on the skull that felled him to the ground like an ox under the stroke of a pole-axe.

In an instant the young Englishman was surrounded by the bandits and their wine-bibbing associates.

Half a score flung themselves simultaneously upon him.

He was soon overpowered; bound hand and foot; and then beaten in his bonds—the village damsels clapping their hands, and by their cries applauding the conquest of brute strength over injured innocence!

CHAPTER XVIII.

THERE was one who witnessed the scene with a sympathizing heart. It is almost superfluous to say that it was a woman, for no man in that community would have dared to take sides against the brigands. While in it, these ruffians were complete masters of the place, and out of it their authority was little less. Their den was not distant; and on any day they could descend upon it with the torch of destruction.

The woman who sympathized with the sufferings of the young Englishman was still only a girl; and although the daughter of the Sindico of the town, she could do nothing to rescue him from his persecutors. Even the intermittent authority exercised by her father would at that moment have been unavailing; and her sympathy only existed in the secret recesses of her heart.

Standing in a balcony of what appeared the best house in the village, she presented a picture that may be seen only in a town of the Roman Campagna—a combination of those antique classic graces which we associate with the days of Lucretia. Beauty of the most striking type —innocence of aspect that betokened the most perfect virginal purity—and below a street crowded with Tarquins!

She looked like a solitary lamb in the midst of a conglomeration of wolves, feebly shepherded by her father and the village priest—by the law and the Church, both on the last legs of a decadent authority.

It was a singular picture to contemplate; nor had it escaped the notice of the young Englishman.

The girl had been standing in the balcony ever since

his arrival ; and, as her position was not very far from the place where the brigands had permitted him to take a seat, he had a fair view of her, and could note her every action.

He could see that she was not accosted like the commoner maidens of the village ; but for all this, bold glances were occasionally given to her, and brutal jests uttered within her hearing.

She had looked toward the captive and he at her, until more than once their eyes had met ; and he fancied that in hers he could read the signs of a sympathetic nature.

It may have been but pity for his forlorn situation ; but it was pity that expressed itself in a most pleasing way.

While gazing on that dark Italian girl, he thought of Belle Mainwaring ; but never, during the whole period of his self-exile, had he thought of her with less pain.

As he continued to gaze, he felt some strange solace stealing over his thoughts, which he could only account for by the humiliation caused by his captivity—by a sorrow of the present expelling a sorrow of the past.

Something whispered him that the relief might be more than temporary : he could not tell why. He only knew, or thought, that if he could be permitted to look long enough into the eyes of that Roman maiden, he might think of Belle Mainwaring with a calmer spirit—perhaps forget her altogether !

In that hour of his captivity he was happier than he had been during the past two years of his free, unfettered life. From the contemplation of that fair form posed in the balcony above him, he had in one hour drawn more inspiration than from all the statues in the Eternal City.

One thing interfered with his newly sprung happiness. He observed that the girl only looked upon him with glances of stealth ; that the moment their eyes met, hers were quickly withdrawn.

This might have gratified him all the more, but that he had discovered the cause. He saw that she was under surveillance.

Had it been her father who was watching the girl there would have been nothing to give him pain. But it was

not. The eyes that seemed so vigilantly bent upon her
were those of the bandit chief, who, .wine-cup in hand,
sat outside the little inn, with his face turned toward the
house of the Sindico.

The young girl seemed uneasy under his glances ; and
at length retired from the balcony.

She came out again at the *fracas* caused by the binding
of the captive.

In the midst of the *mêlée*, Henry Harding had his eyes
upon her—even after he was bound and beaten. He bore
all this the better from the glance she gave him. It
seemed to say—

"I should spring down into the street, and rush to your
rescue, but my doing so would be the sealing of your doom."

So construed he the expression upon her face—a construction that imparted pleasure, but also pain.

       *   *   *   *   *

The shadows of night descended over the town.

There were no lamps to illuminate the place; and the
graceful shape in the balcony gradually blending with the
gloom, became lost to his eyes.

The bandits had entered the inn, where they were joined
by the more *bizarre* of the village belles.

Soon came forth the sound of stringed instruments, the
violin and the mandolin, mingled with the tread and
shuffling of many feet. Occasionally loud talk could be
heard, and the clinking of cups ; then curses and quarrels
—one of which terminated in a street fight and the shedding of blood.

All this the young Englishman heard or saw from the
place where he had been fast bound, outside the open window of the inn. He was not left alone. The bandits
stood sentry over him—watching him with a vigilance in
strange contrast with the negligence before displayed.

The captive took note of this change in the behaviour of
the brigands toward him. It was still more notable when
the chief, staggering past at a late hour, addressed some
words to the men in charge of him.

He could hear what was said. It was in the form of an

injunction, terminating in a threat, to the effect that if he —the prisoner—should not be forthcoming next day, they —the sentries—might expect punishment of the severest kind—in short, they should be shot.

So hiccoughed out their intoxicated chief, as he staggered off in the company of the flaunting belle who had taken part in the bandit's ball.

That it was no empty threat made under the influence of drink became evident to the captive, in the increased vigilance with which he was tended. As soon as their chief was out of sight the two sentries made a fresh examination of his fastenings; retightened the cords wherever they had become loose ; and added others for greater security.

Skilled in this peculiar craft by long practice, their prisoner was left but little chance of releasing himself, had he been ever so inclined to attempt it.

And now he was, as he had not been before, not only inclined, but eagerly desirous, of making his escape. The stringent orders of the chief, with the elaborate precautions taken by the two sentries, had naturally awakened within him a degree of apprehension. Such pains would scarce have been taken for the sake of merely keeping him all night, to let him go free in the morning.

Moreover, the messenger who had been sent to the city had already returned. He had seen the man go into the inn while the dance was in progress, and no doubt he had delivered the four score scudi to his chief. It could not be this that was waited for to obtain his delivery.

There was to be another chapter added to his imprisonment—perhaps some cruel torture in store for him. He could only attribute it to the incident that had occurred previous to his being bound. The knock-down blow given to Doggy Dick would be looked upon as an insult to the whole band, and, little as that English renegade might be esteemed by his Italian comrades, he would still have sufficient influence to instigate them to hostility against their captive.

This was the cause to which the latter ascribed the altered treatment he was receiving, and he regretted having given it.

Could he have guessed the true reason, he might have spared himself such self-recrimination. The prolonged imprisonment before him—and such in reality there was—had for motive a scheme far deeper than the hostility of Doggy Dick, either on account of the conflict that had occurred between them, or that of older and earlier date. It was a scheme likely for a long time not only to restrain Henry Harding from his liberty, but perhaps deprive him of his life.

Though apprehensive of receiving some severe castigation at the hands of the brigands, he did not believe himself to be in any danger of this kind; and he was hindered from sleeping less by the prospect of punishment than the pain caused by the cords too tightly looped around his limbs.

Despite this—despite his hard couch, which was the stone pavement of the street—he at length fell asleep, and slept on till the crowing of the village cocks, aided by a kick from one of the brigand sentries, aroused him once more to a consciousness of his situation.

CHAPTER XIX.

At daybreak the brigands were upon the march.

The town where they had spent the night was not one of their safe places. They might halt there for a day, or a night, and refresh or amuse themselves; but a prolonged stay in it might subject them to a surprise by the Papal troops when these chanced to be on the alert.

This was only upon occasions when some unusual outrage committed by the bandits called the latter forth to make a show of chastisement.

Something of the kind was just then reported upon the *tapis*. He who had gone to rifle the chest of the poor artist had brought back word of it. Hence their quick decampment.

When the villagers made their appearance upon the streets they could congratulate one another on a happy riddance of their ruffian guests; though there were some among them to whom this would be no satisfaction—the keepers of the wineshops, for example. To them robbers' gold was as good as any other.

The band proceeded through the hills, evidently making homeward. They were already laden with booty, captured before they had fallen in with the artist. It was, in fact, the report of this foray that was tempting the troops to pursue them.

They had no prisoners—only plunder, in the shape of plate, jewellery, trinkets, and other light personal effects. The *villa di campagna* of some old Roman noble had been the scene of their late raid; and they were carrying the spoils to their den.

That this was in some secluded part of the country was

evident from the roads taken to reach it. Now it was a rough causeway traversing a ridge; anon a mere *scorzo* or cattle-track, zigzagging through the hills, or following the bed of a rivulet.

Long before reaching the end of their journey, the captive was fatigued and footsore. His shoes, none of the strongest, had yielded to the abrasion of the sharp stones; while the long tramp of the preceding day, with a half-sleepless night on the street pavement—to say nothing of the beating the brutes had given him—had but ill prepared him for such an irksome march.

His hands, too, were tied behind his back, and this spoiling his balance, made progress still more difficult and disagreeable. The terrible depression of his spirits also detracted from his strength.

He had good reason for being dispirited. The rigorous watch kept upon him all along the route told him that he was not going to be easily let off. Already the brigand had broken faith with him; for he knew that the courier had come back, and of course brought the scudi along with him.

Once only had he an opportunity of talking to the chief —just before starting out from the village. He reminded him of his promise.

"You have released me," replied the ruffian with a savage oath.

"In what way?" innocently asked the prisoner.

"*Hola!* how simple you are, Signor Inglese! You forget the blow you gave to one of my band."

"The renegade deserved it."

"I shall be judge of that. By our laws your life is forfeit. With us it is blow for blow."

"In that case I should be absolved. Your fellows gave me twenty for one; good measure, as I can tell by my aching ribs."

"Ah!" contemptuously rejoined the bandit, "be satisfied it's no worse with you. Thank the Virgin you're still alive; or perhaps you may come nearer the mark by thanking that scar upon your little finger."

The look with which this last remark was accompanied

spoke of some secret meaning. The captive could not tell what it was; but it gave him food for reflection that lasted him all along the route. Taken in connection with the close watch kept upon him, he could forbode no good from it. On the contrary, there was evil in the innuendo; though of what sort was beyond his intelligence to discover.

On the second day after leaving the town the march continued on through a mountainous country, most of it covered with forest. The track was rougher and more difficult to travel—at times ascending steeps almost precipitous, at others winding through clefts of rocks, so narrow as only to admit the passage of one at a time.

Both brigands and captives suffered from thirst; which they were at length able to quench with the snow found upon the colder exposure of the ridges.

Just before sunset a halt was made, and one of the bandits was sent forward as a scout.

A mountain summit, shaped like a truncated cone, was seen a short distance in front, and toward this the path was trending.

About twenty minutes after the man had disappeared from view, the howl of a wolf came back from the direction in which he had gone, while another similar sound was heard still further off.

Following this there was the bleating of a goat, on hearing which the brigands once more resumed their march.

Rounding an angle of rock, the face of the conical hill was seen from base to top, scarred by a deep ravine that trended to the summit.

Up this lay the path, until the highest point was reached, when a strange picture lay spread before the eye of the captive. He was looking down into a cup-like hollow, nearly circular in shape, sloping sides covered with a straggling growth of timber, in places close packed into groves. At the bottom there was a pond of water; and not far from its edge through the trees, some patches of grey wall, with smoke rising above, declared the presence of human habitation.

It was the rendezvous of the bandits, which they reached just before the going down of the sun.

Their home then was no cave, no mere lair, but something that more resembled a hamlet or village. Two or three of the houses were substantial structures of stone; the rest were simple *pagliatti*, or straw huts, such as are common in the remote mountain districts of the Italian peninsula.

A forest of beech-trees overshadowed the group, while the ridges around were covered with a thick growth of ilex and pine.

A deep dark tarn glistened in the centre, looking like some long-extinct crater, that acted as a reservoir for the rain and melted snow from the mountain slope.

The stone houses could never have been built by the bandits. The straw cabins may have been erected to afford them additional accommodation; but the more substantial dwellings told of times long gone by, before the enervating influence of a despotic government had brought decay upon the territory of Italia. Some miner, perhaps, who extracted ore from the neighbouring mountains, had found here a convenient smelting-place in proximity to the tarn.

Around, the mountains sloped up into ridges that formed a sort of amphitheatre, with apparently two passes leading outward—one to the north, the other to the south. By each of these passes was a peak that rose bald and herbless above the fringe of the forest, and on each of these close to its extreme summit could be seen the figure of a man—visible only from the valley below.

They were the bandit pickets upon their post. Now and then, as they changed attitude, their accoutrements and carbine-barrels could be seen glancing in the golden sunset.

The young Englishman noted all this as he stood in the open plazza of the robber quarters.

It recalled the song of the famed Fra Diavolo, and a night at Her Majesty's Theatre—his box shared by Belle Mainwaring!

He was not allowed long to indulge in such reminiscences—at least in the open air.

Acting under orders from their chief, two of his captors conducted him into a dark chamber in one of the stone houses, and giving him a push that almost sent him face forward upon the floor, closed the door behind him.

There was the harsh grating of a bolt, and then all was silence. For the first time in his life he felt that he was inside a prison !

CHAPTER XX.

THERE was at least relief in being left alone, and Henry Harding felt it so much that scarce had his jailers drawn the key from out the lock than he stretched himself along the floor of his prison, and fell fast asleep.

Some fern-leaves strewn over the stones served him for a couch; though he was too tired to care much for that.

He didn't wake until the sunlight, shooting in through the window, fell slanting upon his face.

Then he arose to his feet, and took a survey of his chamber.

A glance convinced him that he was inside the cell of a prison; for whatever may have been the original design of the room, its adaptability to this purpose was at once apparent.

The window was high above the level of the floor, and so narrow that a cat could barely have squeezed through it. Besides, there was a strong bar set vertically into the sill that rendered egress absolutely impossible.

The door was alike forbidding, and ten minutes' contemplation of the place told the prisoner there was no chance of escape—save in the corruptibility of his jailers.

To Henry Harding there was no hope of that, and he did not even think of it. He saw no alternative but to wait for the development of events.

He was hungry, and would have eaten—anything.

He listened in hopes of hearing a footstep—the tread of a brigand bringing him his breakfast.

He could hear a tread, but it was that of the sentry outside his door.

It came and went, and came and went again, but no sound of drawn bolt or key turning in the lock.

An hour was passed in this hungry uncertainty, and *then* the tread of the sentry became commingled with other footsteps.

A short parley outside. The key was inserted, the bolt clicked back, and the door stood open.

" Good-mornin', Muster Hardin' ! I hope ye ha' passed a pleasant night o't. Compliments o' the captain, an' wants ye to come and see him."

Without further speech Doggy Dick seized the prisoner by the collar. Then with a spiteful shake, such as might have been given by an irate policeman, dragged him out of the cell and conducted him to the quarters of the bandit chief.

As a matter of course, these were in the best house of the place, but the young artist was not prepared to witness the splendour inside. Not only was the furniture well made, but there were articles of *luxe* in abundance— plate, pictures, looking-glasses, clocks, girandoles, epergnes, and the like, not very artistically arranged, but plenteous everywhere. It was a somewhat grotesque admixture of the ancient and modern, such as may be seen in a curiosity shop, or the chambers of a London money-lender.

In the apartment to which the prisoner was introduced there were two individuals seated among this glittering *bijouterie.* One was the brigand chief, whose name he now knew for the first time to be Corvino. He knew it from hearing him so addressed by the other occupant of the chamber, who was a woman ; and who in her turn was called by the chief Cara Popetta—the " Cara " being merely a prefix of endearment.

Corvino, the chief, has been already delineated. Popetta, as being his spouse, also deserves a word.

She was a large woman, nearly as tall as Corvino himself, and quite as picturesquely attired. Her dress was glittering with beads and bugles, and with her dark, almost chestnut-coloured skin and crow-black hair she would have passed muster among the belles of an Indian encampment.

She had once been beautiful, and her teeth were still so when displayed in a smile. Otherwise, they resembled the incisors of a tigress preparing to spring upon her prey.

The beauty that had once shone in her countenance might still to some extent have remained—for Cara Popetta was scarce turned thirty—but a scar of cadaverous hue, that traversed the left cheek, had turned what was once a fair face into a visage disfigured even to ugliness.

And if her eyes spoke the truth, many a scar had equally disfigured her soul; for as she sat eyeing the prisoner as he entered, there was that in her aspect that might have caused him to quail.

Just then he had no opportunity for scanning her very minutely. On the instant of his entrance, he was accosted by the chief, and commanded, rather than requested, to take a seat by the table.

"I need not ask you if you can write, Signor Artista," said the bandit, pointing to the "materials" upon the table. "Such a skilled hand as you with the pencil cannot fail to be an adept with the pen. Take hold of one of these and set down what I indite, translating it, as I know you can, into your native tongue. Here is a sheet of paper that will suit for the purpose."

As he said this, the brigand stretched forth his hand and pointed to some letter-paper already spread out upon the table.

The prisoner took up the pen without having the least idea of what was to be the subject of his first essay at secretaryship. Apparently it was to be a letter, but to whom was it to be written?

He was not long kept in ignorance.

"The address first," commanded the brigand.

"To whom?" asked the amanuensis, making ready to write.

"Al Signor Generale Harding," dictated the bandit.

"To General Harding!" translated Henry, dropping the pen and starting up from his seat. "My father! What know you of him?"

"Enough, Signor Pittore, for my purpose. Sit down again and write what I dictate. That is all I want of you."

Thus commanded, the secretary resumed his seat, and once more taking up the pen, wrote the address as dictated.

As he did so, he thought of the last time he had penned the same words, when directing that angry letter from the inn outside his father's park.

He had no time to give way to reminiscences, for the bandit showed impatience to have the letter completed.

" Padre caro! " was the next phrase that required translation.

Again the secretary hesitated. Again went his memory back to the letter from the roadside inn, in which he had addressed that epistle without the prefix "dear." Was he now to use it at the dictation of a brigand?

The command was peremptory. The bandit, chafed by the delay, repeated it with a menace. His captive could only obey, and down went the words " Dear father."

" And now," said Corvino, " continue your translation; don't stop again. Another interruption may cost you your ears."

This was said in a tone that told the chief to be in earnest.

Of course, in the face of such a terrible alternative, the secretary assented, and continued the writing of the letter to its end.

In the translation it ran as follows:

" DEAR FATHER,—This is to inform you that I am a prisoner in the mountains of Italy, about forty miles from the city of Rome, and upon the borders of the Neapolitan territory. My captors are stern men, and if I be not ransomed will kill me. They only wait till I can hear from you, and for this purpose they send a messenger to you, upon whose safety while in England my life will depend. If you should cause him to be arrested or otherwise hindered from returning here, they will retaliate upon me by a torture too horrible to think of. As the amount of my ransom they demand 30,000 scudi—about £5,000. If the bearer bring this sum back with him in gold—or a circular note on the Bank of Rome will do—they promise me my liberty, and I know they will keep their promise;

for these men, although forced to become bandits by cruel treatment on the part of their government, have still true principles of honesty and honour. If the money be not sent, then, dearest father, I can say with sad certainty that you will never more see your son."

"Now sign your name to it," said the brigand, as the writing was completed.

Henry Harding once more started from his chair, and stood irresolute, still holding the pen in his hand.

He had written the letter as dictated, and while occupied in translating it into his native tongue he had given but little heed to its true signification.

But now that he was called upon to append his name to this piteous appeal to his father, with the remembrance still vivid in his mind of the defiant epistle he had last penned to him, he felt something more than reluctance—he felt shame, and a determination to refuse.

"Sign your name," cried the brigand, half rising from his seat. "Sign it, I say."

Henry still hesitated.

"Lay down the pen again without putting your *firma* to that letter, and, by our Holy Virgin, before the ink becomes dry, your blood will redden the floor at your feet. *Cospetto!* to be crossed by a poor devil of a *pittore*—a cur of an *Inglese!*"

"Oh, signor," interposed the brigand's wife, who up to this moment had not spoken a word, "do as he bids you, *buono cavalier!* There is no harm in what my husband tells you; it is only his way with every one who strays here from the great city. Sign it, *caro*, and all will be well. You will be free again, and can return to your friends."

While delivering this appeal, Popetta had risen up from her chair, her hand upon the young Englishman's shoulder.

The tone in which she spoke, with a certain expression detectable in her fiery eyes, did not seem altogether to satisfy her "spouse," who, rushing round the table, seized hold of the woman and flung her to the furthest corner of the room!

" Stay there, *puttana*," he cried, "and don't interfere with what's no concern of yours."

Then suddenly turning upon his prisoner, and drawing a pistol from his belt, he vociferated, " Sign ! "

The obstinacy that should have resisted such an appeal would have been sheer foolhardiness—a reckless indifference to life. There could be no mistaking the intent of the robber, for the click of his cocked pistol sounded sharp in his captive's ear.

For an instant the young Englishman, whose hands were for the time untied, thought of flinging himself upon his fierce antagonist and trying the chances of a struggle.

But then outside there was Doggy Dick, with a score of others, ready to shoot him down in his first effort to escape.

It was sheer madness to think of it. There was no alternative but to sign—at least, none except dying upon the spot.

The young artist was not inclined for this; and, stooping over the table, he added to what he had already written the name, " Henry Harding."

" Signor Ricardo " was called in and asked if he could read.

" I bean't much o' a scholard," replied Doggy Dick, " but I dar' say I can make out that bit o' scribble."

The letter was slowly spelled over, and pronounced " all right."

It was then enveloped, and directed, " Signor Ricardo " giving the correct address; after which the next duty this Amphitryon was called upon to perform was the re-tying of the captive and transporting him back to his cell.

That same night the epistle that had come so near costing Henry Harding his life was despatched by the peasant messenger to Rome.

CHAPTER XXI.

UNDER THE CEDAR

THE world has become just one year older from the day that Belle Mainwaring "refused" the young son of General Harding.

The crake had returned to the cornfield, the cuckoo to the grove, and the nightingale once more filled the dells with its sweet nocturnal music.

As a tourist straying among the Chiltern Hills—with me almost an annual habit—I could perceive no change in their aspect.

Nor did I find that much had taken place in the "society" introduced in the early chapters of our story.

I met Miss Mainwaring at a private ball that concluded an outdoor archery gathering. She was still the reigning belle of the neighbourhood, though there were two or three young sprouts that promised soon to dispossess her.

There was less talk of her becoming a bride than had been twelve months ago, though she was followed by a train of admirers that appeared to have suffered but slight diminution—Henry Harding being the only one missing from the muster.

I heard that his place had been supplied by his brother Nigel, though this was only whispered to me in conjecture by one that was present at the gathering, where was also Nigel Harding himself.

Knowing something of the nature of the young fellow, I did not believe it to be true; but, strange enough, before leaving the ground, I had convincing evidence that it was so.

These summer *fêtes*, when extended into the night, afford wonderful opportunities of flirtation; far more than the winter ball-room. The promenade, which occurs during the intervals of the dance, may be extended out of doors, along the gravelled walks, or over the soft grassy turf of the shrubbery. It is pleasant thus to escape from the heated air of the drawing-room, improvised for the night into a ball-room—especially pleasant when you take along with you your partner of the dance.

Strolling thus with one of the afore-mentioned maidens, I had halted by the side of a grand deodora, whose drooping branches, palmately spread, swept the grass at our feet, forming around the trunk of the tree a tent-like canopy by day, by night a cave of amorphous darkness.

All at once a thought seemed to strike my companion.

" By the way," said she, " I was wondering what I had done with my sunshade. Now I remember having left it under this very tree. You stay here," she continued, disengaging herself from my arm, " while I go under, and see if I can find it."

" No," said I, " permit me to go for it."

"Nonsense," replied my agile partner—she had proved herself such in the galop just ended—" I shall go myself. I know the exact spot where I laid it—on one of the great roots. Never mind, you stay here ! "

Saying this, she disappeared under the shadow of the deodora.

I could not think of such a young creature venturing all alone into such a dismal-looking place ; and, not heeding her remonstrance, I bent under the branches and followed her in.

After groping about for some time, we failed to find the parasol.

" Some of the servants may have taken it into the house," she said. " No matter, I suppose it will turn up along with my hat and cloak."

We were about returning to the open lawn, when we saw, coming through the same break in the branches through which we had entered, a pair of promenaders like ourselves. *Their* errand we could not guess.

Though ours had been innocent enough, it occurred to me that it might have a compromising appearance.

I cannot tell if my companion had the same thought; but whether or no, we stood still, as if by a mutual instinct, waiting for the other pair to pass out again. We supposed they had stepped under the tree actuated by curiosity or some other caprice that would soon be satisfied.

In this we were mistaken. Instead of immediately returning into the light—faint as it was, and only springing from the glimmer of a starlit sky—they stopped, and entered into a conversation that promised to be somewhat protracted.

At the first words, I could tell it was only the resumption of one that had already made some progress between them.

"I know," said the gentleman, "that you still bear him in your mind. It's no use telling me you never cared for him. I know better than that, Miss Mainwaring."

"Indeed, do you? What a wonderful knowledge you have, Mr. Nigel Harding! You know more than I ever did myself; and more than your brother too; else why should I have refused him? Surely that should convince you there was nothing between us—at least on my side there wasn't."

There was a short pause, as if the suitor was reflecting on what the lady had just said.

My companion and I were puzzled as to what we should do. I knew it by the trembling of her arm, that spoke irresolution; and, by a familiar sign, I felt that we agreed upon keeping silent and hearing this strange dialogue to its termination. We had already heard enough to make discovering ourselves exceedingly awkward, to say nothing of our own compromising position.

We stood still, like a couple of linked statues.

"If that be true," said Nigel Harding, who appeared to have brought his reasoning process to a satisfactory conclusion, " and if also true that no other has your heart, may I ask, Miss Mainwaring, why do you not accept the offer I have laid before you? You have told me—I think you have said as much—that you could like me as a husband. Why not go further, and say you will have me?"

"Because—because—Mr. Nigel Harding, do you really wish to know the reason?"

"If I did not, I should not have spent twelve months in asking—in pressing for it."

"If you promise to be a good boy, then, I shall tell you."

"I will promise anything, If it be a reason that I can remove, you may command me and all the means in my power. My fortune—I won't speak of that—my life, my body, my soul, are all at your service."

The suitor spoke with an enthusiasm I had not deemed him capable of.

"I shall be candid, then," was the response, half whispered, "and tell you the exact truth. Two things stand between you and me, either of which may prevent us becoming man and wife. First, there is my mother's consent to be obtained, and without that I will not marry. To my dear mother I have given my promise—I have sworn to it. Second, there is *your father's consent*—without it I *cannot* marry you. I have equally sworn to that— my mother exacting the oath. Much, therefore, as I may like you, Nigel Harding, you know I cannot perjure myself. Come! we have talked of this too often. Let us return to the dancing, or our absence may be remarked."

Saying this she swept out from beneath the branches.

The foiled suitor made no attempt to detain her. The conditions could not be answered, at least not then ; and with a vague hope of being able at some future time to obtain better terms, he followed her back into the house.

My companion and I, as soon as released, sauntered the same way.

Not a word passed between us as to what we had heard.

To me it did not throw much new light either on the ways of the world or the character of Miss Mainwaring, but I could not help regretting the lesson of deception thus unavoidably communicated to the young creature on my arm, who might afterwards practise it on her own particular account.

CHAPTER XXII.

A QUEER TRAVELLER

THE swells who diurnally take their departure for Windsor and the West, were one afternoon in the year 1849 called upon to use their eyeglasses upon a somewhat strange-looking traveller, who, coming from Heaven knows where, made his appearance on the platform of the Paddington station.

And yet there was nothing so very remarkable about the man—except on the Paddington platform. At London Bridge you might see his like any day in the year—a personage of very dark complexion, dressed in black cloth, with a loose poncho-like garment hanging from his shoulders, and a hat upon his head—half wide-awake, but tending toward a steeple-crown—in short, a "Calabrian."

Of such sort was the costume of the individual who had caused the raising of eyeglasses on the Paddington platform.

In an instant they were down again; the object of supercilious attention having dissipated scrutiny, by diving into the interior of a first-class carriage.

"Dem'd queer-looking fella!" was the remark; and with this he was forgotten.

At Slough he appeared again upon that gloomiest of platforms, commanded by a man with the loudest voice and most cheerful face upon all the G.W.R. line. The strange traveller did not show himself until the swells, such of them as made stop at Slough, had given up their tickets, and passed through the gate.

Then tumbling out of the carriage the queer traveller, with a small portmanteau in his hand, placed himself in communication with the great Boanerges who directs the startings and departures at the Slough station.

Between the two individuals thus accidentally coming together there was a contrast so striking that the most careless lounger on the platform could not have restrained himself from giving them attention. Standing *en rapport*, they appeared the very types of the extreme—the negative and positive. A grand colossal form of true Saxon physiognomy, *vis-à-vis* with a diminutive specimen of Latinic humanity—for such the traveller appeared.

At the time I chanced myself to be on the platform, waiting for a down train. I was so struck with the tableau that I involuntarily drew nigh, to hear what the little dark man in the *capote* had to say to the giant in green frock and gilt buttons.

The first word that fell upon my ears was the name of General Harding!

It was not pronounced in the ordinary way, but with an accent, plainly foreign, and which I could distinguish as Italian.

Listening a little longer I could hear that the stranger was inquiring the direction to General Harding's residence.

I should have myself volunteered to direct him, but from the station-master's reply I could perceive that this functionary was capable, and just then the down train gliding alongside, admonished me to look out for myself.

Just then it occurred to me that I had stupidly forgotten to take a ticket; and I hastened into the office to procure one.

As I came out again upon the platform I saw the strange traveller disappear within the doorway of a fly, the driver of which, giving the whip to his horse, trundled off from the station.

In ten seconds after I had taken my seat in the railway carriage—an empty one—an incident occurred that drove the queer-looking traveller as completely out of my head as if he had never been in it.

The whistle had already screamed, and the train was about to move off, when the door was opened by the Titanic station-master, who was saying at the same time—

"This way, ladies!"

The rustle of silk. with some hurried exclamation out-side, told of the late arrival of at least two passengers feminine, and the moment after two entered the carriage and took their seats nearly opposite me.

I had been cutting open the pages of *Punch*, and did not look up into their faces as they entered. But on finishing my inspection of the cartoon, I raised my eyes to see of what style were my two travelling companions, then beheld—Belle Mainwaring and her mother !

It was just about as awkward a position as I ever remembered occupying in my life. But I managed to sustain it by appealing once more to the pages of *Punch*. Not even as much as a nod was exchanged between us, and had there been a stranger in the carriage he could not have told that Miss Mainwaring and I had ever met, much less danced together.

I did *Punch* from beginning to end, and then turning back to the advertisements on the back of the title-page, made myself acquainted with the qualities of " Gosnell's Soap " and the mysteries of the " Sansflection Crinoline."

Despite these studies I found time to give an occasional side-glance at Miss Mainwaring, which I saw she was returning by a similar slant. What she may have seen in my eye I cannot tell, but in hers I read a light—that had my heart not been of the dulness of lead might have set it on fire. It had at one time come very near melting under that same glance ; but after the cooling process experienced, it had become hardened to the temper of steel, and now passed through the crucible unscathed.

When I had finished reading *Punch*, three columns of advertisements, and for the hundredth time in my life had made an examination of Toby, and the procession of nymphs, dancing buffoons, and bacchantes, the train made stop at Reading.

Here my travelling companions got out.

So did I. I had been asked to a park *fête* to be held at a gentleman's residence in the neighbourhood—the same mentioned in a previous chapter. I suspected the Mainwarings were bound for the like place, and from the direction taken by the fly in which they drove off, became sure of it.

On arriving at my friend's residence I found them upon the lawn—Miss Belle as usual surrounded by simpering swells—among whom, not to my surprise, I recognised Mr. Nigel Harding.

I noticed that during the process of the game he refrained from showing her any marked attention—leaving this for the others. For all that he was evidently uneasy, and stealthily watched her every glance and movement.

One or twice, when they were apart, I could hear him say something to her in a low tone, with the green of jealousy in his eyes, and its pallor upon his lips.

On leaving the place, which the company did at an early hour, I saw that he accompanied her and her mother to the railway station. The three rode back in the same fly.

We all returned to Slough in the same train—I going on to London.

From the carriage in which I sat I could see Miss Mainwairing's pony phaeton, with the page at the pony's head; and close by a dog-cart with a groom in the Harding livery.

Before the train parted I saw the ladies step into the phaeton. Nigel Harding climbed to the seat behind them, while "Buttons" was dismissed to take his seat in the dog-cart. With their freights thus assorted the two vehicles drove off, just as the train was slipping out of the station.

From what I had seen that day, and what I had heard under the great Cedar of Lebanon, and more than all from what I knew of both parties to the suit, I had made up my mind before reaching London, that Belle Mainwaring was booked to be the better half of Nigel Harding, if "*consent*" could be squeezed out of his father, either by fraud or by force.

CHAPTER XXIII.

DISSIMULATION

ON that same night, as upon almost every other of the year, General Harding was seated in his dining-room with a decanter of crusted port on his right hand, a glass a little nearer, and a Trinchinopoly cheroot between his teeth.

His maiden sister was on his left round a corner of the table, upon which stood before her another wine-glass, with an epergne of flowers, and a hand-dish containing fruit. It was the hour after dinner, the cloth had been removed, the dessert decanters set upon the table, and the butler and footman dismissed.

" It's gone nine," said the General, consulting his chronometer watch. " Nigel should be back by this. He wasn't to stop for dinner, only luncheon; and the train leaves Reading at 7.16. I wonder if those Mainwarings were there? "

"Pretty sure to be," replied the ancient spinster, who was shrewd at conjectures.

" Yes," thoughtfully soliloquized the General, " pretty sure, I suppose. Well, it don't much matter. I've no fear for Nigel, he's not the sort to be humbugged by her blandishments, like that hot-headed simpleton, Hal. By Jove, sister, isn't it strange we have not heard a word from the lad since he left us? "

"You will when he's spent the thousand pounds you gave him. When that comes to an end he'll not be so chary of his correspondence."

" No doubt—no doubt—not a single letter since that disagreeable epistle from the inn—not even to acknowledge the receipt of the money. I suppose he got it all

H

right. I've not looked into my bank-book since I don't know when."

"Oh, you may be certain of his having got it. If he hadn't you'd have heard from him long ago. Henry isn't one to go without money, where money can be had. You've good reason to know that. I should say you needn't trouble about him, brother; he's not been living all this time upon air."

"I wonder where he is? He said he was going abroad; I suppose he has done so."

"Doubtful enough," rejoined the spinster, with a shake of her head. "London will be the place for him so long as the money lasts. When that is spent you'll hear from him. He'll write for a fresh supply. Of course, brother, you'll send it?"

The interrogatory was spoken ironically and in a taunting tone, intended to produce an effect the very opposite to what it might seem to serve. "Not a shilling!" said the General, determinedly, setting his wine-glass down on the table with an emphatic clink. "Not a single shilling; if within twelve months he has succeeded in dissipating a thousand pounds, he shall go twelve years before he gets another thousand—not a shilling before my death, and then only enough to keep him from starvation! So, Nelly dear, I've made up my mind about that—Nigel shall have all—except a little something which must be left for yourself. I gave him every chance. He should have had half. Now, after what has happened—there's wheels upon the gravel! Nigel with the dog-cart, I suppose?"

It was, and in ten seconds more Nigel, without the dog-cart, stepped softly into the room.

"You're a little late, Nigel!"

"Yes, papa. The train was behind time."

This was a lie. The delay was caused by a stoppage nearer home—at the widow Mainwaring's cottage.

"Well, I hope you have had a pleasant party."

"Passable."

"That all? and such weather; who was there?"

"Oh, for that matter, there was company enough—half

of Bucks and Berkshire I should say—to say nothing of a score of snobs from London——"

" Any of our neighbours ? "

" Well—no—not exactly——."

" It's a wonder the widow Mainwaring——"

" Oh, yes ! she was there ; I didn't think of her."

" The daughter, of course, along with her ? "

" Yes—the daughter was there too. By the way, aunt," continued the young man, with the design of changing the subject, " you haven't asked me to join you in a glass of wine ! and I'd like to have a morsel of something to eat. We got only a tent lunch, standing at that, and I feel as if I'd had nothing at all ; I think I could eat a raw steak if I had it."

" There was roast duck for dinner," suggested the aunt, " but it's cold now, dear Nigel, and so is the asparagus. Will you wait till it's warmed up, or perhaps you would prefer a slice of the cold boiled beef with some West Indian pickles ? "

" I don't care what so long as it's something to eat."

" Have a glass of port wine, Nigel," said the General, while his sister was directing Williams as to the arrangement of the tray. " From what you say, I suppose you don't want a nip of cognac to give you an appetite ? "

" No, indeed. I've got that already. How late is it, father ? Their clocks appear to be all wrong down the road, or else the trains are. It's always the way with the Great Western. It's a bad line to depend on for dining."

" Ah ! and a worse for dividends," rejoined the General, the smile at his own pun being more than neutralized by a grin that told of his being holder of shares in the G.W.R.

With a laugh Nigel drank off his glass of port, and then sat down to his cold duck, boiled beef, and pickles.

CHAPTER XXIV

A STRANGE VISITOR

GENERAL HARDING's butler, with the assistance of the foot-man, had just carried out the supper-tray, when there came a ring at the hall-door bell, succeeded by a double knock.

Neither were of the kind which the butler would have called "obstreperous," but rather bashful and subdued. For all that they were heard within the room where the General sat.

"Very odd—at this hour of the night!" remarked the General. "Ten o'clock!" he said, consulting his chrono-meter. "Who can it be?"

No one made reply, as all were engrossed in listening.

They heard the opening of the door, and then a parley between Williams upon the step and somebody outside in the porch.

It lasted some time longer than need have been necessary for a visitor who was a friend of the family. The voice too —answering the butler's—was evidently that of a stranger, and, as the occupants of the dining-room thought, one who spoke with a foreign accent.

The General bethought him whether it might not be some of his old chums freshly arrived home from India, and who had come down *sans ceremonie* by a late train.

But, then, he could think of none of them who spoke with a foreign accent.

"Who is it, Williams?" asked he, as the latter appeared in the doorway of the dining-room.

"That I can't tell, General. The gentleman, if I may so call 'im, will neither give his name nor his card; he says he has most important business, and must see you."

" Very odd! What does he look like ? "

" Like a furriner, and a rum 'un at that. Certain, General, he arn't a gentleman, that can be seen plain enough."

" Very odd ! " again repeated the General, " very odd ! Says he *must* see me ? "

" Said it over and over. That it's important more to *you* than him. Shall I show him in, General ? Or will you speak to him at the door ? "

" Door be d——d ! " testily replied the old soldier. " I'm not going out there to accommodate a stranger, without either name or card—maybe some begging-letter impostor. Tell him I can't see him to-night. He may come back in the morning."

" I've told him so, General, already. He says no—you must see him *to-night*."

" Must the devil ! "

" Well, General, if I'd be allowed to speak my opinion, he looks a good bit like that same gentleman you've mentioned."

" Who the deuce can it be, Nigel ? " said the old soldier, turning to his son.

" I haven't the slightest idea myself," was Nigel's reply. " It wouldn't be that lawyer Woolet ? He answers very well to the description Williams gives of his late intruder."

" No, no—Master Nigel. It's not Mr. Woolet. It's an article of hoomanity even uglier than him ; though certain he have got somethin' o' a lawyer's look 'bout him. But then he be a furriner. I can swear to that."

" By Jove ! " exclaimed the General, using one of his mildest asseverations ; " I can't think of any foreigner that can have business with *me ;* but whether or no, I suppose I must see him. What say you, my son ? "

" Oh, as for that," answered the latter, " there can be no harm in it. I'll stay in the room with you ; and if he become troublesome, I suppose, with the help of Williams here and the footman, we may be able to eject him."

" Lor', Master Nigel, he isn't bigger than our page-boy. I could take him up in my arms, and swing him half way across the shrubberies. You needn't 'have no fear 'bout that."

" Come, come, Williams," said the General ; " none of this idle talking. Tell the gentleman I'll see him. Show him in."

Then turning to his sister, he added—

" Nelly, dear, you may as well go up to the drawing-room. Nigel and I will join you as soon as we've given an interview to this unexpected guest."

The spinster, gathering up some crochet-work that she had made a commencement on, sailed out of the room, leaving her brother and nephew to receive the nocturnal caller, who would not be denied.

CHAPTER XXV

AN UNCOURTEOUS RECEPTION

THE old soldier and his son stood in silent expectation, for the oddity of an interview thus authoritatively demanded had summoned both to their feet.

Outside they could hear the resumed exchange of speech between Williams and the stranger, and their two sets of footsteps sounding along the flagged pavement of the hall.

Two seconds after the stranger was shown inside the room; and the three were left alone, Williams having retired at a sign from the General.

Perhaps a queerer specimen of the *genus homo*, or one less in keeping with the place, had never made appearance inside the dining-hall of an English country gentleman.

As Williams had asserted, he was not much bigger than a page-boy, but, for all that, he could not be less than forty years of age. In complexion he was dark as a gipsy, with long straight hair of crow's-wing blackness, and eyes scintillating like chips of fresh broken coal.

His face was of the Israelitish type, while his dress, with the exception of a sort of *capote*, which he still kept upon his shoulders, had something of a professional cut about it—such as might be seen among men of the law in the Latinic countries of Europe. He might be an "avocato," or notary.

In his hand he held a hat—half wide-awake, half Calabrian—which on entering the dining-room he had the courtesy to take off. Beyond this there was not much politeness shown by him either in aspect or action, for notwithstanding his diminutive person he appeared the very picture of pluck, of that epitomized kind seen in the terrier or weasel.

It showed itself not so much in swagger as in an air of self-reliance, that seemed to say: "I have come here on an errand that will be its own excuse, and I know you won't send me back without giving me a satisfactory answer."

"What is it?" asked the General, as if this very thought had just passed through his mind.

The stranger looked towards Nigel, as much as to say, "do you wish him to be present?"

"That is my son," continued the old soldier; "anything you have to say need not be kept secret from him."

"You have another son?" asked the stranger, speaking in a foreign accent, but in English sufficiently intelligible. "I think you have another son, Signor General."

The question caused the General to start, while Nigel turned suddenly pale. The significant glance that accompanied the interrogatory told that the stranger knew something about Henry.

"I have—or should have," replied the General. "What do you want to say of him, and why do you speak of him?"

"Do you know where your other son is, Signor General?"

"Well, not exactly at present. Do *you* know where he is? Who are you? and whence do you come?"

"Signor General, I shall be most happy to answer all three of your questions if you only allow me to do it in the order inverse to that in which you have put them."

"Answer them in what order you please, but do it quickly. The hour is late, and I've no time to stand here talking to an entire stranger."

"Signor General, I shall not detain you many minutes. My business is of a simple nature, and my time, like yours, is precious. First, then, I come from the city of Rome, which I need not tell you is in Italy. Second, I am *un procuratore*—an attorney, you call it in English. Thirdly, and lastly, I do know where your other son is."

The General again started, Nigel growing pale.

"Where is he?"

"This, Signor General, will inform you."

As he spoke the *procuratore* drew a letter from under his *capote*, and presented it to the General.

It was that which had been written by Henry Harding in the mountains, under the dictation of Corvino, the bandit chief.

Putting on his spectacles and drawing the light nearer him, General Harding read the letter with a feeling of astonishment, though tinctured with credulity.

" This is nonsense ! " said he, handing the document to Nigel. " Sheer nonsense ! Read it, my son."

Nigel did as he was desired.

" What do *you* make of it ? " asked the General, addressing himself in another tone to his son.

" That's just what it is, father ; or perhaps something worse. It looks to me like a trick to extort money."

" Ah ! "

" But do you think, Nigel, that Henry has any hand in it ? "

" I hardly know what to think, father," answered Nigel, continuing the whispered conversation. " It grieves me to say what I think. But, I must confess, it looks against him. If he has fallen into the hands of brigands—which I cannot believe, and I hope is not true—how should they know where to send such a letter ? How could they tell he has a father, capable of paying such a ransom for him —unless he has put them up to it ? It is probable enough that 'he's in Rome, where this fellow says he has come from. That may all be ; but a captive in the keeping of brigands ! The tale is too preposterous ! "

" Most decidedly it is. But what am I to make of this application ? "

" To my mind," pursued the insinuating counsellor, " the explanation is easy enough. He's run through his thousand pounds, as might have been expected ; and he now wants more. I am sorry to believe such a thing, father ; but it looks as if this is a story got up to work upon your feelings for a fresh remittance of cash to him. At all events, he has not stinted himself in the sum asked for."

" Five thousand pounds ! " exclaimed the General, again

glancing over the letter. "He must think me crazy. He shall not have as many pence—no, not if it were even true what he says about brigands."

"Of course that part of the story is all stuff, although it's clear he has written the letter. It's in his own hand, and that's his signature."

"Certainly it is. My God! to think that this is the first I should hear from him since that other letter. A pretty way of seeking a reconciliation with me! Bah! the trick don't take. I'm too old a soldier to be deceived by it."

"I'm sorry he should have tried it. I fear, papa, he has not yet repented of his rash disobedience. But what do you mean to do with this fellow?"

"Ay, what?" echoed the General, now remembering the man who had been the bearer of the strange missive. "What would you advise to be done?"

"Send over for the police and give him in charge."

"I don't know about that," answered Nigel, reflectingly. "It seems hardly worth while, and might lead to some unpleasantness to ourselves. Better the public should not know about the unfortunate affair of poor Henry. A police case would necessarily expose some things that you, father, I'm sure, don't wish to be made public."

"True—true. But something should be done to punish this impudent impostor. It's too bad to be so bearded—almost bullied—in one's own home, and by a wretch like that."

"Threaten him, then, before dismissing him. That may bring out some more information about the scheme. At all events, it can do no harm to give him a bit of your mind. It may do good to Henry to know how you have received his petition, so cunningly contrived."

CHAPTER XXVI.

AN UNCEREMONIOUS DISMISSAL

THE side conversation between General Harding and his son was at length suspended by the old soldier facing abruptly toward the stranger, who all the while had been standing quietly apart. "You're an impostor, sir!" exclaimed the General. "An impostor, I say!"

"*Molto Grazie*, Signor General!" replied the man, without making other movement than a mock bow. "Rather an uncomplimentary epithet to apply to one who has come all the way from Italy to do you a service, or rather your son. Is this all the answer I am to take back to him?"

"If you take any back to him, that's it," interposed Nigel. "Do you know, sir!" he continued, in a threatening manner, "do you know that you've placed yourself within the power of our laws; that you can be arrested and thrown into prison for an attempt to extort money under false pretences?"

"His Excellence, the General, will not have me arrested. First, because there are no false pretences; and second, that to do so would be to seal the doom of your son. The moment the news should reach those who have him in their keeping—that I've been arrested or otherwise molested here in England, that moment he will be punished far more than you can punish *me*. You must remember that I am only a messenger, who have taken upon me the delivery of this letter. I know nothing of those who have sent it, except in the way of my profession, and in the cause of humanity. I am as much your son's messenger as theirs. I can only assure you, Signor General, that it is a serious mission, and that your son's life depends on my safety, and the answer you may vouchsafe to send back."

"Bah!" exclaimed the old soldier, "don't tell a cock-and-bull tale to an Englishman. I don't believe a word of it. If I did, I'd take a different way of delivering my son from such a danger. Our government would soon inter-fere on my behalf, and then, instead of five thousand pounds, your beautiful brigands would get what they deserve, and what I wonder they haven't had long ago—six feet of rope around each of their necks."

"I fear, Signor General, you are labouring under a delusion. Allow me to set you right on this question. Your government can be of no service to you in this affair, nor all the governments of Europe to boot. It is not the first time such threats have been used against the freebooters in question. Neither the Neapolitan Govern-ment in whose land they live, nor that of his Holiness, upon whose territory they occasionally intrude, can coerce them if even so inclined. There is but one way for you to obtain the release of your son—by paying the ransom demanded for him."

"Begone, wretch!" shouted the General, losing all patience at the pleading of the procuratore; "begone! out of my house!—off my premises instantly! or I shall order my servants to drag you to the horse-pond! Begone! I say."

"And you would rue it if you did," spitefully rejoined the little Italian as he edged off toward the door. "*Bueno notte, Signor General!* Perhaps by the morning you will have recovered your temper, and think better of my errand! If you have any message to send to your son—whom it is not very likely you will ever see again—I shall take upon myself to transmit it for you, notwithstanding the uncourteous treatment of which, as a gentleman, I have the right to complain. I stay at the neighbouring inn all night; and will not be gone before twelve o'clock to-morrow. *Bueno notte, Bueno notte.*"

So saying the swarthy little stranger backed out of the room, and, conducted by the butler, was not very courteously shown into the night.

The General stood still, his beard bristling with passion.

For a time.he seemed irresolute as to whether he should have the stranger detained and punished in some summary way.

But he thought of the family scandal, and restrained himself.

" You won't write to Henry ? " asked Nigel, in a tone that said " don't."

" Not a line ! If he's got into a scrape for want of money, let him get out of it again the best way he can. As to this story about brigands——"

" Oh, that's too absurd," insinuated Nigel; " the brigands into whose hands he has fallen are the swindlers and harpies of Rome. They have no doubt employed this lawyer, if he be one, to carry out their scheme, certainly a cunningly contrived one, whoever originated it."

" Oh, my son ! my wretched son ! " exclaimed the General, " to think he has fallen into the hands of such associates ! To think he could lend himself to a conspiracy like this, and against his own father ! Oh, God ! "

And the old soldier uttered a groan of agony, and sunk down upon a sofa !

" Had I better not write to him, father ? " asked Nigel, " just a line, to say how much his conduct is grieving you. Perhaps a word of counsel might yet reclaim him ? "

" If you like. If you like, though, after such an experience as this, I feel there is little hope of him. Ah, Lucy ! Lucy ! it is well that you are not here, and that God has taken you to himself. My poor wife ! My poor wife ! This would have killed you ! "

The apostrophe was spoken in a low, muttered tone, and after Nigel had left the room, having gone out apparently with the intention of writing the letter which was to reclaim his erring brother.

It was written that night, and that night reached the hands of the strange procuratore, to whom it was entrusted for delivery ; and who next day, true to his word, re-mained at the roadside inn till the hour of twelve, at which hour he was seen driving off in the inn " fly " for the Slough station ; thence to be transported by rail and steam to his home in the seven-hilled city.

CHAPTER XXVII.

DOMESTIC BRIGAND LIFE

For several days Henry Harding was kept confined to his cell, without seeing a face—except that of the brigand who brought him his food—always the same individual.

This man was a morose wretch, and uncommunicative as if he had been an automaton. Twice a day he would bring in a bowl of *pasta* (a sort of maccaroni porridge, boiled in bacon fat, and seasoned with salt and pepper). He would place the vessel upon the floor; take away the empty one, that had contained the previous meal; and then leave the captive to himself, without saying a word!

The repeated attempts of the young Englishman to bring him to a parley were met either by complete inattention or rude repulse.

Seeing this, they were abandoned, and the captive ate his *pasta* and drank his cold water in silence.

Only at night was there quiet in his cell. All day long through the slender slit of window came noise enough. Just in front of it seemed to be the favourite loitering place of the brigands, where they passed most of their time.

It was spent almost exclusively in gambling, except during intervals, when quarrelling took the place of playing.

Those intervals were not rare. Scarce an hour elapsed without some dispute ending either in a fight between two individuals or a general row, in which more than half the band appeared to take part. Then would be heard the voice of the capo thundering in authoritative tones as he delivered cudgel blows and curses upon the quarrelers.

Once there was the report of a pistol followed by groans. The young Englishman believed that a summary punishment had been inflicted on some offender, for after the groans there was an interval of solemn stillness such as might be observed in the presence of death.

If such were the dread impression upon the scoundrels, it did not last long, for soon after they were heard resuming play, and the cries, " Cinque a cinque a capo ! Vinti a vinti croce ! " the game being that common among the Italian peasantry, " Croce a capo," and which differs but little from the English " Heads or tails ? "

By standing on tiptoe, the prisoner could see them playing it.

The gaming-table was simply a level spot of turf in front of his cell and nearly opposite to the window. The brigands knelt or squatted in a ring. One held an old hat from which the lining had been torn out. In this were placed a number of coins—odd—usually three. These were first rattled about the hat and then thrown down upon the turf; the hat—unlike as with a dice-box —still covering them. The bets were then made upon " capo " or " croce " (head or cross), and the raising of the hat determined who were winners or losers.

It is in this game that the bandits find their chief source of distraction from a life that would otherwise be unendurable—even to such ruffians as they. *Capo a croce*, with an occasional quarrel over it ; plenty of *pasta confetti*, fat mutton cheeses, *rocattas ;* and *Rosolio*—a *festa* when wine and provisions were plenty—songs usually of the most vulgar kind—now and then a dance, accompanied by some coarse flirting with the half-dozen women who usually keep company with a *banda*—these, and long hours of listless basking in the sun, compose the joys of the Italian brigand's life.

When on a foray to the peopled plain he finds excitement of a far more different character. The surprise— the capture—the escape from pursuing soldiers ; perhaps an occasional skirmish while retreating to his hill fortress —these are the incidents that occur to him on a plundering expedition. And they are sufficiently exciting to preserve him from *ennui*.

This last only steals upon him when the divided plunder, which is generally in the shape of *denaro di riscatta* (ransom money), has, by the inexorable chances of the *capo a croce*, become consolidated in a few hands, the universal result of the game.

Then does the bandit become dissatisfied with listless idleness, and commences to plan new surprises—the sack of some rich villa, or, what is more much to his mind, the capture of some *galantuomo*, by whose ransom his purse may be again replenished—again to be staked on " Heads or tails."

Unseen himself, the young Englishman had an excellent opportunity of studying the life of these lawless men.

Between them and their chief there appeared to be but slight distinction.

As a general rule, the spoils were shared alike, as also the chances of the game—for Corvino could at any time be seen in the ring along with the rest, staking his *pezzos* on the *capo* or *croce*.

His authority was only absolute in the administration of punishment. His kick, or cudgel, were never disputed, for if they had been it was well understood these modes of castigation would be instantly changed for a stab of his stiletto, or a shot from his pistol.

His chieftainship may have been derived from his being the originator of the band, but it was kept up and sustained by his being its bully. A chief of low courage or less cruelty would soon have been dispossessed, as not unfrequently happens among the *banditti*.

One thing caused Henry Harding much wonder, as standing on tiptoe he looked out of the little window— the women, the *banditas*.

In Corvino's band there were nearly a score of them. He had at first taken them for boys—beardless members of the gang. There was but little in their dress to distinguish them from the men. They wore the same polka jacket, vest, and pantaloons, only with a greater profusion of ornaments around their necks, and a larger number of rings upon their fingers.

Some of them were absolutely loaded with jewels of all kinds — pearls, topaz, rubies, torquoise stones, even diamonds sparkling among the rest —the spoils drawn from the delicate fingers of many a rich *signorina*.

The hair of all was close cropped, like that of the men, while several carried carbines—all of them *poignards* or *pistols*, so that only by a certain rotundity of form could they be distinguished from their male companions, and not all of them by this. They were not allowed to take part in the gaming, as they never shared in the *riscatta*. For all that, most of them shared in the perils of army enterprise, accompanying the men on their expeditions.

At home they laid aside the carbine to take up the needle, though they were seldom called upon to wet their fingers in the washing-tub. That was regarded as an occupation beneath the dignity of a bandita, and was left to the wives of those peasants in communication with the band, and who are termed *manutengoli* or "helpers!"

These are well paid for the labour of the laundry—a clean shirt costing the bandit almost the price of a new one!

It was not often that any of Corvino's band cared to incur the expense—only its *damarinos* or dandies, and they only upon the occasion of a *festa*.

Most of these observations were made by the English captive during the first few days of his captivity. He saw many strange scenes through the little window of his cell. He might have seen more had the window been lower in the wall, but high up as it was he was obliged to stand on tiptoe, and this became tiresome after a time, so that he only assumed the irksome attitude when some scene more exciting than common summoned him from his lair of dried fern-leaves.

CHAPTER XXVIII.

SEVERAL days had elapsed without any change either in the prisoner's prospects or situation. He had come to the conclusion that his capture was no longer a farce, nor his imprisonment likely soon to terminate. The stories he had heard told during his short sojourn in Rome of brigand life, and which, like others of his incredulous countrymen, he had been loth to believe in, were no longer doubted. He was himself a sad example of their reality, and he almost felt angry at his friend Luigi for having given him that letter of introduction which had introduced him to such a pitiful dilemma. It was still upon his person, for beyond robbing him of his slender purse and his other metallic movables, the brigands had left everything else untouched.

By way of passing the time, he took the letter out and re-read it. One paragraph which he had scarcely noted before now particularly impressed him—" I suppose my sister Lucetta will by this time be a big girl. Take good care of her till I come back, when I hope I shall be able to carry all of you out of that danger we dreaded."

When Henry Harding first read these words on his way to Rome—for the letter of introduction was an open one—he thought nothing of their signification. He supposed it could only refer to the straitened circumstances of his family, which the young artist expected at some time to relieve by the proceeds of his successful pencil. Besides, Belle Mainwaring was too much in his mind to leave room for more than a slight thought of anything else—especially for the little sister of Luigi, big as she might be at the writing of the letter.

Now, however, reflecting in his lone cell, with the image of that fair face first seen on the day of his captivity, and since constantly recurring to his thoughts, he began to shape out a different interpretation to the ambiguous phrase. What if the danger spoken of was less of poverty than peril—such, in short, as appeared to threaten that young girl, the daughter of the village Sindico? To reflect even upon this gave the captive pain. How much more would he have been pained to think that the sister of his dear friend Luigi was in like peril!

Sunset declaring itself by the increasing gloom of his cell, caused him to refold the letter and return it to his pocket. He was still pondering upon its contents, when voices outside the window attracted his attention. He listened: anything to vary the monotony of his prison life—even the idle talk of a brace of bandits, for it was two of these who were heard outside. In less than ten seconds after he was listening with all his ears, for in the midst of their conversation he fancied he heard a name that was known to him.

He had just been thinking of Luigi Torriani! This was not the name that passed from the lips of the bandit, but one of like signification—Lucetta. It was the name of Luigi's sister, of which he had been reminded by the letter.

Henry Harding had often heard his friend speak of his sister—his only one. It was not strange, therefore, he should listen with quickened attention. And so did he; grasping the solitary bar of his window and holding his ear close up to the sill. True, there might be scores of Lucettas in this part of the country, but for all that he could not help listening with eager interest.

" Shall be our next *riscatta*," said the brigand who had pronounced the name, " you may make up your mind to that." •

" *E por che?* " inquired the other. " The old Sindico, with all his proud name, and his syndicate to boot, hasn't enough to pay ransom for a cat—what would be the object of such a capture? "

" Object! Ah, that concerns the capo—not us. All I

know is that the girl has taken his fancy! I saw it as we
passed through the town the other night. I believe he'd
then carried her off only for fear of Popetta; she's a she-
devil, is the signorina, and though for ordinary she takes
kindly to her kicks and cuffings, she wouldn't if there was
a woman in the case. Don't you remember when we had
the dancing bout down in the valley of Malfi? What a
row there was between our captain and his cara sposa!"

"I remember. What was it all about? I never
heard."

"About a bit of kissing. Our capo was inclined upon
a girl—that coquettish little devil, the daughter of the old
charcoal-burner, Poli. The girl seemed kindly. He had
slipped a charm round her neck, and I believe had kissed
her. Whether he did that or no I won't be certain. But
the charm was seen and recognised by the signorina; she
plucked it from the girl's neck, and as she did so almost
dragged her off her feet. Then came the scene with the
capo."

"She drew a stiletto upon him, did she not?"

"Ay, and would have used it, too, if he had not made
some excuse, and turned the thing into a laugh—that
pacified her. What a fury she was while the fit was on
her, Cospetto! Her eyes glittered like hot lava from
Vesuvius."

"The girl stole away, I think?"

"That did she, and a good thing for her she did; though
if she had stayed I don't think Corvino would have dared
look at her again that night. I never saw him cowed
before: he lost both his sweetheart and his gold charm,
for the Cara Popetta appropriated that to herself, and wears
it regularly whenever he holds festa among the peasant
girls—by way of reminder, I suppose."

"Did the captain ever see Poli's daughter again?"

"Well, some of us think he did. But you remember
after you left us we moved away from that part of the
country. The soldiers became too strong for us about
there, and there was a whisper the signorina had something to do with making the place too hot for us. After
all, I don't think Corvino cared for the carbonero's

daughter. It was only a shortlived fancy, because the girl showed sweet upon him; this of the Sindico's daughter is a very different affair, for I know he's fond of going in that direction, and shouldn't wonder if we get into danger by it. Danger or no danger, he'll have her sooner or later, take my word for it."

"I don't wonder at his fancy, she's a sweet-looking girl; one likes her all the better for being so proud upon it."

"Her pride will have a fall once Corvino gets her in his clutches—he's just the man to tame such shy damsels as she."

"*Povera!* it's a pity, too."

"Bah! you're a fool, Thomasso, your short sojourn in the Pope's prison has spoiled you for our life, I fear; what are we poor fellows to do if we don't have a sweetheart now and then? Chased like wolves, why shouldn't we take a slice of lamb when we can get it? Who can blame the capo for liking a little bit of tender liver? and such a sweet bit as Lucetta Torriani?"

With a laugh at his brutish jest the brigand moved off, followed by his unsympathetic companion.

Henry Harding, who had been all this while listening with disgust to the dialogue between the two brigands, felt as if a huge stone had struck him; the presentiment that had just commenced shaping itself in his mind, seemed all at once become circumstantially confirmed. The young girl spoken of is Lucetta Torriani! It could be no other than the sister of Luigi, the same, too, he had seen standing in the balcony, and who often since had been occupying his thoughts.

It was a strange collocation or coincidence of circumstances—alike strange and painful. Under the blow he relaxed his hold of the bar, and, staggering back, sank down upon the floor of his cell.

CHAPTER XXIX.

PAINFUL SPECULATION

FOR some time the young Englishman sat where he had sunk down in a state of mind not far removed from bewilderment. His captivity, if irksome before, was now changed to torture. Of his own misfortunes he no longer thought nor cared. His soul was absorbed in contemplating the perils that beset the sister of his friend—that fair young girl—that although seen but for a moment, and then looked upon only in the light of a stranger, had made such an impression on his imagination—even without knowing that she was Luigi's sister, what he had just heard was of itself sufficient to make him unhappy in her behalf. He knew the terrible power exercised by these bandits. He had proofs of it in his own experience. A power all the more dangerous, since to men, with lives already forfeited, there can be no restraint arising from fear of the law. One crime more could not further compromise them, and to commit such crime there needed only the motive and the opportunity. In this case both appeared to be present. He had himself seen something of the first by the behaviour of the brigands on the night of their bivouac in the village. Perhaps he might have seen more but for the presence of Popetta, who in their late maraud had made one of the band. What he had now listened to placed the thing beyond doubt. The eyes of Corvino had turned longingly on the sister of Luigi Torriani. What must be the sequel when the wolf thus looks upon the lamb—only destruction.

About the opportunity there was not much left to conjecture. It appeared like a sheepfold without either watch-dog or shepherd. The behaviour of the bandits while occupying the town told that they could reoccupy at any moment they had a mind. They might not be allowed long to remain there, but the shortest flying visit would be sufficient for such purpose as that. Such *razzai* and rape were both the ordinary incidents of their life, the tactics of their calling, and they were accustomed to execute them with the most subtle skill and celerity.

Corvino and his band could at any moment carry off Lucetta Torriani with half the damsels of Val di Torno—the young Englishman now knew this to be the name of the village—without danger of either resistance or interruption. After such an outrage they might be pursued by the Papal gendarmes and soldiery, and they might not. That would depend upon circumstances—or whether the *maunlengole* willed it !

There would be a show of pursuit perhaps, and perhaps with this it would end.

In his own land the young Englishman could not have given credit to such a state of things. He could not, nor would his countrymen until later times when it was brought home to them by testimony too substantial to be discredited. Besides, since his arrival in Rome he had become better informed about the social and political status of Italian life—upon the topic of the banditos. He had no doubt, therefore, of the danger in which stood the sister of Luigi Torriani.

There seemed but one who could save her from the fearful fate that hung over her head, and that one a woman, if the word could be used in speaking of such a thing as Cara Popetta. To the brigand's wife, companion, whatever she was, the thoughts of the captive turned as he sat reflecting in his cell, devising schemes for the protection of Lucetta Torriani.

If he were only free himself, knowing what he now did, the thing might have been easy enough, without appealing to such uncertain aid. But his own freedom was out of the question. He felt convinced that from that prison he would never go forth, unless to be carried to some equally secure—until the messenger returned from England, bearing the ransom for which he had written. And now, for the first time, did he feel satisfied at having written as he had done. Had he known what he now knew, it would have needed no dictation of the bandit chief to strengthen the appeal to his father. He earnestly hoped that the appeal he had made would receive a favourable response, and the money come in time to make liberty worth regaining. He had already traced out the course to which he would devote it.

What if it came not at all? There was, too, much probability in this. Lately he had become reckless by the curse that had been resting upon him—the remembrance of Belle Mainwaring. The remembrance of that dis-inheritance he deemed cruel, added to the still later act of paternal harshness by his father's refusal to forestall the paltry legacy promised to be left him. In like manner might he refuse the ransom. All that night sat the captive in his cell without sleeping, or now and then paced its fern-covered floor, by the movement hoping to stimulate his thoughts into the conception of some plan that would ensure less his own safety than that of Lucetta Torriani.

But daylight glimmered through the little window, and he was still without scheme to cheer him. There was only the slender hope that the ransom might arrive in time to enable him to act outside; this and the equally slender expectation that pointed to assistance from Popetta.

CHAPTER XXX.

BRIGANDAGE AND ITS CAUSE

BRIGANDAGE, as it exists in the southern countries of Europe, is only beginning to receive its full measure of credit.

There was always a knowledge, or supposition, that there were robbers in Spain, Italy, and Greece, who went in bands and now and then attacked travellers and plundered them of their purses, now and then also committing outrages on their persons.

Americans, however, supposed these cases to be exceptional, and that the stage representations of brigand life, to which we are occasionally treated, were simple exaggerations, both as regards the power and picturesqueness of these banded outlaws.

There were banditti, of course conceded every one; but these were few and far between, confined to the fastnesses of the mountains, or concealed in some pathless forest, only showing themselves by stealth, and on rare occasions upon the public highways, or in the inhabited districts of the country.

Unhappily, this view of the case is not the correct one. At present, and for a long time past, the brigands of Italy, so far from skulking in mountain caves or forest lairs, openly disport themselves in the peopled plains even where thickly peopled, not unfrequently making themselves masters of a village, and retaining possession of it for days at a time. You may wonder at the weakness of the Italian government that permits such a state of things to exist; but it does exist, sometimes in spite of these governments, but sometimes also with their secret support and connivance, notably in the territories of Rome and Naples.

To explain why they connive at it would be to enter upon a religio-political question which we do not care to discuss, since it may be deemed out of place in the pages of a mere romantic tale.

The motives of these governments for permitting brigandage is similar to that which gives " comfort and support " to Orangeism in Ireland—an association almost as despicable as brigandage.

It is the old story of despotism all over the world, " *Divide et imperia ;* " and prince or priest, if they cannot divide a people otherwise, will even rule them through the scourge of the robber !

Were there two forms of religion in Italy, as in Ireland, there would be no brigands, for then there would be no need of them ; since, in aspiring to political liberty, the two parties would satisfactorily checkmate one another, as they have done and still do in Ireland, each preferring serfdom for itself rather than to share freedom with his hated rival.

As in Italy there is but one religion, some other means was required to check and counteract the political liberty of the people. Despotism has hit upon the device of brigandage, and this is the explanation of its existence.

The nature of this hideous social sore is but imperfectly understood outside Italy. It might be supposed an irksome state of existence to dwell in a country where robbers can ramble about at will, and do pretty much as they please

And so it would be to any one of sensitive mind or educated intelligence.

But where the bandits are there are few of this class ; the districts infested by them having been long since surrendered to small tenant farmers and peasantry.

A landed proprietor does not think of residing on his own estate. If he did he would be in danger every day of his life of being—not assassinated, for that would be a simple act of folly on the part of the brigands—but hurried away from his home to some rendezvous in the mountains, and there held captive till his friends could raise a ransom sufficient to satisfy the cupidity of his captors! This refused, supposing it possible of being obtained, then he would certainly be assassinated, hanged, or shot without further equivocation.

Knowing this from either his own or his neighbours' experience, the owner of an Italian estate takes the precaution to reside in the town where there is a garrison of regular soldiers, or some other source of protection for his person.

Only inside such a town is he safe. A single mile beyond the boundary of its suburbs, sometimes even within them, he runs the risk of getting picked up and carried off before the very faces of his friends and fellow-citizens.

To deny this would be to contradict facts of continual occurrence; scores of such instances are constantly reported both in the Roman States and in the late Neapolitan territory, now happily included in a safer and better *régime*, though still suffering from this chronic curse.

But the peasantry themselves—the small farmers, shop-keepers, artificers, labourers, shepherds, and the like—how do they live under such an abnormal condition of things?

That is what the world is wondering at, especially the world of England. It is not very intelligent on any foreign matter, and dull at comprehending even that which concerns itself. Did it ever know one of its own farmers raise his voice against a war, however cruel or destructive, against the people of another country, provided it raised the price of corn and bacon in his own? Certainly not. And in this we have the explanation why the peasant people of Italy bear up so bravely against brigandage.

When a village baker gets a pezzo (something more than a greenback dollar) for a loaf of bread weighing less than three pounds, the real price in the nearest town being only three pence; when a labourer gets a similar sum for his brown bannock of light weight; when his wife has another pezzo for washing a brigand's shirt, the brigandesses being above such work; when the shepherd asks and obtains a triple price for his goat, kid, or sheep; and when every other article of bandit clothing or consumption is paid for at a proportionate famine price, one need no longer be astonished at the tolerance of the Italian peasantry toward such generous customers.

But how about the insults, the annoyances, the dangers to which they are subject at the hands of the outlaws?

All nonsense. They are not in any danger. They have little to lose but their lives, and these the brigands don't care to take. It would be to kill the goose, and get no more eggs!

In the way of annoyance the English labourer has to submit to quite as many, if not more, in the shape of heavy taxation or the interference of a prying policeman; and when it comes to the question of insult, supposing it to be offered to a wife or pretty daughter, the Italian peasant is in this respect not much worse off than the tradesmen of many an English town annually abandoned to the tender mercies of a scurvy militia.

Brigandage, therefore, in the belief of the Italian peasant, may not after all be so unendurable.

For all this there are times when it is so, and people who suffer from it grievously. Scenes of cruelty are often witnessed, episodes and incidents absolutely agonizing.

These usually occur in places that have hitherto either escaped the curse of brigandage, or have been for a long period relieved from it; where owners of estates, deeming themselves safe, have ventured to reside on the properties in hope of realizing that income, more than a moiety of which, under the robber *régime,* goes into the pockets of their tenantry, the peasant cultivators.

And to prevent this residence of the proprietors on their estates is the very thing desired by their proletarian retainers, who benefit by their absence—another motive, perhaps the strongest of all, for their toleration of the banditti.

When, in districts for a time abandoned by them, brigands once more make their appearance, either on a running raid or for permanent occupation, then scenes may be witnessed that are indeed deplorable.

Owners for a time remain, either hating to break up their households, or unable to dispose of the property in hand, such as stock or chattels, without ruinous sacrifice.

They live on, trusting to chance, sometimes to favour, and not unfrequently to a periodical bleeding by black-mail to gain them the simple indulgence of non-molestation.

It is at best but a precarious position—painful as uncertain.

In just such a dilemma was the father of Luigi Torriani. "Sindico," or chief magistrate of the town in which he lived, owning considerable property in the district, up to a late period he had felt secure from the incursions of the bandits. He had even gone so far as to gain ill-will from these outlaws, by the prosecution of one or two of their number at a time when there was some safety in the just administration of the laws.

But times had changed. The Pope, occupied with his heretical enemies from without his dominions, gave but little heed to interior disturbances; and as for Cardinal Antonelli, what cared he for the complaints of brigand outrages daily poured into his ears! Rather had he reason for encouraging them, this true descendant of the Cæsars and type of the Cæsar Borgias.

It was to this peril in which his father was placed, that the paragraph in Luigi's letter referred. Henry Harding had hit upon its correct explanation.

CHAPTER XXXI.

THE TORRIANIS

On that same night in which the brigands had strayed in the town of Val-di-Orno, the Sindico had learned something which caused him more than ever to fear for the future.

The bold, bullying behaviour of the men was itself sufficient to tell him of his own impotence in case they had chosen to violate the laws of hospitality.

But he had been told of something more—something personal to himself, or rather to his family—that family consisting solely of his daughter Lucetta.

She and Luigi were his only children, and now had been motherless for many a year.

What he had learned is already known to the reader— that Corvino had been seen to cast longing looks upon his child. This is the Italian parlance when speaking of a preference of the kind supposed to exist in the bosom of a brigand.

Francisco Torriani knew its significance. He was well aware of the personal attractions possessed by his daughter. Her great beauty had long been the theme, not only of the village of Val-di-Orno, but of the surrounding country. Even in the city itself had she been spoken of, and once, while on a visit there with her father, she had been beset by blandishments, in which counts and cardinals had taken part—for these red-legged gentry of the Church are not callous to the smiles of witching women.

It was the second time that Corvino had seen Lucetta Torriani, and her father was admonished that he had perhaps seen her twice too often, and that once more might bring misery to his house—leaving it with a desolated hearth.

There was no insinuation against the girl; no hint that she had in any way encouraged the bold glances of the brigand chief. On the contrary, it was known that she hated the sight of him, as she should do. It had been simply a warning, whispered in the father's ear, that it would be well for her to be kept out of Corvino's way.

And how was this to be done?

On the day after the visit of the band Francisco Torriani noticed something strange in his daughter's manner. There was an air of dejection—not usual to her, for the pretty Lucetta was not given to gravity. Why should she be low-spirited at such a crisis?

Her father inquired the cause. " You are not yourself to-day, my child ? " he said, observing her dejected air.

" I am not, papa, I confess it."

" Has anything occurred to vex you ? "

" To vex me—no, not quite that. But something of another that gives me an unhappy thought."

" Of another! who, *cara figlia ?* "

" Well, papa, I've been thinking of that poor young Inglese who was carried through by those infamous men. Supposing it had been brother Luigi ? "

" Ay, indeed ! "

" What do you think they will do with him ? Is his life in any danger ? "

" No—not his life—that is, if his friends will only send the money that will be demanded for his ransom."

" But if he has no friends ? He might not. His dress was not rich, and yet for all that he looked a *galantuomo*. Did he not ? "

" I did not take much notice of him, my dear. I was oo busy with the affairs of the town."

" Do you know, papa, what our girl Annetta has heard ? —some one told her this morning."

" What ? "

" That the young Inglese is an artist—just like our Luigi. How strange if it be so ! "

" 'Tis probable enough. Many of these English residents in Rome are artists by profession. They come here to study our old paintings and sculptures. He *may* be one, and very likely is. 'Tis a pity, poor fellow; but it can't be helped. Perhaps if he were a great *milord* it would be all the worse for him. His captors would require a much larger sum for his ransom. If they find he can't pay they'll be likely to let him go."

" I do hope they will. I do, indeed."

" But why, child?—why are you so much interested in this young man? There have been others. Corvino's band took three with them the last time they passed through. You said nothing about them? "

I did not notice them, papa; and he—think of his being a *pittore!* Suppose brother Luigi was treated so in his country ! "

" There is no danger of that. I wish we had such a country to live in—under a government where everything is secure, life, property and——"

The Sindico did not say what besides. He was thinking of the admonition he had recently received.

" And why should we not go to England? Go there and live with Luigi! He said in his last letter he is very successful in his profession, and would like to have us with him. Perhaps this young Inglese on his return may stop at the inn, and if you would question him he could tell us all about his country. If it be true what you say of it, why should we not go there? "

" There, or somewhere else. Italy is no longer a home for us. The Holy Pontiff is too much occupied with his foreign affairs to find time for the protection of his people. Yes, *cara figlia*, I've been thinking of leaving Val-di-Orno this day, more than ever. I've almost made up my mind to accept the offer Signor Bardoni has made for my estate. It's far below its value; but in these times—what's that noise in the street? "

Lucetta ran to the window and looked out.

" *Che vedete ?* " inquired her father.

" Soldiers," she replied. " There's a great big string

of them coming up the street. I suppose they're after the brigands ? "

" Yes. They won't catch them for all that. They never do. They're always just in time to be too late ! Come away from the window, child. I must go down to receive them. They'll want quartering for the night, and plenty to eat and drink. What's more, they won't want to pay for it. No wonder our people would rather extend their hospitality to the brigands who pay well for everything. Ah, me ! It's no sinecure to be the Sindico of such a town. If old Bardoni wishes it, he can have both my property and place. No doubt he can manage better than I. He is better fitted to deal with the brigands."

Saying this, the Sindico took up his official staff, and putting on his hat, descended to the street, to give official reception to the soldiers of the Pope.

" A grand officer ! " said Lucetta, glancing slyly through the window bars. " If he were only brave enough to go after those brutes of brigands, and rescue that handsome young Inglese ! Ah ! if he'd only do that, I'd give him a smile for his pains. *Povero pittore !* Just like brother Luigi. I wonder, now, if he has a sister thinking of him ! Perhaps he may have a—— "

The girl hesitated to pronounce the word "sweetheart," though as the thought suggested itself there came a slight shadow over her countenance, as if she would have preferred knowing he had none.

" Oh ! " she exclaimed, once more looking out of the window. " The grand officer is coming home—with papa ; and there's another—a younger one along with him. No doubt they will dine here ; and I suppose I must go and dress to receive them."

Saying this, she glided out of the room, which was soon after occupied by the Sindico and his two soldier guests.

CHAPTER XXXII.

THE town of Val-di-Orno was now in military possession, and there was no longer any fear of a revisit from the bandits.

The soldiers—in all about a hundred—were distributed by billet into the best houses, while the officers took possession of the Albergo.

The captain, however, not contented with such shelter as the humble inn afforded, contrived to insinuate himself into more comfortable quarters—in the house of the chief magistrate of the town, who was the Sindico himself.

It was a hospitality somewhat reluctantly offered; and, under other circumstances, the offer might not have been made.

But the times were troublous; the brigands were "abroad;" and people could not well act with churlishness towards their professed protectors.

Besides, Francesco Torriano, on his own account, had need to show courtesy—or pretend it—to the soldiers of the Pope. It was suspected that he sympathized with that party of liberal views, fast growing in influence, and who, under the inspiration of Mazzini, was threatening a Republic in Rome.

Compromised by this suspicion, the Sindico of Val-di-Orno required to act with circumspection in the presence of the Pope's officer.

The proposal for quarters in his house had come from the latter. It was made deferentially, and under some trifling excuse, but in a way to make refusal a delicate and difficult matter.

The Sindico was constrained to give consent; and the

officer brought his luggage along with his body-servant from the inn, leaving more room for his subalterns.

The Sindico thought it strange, but said nothing. The explanation he gave to himself was not very consolatory:

"To spy upon me, I suppose. No doubt he has his orders from Antonelli."

Though plausible to him who made it, the conjecture was not true. Captain Count Guardioli had received no orders of the kind; though likely enough he had given the Vatican some hints of the political proclivities of the Sindico of Val-di-Orno.

His desire to share the hospitality of the magistrate's mansion was a thought that came after his entering the house on that first merely official visit.

The cause was simple enough. He had caught sight of the Sindico's daughter as she was crossing one of the corridors, and Captain Count Guardioli was not the man to shut his eyes to such attraction.

Poor Lucetta! Beset on every side—on one hand a capo of bandits, on the other a captain of Papal soldiers. In truth was she in danger!

Fortunately for her peace of mind, she knew nothing of the designs of Corvino; though she was not long in discovering the inclinations of Captain Count Guardioli.

His countship was one of those men who believe themselves irresistible—a true Italian lady-killer, with a semi-piratical aspect, eyes filled with intellectual fire, teeth of snow-white sheen, and coal-black moustache, turning spirally along his cheeks. A maiden must have her mind powerfully preoccupied who could withstand his amorous attack.

So was he accustomed to declare in the ears of his military associates.

No doubt, in the corrupt circles of the apostolic city, he had had his successes. Count, captain, and cavalier, above all a keen seeker of love adventures, it could scarce be otherwise.

At first sight of Lucetta Torriani, the captain-count experienced a sensation akin to ecstasy. It was like one who has discovered a treasure hitherto unseen by the eyes of man.　What a triumph there would be in revealing it!

To obtain it there could be no great difficulty.　A village damsel—a simple country girl!　She would not be likely to resist the fascinations of one who brought along with him the accomplishments of the Court, backed by the prestige of title and position.

So reasoned Captain Count Guardioli, and from that moment commenced to lay siege to the heart of Lucetta Torriani.

But although from the city of the Cæsars, he could not say, as the first Cæsar had done, *Veni, vidi, vici.*　He came and saw ; but after residing a week under the same roof with the simple village damsel, he was so far from having subdued her heart, that he had not made the slightest impression upon it.　On the contrary, he had himself become completely enslaved by her charms.　He had grown so enamoured of the beautiful Lucetta, that it was apparent to every one in the place—his own soldiers and subalterns included.

Blinded by his ill-starred passion he had abandoned even the dignity of concealing it; and followed his *ignis fatuus* about—constantly forcing his company upon her in a manner that rendered him ridiculous.

All this the Sindico saw with chagrin, but could not help it.　He consoled himself, however, with the reflection that Lucetta was safe—so far as her heart was concerned.

And yet every one did not believe this.　In the character of the Sindico's daughter there was nothing that could be called coquetry.　It was rather an amiability that hesitated about giving pain ; and influenced by this, she listened to the solicitations and flatteries of the captain-count, almost as if she liked them.

It was only her father who thought otherwise.　Perhaps he might be mistaken.

As usual the soldiers did but little service—none at all that was of any avail toward clearing the country of the bandits.

They made occasional excursions to the neighbouring

valleys where the brigands had been heard of—but where they could never be found.

In these expeditions they were never accompanied by their *commandante*. He could not tear himself away from the side of Lucetta Torriani, and the field duty was left to his lieutenants.

By night the soldiers strayed about the town—got drunk in the liquor-shops—insulted the townsmen—took liberties with their women—and made themselves so generally disagreeable, that before a week had elapsed the citizens of Val-di-Orno would have gladly exchanged their military guests for Corvino and his cut-throats.

About ten days after their entry into the place, there came a report which by the townspeople was received with secret satisfaction ; not the less from their having heard a whisper as to the cause.

The soldiers were to be recalled to Rome to protect the Holy See from the approach of the Republic.

Even to that secluded spot had rumours reached that a change was coming, and there were men in Val-di-Orno, where it might be supposed such an idea could scarce have penetrated, ready to vociferate " Erviva la Republican."

Its Sindico would have been among the foremost to have raised the regenerating cry.

CHAPTER XXXIII.

IMPROVED PRISON FARE

A WEEK had elapsed from the day the brigands had got back to their mountain den.

The plunder had all been appropriated by three or four, to whom fortune had been most favourable.

These were already the richest individuals in the band, for amid the mountains of Italy, as in the towns of Homburg and Baden, the banker in the end is sure to sweep in the stakes of the outsiders. Dame Fortune may give luck for a run; but he who can afford to lose longest will outrun her in the end.

Among the winners was the capo, of course; and Cara Popetta put fresh rings upon her fingers, new brooches upon her hair, and additional chains round her neck.

A new expedition began to be talked about, to provide fresh stakes for another spell of *capo or croce.*

It was not to be either a grand or distant one. Only a little spurt into one of the neighbouring valleys, the capture, if chance allowed it, of some petty proprietor, who might have ventured from the great city to have a look at his estates, or the seizure of such chattels as might be found in a country village.

It was intended rather to fill up the time until the return of that secret messenger, who had been despatched to England, and from whose mission much was expected.

Their English *confrère* had given the brigands a hint of the great wealth of 'their captive's father, and all were hopeful of receiving the grand ransom that had been demanded by the capo. With five thousand pounds, nearly thirty thousand pezzos, they might play for a month, and go to sleep for another, without much troubling themselves about the soldiers in pursuit of them.

The little expedition that was to form the interlude, while this was being waited for, was soon organized, only about three-fourths of the band being permitted to take part in it.

On this occasion the women were also left behind, Cara Popetta among the rest.

The captive inside his cell only knew of its having started by the greater tranquillity that reigned around the place. There were still quarrels occurring at short intervals; but these appeared to be between the women, whose voices, less sonorous, were not less energetic in their accents of anger or more refined in their mode of expressing it.

Like their short, cropped hair, their vocabulary appeared to have been shorn of all its elegance; both perhaps having been parted with at the same time. Had Henry Harding been in a mind for amusement, he might have found it in witnessing their disputes, oft occurring right under his window.

But he was not. On the contrary, it but disgusted him to think of the degradation to which the angel woman may reach when once she has fallen from virtue.

And many of these women were beautiful, or had been before they became vicious; no doubt more than one of them the fond hope of some doting parent, perhaps the stay of some aged mother, and the solace of her declining days, who, having one day strayed beyond the confines of her native village, like the daughter of Pietro, returned home "sad and slow," or never returned at all!

The heart of the young Englishman was lacerated as he reflected upon their fate. It was torture when he thought of them in connection with Lucetta Torriani. To think of that pure, innocent girl—the glance he had had of her convinced him she was this—becoming as one of those feminine fiends daily jarring and warring outside his window. Surely, it could never be! And yet what was there to hinder it? This was the inquiry that now occupied his attention, and filled him with unpleasant forebodings.

Since the departure of the expedition a ray of hope had shone into his cell. It was light as the sunlight that there entered. But the mind of the captive, quickened by captivity, like a drowning man, will catch even at straws, and one seemed to offer itself to the young Englishman.

In the first place, he perceived that there was a chance of corrupting his jailer. He was no longer the morose taciturn fellow who had hitherto attended upon him, but one who, if not cheerful, was at least talkative. On hearing his voice, the prisoner could at once recognise the voice as that of one of the brigands who had held conversation under his window. It was the one whose sentiments showed him the least hardened of the two, and whom the other had called Thomasso. The captive fancied something might be done with this man. From what he had heard him say, Thomasso did not appear altogether dead to the dictates of humanity.

True, he had made confession to having spent some time in a Papal prison. But many a martyr had done that— political and otherwise.

The worst against him was his now being where he was; but this also might have come from a like cause.

So reflected Henry Harding, and the more did he think of it after his new jailer had held converse with him.

But he had found something else to reflect upon, also of a hopeful character. The breakfast brought by Thomasso, which was his first meal after the departure of the band, was altogether different from those of former days. Instead of maccaroni paste, often unseasoned and insipid, there came broiled mutton, sausages, *confitti*, and a bottle of Rosolio !

"Who sent these delicacies?" was the thought of him who received them.

He did not give it speech until after dinner, which, in a like way, was different from the dinners of previous days.

Then he put the question to his new attendant.

"La signorina," was the answer of Thomasso, speaking in such courteous tones that but for the small chamber and the absence of chattels, the captive might have fancied himself in an hotel, and specially cared for by one of its waiters.

Throughout the day did this solicitude show itself, and at night the signorina herself brought him his supper without either the intervention or attendance of Thomasso.

Shortly after the sun had gone down the young English-man was startled at seeing a woman coming inside his cell, for it was an apparition strange as unexpected.

The small chamber in which he was imprisoned was but the adjunct of a larger apartment, a sort of store-room where the brigands kept the bulkier articles of their plunder, as also provisions.

In this last was a large window through which the moon was shining, and it was only on the door of his cell being opened that he perceived the entrance of his new visitor. Though but dimly seen in the borrowed light of the outer chamber he could tell that it was a woman.

" Who was she ? "

Only for a second was he in doubt, her large form as she stood outlined in the doorway, as also the drapery of her dress, told him it was the wife of the chief! He had observed that only she, of all the women belonging to the band, affected female habiliments.

He wondered what she could want with him—all the more as she came stealing in, apparently in fear of being watched or followed by some outsider.

She had noiselessly opened the outer door, as noiselessly closed it behind her, and in the same way opened and closed that communication with his cell.

CHAPTER XXXIV.

POPETTA

THE prisoner had started up, and was standing in the centre of his cell.

"Don't be alarmed, Signor Inglese!" said his strange visitor, speaking in a half whisper.

While speaking she had groped her way through the gloom, and was now so near that he felt her breath upon his cheek, while her hand was laid gently upon his shoulder.

"What is it?" he asked, starting at her touch, and slightly recoiling, though not from fear.

"Do not be alarmed!" she said, soothingly; "I am not a man come to do you any injury. Only a woman. It is I, Popetta; you remember me."

"I do, signorina; you are the wife of the chief Corvino."

"Wife! ah, if you'd said slave, it would be nearer the truth. No matter, signor; that can signify nothing to you."

A sigh, distinctly audible in the still darkness, accompanied the speech.

The captive remained silent, wondering what was to come next. She had taken her hand from off his shoulder, or rather it had dropped from it on his starting away.

"You will be surprised at my being here?" she continued, speaking in the tongue and tone of a lady. "From what you have seen, you will think there can be no compassion in a heart like mine! You may well think so."

"No, no," asseverated the captive, now really feeling surprise; "no doubt you have been unfortunate."

"True, true," she hurriedly rejoined, as if not caring to dwell upon the recollections called up by his speech. "Signor, I am here, not to talk of the past—my past—but of your future."

"Mine!"

"Yours, signor. Oh, it is fearful!"

"In what way fearful?" asked the young Englishman. "Surely I shall soon be set free. What do I care for a few days, or even weeks of imprisonment?"

"Caro signor, you deceive yourself! It is not imprisonment, though you may find that hard enough : harder still when he comes back again, brute that he is!"

Strange language for a wife to use toward her husband, thought Henry Harding.

"Yes, harder," continued she, "if the letter you have written receives no response : I mean, if it brings no ransom. Tell me, signor—what did you say in that letter? Tell me all!"

"I thought you were acquainted with its contents. It was dictated in your hearing and written in your presence."

"I know, I know; but was that all? I saw that you were unwilling to sign it. You had a reason?"

"I had."

"Some difference with your family? You are not friends with your father—am I right?"

"Something of that," answered the young Englishman, knowing no reason why he should conceal a quarrel, so far away from them whom it might concern.

"I thought so," said the woman. "And this," she continued, changing her tone to one of greater earnestness, "this quarrel may prevent your father from sending the *riscatta.*"

"Possibly it may."

"Possibly, signor; you treat the matter lightly, you have done so all along. I have noticed it. One cannot help admiring your courage. I have. Perhaps that is why I am here."

Again there was something like a sigh, which only added to the surprise of the captive.

"You know not," continued Popetta, "the fate that is before you, if the *riscatta* should not come."

"What fate, signora?"

"Cruel! cruel!"

"Tell me what it is. By what you say it seems to have been already determined on."

"It is determined—always determined. It is the custom of Corvino."

"Explain yourself, signora."

"First, your ears will be cut off. They will be enclosed in a letter, and sent to your father. The letter will be a renewed demand for the money; and then——"

"Then?" demanded the captive, with some impatience, for the first time giving credence to the threat that had already been twice made by Corvino himself.

"If the money be not sent, you will be still further mutilated."

"How?"

"Signor, I cannot tell you. There are many ways. I may not mention them. Better for you if the answer should leave no hope of your being ransomed—you would escape torture, by being immediately shot!"

"Surely, signora, you are jesting with me?"

"Ah, signor, it is no jest. I have witnessed it, once—twice—often! It is the custom with him, Corvino—this wretch with whom I have the misfortune to be associated. It is the custom of the band. It will be carried out to a certainty."

"You come to me as a friend?" inquired the captive as if to test the sincerity of her speech.

"I do! I do!"

"You have some counsel to give me? What is it?"

"It is that you should write again, write to your friends; you must have some, signor, you the son of a great *galantuomo*—your countryman Ricardo tells us you are. Write to your friends to see your father, and urge upon him the necessity of sending the sum stated for your ransom. It is your only chance of escaping from the fate I have told you of, escaping from being fearfully mutilated!"

"There is another," said the captive, for the first time speaking in a tone of complaisance to his strange counsellor.

"Another? I do not know it; say what it is."

"Your favour, signora."

"How?"

"You can find me the means of escaping from this prison."

"'Tis possible; just possible, but not certain. And if I succeeded, it could only be by giving my life for you. Would you wish that, signor?"

"No, not such a sacrifice."

"Such a sacrifice would be certain; you know not how I am watched. 'Tis only by stealth and a bribe to Thomasso I've been able to come here—Corvino's jealousy —ah, Signor Inglese, I have been thought handsome—*you* may not think me so?"

Her hand once more rested on the young Englishman's shoulder—once more to be repelled, but this time with greater gentleness. He feared to wound her self-esteem, and stir the tigress that slumbered in that strange Italian heart.

He made reply as he best could with a compliment evasive, insincere.

"Even were he to know of this interview," she continued, still speaking of Corvino, "by the laws of our band my life would be forfeited—you see, signor, that I am ready to serve you."

"You would have me write then? How is it to be done, how can a letter be sent?"

"Leave that to me. Here are some sheets of paper, ink and a pen. I have brought them with me; you can have no light now; I dare not give it you. Corvino's captives must not be made too comfortable else they would be less urgent for their friends to set them free. When the sun shines in through your window in the morning, write. Thomasso will bring you your breakfast, and take your letters in exchange. It will be my care to see that they are sent."

"Oh, thanks, thanks!" exclaimed the grateful captive,

seizing hold of the writing materials with an eagerness he had not hitherto shown, a new idea had come suddenly into his mind. "A thousand thanks!" he repeated, "I shall do as you say."·

"*Buono notte!*" said the brigandess, putting the writing materials into his hand, at the same time pressing it with a fervour that showed something more than friendship. "*Buono notte, galantuomo!*" she added, "sleep without fear! If it should come to that, you may command even the life of her you have heard called Cara Popetta."

Henry Harding was but too happy when she permitted him to disengage himself from her clasp, which, though ho scarce understood, filled him with a feeling somewhat akin to repulsion.

He was happier still when she stole silently out of his cell, and he heard the door closing cautiously behind her.

CHAPTER XXXV.

As soon as the captive became convinced that his visitor was gone for good, he lay down upon the fern-leaves and gave way to profound reflection, the subject, of course, being what had just passed between him and Popetta.

What could be her motive for the counsel thus voluntarily given ? Was it a trap to betray him ?

It could hardly bear this construction : for what was there to betray ?

He was already in the power of the bandits for life as for death. What more could they want ?

" Ah ! " thought he, " I see through it now ! After all, it may be Corvino's doing. He may have put her up to this, to make more sure of getting the money for my ransom. He thinks that her counsel, given in this sly way, will terrify me, and make me write a stronger letter to my father."

But the answer to these self-asked interrogations did not quite satisfy. What need was there for any scheme of the kind on the part of the bandit chief ? He had dictated the letter sent ; if stronger terms had seemed necessary, he would have insisted on their being inserted.

The former conjecture fell through.

Then, supposing Popetta's counsel to have been loyal, what could be her object—her motive ?

Henry Harding was yet young, and but little experienced in the ways of a woman's heart. He could count but one experience, and that of a different kind. Only by some ill-understood whisperings of Nature was he guided to a suspicion of what this strange woman meant ; and he cared not to continue the reflection.

Leaving her motives to make way for themselves, he eagerly seized at her suggestion. It promised to assist him in a design he had already been running over in his mind, without much prospect of being able to carry it into execution. It was to write to Luigi Torriani, in London, and warn him of the peril in which his sister was placed.

He could write to his own father all the same, and in stronger terms, as he had been counselled; for he had now become sensible of dread impending danger.

The behaviour of the brigands, which for more than a week he had been witnessing, had produced upon him a serious impression, altogether effacing that imbibed by contemplating the stage bandit of picturesque habiliments and courteous carriage. However he might have felt about the representative, looking upon him from the stall of a theatre, he could now tell there would be no trifling with the real character, when contemplated by one completely in his power, upon the summit of an Italian mountain!

Everything around proclaimed the seriousness of his situation. It had become too critical for him to affect further nonchalance, or feel in any way contented; and, scarce able to sleep, he watched anxiously for the light of morning.

No sooner did the dawn show itself through the window of his cell than he spread out the paper with which Popetta had provided him, and commenced writing the letters. His table was the stone-paved floor; the chair the same. He wrote lying flat along the flags!

There were two letters, as intended. When finished, they were as follows—the first to his father:—

"DEAR FATHER,—By this time I suppose you will have received a letter, which I wrote to you eight days ago, and which I have reason to believe was carried to you by a. special messenger. I have no doubt that its contents will have surprised and perhaps pained you. It was an appeal which I must confess I was very little inclined to make, but it was done at the dictation of a brigand, with a pistol held to my head, and there was no help for it. I am now writing one under different circumstances, on the floor of the cell where I am imprisoned—I am doing it without the knowledge of my jailers. I can add but little to what I have said before, only that I am not now speaking under compulsion. From what I have lately learned, I can assure you that my former letter—though I thought so at the time—contained no idle words.

"The threat made in it by the brigand chief he means most surely to execute, and if the sum named be not sent to him, he will.

"The first part of his performance is to be the cropping of my ears, and forwarding them to your address. The latter he has learned from a strange source of which I may as well inform you: from our old discharged game-keeper—Doggy Dick—who happens to be one of his band. How the scoundrel came to be here I cannot tell. I only know that he is here and the most hostile to me of the whole fraternity. He remembers the thrashing I gave him, and takes care to keep me in mind of it.

"Now, dear father, I have told you all about how I am situated; and if you deem it worth while to extract your unworthy son from his dangerous dilemma, send on the money. You may think £5,000 rather a high figure to pay for such a life as mine. So do I, but unfortunately I am not permitted to name my own price. If it appears too much, perhaps you will not object to send the £1,000 you promised I should have at your death, and I shall make the best bargain I can with the scoundrels who've got me in pawn.

"Hoping to hear from you by return of post—this I believe is to go by post—I remain your closely guarded son, "HENRY HARDING.

"To General Harding,
 "Beechwood Park, Bucks, England."

Such was the letter from Henry Harding to his father.

That to his friend Luigi was shorter, though, perhaps, more stimulative in its suggestions. It ran as follows:—

"DEAR LUIGI,—I have only time to say three words to you. I am prisoner to a band of brigands—the band of

L

Corvino, of whom, if I mistake not, I have heard you speak. The place is in the Neapolitan mountains, about forty miles from Rome and twenty from your native town. I saw your sister while on my way through it as a captive. I did not know her at the time, but I have since learned something I almost hesitate to tell you. It must be told, however, and it is for that I write you this letter. Lucetta is in danger! The brigand chief has designs upon her. I learned it by a conversation between two of the band whom I chanced to overhear. I need not add more. You will best know how to act; and there is no time to be lost. God speed you! Yours,

"HENRY HARDING."

The letters were ready for the post long before Thomasso brought the writer his breakfast.

Without saying a word, Thomasso slipped them into the breast-pocket of his coat, and carried them away with him.

That same night they were in the mail-bag of the steamer plying from Civita Vecchia to Marseilles.

CHAPTER XXXVI.

A SHORT TRIAL

THE brigands returned from their raid two days earlier than they had been expected.

The captive became aware of their arrival by the increased clamour outside. On peering through his cell window, he saw the men who had been upon the expedition. They were all in ill-humour, looking sulky, and cursing beyond their usual quantity.

They had been unsuccessful in the raid, having found soldiers in the district into which it had been made. They had, moreover, heard a rumour that a combined force, both from the Roman and Neapolitan territory, was marching upon their mountain retreat.

The captive could hear them talking of treason.

He caught sight of Corvino in front of his window. Something special seemed to have enraged the chief. He was swearing at Popetta and calling her foul names in presence of his followers.

One of the other women—a sort of rival in the regards of the ruffian—was standing by, and appearing to act as instigator. She talked as if she was bringing some accusation against the *sposa* of the *capo*.

The prisoner could see that Popetta was in trouble, though he had no clue to the cause. They talked so fast, several clamouring at the same time, that it was impossible for him, with his slight knowledge of Italian, to make out much of what was said.

Soon the colloquy assumed a different phase, Corvino separating from the crowd, and along with two or three others coming toward the cell.

L 2

In an instant the door was dashed open, and the brigand chief stepped inside the dismal apartment.

"Le signor!" he cried, hissing the words through his teeth, "I understand you've been very comfortable during my absence? Plenty to eat and drink. *Rocatti, confetti,* cordials, the best of everything, ah! and a companion too in your solitude! no doubt a pleasant companion! I hope you both enjoyed yourselves. Ha! ha! ha!"

It fell upon the ears of the captive with a fearful significance. It boded evil either to himself, or Popetta— perhaps to both.

"What do you mean, Captain Corvino?" mechanically exclaimed the young Englishman.

"Oh! how innocent you are, my beardless lamb—my smoothed-faced Adonis. What do I mean? Ha! ha! ha!"

And again the cell resounded with his fierce exultant laughter.

"*Cospetta!*" cried the chief, suddenly changing tone as his eye fell upon a white object lying in a corner of the cell; "what's this? *Una lettera?* And *carta bianca!* And here, pen and ink! So, so, signor! you've been carrying on a correspondence? Bring him out to the light," he vociferated. "Bring everything."

And with a fierce oath, he rushed into the open air, one of his followers dragging the captive after him. Another carried the sheet of paper—surplus of the supply left by Popetta—as also the ink-horn and pen.

The whole band had by this time gathered upon the ground.

"Comrades!" cried their capo, "there's been treason in our absence. See what we've found. Paper, pens and ink in the cell of our prisoner, and look! On his fingers the stain! He's been writing letters! What could they have been about but to betray us? Examine him. See if they be still upon his person!"

The search was instantly made, extending to every pocket of the prisoner's dress, every fold where a letter might be concealed.

One was brought to light, but evidently not of recent
writing

It was the letter of introduction to the father of Luigi
Torriani.

" To whom is it addressed ? " asked the chief, snatching
it from the hands of his satellite.

"Diavolo!" he exclaimed, on reading the superscription,
"here's correspondence unexpected ! "

Without further delay he pulled the letter out of its
envelope, and commenced making himself master of the
contents.

He did not communicate them to the bystanders, but
the expression that passed over his countenance told them
that the letter contained something strangely interesting
to him. It was like the grim smile of the tiger who feels
that his prey has been already secured, and lies helpless
within reach of his claws.

"So, signor!" he exclaimed, once more bending his eyes
upon the young Englishman. " You told me you had no
friends in Italy—*una menzoqua, signor!* Rich friends you
have. Powerful friends. The chief magistrate of a town,
with "—he satirically whispered, placing his lips close to
the captive's ear—" with a very pretty daughter ! What
a pity you did not have an opportunity to present your
letter of introduction. Never mind ; you may make her
acquaintance yet—soon, perhaps, and here among the
mountains! That will be all the more romantic, *signor
pittore !* "

The whispered insinuation, as also the satirical tone in
which it was made, passed like a poisoned shaft through
the heart of Henry Harding. Every hour since the first
of his captivity the interest concerned for the sister of
Luigi Torriani had been growing stronger, while that
hitherto felt for Belle Mainwaring had passed altogether
out of his mind.

Stung by the speeches of the brigand, he made no reply.
Anything he could have said would have served no purpose, even had there been time to say it.

But there was not. The tormentor thought not of listening to the response of the prisoner, and, without waiting for it, he continued :

"*Compagnos !*" cried he, addressing himself to his band, "you have here before you the proofs of treason—no wonder the soldiers are gathering upon our track. It remains for you to discover who have been the traitors !"

"Yes, yes!" cried a score of voices; "the traitors! Who are they? Let us know that, and we'll settle the score with them!"

"Our prisoner here," continued the chief, "has written a letter, as you can all see for yourselves. It has been despatched, too, since it is not upon his person. To whom has it been sent? Who carried it? Who supplied him with the pen, ink, and paper? These are the questions to be considered."

"Who was left to guard over him?" inquired one of the men.

"Thomasso," answered several.

"Where is Thomasso?" shouted a score of voices.

"I am here," responded the brigand who bore that name.

"Answer us, then. Did you do this?"

"Do what?"

"Furnish these writing materials to our prisoner?"

"No," firmly replied Thomasso.

"You need not waste your time questioning him!" interposed a voice recognised as that of Popetta. "It was I who furnished them!"

"Yes!" said the rival brigandess, speaking aside to several members of the band. "Not only found them, but carried them to the cell herself."

"*Tutti !*" cried the chief, in a voice of thunder, that stilled the murmurs produced by the communication. "For what purpose did you supply them, Cara Popetta?"

"For the common good," replied the woman, seemingly with the intent to give colour to what she had done.

"How?" shouted a score of voices.

"*Cospette,*" replied the accused, "it is simple enough."

" Explain it ! Explain it ! "

" *Buono ! buono !* Listen, and I will."

" We listen."

" Well, like yourselves, I wanted to see the *riscatta*. I didn't think the Inglese would get it for us. The letter directed by him wasn't strong enough. While you were gone, having nothing else to think of, I prevailed upon the *galantuomo* to write another. What harm was there in that ? "

" It was to his father, then ? " asked one of the spokesmen.

" Of course it was," replied Popetta, with a scornful inclination of the head.

" How was it sent ? "

" To the posta at Rome. The young man knew how to address it."

" Who carried it to Rome? "

To this question there was no answer. Popetta had turned aside, and pretended not to hear it.

" *Compagnos !* " cried the chief, " make inquiry, and find out who of those left behind has been absent during our absence."

A man was pointed out by the accuser of Popetta.

He was a greenhorn, one of the recent recruits of the band, not yet admitted to the privileges of the " giro."

The cross-questioning to which he was submitted soon produced its effect. Notwithstanding his promise of secrecy given to her who had selected him for a messenger, he confessed all.

Unfortunately for Popetta, the fellow had been taught to read ; and enough arithmetic to know that he had carried two letters instead of one. He was able to tell that one was for the father of the prisoner. So far, Popetta had spoken the truth.

It was the second letter that condemned her. That had been directed to the " Signor Francesco Torriani."

" Hear that ! " cried several of the brigands, as soon as the name was announced, and without listening to the address. " The Signor Torriani ! Why, it is the Sindico of Val-di-Orno! No wonder we're being beset by soldiers! Every one knows that Francesco Torriani has never been our friend!"

"Besides," remarked the brigandess, who had started the accusation, "why such friendship to a prisoner—an Inglese? All that *confetti*, *rosolio*, the best tidbits in the place, to say nothing of the company of the signorina herself! Depend upon it, *compagnos*, there has been *untratimento !*"

Poor Popetta! her time was come. Her husband (if such he was) had found the opportunity long wanted—not to protect, but to destroy her. He could now do so with perfect impunity, even without blame.

With the cunning of a tiger he had approached the crisis, with the ferocity of a tiger he seized upon it.

"*Compagnos*," appealed he in a tone pretended to be sad, "I need not tell you how hard it is to hear these charges against one who is dear to me—my own wife. And it is harder to think they have been proved! But we are banded together by a law which must not be broken —the law of self-preservation, and it must be mutual among us. To infringe that law would lead to our dissolution—our ruin; and we have sworn to one another that he or she who does aught to lead to its infringement shall suffer death! Death, though it be brother, sister, wife, or mistress. I, whom you have chosen for your chief, shall prove myself true; and by this may you believe me."

While in the act of speaking the last words the brigand sprang forward till he stood by the side of his supposed wife, Popetta.

Her cry of astonishment was quickly followed by one of a different intonation. It was a sharp scream of agony, gradually subdued to the expiring accents of death, as the woman sunk back upon the grass with a poignard transfixed in her heart!

The scene that followed calls for no description. There was sign of neither weeping nor woe in that savage assemblage. There may have been pity, but if there was, it did not declare itself.

The murderous chieftain strode quietly away to his quarters, and there sought concealment. He was too hardened to feel remorse.

Some of his subordinates removed from the spot the ghastly evidence of his crime, burying the body of the brigandess in a ravine close by, but not before they had stripped it of its glittering adornments—the spoils of many a fair maid of the *Compagna*.

The prisoner was carried back to his cell, and there left to reflect on the tragedy just enacted, the fate of poor Popetta.

To his excited imagination it appeared but the over-shadowing of a still more fearful fate for himself.

CHAPTER XXXVII.

A TOUGH AMPUTATION

DURING three days succeeding the tragical event recorded, there was tranquillity in the bandit quarters—that gloomy quiet that succeeds some terrible occurrence alike telling that it has occurred.

So far as Henry Harding saw, the chief kept himself within doors, as if doing decent penance for the brutish-like crime he had committed.

On the fourth day there transpired an event which roused the rendezvous to its usual activity—to an excitement under which the late sanguinary scene was for a time buried in oblivion.

A little before sunrise, the signals of the sentinel announced the approach of a messenger, and shortly after the man came into the quarters. He was in peasant garb, the same who had carried the requisition on the landlord of the lodgings, and brought back the three score scudi.

This time he was the bearer of a despatch of somewhat portentous appearance, a large envelope, inclosing a letter with still another inside.

It was addressed to the brigand chief, and to him delivered direct. The captive knew of the arrival of the messenger by the excited talking outside, which also proclaimed it to be an event of some importance.

He only learned that it was a letter, when the brigand chief burst angrily into his cell, holding the opened despatch in his hand.

"So!" cried the latter, in fierce vociferation, "so, Signor Inglese, you've quarrelled with your father, have you? Well! that won't help you. It only shows that, for being such an undutiful son, you deserve a little punishment. If you'd been a better boy, your worthy parent might have acted differently, and saved you your ears. As it is, you are about to lose them. Console yourself with the thought that they are not going out of the family. They shall be cropped off with the greatest care, and sent under cover to your father! Bring him out, comrades! Let us have light for this delicate amputation! "

The young Englishman was led, or rather dragged forth, from the cell, and on to the open space in front of it. There he was surrounded by all the brigands in the band, both men and women, but not children. There were none in that motley community.

Doggy Dick was ordered by the chief to go into the house for a knife, while two others retained the captive in their grasp, holding as if to keep him steady for an operation. A third knocked his hat from his head; while a fourth pulled his long brown curls up over his crown, leaving his ears naked for the knife.

All seemed to take delight in what they were doing— the women as well as the men—more especially she who had been instrumental in causing the death of Popetta.

There was anger in the eyes of all. They were spited at not receiving the *riscatta*.

The renegade had told an exaggerated story of the wealth of the captive's father, and they had founded high hopes upon it.

They charged their disappointment to the prisoner, and were paying him for it by gibes and rough usage. They could see his ears cut off without a single sentiment of pity!

In a few seconds the knife-blade was gleaming beside them!

It was first raised to the left ear, which in another instant would have been severed from his head, when the captive, by a superhuman wrench, released his left hand, and instinctively applied it over the spot! It was a mere convulsive effort caused by the horror of his situation.

It would have been utterly unavailable, and he knew it. He had only made the movement under the impulse of a physical instinct.

And yet it had the effect of saving his ears !

Corvino, who stood near to superintend the amputation, uttered a loud shout, at the same time commanding the amputation to desist. The cry was called forth at the sight of the uplifted hand, or rather its little finger.

"Diavolo ! " he exclaimed, springing forward and seizing the captive by the wrist, " you've done yourself a service, signor ! you've saved your ears at least for this time ! Here's a present for your father much more appropriate, since it will point out to him the line of his duty which he has shown himself so inclined to neglect. The hand to guard the head—that's the motto among us ; we shall permit you to adopt it to a proportionate extent, by allowing your little finger to protect your ears. Ha! ha! ha! "

The brigands echoed the laughter of their chief, without exactly comprehending the witticism which had called it forth.

They were soon enlightened as to the significance of the jest. The scarred finger was before their eyes, they saw it was an old cicatrice, sure to be recognised by any father who had taken the slightest interest in the physical condition of his son. This was the explanation of Corvino's interference to stay the cutting off their captive's ears.

" We don't wish to be unnecessarily cruel," continued the chief in a tone of mock mercy. "No more do we wish to spoil such a pretty countenance as that which has made conquest of Popetta, and might have done the same for " —here he leaned close to his captive and hissed spitefully into his ear, " Lucetta !"

The cutting off of his ear, or both of them, would not have given Henry Harding so much pain as the sting of that cruel whisper. It thrilled him to his heart's core. Never in all his life had he felt as at that moment the despair, the absolute horror of helplessness.

His tongue was still free, and he could not restrain

it. He would speak, though he knew that speech might cost him his life.

"Brute!" he vociferated, fixing his eye full upon the brigand chief. "If I had you upon fair ground, I'd soon change your sham exultation to an appeal for mercy. You dare not give me the chance. If you did, I would show these ruffians around you that you're not fit to be their captain. You killed your wife to make way for another—not you, madam!" he continued, bowing derisively to the betrayer of Popetta, "but another whom God preserve from ever appearing in your place; you may kill me, cut me into pieces, if you will, but depend upon it, my death will not go unavenged. England, my country, shall hear of it, and though you fancy yourself secure, you will be tracked into the very heart of your mountain fortresses, hunted up and shot down like dogs—like wolves as you are—that's what will come!"

He was not allowed to proceed.

Three score angry voices breaking in upon his impetuous speech put an end to it.

"What care we for your country?" cried they. "England indeed!"

"Dom England!" shouted Doggy Dick.

"*Inglatena al inferno!*" vociferated others. "France and Italia the same—the Pope too, if you choose to throw him in, what can they do to us? We are beyond their power. But you are in ours, signor, and now let us show it to you!"

A score of stilettos suddenly drawn from their sheaths were gleaming in the eyes of the captive, as he listened to these words.

He was half repenting his hasty speech, believing it would be his last, when he saw the brigand chief interfering to protect him.

He saw this with surprise, for Corvino had quailed before his challenge with a look of the most resentful malice.

His surprise was of short duration, and ended on hearing what the chief had to say.

"Hold!" shouted he, in a voice of thunder. "Simple-

tons that you are, to care for the talk of a cur like this?
Your own captive too! Would you kill the goose that is
to lay us a golden egg? And an egg worth thirty thousand
scudi! You are mad, *compagnos*. Leave me to manage
this matter. Let us first get the egg, which, by the
grace of God, and the help of the Madonna, we shall yet
extract from the parental nest, and then——"

"Yes, yes!" cried several, interrupting the figurative
speech of their leader; "let's get the egg, let's make the
old bird lay it. Our comrade, Ricardo, says he is able to
lay a big one."

"That do I," interposed Doggy Dick. "And I should
know something about the egg he's got, since I was three
years his gamekeeper."

At this *jeu d'esprit*, which seemed rather dull to his
Italian audience, though better understood by the captive,
the renegade laughed immoderately.

"Enough!" cried Corvino, "we're wasting our time,
and perhaps," he added, with a ferocious leer, "the
patience of our friend, the *pittore*. Now, signor, we shall
leave that handsome head unshorn of its auricular append-
ages. The little finger of your left hand is all we require
at present. If it don't prove strong enough to extract the
egg we've been speaking of, we shall try the whole hand;
and if that too fail, we must give up the idea of an omelet
altogether."

A yell of laughter hailed this sally.

"Now," continued the jocular ruffian, "we shan't have
done with you; but to show the grand Inglese, your
father, that we are not spiteful, and how far we Italians
can outdo him in generosity, we shall send him a calf's
head with skin, ears, and everything attached to it."

Roars of laughter succeeded this fearful speech, and
the stilettos were returned to their respective sheaths.

"But," commanded the chief, once more calling the
knife into requisition, "off with his finger; you needn't go
beyond the second joint. Cut off by the knuckle, which,
I've heard, is in great request among his countrymen.
Don't spoil such a pretty hand. Leave him a stump to

help fill out the finger of his glove; when that is on, no one will be wiser of what's wanting. You see, signor," concluded the ruffian, in a taunting tone, " I don't wish to damage your personal appearance any more than is absolutely necessary for our purpose. I know you are proud of it, and considering what has happened with Popetta, I should be sorry it should hinder you from a like success with the charming Lucetta."

The last speech was delivered in a satanic whisper again hissed into the ear of the captive.

It elicited no reply, nor did the young Englishman make either remark or resistance when the cruel executioner caught hold of his hand, and severed from it the little finger—*carte* and *tierce*—by a cut of his knife-blade !

The amputation was the cue for terminating the strange scene. As soon as it was over, the captive was conducted back to his gloomy chamber, and left to the contemplation of a hand thus unsymmetrical for life.

CHAPTER XXXVIII.

THE FAMILY SOLICITOR

THOUGH within less than an hour by rail from London, General Harding rarely visited the metropolis more than once a year.

Once, however, was it his custom to go, less to keep up his acquaintance with the great world, than with his old associates of the service, and the Oriental Club.

He would stay at a hotel for a couple of weeks, spending most of his time in the streets, or at his club, and then return to his retirement among the Chilterns, with *souvenirs* sufficient to last him for the remainder of the year.

During his annual sojourn in the City, he did not waste all his time in mere gossiping with his ancient comrades in arms. He gave some portion of it to the management of affairs connected with his estate, which, of course, included a call upon his solicitor in Lincoln's-Inn-Fields.

The time of his annual visit to the metropolis was in the "season," when all London and a goodly number of its "country cousins" are in town. The "House" is then sitting, concerts are the rage, and the "Row" affords its varied attractions.

It was not any of these allurements, however, that called the old Indian from his country seat; it was simply because that in the season he would meet men in London, who, like himself, were not to be met there at any other period of the year.

It was on one of the earliest days of the London season that the dark-visaged messenger who declared himself to have come from the dominions of the Pope had made his appearance at Beechwood Park; and a few days later General Harding made his annual trip to London.

This visit to the metropolis had nothing to do with the strange communication he had received through this very strange individual. It remained in his mind only from the painful impression it had made; he grieved that his son could be capable of practising such a deception, otherwise he thought very little about it, or, if he did, it was not with the belief that there was any truth in the story about the brigands.

He believed it to be a very skilful concoction, and it was just this that gave him more pain, revealing, on the part of his son, not only a talent for, but a practice in, deception.

How Henry had spent the time during the twelve months that had elapsed, he had not the slightest idea; he had not heard a word of him or from him.

He had written once to his solicitor to make an inquiry, but it was simply whether the lawyer had seen him.

The answer had been " yes."

Henry Harding had called at the solicitor's office some twelve months before.

There was nothing said about the payment of the thousand pounds, for the question had not been asked in the General's letter, and the formal old lawyer, habituated to laconic exactness, had limited the terms of his answer to a simple response to such inquiry as had been made.

Henry, in his parting letter, had spoken of going abroad; this would to some extent account for his not being heard of in London, and there was no reason why he should not find his way to Rome, or any other continental capital. The General had the idea that it would serve him for a tour of travel, and keep him out of perhaps worse company in London. He would have been satisfied enough to hear of his son being in Rome but for the contents of that same letter that brought the information.

In it there was proof that, if not actually in the hands of brigands, he had fallen into company almost, if not altogether, as bad.

M

Such were the reflections of his father as he meandered through the streets of the metropolis, reminded of his son's existence only by knowing that he had first gone there, but not from any expectation of meeting him.

Henry was, he no longer doubted, in the city of Rome, though not among the Neapolitan mountains, as the letter had alleged, a supposed falsehood that much embittered his father's remembrance of him.

After having made the round of the clubs, the General as usual called on his solicitor—Mr. Lawson, of the respectable firm of "Lawson & Son," Lincoln's-Inn-Fields.

"You have heard nothing of my son Henry since I wrote you?" asked he.

The question was put after other business had been transacted.

"No," said Lawson *père* to whom the inquiry was directed—Lawson *fils* having gone out of the way.

"I have had a singular letter from him—there it is—you are at liberty to read it, you may put it among my papers. It's a document that has grieved me. I don't wish it lying in my own desk."

Mr. Lawson adjusted his spectacles, and perused the epistle that had been dictated by the brigand chief.

"This is strange, General! How did it reach you?" he asked on finishing; "there does not appear to be any postmark."

"That is perhaps the strangest part of it—it came by hand, and was delivered to me in my own house."

"By whom?"

"An odd-looking creature of a Jew, or Italian, or something of the kind. He proclaimed himself to be one of your own craft, Mr. Lawson. A *procuratore* he said, which, I believe, in the Italian lingo means an attorney or solicitor."

"What answer did you send to your son?"

"I sent no answer at all—I didn't believe a word of what's in the letter. I saw, and so did my son Nigel

—that it was a scheme to get money—Nigel wrote to him."

"Ah! your son Nigel wrote to him. What did he write, General? You will excuse me for asking the question?"

"Of course! I'll excuse you. But I can't tell you for all that. I don't know what was in my eldest son's letter, something I think to the effect that I saw through his deception, and also a word to reproach him for the attempt to play such a shabby trick on his own father. Nigel thought this might have some effect on him—perhaps shame him if there was any shame left—though I fear, poor fellow, he has fallen into bad hands, and it will take a severe lesson to reclaim him."

"You don't believe then that he has fallen into the hands of brigands?"

"Brigands! Bah! Surely, Mr. Lawson, you're not serious to think such a thing possible with your experience?"

"It's just my experience, General, that suggests not only its possibility, but its probability. It is now some years since, during one of my vacations, I made what is usually called the Italian tour, and learned while in Italy some strange facts about the bandits of Naples and Rome. I could not have believed what I heard but for circumstantial testimony almost equal to the evidence of my own eyes, in the fact of one of the gentlemen having fallen into their clutches, and who had to pay a ransom to get clear.

"Indeed, it was by the merest accident I was not myself taken prisoner by them at the same time. I owed immunity to the lucky breakdown of a post-chaise, in which I was travelling over the horrid roads of the Romagna. The trouble caused my return to Rome, whereas, had I gone five miles further, the house of Lawson & Son, Lincoln's-Inn-Fields, might have had to pay ransom for my person, just as this is demanded for that of your son."

"Demanded for my son! Pooh, pooh! Demanded *by* my son, you mean?"

"I do not believe it, General. I am sorry to say I have reason to differ with you."

"But I do believe it. I have not told you how he left home in a 'huff' about a girl he wanted to get married to. I was determined he shouldn't, and made use of a trick to prevent it. I shall some day tell you of this trick. It deceived a very tricky party—a pair of them, for that matter. It was then that I wrote you to give him the thousand pounds. He's spent it, I suppose, upon idle vagabonds like himself, who have put him up to this thing to get more money. It's a cunning dodge, but, for all that, didn't do."

"Wrote to me to give him a thousand pounds!" exclaimed the old solicitor, half starting from his chair, and pulling the spectacles from his nose. "What do you mean, General Harding?"

"What should I mean, Mr. Lawson? I mean the thousand pounds I directed you to draw from the bank and pay over to my son Henry, whenever he should call for it?"

"When?"

"When? only twelve months ago. Let me see. Yes. Just twelve months ago. It was only a week or so after I saw you on my last visit to London. You told me yourself, in your letter, that he had been to your office about that time."

"I did, and so he had—twice, I think, he called—but not to receive a thousand pounds, or ask money of any kind. He did not ask for it. If I remember aright, he only called to inquire if there was any message for him from you. I did not see him myself—my head-clerk did. He can tell what passed with your son. Shall I summon him?"

"Do so," said the General, almost beside himself with astonishment. "Damme, it's very strange, very strange, damme."

A hand-bell was touched, and in an instant the head-clerk came into the room.

"Jennings," said the solicitor, "do you remember General Harding's son—his younger son, Henry—you know him, I believe—having called here about twelve months ago?"

"Oh, yes," responded the clerk, "I remember it very well. It is just twelve months ago. I can find the entry if you wish. He called twice—the second time a day or two after the first. They were both entered in the call-book."

"Bring in the call-book," commanded Mr. Lawson.

The clerk hurried off into the front office, leaving General Harding once more alone with his solicitor.

CHAPTER XXXIX.

THE General could no longer keep his seat.

At the unexpected information communicated by Mr. Lawson he had started up, and commenced pacing the floor in short irregular strides, at intervals exclaiming, " Strange, damme ! "

" If I had known this," he said more continuously—"if I'd have known this, all might yet have been well. Never got the thousand pounds, you say ? "

" Never a penny of it—from me."

" I'm so glad to hear it—so glad ! "

" True, you should be. It's no doubt so much money saved—that is, if you think it would have been spent foolishly."

" Nothing of that, sir; nothing of the sort ? "

" Pardon me, General, I did not mean——"

The lawyer's apology was interrupted by the re-entrance of his clerk, carrying a large volume on whose covering of vellum were the words " CALL-BOOK."

Mr. Lawson had hold of the book, glad to escape from further explanation.

" There it is !" said he after turning over a number of pages. " Two entries of different dates both relating to your son. The first is on the 4th day of April, the other on the 6th. Shall I read them, General, or will you look at them yourself? "

" Read them to me."

The solicitor, readjusting his spectacles, read aloud :—

" *April 4th*, half-past 11 A.M.—Called at office, Mr. Henry Harding, son of General Harding, of Beechwood

Park, county of Bucks. Business, to ask if any communication received from father, intended for self. Answer—
None received."

"*April 6th*, half-past 11 A.M.—Called again, Mr. Henry
Harding; same question put; same answer given as on
April 4th. Young gentleman said nothing, but went away,
seeming dissatisfied."

" Of course, General," said the lawyer apologetically ;
" we are obliged to make these remarks in the way of our
profession. Are these the only entries, Mr. Jennings? I
mean that have reference to Mr. Harding? "

" There are no others in the book, sir, except one made
about six months ago, relating to a letter you received
from his father—shall I find it, sir ? "

" No ; that is not necessary ; you can take the book
out."

" And so you never paid my son Henry that thousand
pounds ? " interrogated the General, after the clerk had
gone out.

" Never—not a thousand pence—no money of any kind,
as you see by the memorandum. He never asked for any
—of course, if he had done so, I should have been obliged
to refuse him until I received your order. A thousand
pounds, General, is too large a sum to be handed over to
a young man—a minor, as your son then was—simply at
his own request."

" But, Mr. Lawson, you astonish me still more ! Do you
mean to tell me that you never received any letter author-
izing you to give him a cheque for that amount ? "

" Never heard of such a letter until this moment."

" Damme, this is strange. He may be among brigands
after all ! "

" I should be sorry if it is so."

" And I shall be glad of it."

" Oh, General ! "

" No, Lawson, you don't understand me. I'd be glad
of it for a good reason. It would prove that the boy
might not be so bad after all. I thought he had spent
the thousand pounds. Is it possible there can be any

truth in the letter from Rome ? Damme, I hope it is true, every word of it !"

" But, General, you would not wish it true that your son is a captive in the hands of banditti ? "

" Of course I would ! Better that than the other. I hope he is. I'd willingly pay the £5,000 to think so. How shall we find out ? What's to be done ? "

" What became of the messenger—my professional brother from the dominions of the Pope ? "

" Oh, him—he's gone back, I suppose, to those who sent him—brigands, or whatever they were. I came nigh kicking him out of the house, and should have done so, or given him in charge of the police, but refrained solely to avoid creating a scandal. Think, Mr. Lawson, what's to be done ? I suppose there's no immediate danger ? "

" I'm not so sure of that," answered the lawyer, reflectingly ; " these Italian bandits are cruel ruffians. There is no knowing how far they may go in the execution of their threats. Did the man leave no clue by which he could be communicated with, no address ? "

" None whatever. He only said I should hear from my son again—as the letter itself says. My God! they surely don't mean to carry out the threat it contains."

" Let us hope not."

" But what had I better do ? Apply to the Foreign Secretary, get him to write to Rome, and make a demand on the Pope's Government, that is, if the story of my boy's captivity be true ? "

" Certainly, General ; of course. But would all that not be too late ? When did you get the letter ? "

" Eight days ago—you will see by the date that it has been written more than two weeks."

" Then I fear that any interference of the Government—either ours or that of Rome—would be too late to anticipate the steps that may have been taken in the event of their having received your answer. I mean that sent by your son Nigel. There appears to be no alternative but wait till you get another communication from them. That will at least give you the means of writing to your son, and forwarding the ransom required. You could proceed with the other all the same. Lay your case before the Government and see what can be done about it."

"I shall go about it this very day," said the General, "this very hour shall I go to Downing Street—can you go with me, Mr. Lawson?"

"Of course," said the solicitor, rising from his desk and putting his spectacles into their case. "I'm at your service, General," he added as they walked toward the door. "I hope after all we shall not be called upon to have any dealings with brigands."

"And I hope we shall," said the General, striking his malacca cane upon the flagged pavement. "Better my boy to be the captive of brigands than the plotter of a deception such as that I have been giving him reproach for. May God forgive me, but I'd rather see his ears in the next letter sent me than to believe him capable of that."

To this fervent speech from a father's heart, the solicitor made no answer, and the two walked side by side in silence.

CHAPTER XL.

A FURNITURE PICTURE

THE man who can make his way out of Lincoln's-Inn-Fields, whether to the east, west, north, or south, without travelling some intricate courts and passages, must do it by mounting up into the air either upon wings or a balloon.

A splendid square—one of the largest and finest in the metropolis—gay with green trees, and showing some worn façades that might shame much of our modern architecture, it is nevertheless inaccessible except by the dirtiest lanes in all London.

Almost exclusively inhabited by lawyers who have attained to the highest eminence in their profession, all these shabby approaches, emblematic of the means by which they have reached it, the idea is suggestive.

In the purlieus that surround this great square art struggles feebly for existence. Here and there there is a picture-shop, where the dauber finds immortality in a cobwebbed window, or *al fresco* on the stone flags outside the door. There is a particular passage, where he may be seen displayed with a conspicuousness that, if granted him by the rulers of the Royal Academy, fortune would be sure to follow.

Through this passage General Harding and his solicitor had to make their way—for the reaching of the Strand *en route* to Downing Street.

In this passage there is a woman whose sharp glance and sharper voice has a tendency to keep it clear. On seeing the one, or hearing the other, the wayfarer will be disposed to hurry on. She is the proprietress of a furniture shop, of which the pictures in question are an adjunct, being usually what are called in the trade " furniture pictures."

Neither Gerald Harding nor his solicitor had any idea of stopping to examine them. They were hurrying on through the passage, when one so conspicuously placed that it could not escape observation caught the attention of the old officer, and caused him to halt, with a suddenness that not only surprised his companion, but almost jerked the latter from his legs.

" What is it, General ? " asked Mr. Lawson.

" My God ! " gasped the General, "look there. Do you see that picture ? "

" I do," answered the solicitor. " A sporting scene. Two young fellows out shooting, accompanied by a gamekeeper. What do you see in it to surprise you ? "

" Surprise me," echoed the General, " the word is not strong enough. It astounds me."

" I do not understand you, General," said the lawyer, glancing toward the old soldier's face to see whether he was still in his senses. " The picture appears to be of very moderate merit—painted by some young hand, I take it—though certainly there is spirit in the conception and the scene ; what is it ? One of the sportsmen has a knife in his hand, looks as if he intended to stab the spaniel with it, while the other is in the act of protecting it. I can't make out the meaning of that."

" I can," said the General with a sigh, deeply breathed, while his frame seemed convulsed by some terrible agitation. " My God ! " he continued, " it cannot be a coincidence ; and yet, how could that scene be here—here upon canvas. Surely I am not dreaming ? "

Once more Mr. Lawson looked into the General's face —doubtful whether he was not dreaming—either that, or demented.

" No ! " exclaimed the old soldier, bringing down his cane upon the pavement with an emphatic stroke. " There can be no mistake about it. It is the same scene—alas ! too real. Those figures, Mr. Lawson, are portraits, or intended to be. The costumes alone would enable me to recognise them. He holding the knife is my eldest son, Nigel—just as he was then some five years ago. The other is Henry. The man in the background is, or was, my gamekeeper—since become poacher and escaped convict. What can it mean? Who can have heard of the occurrence? Who painted this picture?"

"Perhaps," suggested the solicitor, "this woman can tell us something about it. I say, my good woman, how came you by this?"

"That picture, ye mean? How should I come by it but by buyin' it? It's a first-class paintin'. Only thirty shillin's, an' 'ud look spicy set in a nice frame. Thirty shillin's the price. Dirt cheap, gentlemen."

"Do you know who you bought it from?"

"In course I do. Oh, you needn't be afeerd of it's bein' honestly come by—if that's what you're drivin' at. I know all about its pedigree, for I know the painter as painted it; he's a reg'lar artist, he is."

"What sort of a man is he?"

"He's a young 'un; they're both young 'uns, for there be two on 'em. One appeared to be a furrener—a Italyin, I think. The other ain't so old as him—he's English, I sh'd say. Don't know which paints the pictures. Maybe both takes a hand at it, for both brings 'em to sell. I had some more o' them, but they're sold. I daresay the old 'un's the one as is the artist."

"Do you know his name?" asked the General, with an eagerness that caused the woman to look suspiciously at him, and hesitate about making reply.

"I am interested," continued he, "in whoever painted this picture. I admire it, and will buy it from you. I want more from the same hand, if you could furnish me with the name and address."

"Oh, that's it. Well then, the black complected chap —that is the old 'un, his name's a furren one, and I've heard it, but don't recollect it. The other's name I never heerd, an' as for him I s'pect he's gone away. I hain't seed him here lately—not for months."

" Do you know the address of either of them—where they live ? "

" In course I do. I've gone there to fetch away some pictures. It's close by here—just the other side of the Fields. I can give it to you on one of my billheads."

" Do so," said the General. " Here is the thirty shillings for the picture. You can send it round to Messrs. Lawson & Son, No. — Lincoln's-Inn-Fields."

The woman took the money, praising the picture all through the transaction, by characterizing it as " dirt cheap," and worth twice as much as she had asked for it. Then scratching out with an indifferent pen upon a soiled scrap of paper the promised address, she handed it to the purchaser, who folding it between his fingers hurried off out of the passage, dragging Mr. Lawson along with him.

Instead of going on toward Downing Street, he had turned sharp round, and retraversed the court in the opposite direction.

" Where now, General ? " inquired the solicitor.

" To see the painter," was the reply. " He may throw some light on this strange—this mysterious affair, that still appears to me like a dream. Perhaps he can tell us what it means."

He could have done so had he been found. But he was not. The address as given by the woman was correct enough. The General and his companion easily found the place—a mean-looking lodging-house, in one of the back streets of High Holborn—and three days before would have found au artist in it, whose description answered to that given by the picture-dealer, and was recognised by the keeper of the lodging-house. Three days before he had gone off in a great hurry—altogether out of London, as his former landlady supposed. She reckoned so, from his having sold all his pictures and things to a few dealers, and at a sacrifice. She did not know his name, nor where he had gone to. He had squared his account, and that was all she seemed to care about.

Had she ever had another lodger, an associate of the one she spoke of? Yes, there had been another—also a painter—a younger one. He was English, but she did not know his name either, as the foreigner paid the bill for both. The young one had gone long ago—quite three months—and the foreigner had since kept the apartment to himself.

This was all the woman could tell beyond giving a description of the young artist.

"My son Henry," said General Harding, as he stepped forth into the street. "He has been living in these wretched rooms, when I thought he was running riot on that thousand pounds! I fear, Mr. Lawson, I have been outrageousiy wronging him."

"It is not too late to make reparation, General."

"I hope not—I hope not. Let us hasten on to Downing Street."

The Foreign Office was reached—the Foreign Secretary seen, and the usual promises given to interfere with all dispatch in an affair of such evident urgency.

Nothing more could be done for the time, and General Harding set out for his country seat, to prepare for any eventuality that might arise. He was now ready to send the ransom, if he only knew where to send it, and in hopes that a Roman letter might have arrived during his absence, he had hurried home directly after his visit to Downing Street.

In this hope he was not disappointed. On reaching home he found several letters upon his table, that had been for several days awaiting him.

There were two that bore the Roman postmark, though of different dates.

One he recognised in the handwriting of his son Henry. He opened and read it.

"Thank Heaven," he exclaimed, as he came to its close. "Thank Heaven, he is yet safe and well."

The second foreign letter was conspicuous—both in size and shape.

It carried a multiplicity of stamps, required by its greater weight.

The General trembled as he took hold of it. Its "feel" told that it contained an inclosure. His hands felt feeble, as he tore open the envelope.

There was still another wrapper with something substantial inside—something in the shape of a packet.

The covering was at length stripped off, and revealed to the sight an object of ashen colour, somewhat cylindrically shaped and nearly two inches in length.

It was a finger cut off at the second joint, and showing an old scar that ran longitudinally to the end of the nail.

A cry escaped from the lips of the horrified father, as in the ghastly inclosure he recognised the finger of his son !

CHAPTER XLI.

A TERRIBLE THREAT

IT would be impossible to depict the expression on General Harding's face, or the horror that thrilled through his heart, as he stood holding his son's finger in his hand.

His eyes looked as if about to start from their sockets, while his fingers shook as if he had become suddenly palsied.

Not for long did he keep hold of the ghastly fragment; and as he attempted to lay it on the table, it dropped out of his now nerveless grasp.

It was some time before he could command sufficient calmness to peruse the epistle that had accompanied the painful present.

He at length took it up, and spreading it before him, read :—

" SIGNOR,—Enclosed, you will find the finger of your son. You will easily recognise it by the scar. If, however, you still continue to doubt, and refuse to send the ransom by next post, the whole hand shall be remitted to you, and you can see whether the finger fits. You shall have ten days allowed for your answer; if at the end of that time it does not reach Rome, and 30,000 scudi along with it, the next post after will take the hand to you. If that fails to open your *borsa*, we shall conclude you have no heart, and that you decline to negotiate for your son's life.

" Do not, therefore, charge cruelty upon us, who by unjust laws have been forced to war with mankind, and who, tracked like wild beasts, are compelled to adopt extreme measures to gain our livelihood.

"In fine, and to close the correspondence, should the negotiation thus fall through unsatisfactorily, we promise that your son's body shall have Christian burial. As a reminder of your inhumanity, the head shall be cut off and sent you by the next steamer that touches at Civita Vecchia. We have paid the post on the finger; we shall do the same with the hand; but we shall expect you to pay the carriage upon the head.

" And now, Signor General, to repeat the advice already given you. Don't mistake what is herein written for an idle menace ; it has no such meaning. Continue incredulous, the threat will be carried out to the letter as stated. Refuse the ransom, and as sure as you are living your son will be put to death. "Il Capo,

(for himself and associates).

" *Postscriptione.*—If you send the money by post, direct to ' Signor Jacopi, No. 9, Strada Volturno.' If by a messenger, he can find our agent at the same place.

" Beware of treason ; it cannot avail you."

Such was the singular communication that had come into General Harding's hand.

" My God ! my God !" was his exclamation, as he finished reading it—the same he had uttered before commencing.

He had no doubt about the truth of its contents. Lying on the table, before his face, was the fearful voucher—still apparently fresh—the gore scarce congealed upon it, as it came out of the wrapper in which it had been carefully put up.

With a trembling hand the General touched the table-bell.

" My son Nigel !" he said to the footman who answered it—send him to me instantly."

The servant turned away, wondering at his agitation.

" My God !" once more ejaculated the sorrowing father, " this is terrible, horrible ; who would have believed it ? *who would* have believed it ? It is true—true beyond a doubt—my God !" And bending down over the table,

N

with eyes that showed the agony of his spirit, he once more scrutinized the ghastly object, as if afraid to take it up or touch it.

Nigel came in.

" You sent for me, father ? "

" I did—look here—look at that ! "

" That! What is it ? An odd-looking object, what is it, papa ? "

" Ah ! you should know, Nigel."

" I know ? What—why, it looks like part of a finger."

" It is part of a finger. Alas, yes ! "

" But whose ? and how did it come here ? "

" Whose, Nigel ?—whose ? " said the General, his voice vibrating with emotion. " You should remember it—you have reason."

Nigel turned pale as his eyes rested upon the cicatrice, showing like a whitish seam through the hard coating of blood. He *did* remember it, but said nothing.

" Now do you recognise it ? " asked his father.

" As a human finger," he answered evasively, "nothing more."

" Nothing more! And you cannot tell to whom it has belonged ? "

" Indeed I cannot—how should I know ? "

" Better than anybody else. Alas ! it is your brother's ! "

" My brother's! " exclaimed Nigel, pretending both surprise and emotion, neither of which he felt.

" Yes ; look at that scar ; you should remember that! "

Another pretended surprise—another feigned emotion, was the answer.

" I do not wish to reproach you for that," said the General, speaking of the scar ; " it is a thing that should be forgotten ; and has nothing to do with the misfortune now before us. What you see there is poor Henry's finger."

" But how do you know, father? How came it here? How has it been cut off? And who——"

" Read these letters ; they will tell you all about it."

Nigel took up the bandit's letter and ran through its contents, at intervals giving utterance to ejaculations that might be considered either expressions of sympathy, surprise, or indignation.

He then ran through the other.

"You see," said his father, as soon as he had finished, "it turns out to be true—too true. I had my fears when I read Henry's first, poor lad; but you, Nigel—you——"

"How could any one have supposed such a thing as this? Why, papa, it appears yet impossible!"

"Impossible!" echoed the General, glancing almost angrily at his son, "look here, upon that table! Look on the truth itself—the finger that points to it. Poor Henry! what will he think of his father—his hard-hearted, cruel, unmerciful father? My God! oh, my God!"

And giving himself up to a paroxysm of self-reproach, the General commenced pacing to and fro over the floor.

"This epistle appears to come from Rome," said Nigel, examining the envelope of the bandit's letter with as much coolness as if it had contained some ordinary communication.

"Of course it came from Rome," replied the General, surprised, almost angered, at the indifference with which his son seemed to be contemplating it; don't you see the Roman postmark upon it, and haven't you read what's inside? Perhaps you still think it a trick?"

"No, no, father," hastily rejoined Nigel, perceiving that he had committed himself; "I was only thinking how it had best be answered."

"There's but one way for that—the letter itself tells how."

"What way, papa?"

"Why, send the money at once—that's the only way to save him. I can tell by the talk of the scoundrel—what's his name?"

"He signs himself 'Il Capo,' but that is only his title as chief of the band."

"It's clear, from what the ruffian writes, that they care for no law or government, human or divine. That lying upon the table is proof sufficient that nothing will deter them from carrying out their threat. Clearly, nothing will prevent them but the payment of the money."

"Five thousand pounds!" muttered Nigel; "it is a large sum."

"A large sum! And if it were ten thousand, should we hesitate about sending it? Is your brother's life not worth that? Ay! his hand is; poor, dear Henry!"

"Oh, I did not mean that, papa. Only it occurred to me that if the money should be sent, and after all, these scoundrels should refuse to give him up. There will need to be some caution in dealing with them."

"What caution can there be? There is no time. Within ten days the answer is required. My God! what if the post has been delayed! Look! see the date of the postmark on the letter."

"Rome, 12th," said Nigel, reading from the back of the brigand's letter. "It is now the 16th—there are still six days to the time."

"Six days! six days are nothing to send a messenger all the way to Rome. Besides, there is the arranging everything—the money—though I thank Heaven that need not cause any delay. But there is the going to London, to Mr. Lawson. He may not be at home. There's not a moment to be lost. I must start at once. Out, my son, and give orders for the carriage to be got ready without delay!"

Nigel, pretending an alacrity he was far from feeling, rushed out of the door, leaving his father alone.

"Where's 'Bradshaw'?" the General asked of himself, scanning around the library in search of the well-known "Guide;" and then laying his hands upon it, he commenced a traverse of its puzzling pages in search of the G.W.R.

The carriage, not very speedily brought to the door, was yet ready before he had become quite certain abo t the exact time of a suitable train. This he had at length ascertained, and then flinging aside the book, and permitting the old butler to array him in proper travelling habiliments—not forgetting to put into his large pocket-book the strange epistle, with its still stranger inclosure— he stepped inside the chariot and was driven to the station.

The wheels of the carriage had scarce cleared the gate of Beechwood Park, when a pedestrian appeared upon the gravelled drive going in the same direction.

It was the son, Nigel. He, too, appeared in a state of agitation, though its cause was very different to that which had taken his father in such haste along the road to the railway station.

Nigel had no intention of going so far. Nor was he at the moment even thinking of the peril in which his brother was placed.

His thoughts were given to one nearer home—one far dearer to him than that brother. He was simply proceeding to the residence of the widow Mainwaring, where for three months—partly owing to a taboo which his father had placed on it—he had been but an occasional and clandestine visitor.

CHAPTER XLII.

AFTER the atrocious cruelty that deprived him of a finger, two days more of gloomy imprisonment were passed by Henry Harding in his cell. The coarse fare by day and hard couch by night—even the loss that he sustained—were nothing compared with the anguish of his spirit. In this lay the pain of his captivity. The chagrin caused by his father's refusal to ransom him, was bitter to bear. His brother's letter had placed the refusal in its worst light. He felt as if he had no friend—no father.

He suffered from a reflection less selfish, and yet more fearful—an apprehension for the safety of his friend's sister; there could be no mistaking what Corvino meant by the words whispered in his ear during that dread scene, and he knew that the savage tragedy then enacted was but in preparation for the still more revolting episode that was to follow.

Every hour—almost every minute—the captive might have been seen standing by the window of his cell scrutinizing what could be seen outside—listening with keen ear, apprehensive that in each new arrival at the rendezvous he might discover the presence of Lucetta Torriani.

Himself a prisoner, he was powerless to protect, even to give her a word of warning. Could he have sent but one line to apprise her of the danger, he could have sacrificed not only another finger, but the hand by which it was written.

He blamed himself for not having thought of writing to her father at the time that he sent the letter to Luigi. It was an opportunity not likely to occur again. He could only hope that his letter to Luigi might be received in time—a slender reed to depend upon. He thought of trying to effect escape from his prison—could he succeed in doing this all might be well. But he had been thinking of it from the first, every hour during his confinement— thinking of it to no purpose. He made no attempt simply because there was no means of making it.

He had well examined the structure of his cell—the walls were thick, constructed of stone and stucco; the floor was a pavement of rough flags, the windows a mere slit, and the door strong enough to have withstood the blows, of a trip-hammer. Besides, at night, a brigand slept transversely across the entrance, while another kept sentry outside. A bird worth thirty thousand scudi was too precious to be permitted the chance of escaping from its cage.

His eyes had often turned upward; in that direction seemed the only chance of escape at all possible. It might have been practicable had he only been provided with two things—a knife in his hand and a stool for his feet. Strong beams stretched horizontally across, over these a sheeting of roughly sawed planks, as if there was a second story above; but he knew it could only be a garret, for the boards were damp and mildewed from the leaking of the roof over them. They looked rotten enough to have been easily cut through if there had been but a chisel or knife to accomplish it. Here was neither. Right and left, behind and before, below and above, egress appeared impracticable.

On the second night after losing his little finger he had ceased to think of it, and with mutilated hand wrapped in a rag torn from the sleeve of his shirt, the only surgical treatment it received, he lay upon the floor endeavouring in sleep to find a temporary respite from his wretchedness, had to some extent succeeded, and was beginning to lose consciousness of his misery, when something striking him on his forehead startled him to fresh wakefulness. It was a hard substance that had hit him; and the blow caused

him pain, though not enough to draw from him any exclamation. He only raised himself on his elbow and
waited for a repetition of the stroke, or something that
might explain it. While listening attentively, he heard a
sound as if some light missile had been chucked through
the window and fallen on the floor not far from where he
lay.

He looked to see what it could have been ; there was no
light, save what came from a starlit sky, and still more
sparingly through the aperture in the wall, so of course
the floor of the chamber was in deep obscurity.

Notwithstanding this, an object of oblong shape was
revealed upon it, distinguishable by its white colour. The
captive, on clutching it, could tell it was a piece of paper,
folded in the shape of a letter.

Supposing it to be one, he was hindered for the time
from perusing it; so he remained holding it in his hand,
but without making any movement, watching the window
through which it had evidently come, to see whether anything else—sound, substance, or sign—should enter by
the same aperture.

He waited for a full half-hour, and as nothing more
seemed likely to come in by the window, he turned his
attention to that which had at first startled him, and which
he now believed to have been something projected into his
cell after the fashion of the folded sheet. Groping over
the floor he became convinced of it. His hand came in
contact with a knife, he felt that its blade was in a sheath
—a covering of goatskin, such as he had seen carried by
the brigands.

Without comprehending the intent of the unexpected
presents, or from whom they had come, he could not help
thinking there was a purpose in them, and after watching
the window another hour or so, he turned to conjecturing
what it might be.

He was not very successful. A variety of conjectures
came before his mind, but none that satisfied him. Under
these circumstances, the gift of a keen-bladed knife suggested suicide, but that could hardly be the intent of the

donor; at all events, the recipient, wretched as he was, did not feel himself reduced to quite such a state of despair. No doubt there was writing on the paper, and no doubt, could he have seen, that it would have enlightened him, but there was no chance to do so, and would not be until morning. His sense of touch was not sufficiently delicate to enable him to decipher it in the darkness, and there was no help for it but to wait till the dawn broke in through the window.

He did wait till dawn, but not one minute after. As the first rays of the aurora came stealing through the aperture, he stood close to it, spreading the unfolded sheet upon the cell. There was writing; it was couched in Italian, and fortunately in a bold, clerkly hand, though evidently written in haste. In the translation it read thus :—

"You must make your escape upward, toward the zenith; there is no chance toward the horizon on any side. The knife will enable you to cut your way through the roof, and take care to slide off the back of the house, the sentry being in front. Once out, make for the pass by which you came up. You should remember it—it lies due north. If you need guiding, look for the polar star. At the head of the gorge there is a picket.

"You may easily steal past him. If not, you have the knife; but with proper caution there need be no occasion for your using it. His duty is not much by night; he has only to listen to any signal that may be given from below, and his post is not in the gorge, but on the summit, to one side. You may easily creep into the ravine, and pass without his seeing you. At the mountain foot it is different; the sentry placed there is only for the night; in the daytime he would be of no use, as the place can be seen from above in time to give warning of any approach. This man will be awake, as his life would be forfeited by his being found asleep. He will be concealed upon the edge of the ravine. You cannot pass without his seeing you; you must do so by using the knife. Better not try,

as he would have the advantage of seeing you first. Instead, conceal yourself in the ravine, and remain there till
morning. At daybreak he will leave his post, as it is
then no longer necessary to keep it, and come up to the
rendezvous. Wait till he has passed you, and wait till he
has got to the head of the gorge—longer, if you like—and
then make your way as you best can. Go with all speed,
for you will be seen and pursued. Make for the house
where you stopped on your way hither. Save yourself!
Save Lucetta Torriani!"

The astonishment caused by this strange epistle hindered
the reader from perceiving there was a postscript. He read
it at length. It ran as follows:—

"If you would also save the writer, swallow this note as
soon as you have read it."

Reading it over again, to make sure of its meaning, and
to memorize the instructions it contained, the postscript
was almost literally complied with; and when his jailer
entered the cell bearing the usual breakfast of boiled
maccaroni, not a scrap of paper was to be seen that might
direct suspicion upon the prisoner.

CHAPTER XLIII.

CUTTING A WAY SKYWARD

His jailer once gone out of the cell, the prisoner was left undisturbed to consider the plan of escape so unexpectedly proposed to him. The first question that occurred was, who could the unknown writer be? It was evidently some one of a refined intelligence, the writing proved this, but more the method in which the instructions were conveyed. These were so acutely conceived and so clearly expressed as to be quite intelligible to him for whom they were intended.

At first, the thought of its being some plot on the part of Corvino, a *ruse* to give the chief a chance of recapturing him or taking him in the act of attempting to escape.

Then came the reflection, *cui bono?* The chief could not want an excuse for taking his life; on the contrary, he had every reason for preserving it, at least until some definite answer about the ransom. If the demand should be again denied, the captive knew this would be plea sufficient for putting him to death.

The threat of the brigand had been backed by the assurance of the unfortunate Popetta. He no longer doubted of their being in earnest.

It could not be Corvino who had furnished him with the means of escape. Who then? Certainly not his own countryman. The renegade was his bitterest enemy—ever foremost in persecuting him—of all the band his thoughts now turned to Thomasso, simply because there was no other who had shown him the slightest sign of sympathy. Thomasso had, during the two days of his attendance, but then the captive presumed it to be at the instance of the *signorina*.

She was dead, and her influence over the man died away with her—what further interest could Thomasso have in him ?

True, there seemed something about this individual different from his outlawed associates. He at least appeared less brutal than they—as if he had seen better days, and had not fallen so far below the normal condition of humanity. Henry Harding had noticed this from slight communication he had with him. Besides, there was evidence of it in the conversation he had heard under his window in relation to the chief's designs on Lucetta Torriani. But then Thomasso's motive for assisting him ? And at such risk to himself. Death would be the reward for any of the band who might aid him in his escape, or even connive at it—death sure and cruel. Why should Thomasso place himself in peril ? What had he, Henry Harding, done to preserve the sympathy of this man—nothing.

The last words in the letter of instruction now occurred to him, not the postscript, but the closing instructions of the epistle itself, " *Save Lucetta Torriani !* "

Was this the explanation ? Was this the clue to Thomasso's conduct ? If so, Thomasso was indeed the writer. It was at all events an injunction well calculated to stimulate the prisoner to action—the thought of Lucetta's danger was never for a moment out of his mind, and now, this scheme brought it before him, he ceased his conjectures, and gave himself up to considering how he should carry out the design conveyed to him in such a mysterious manner.

Plainly he should do nothing before night—any attempt during daylight might be detected by his jailer coming in with his food. The last meal having been brought him would be the cue for commencement. During the day, however, he was not idle, he made a careful survey of his cell, but chiefly the wood-work overhead; the boards appeared in a dilapidated condition as if they would easily

give way to the knife—but what was his chagrin on
discovering that the ceiling was too lofty to be reached—
nearly twelve inches beyond the tips of his fingers held
aloft to their full stretch. If it had been absolutely rotten,
he could not have reached it.

He looked around the cell with despair—there was
nothing on which he could stand—neither stool nor stone
—nothing to give him the necessary elevation.

The chapter of instructions had been written in vain,
the writer had not contemplated this necessary point for
their fulfilment. For a moment the captive believed he
would have to abandon the scheme, it seemed impossible
even to commence its execution.

Ingenuity becomes quickened under circumstances of
dire necessity, and in his own case the truth was illus-
trated. Once more scanning the floor of his cell, he
perceived the litter of fern-leaves that formed his sty-like
couch; it might be possible to collect them into a lump,
and so obtain the standpoint he required. In his mind he
made a calculation of the quantity, and the probable
height to which they would elevate him. He did not
experiment practically, by massing the ferns and so making
a trial. Any disturbance of the litter might excite
suspicion. It would be a thing easily done; and should
be left till the last moment.

And till the last moment it was left. As soon as the
morose attendant took his departure for the night, though
without even the salutation, "*Buono notte,*" the captive
entered upon his task.

The fern-leaves were collected, and piled one upon the
other in the middle of the floor. He took great care in
packing them firmly, so as to form a sort of cushion, and
also in a small space, to increase the elevation. He also
observed the precaution to select a part of the ceiling that
seemed most assailable.

The dais erected, he mounted on it, knife in hand.

He could just reach the boards with his knife, but this
appeared enough, and he commenced making an incision.

As he conjectured, the wood was half decayed, with

damp or dry rót, and gave way before the blade, which, by good luck, was a sharp one.

But he had not worked long, when he found his support sinking gradually beneath him, and before he had accomplished one-tenth part of his task, the fern footstool had become so flattened that he was unable to proceed.

He descended to the floor and rearranged it, and then recommenced his cutting and carving all in silence, and with the least noise possible, for there was the knowledge of a sharp-eared sentry in the ante-chamber, and another keeping guard close by the window of his cell. Again the cushion sunk, with only another fraction of the task accomplished. Again was it repeated, and the work went on again for another short spell.

A new idea now helped him to keep on continuously; he took off his coat, folded it into a thick roll, placed it on the summit of the fern heap and then set his feet upon it. This gave him a firmer pedestal to stand upon, and enabled him to complete the task he had undertaken, which was the cutting a trap-like hole through the floor-boards big enough for his body to pass through.

It was done before twelve o'clock. He could tell this by the brigands still keeping up their carousal outside.

Hitherto the sound of their voices had favoured him, drowning any noise he might make to the ears of the sentries—moreover, they would be less on the alert during the earlier hours.

About midnight the sounds ceased, and the band seemed to have gone to sleep. It was time for him to continue the attempt at escape. Putting on his coat he caught hold of one of the joists and drew himself up through the hole he had recently cut. As anticipated, he found himself in a sort of garret-loft. He then commenced groping round to discover some means of egress. At first he could find none, and supposed the space to be closed in without any aperture. His head coming in contact with the roof, he perceived that it was a thatch of either straw or rushes, and was planning how he should cut his way through it, when a glimmer of light came under his eye, paling faintly along the floor.

Approaching the spot where the light was admitted, he discovered a sort of dormer-window, without glass, but closed by a dilapidated shutter pushed open to the outside. He looked cautiously through, and scanned the ground beneath as well as the premises adjoining. He saw that it was the back of the house, and there were no others to the rear of it. There was no light, or anything to show that human beings were astir.

He could perceive a clump of trees, standing a short distance off, and others straggling up the sides of the mountain. If he could succeed in getting under this cover without disturbing the two who kept guard over his cell, he would stand a good chance of escape, at least so far as the main line of sentries was concerned. As to those keeping the pass—that would be an enterprise altogether distinct in effect ; the *present* was the thing now to be thought of, and he proceeded to take his measures. To creep through the dormer-window and let himself down outside were naturally the movements that suggested themselves.

The night was dark, though with a sky apparently starry. It was the sombre gloom that in all its obscurity shrouded the extinguished crater. He could not see the ground beneath ; but knowing how high he had climbed to the garret, the descent could not have been a deep one, unless, indeed, the house stood on the edge of some scarped elevation. The thought of this caused him to hesitate, and once more craning his neck over the sill, he endeavoured to penetrate the obscurity below. Still, he could not see the ground, and as it would not do to remain any longer, he turned face inward, and backing through the window, let his legs down the wall. A wooden bar stretched transversely across the sill seemed to offer the proper holding-place for his hand. He grasped it to balance his body for the drop, but the treacherous support gave way, and he fell in such a fashion as to throw him with violence on his side.

He was stunned, and lay still in what appeared to be the bottom of a drain or trench. Fortunately for him he did so, for the crack of the breaking bar had been heard by the sentries, who came quickly round to the rear to discover the cause.

"I'm sure I heard something," said one of them.

"Bah! nothing of the kind; you must have been mistaken."

"I could swear to it; a noise like a blow with a stick or the falling of a bundle of faggots."

"Oh! that was it—there's the cause there, over your head, that window shutter flapping in the wind."

"Ah! like enough it was. To the devil with the rickety old thing! What good does it do there?"

And the satisfied alarmist, following his less suspicious comrade, returned towards the front.

By the time they had regained their respective posts, the prisoner had crept over the dark ditch and was skulking cautiously toward the cover, which he succeeded in reaching without further interrupting the tranquillity of the watch.

CHAPTER XLIV

A COUNT IN COUNTRY QUARTERS

ABOUT two weeks were elapsed since the Papal soldiers had first quartered themselves in the village of Val-di-Orno.

The sun had sunk quietly down into the blue bosom of the Tyrrhenian Sea, and the villagers were, most of them, indoors. They were not desirous to encounter their military guests upon the streets by night, lest in the darkness the latter might mistake them for the enemy, and make free with any little pocket cash they might have acquired during their tradings of the day.

The captain of this protecting force was at the time seated in the best sitting-room of the Sindico's house; making himself as agreeable as he could to the Sindico's daughter, the father himself being present.

The conversation that had been carried on upon various themes at length reverted to the brigands, as may be supposed, a stock topic in the village of Val-di-Orno. On this occasion it was special, relating to the captive *Inglese*, of whom, as a matter of course, Captain Count Guardioli had heard, having been officially furnished with the particulars on his first arrival in the town.

" *Pivero !* " half-soliloquized Lucetta, " I wonder what has happened to him ? Do you think, papa, they have set him free ? "

" I fear not, *figria mia.* They will only do so when the *riscatta* reaches them."

" Oh, me ! how much do you think they will require ! "

" You speak, signorina," interposed the captain-court, " as if you had a mind to send the ransom yourself."

o

" Willingly, if I were able. That would I ! "

" You seem greatly interested in the *Inglese*. *Uno povero pittore !* " the last words were uttered in a tone of sneering contempt.

" *Uno povero pittore !* " repeated the girl, her eyes kindling with indignation. " Know, Signor Count Guardioli, that my brother is *uno povero pittore,* and proud of it too, as so am I, his sister."

" A thousand pardons, signorina, I did not know that your brother was an artist. I only meant this poor devil of an *Inglese*, who after all may be no artist, but a spy of that monster Mazzini. It isn't at all improbable. Our last news tells us that the arch impostor has arrived in Genoa ; and as he has come direct from England, this fellow may be one of his pilot-fish—sent in advance to spy out the land. Perhaps he has been unfortunate in having fallen into the hands of the brigands. Should he come into my clutches, and I find any traces of the spy about him, I won't wait for a *riscatta* before consigning his neck to a halter."

The indignation which was rising still higher in the heart of Lucetta Torriani, becoming more perceptible in the pallor of her cheeks, and the quick flashing of her eyes, was hindered from declaring itself in speech. Before she could reply, a voice was heard outside the door, accompanied by a knock, of some one seeking admission. This was granted, less by the host of the house than his military guest, who had by this time grown to regard himself as its master. The door was opened, and a sergeant stepped into the room, saluting as he did so. He was the orderly of the troop.

" What is it ? " inquired the officer.

" A prisoner," replied the man, making a second obeisance.

" One of the banditti ? "

" No, Signor Captain. On the contrary, a man who pretends to have been their prisoner, and escaped from them."

" What sort of a man ? "

"A young fellow in the dress of a *cittidino*. *Un Inglese*, I take it, though he speaks our tongue as well as myself."

The Sindico rose from his chair. Lucetta had already started from hers with a joyous exclamation on hearing the word *Inglese*.

The escaped captive could be no other than he of whom they had been lately speaking; and of whom also she had been long thinking.

"Signor Torriani," said the captain, turning toward his host, with an air that showed he too was gratified by the announcement, "I do not wish to disturb you in the performance of my duty. I shall go downstairs and examine the prisoner my men have taken."

"It is not necessary," said the Sindico, "you are welcome to bring him up here."

"Oh, do!" added Lucetta. "Let him come in here. If you wish, I can retire."

"Certainly not, signorina; that is, if you are not afraid to look upon one who has been a captive among the bandits. If I mistake not, this is the *povero pittore* in whom you have expressed yourself so much interested. Shall I order him to be brought in?"

It was evident that Guardioli wished it. So did Lucetta, from a different motive; the former wished to display his power in the presence of a prisoner—degraded by a double captivity; the latter was inspired with an instinct for his protection, and a secret partiality which she herself scarce understood.

It ended by the sergeant conducting his charge into the room.

The prisoner was Henry Harding.

The young Englishman seemed less surprised at the company to which he was introduced, than by the character of the introduction. Having escaped from the brigands, he could scarce comprehend why he should again be a prisoner. That he was so, he had been already made aware by some rough treatment received at the hands of his new captors—who gave no heed, either to his story or his protestations. He saw that he was now in the presence of their chief. Perhaps the interview would end by his being released.

At a glance he had recognised the other occupants of the apartment.

The Sindico he had seen when passing through as a prisoner to the brigands. He now remembered him; but still more his daughter.

And she remembered the captive. His bare head, for he was hatless; his brown locks, tossed over his temples; his tattered surtout and trousers; his feet next thing to shoeless—all this *delabrement* of dress and person did not conceal from the eyes of Lucetta Torriani the handsome face and manly form she had once before looked upon, but with an interest that had made a strange impression upon her memory. Even in his rags he looked noble as ever. The very scantiness of his garments displayed the fine symmetry of his figure; while his face, flushed with defiant indignation, gave him the look of a young lion, chafing at the toils once more thrown around him. He was not tied, but he was not at liberty; at the same time that he might have supposed himself standing in the presence of friends.

He knew that the gentleman in civilian costume was father of his friend Luigi—that the young lady was his sister—that "little Lucetta," of whose stature the letter had conjectured a grand increase. And truly she was full-grown, stately, statuesque, a fully developed woman.

Of course, neither of them could know him—except what they had seen of him while *in transitu*, as a captive to the banditti. He saw that in such company it was not the time to declare himself, though in a glance exchanged with Lucetta, as he entered the room, he felt gratified to think that the sympathy silently shown for him on that occasion had not yet passed away.

CHAPTER XLV

QUICKLY and surreptitiously as was that glance exchanged between Henry Harding and the Sindico's daughter, it did not escape the notice of Captain Guardioli.

Warned by the conversation that had passed, he was watching for it; it gave him the cue for a swaggering excercise of his authority.

"Where have you taken this ragged fellow?" asked he of the sergeant, nodding superciliously toward the prisoner.

"We found him skulking in the town."

"Skulking!" cried the young Englishman, turning upon the man a look that caused him to quail. "And if I am a ragged fellow," he continued, directing his address to the officer, "it is not to your credit—much less that you should taunt me for it. If you and your valiant followers were to perform your duty a little more efficiently, there would have been less chance for my getting my clothes torn, as you see them."

"*Titti! titti!*" hissed out the officer. "We don't want such talk from you, signor; reserve your speech till you are questioned."

"It is my place to ask the first question. Why am I here a prisoner?"

"That remains to be seen. Have you a passport?"

"A rational question to ask a man who has just escaped out of the clutches of brigands!"

"How are we to know that, signor?"

"Well," said the young man, "the situation, and," he continued, looking quizzically toward his own person, "I

think my appearance might corroborate the assertion.
But if not, I shall have to make my appeal to the signorina,
whom, if I mistake not, I have had the honour of seeing
before, and she perhaps may remember the prisoner who
for some hours had the misfortune to furnish her with a
melancholy spectacle upon the pavement underneath her
balcony."

" I do, I do, signor ; yes, papa, it is the same."

" And I also saw him, Captain Guardioli ; he was carried through here by Corvino—it is the *pittore Inglese*, of
whom we have been just speaking."

" That may be," rejoined Guardioli, with an incredulous
smile, "Englishman, painter, and prisoner to the bandits—
all these in one. But the signor may still have another
character, not yet declared."

" What other ? " demanded the signor in question.

" *Una spia.*"

" Spy ! " echoed the prisoner, "for whom—and what
purpose ! "

" Ah, that becomes the question ! " sarcastically replied
Guardioli. "It is for me to discover it. If you will be
frank, and declare yourself, you may get better treatment ;
besides, it may shorten your imprisonment."

" My imprisonment ! By what right, sir, do you talk
to me of imprisonment ? I am an Englishman ; and you,
I take it, are an officer in the Pope's army—not a captain
of banditti. Make me a prisoner, and it shall cost you
dear."

" Cost what it may, signor, you are my prisoner, and
shall remain so till I can ascertain in what character you
have been travelling through these parts. Your story is
suspicious. You have passed yourself off for a *pittore !* "

" I have not passed myself off, though I am one, in a
humble sense. What has that got to do with it ? "

" Much ; why should you, a poor *pittore* " (this was
said with a sneer), be staying out here in the mountains ?
If you are an English artist, as you say, you must have
come to Rome to paint ruins and sculptures, not rocks and

trees. What then was your errand up here? Answer me that, signor."

The young artist hesitated. Should he make a clean breast of it and declare his errand? Had the time come?

Why should he not? He was in a dilemma, out of which he might escape more easily than he had done from the brigands' den.

Why should he procrastinate the term of his second captivity, for it was clear that the officer intended continuing it. A word would release him—so at least he supposed. There seemed no reason why it should not be spoken.

After a moment's reflection, he determined on speaking it.

" If, Signor Captain," said he, " in the execution of your duty you must necessarily know why I am here, you shall be welcome to know it. Perhaps my answer may give a slight surprise to the Signor Francesco Torriani, and also to the Signorina Lucetta."

"What! Signor Inglese, you know our names?" exclaimed simultaneously the Sindico and his daughter.

" I do."

" From whom have you heard them?" inquired the father.

" From your son, Signor Torriani."

" My son? He is in London."

" Just so, and it was there I first learned the names of Francesco Torriani and his daughter, the Signorina Lucetta."

" You astonish us! You know Luigi?"

" As well as any one man may know another, who for twelve months has been his daily companion, who has shared his apartments and his studio, who——"

" Saved his purse—perhaps his life," interrupted the Sindico, approaching the Englishman and holding out his hand. " If I mistake not, you are the young gentleman who rescued my son from thieves—from bandits—for from all I have heard they were no better. It is you of whom Luigi has oft written to us. Is it not, signor?"

" Oh, yes!" exclaimed Lucetta, also coming nearer and

contemplating the stranger with increased interest. "I'm sure it is, papa. You are so like the description Luigi has given of you."

"Thanks, signorina!" answered the young artist, with a smile. "I hope you except my habiliments. As for my identity, Signor Torriani, I might have been better able to establish it, but for my kind friend Corvino, who, not satisfied with the little cash I carried, has also stripped me of the letter of introduction from your son. I intended to have presented it in person, but was prevented by the circumstances already known to you."

"But why did you not make yourself known to me while you were here?"

" I did not then know you; I was ignorant of the name of the town into which my captors had carried me. Kept so, I suppose, on purpose. I had not the slightest idea that the Sindico I saw was the father of Luigi Torriani, or more, that the young lady I saw in the balcony was my dearest friend's sister."

At the conclusion of this speech, which was made with *empressement*, Lucetta blushed as if from some souvenir of that balcony scene.

"What a pity!" said the Sindico, "I did not know this before. I might have done something to get you off."

"Thanks, Signor Torriani! But it would have cost you dearly—at least 30,000 scudi."

"Thirty thousand scudi!" exclaimed the company.

"You put a high price on yourself, Signor Pittore!" sneeringly insinuated the officer.

"It is the exact sum fixed by Corvino."

"Mistaken you for some milord, I suppose? He has discovered his error and let you off scot-free."

"Yes; and finger-free, too," rejoined the escaped captive, in a jovial tone, as he said so presenting his left hand to the gaze of the company.

Lucetta screamed while her father leaned forward and examined the mutilated hand with a compassionate air.

"Yes," he said; "this is indeed a sign. I could have

done little for you. Tell us, signor, how did you escape from these cruel ruffians?"

"Time enough for that to-morrow," interrupted Guardioli, who seemed stung with the sympathy the stranger was receiving. "Sergeant," he continued, turning to the soldier, "this interview has lasted long enough, and to little profit. You can take your prisoner back to the guard-house. I shall examine him more minutely in the morning."

"Prisoner still!" was the thought of the Sindico and his daughter.

"I warn you against what you are doing," said the Englishman, addressing himself to the officer. "You will find that even your master, the Pope, will not be able to screen you from punishment for this outrage on a British subject."

"And your master, Guiseppe Mazzini, will not be able to protect you for practising as a Republican spy, Signor Inglese."

"Mazzini! Republican spy! What do you mean?"

"Come, your Excellency," interposed the Sindico, "you are altogether mistaken about this young man. He is no spy, but an honest English *galantuomo*—the friend of my son Luigi. I shall be answerable for him."

"I must do my duty, Signor Torriani. Sergeant, do yours. Take your prisoner back to the guard, and bring him before me in the morning."

The order was obeyed. The prisoner offered no resistance to it. There were other soldiers outside the door, and as any attempt to escape would have been idle, Henry Harding had to submit to this additional degradation; not, however, before exchanging a look with Lucetta that consoled him for the insult, and another with Captain Guardioli, that disturbed that gentleman's equanimity for the remainder of the evening.

CHAPTER XLVI.

NEXT morning Captain Guardioli was in a somewhat different frame of mind. On his examination of the prisoner he could find no proof of his being a spy; on the contrary, there was ample evidence of his story being true.

A score of townsmen could identify him as having been in the hands of the banditti. Indeed, this was not doubted by any one, and the fact of his being an *Inglese* was in his favour.

Why should an Englishman be meddling in the political affairs of the country?

The commandant saw that to detain him might end in trouble to himself. He was too intelligent not to understand the power of the English Government, even in the affairs of Italy; and, looking forward to future events, he thought it safer upon the whole to release the artist, which he at length did, under the pretence of doing an act of grace to the Sindico, who had renewed his intercession on the young man's behalf.

Henry Harding was once more free.

Not a little to the disgust of Guardioli, he became the Sindico's guest. But there was no help for it, unless by an act of authority too arbitrary to be passed over without investigation; and the captain was compelled to swallow his chagrin with the best grace he could.

By chance there was a spare suit of clothes left by Luigi on his setting out for England. They were of the *cacciatore* cut, too fantastic for the streets of London. For this reason had they been left behind. They were just the sort for the mountains of the Romagna ; and of a size to suit the young Englishman, fitting him as if he had been measured by the Italian tailor who made them.

The Signor Torriani insisted upon his receiving them. He could not well refuse, considering the state of dilapidation to which his own had been reduced, and also the necessity of a decent appearance, as the guest of the donor.

An hour after his release from the guard-house, he was seen in the velvet jacket, buttoned breeches, and gaiters of a *cacciatore*, with a plumed Calabrian hat upon his head, in almost everything, except facial physiognomy, a brigand.

The costume became him.

Lucetta smiled at seeing him in his new dress. She was pleased with his appearance. He reminded her of brother Luigi. And then he was called upon for the story of his adventures among the bandits, from the date of his capture to the hour óf his re-arrival in the town. Of course only such details were given as were fitted for the ear of Lucetta.

The mode of his escape from the cell was particularly inquired into.

It was given—some points kept back—some expressions in the letter that had been chewed into pulp, and which Henry Harding intended soon to communicate to the Sindico himself—along with that other intelligence which had been his chief motive for making his escape.

His auditors—for there was both father and daughter present at this interview—were strangely interested when he spoke of the mysterious interference on his behalf. Who could have helped him to the knife ? Who could have written the letter ? He did not say anything to assist them in their conjectures, nor mention the name of Thomasso. All that was for the ears of Torriani himself at another time.

He merely described the cutting his passage through the floor above his cell, his dropping from the dormer-window, the alarm given to the sentinels, and its instant subsidence. He told them, too, how he had succeeded in passing the first vedette, stationed at the top of the gorge, by crawling on his hands and knees; how he had got so close to the other as to perceive that passing him in the same way would be impossible; how, knife in hand, he had stood for a time half determined to take life or lose it —how he had recoiled from the shedding of blood, and concealing himself in some bushes he had remained awake till daylight—had seen the second sentry pass up the hill, and then, unseen himself, had continued his retreat. As good luck would have it, a sort of filmy haze hung over the valley below, under the curtain of which he escaped; otherwise he would have been seen, either by the vedette above, or the night-sentinel on his return to the rendezvous.

He could not tell whether he was pursued. Of course he must have been, though not immediately. It was not likely he was missed till an advanced hour in the morning, and then he was far on his way. Fortunately he remembered the track by which they had conducted him, and kept along with an eager celerity, inspired not only by the peril of his own situation, but that of those unconscious of it, to whom he was describing his escape.

He reached the skirts of the town a little after nightfall, once more to be made a prisoner.

He was now again in a fair way of getting into chains less irksome to endure. This, however, did not form part of his confession.

The conversation now turned upon Luigi, and it also became a dialogue between him and Lucetta—her father having gone out on business of the town.

Need we say that Lucetta was very fond of Luigi, being an only brother?

How was he in health? How did he like *Ingleterre?* Was he making progress in his profession?

These, with a score of like questions, were rapidly asked and answered; and then a detailed description had to be given of that episode which had introduced the two young men to one another, with something of their after association; and then there was a sly inquiry as to what Luigi thought of the English ladies, with their blonde complexions and bright golden hair, so different from the daughters of Italia. And there was a hint about a young lady in Rome—a sort of semi-cousin of the Torrianis to whom Luigi ought to be true. Would it be right for a young man in any way out of his own country? And did the signor believe there was any sin in marriages between people of his own faith—he had confessed himself a Protestant—and those of the Holy Church?

These and other topics—perhaps few so pleasant—were talked of, the young Italian girl asking questions and giving answers with that innocent *naïveté* so charming to the listener.

It so charmed Henry Harding, that before he had passed a single day in her company he could think of Buckinghamshire and Belle Mainwaring without a shadow of regret. He was in a fair way of forgetting both.

*   *   *   *   *

That same night the escaped prisoner completed the revelations he had to make to the Sindico alone; first telling him what he had learned about the designs of Corvino upon his daughter, and how he had learned it; and then of the letter he had written to Luigi, asking him to hasten home.

His listener, though pained, was least surprised by the first part of this strange communication.

As is known, he had already been warned elsewhere. It was the letter to his son, written under such circumstances, that filled him alike with surprise and gratitude; with a warm embrace he thanked the young Englishman for his thoughtful interference.

During the explanations, a point that had hitherto puzzled the escaped captive found a presumptive solution.

He had all along wondered who could have been his mysterious protector. Who had furnished the knife, with the chapter of instructions that accompanied it.

At the mention of the word Thomasso, the Sindico started, as if he had guessed the hidden hand that had interfered in his favour. On a further description of the

man, he was sure of it.   An old retainer of the Torrianis,
who had held service in the Pontifical army, had fallen
into evil ways, had been thrown into a Roman dungeon,
from which he escaped, and no doubt had afterward found
an asylum among the mountain bands.   This was the probable explanation—a long remembered gratitude for some
service the Sindico had rendered him.

The latter now acknowledged the danger in which his
daughter was placed, and the necessity of steps being
taken to avert it.

He had already determined on removing from the
place, and taking his *penates* along with him.   In truth,
he had that very day concluded the sale of his estate, and
was now free to go in quest of a new home into whatever
part of the world it might be found.

Meanwhile there was no immediate danger.   The Papal
soldiers intended staying some time in the town.   The
Sindico could retain his post, and await the arrival of his
son, who, if the post kept true to time, might be expected
in a day or two.

To hear that Luigi was coming home was news to his
sister.   How had her father heard it ?   There had been
no letter from London, no message from Rome.   It was a
mystery to Lucetta, and for reasons was permitted to
remain so.

But why need she care so long as Luigi was coming,
her dear brother ?   And so soon too, and the time would
not seem long since his friend was there, and she could
talk to him about Luigi.

It had become pleasant to converse about her dear
brother with her dear brother's friend ; and once again
were the same questions asked as to how Luigi looked and
lived, and prospered at his painting, and whether he was
given to admiring the English girls ; and would it be
wrong for him, a " Cattolico," to marry one, or would it be
wrong the other way.   And so were the artless interrogations repeated.

These were pleasant conversations ; but it was not
pleasant to have them interrupted, as they usually were,

by Captain Guardioli. Why should the officer force himself into their company as he daily, hourly did? Why did he not take his troops, as he ought to have done, and go after the brigands? He could easily have found them.

The young Englishman, still burning with indignation at the treatment he had endured—frantic when he looked at his left hand—would have gladly guided him to the spot. He proposed doing so: but his proposal was not only received with coldness, but repelled with a rebuke that kept the blood warm and bad between Guardioli and himself. From that time there was no communication between them, even when both were in attendance upon Lucetta.

Both were with her upon the hill that rose directly over the town. There was a cave upon the summit of this hill, that had once been the abode of an anchorite. It was one of the curiosities of the neighbourhood, and the young lady, at her father's suggestion, had invited her father's English guest to go up with her and see it.

The invitation was not extended to the other guest, the captain-count.

For all that, he invited himself, under pretence of protection to the signorina. His protection, though not asked for, could not well be refused, and the three proceeded to climb the hill, Guardioli beside himself with jealousy. In his heart he was cursing the young Englishman, and could he have found an excuse for pushing him over a cliff, or running him through with the sword that hung by his side, he would have done either on the instant.

CHAPTER XLVII

WOLVES IN SHEEP'S CLOTHING

OUR excursionists had reached the summit and looked into the cave. Lucetta related the legend of the hermit. How he had sojourned there for several years, never descending to the town, but trusting to the shepherds and others who strayed over the mountains to furnish him with his frugal fare. How he had at last mysteriously disappeared from the place. No one knew where he had gone; but there was a story of his having been carried off by the brigands, and another that he was a brigand himself; and had kept his post for purposes of observation.

"What did the shepherds say?" asked the captain-count, by way of showing his superior intelligence. "They should have known something of the fellow's daily avocations, since, as you say, they provided him with his daily food. But perhaps his doings, like those of many others, were in the dark."

"Suppose you ask them, Signor Captain," said Lucetta, with a languid smile, at the somewhat cloudy insinuation. "There they are coming up the mountain."

The young lady pointed downward to a ravine that that scarred the hill on the side opposite to that on which lay the town. Along its bed five men were seen, driving before them a flock of sheep, bringing them up on the mountain to browse. They were already within a hundred yards of the summit, upon which the spectators stood.

The men were all dressed in coarse *frezadas*, hanging down to their thighs, with the usual straw hat upon their head, and sandals upon their feet. They carried a long stick, which they occasionally used in conducting their charge up the ravine.

One of them wore the *capuce*, hooded over his head, which seemed strange under the hot noonday sun.

The officer had promised to respond to the challenge of the signorina as soon as the shepherds should be near enough for a conversation. They were coming direct toward the spot, and the excursionists awaited their approach.

"How very odd," said the young Englishman, addressing himself to the sister of Luigi, "are some of the customs of your country—at least they seem so to me. Your countrymen appear to lack economy in the distribution of labour : for example, with us in England, one man will easily manage a flock of five hundred sheep, having only a dog to assist him, while here you have five men driving a fifth of the number, and not very skilfully as it appears to me."

"Oh," rejoined Lucetta, in defence of the native industry, "our shepherds have usually more than you see. No doubt these have far more, but have left them on the mountains opposite—perhaps because there would not be enough——"

The explanation was interrupted by the approach of the sheep, whose tinkling bells drowned the discourse.

Soon after the shepherds came up, leaving their charge to go scattering over the summit. Instead of waiting for the captain-count to begin the conversation, one of the *pastores* took the initiative, bluntly opening with the salutation :

"*Buono giorno, signore ! Molto buono giorno, signora bella !* " ("Good-day, gentlemen ! Again good-day, beautiful lady !")

The speech was complimentary; but the manner seemed to have a different meaning. There was something in the tone of voice that jarred on the ear of the young Englishman.

"Free speakers, these Italian *pastores*," was the reflection he was making to himself, when the spokesman continued :

" We've been seeking one of our sheep," said he, " and have been hitherto unable to find it. We fancy it has strayed to this mountain. Have you seen anything of it ? "

" No, my good friends," answered the officer, smilingly, and in a tone intended to conciliate the inquirers, whose rude style of address could no longer be mistaken.

" Are you sure, Signor Capitano ? Are you sure of what you say ? "

" Oh ! quite sure. If we had seen the animal, we should be most happy."

" Your sheep is not here," interrupted the young Englishman, who could no longer stand the *pastore's* impertinence; " you see it is not. Why do you repeat the question ? "

" You lie ! " cried one of the shepherds who had not yet spoken—he who wore the hood. " It is here. You, Signor Inglese, are the stray we are in search of. Thank our gracious Virgin, we have found you in such goodly company ! We shall take back to our flock three sheep instead of one, and one of them such a beautiful ewe—just suitable for our mountain pastures ! "

Before the man had done speaking, Henry Harding recognised him. The voice was sufficient, but the *capuce* now thrown back upon his shoulders revealed the sinister countenance of Corvino.

" Corvino ! " was the exclamation that passed 'mechanically from the lips of his late captive ; and before its echo could reverberate from the adjoining cave, he was seized by two of the disguised bandits, the other two flinging themselves on the officer, while the chief himself laid hold upon Lucetta.

With a desperate effort the young Englishman wrenched his arm free ; but he had no weapon, and of what use would be his fists against his two assailants, who had now drawn their daggers, and were again advancing upon him.

The young lady was still struggling in the embrace of the brigand chief—her cries loud enough to be heard all over the town ; while Guardioli was making no resistance—not even to the drawing of his sword, which was still dangling uselessly by his side.

With a quick eye Henry Harding perceived it, and dashing between the two brigands, who were closing upon him, he caught the weapon by the guard, plucked it out of its sheath, and turned like a tiger upon his special opponents.

The cowards shrank back, as they did so drawing their pistols and firing at random.

None of their shots took effect, and in another instant the swordsman was by the side of Corvino.

With a cry the brigand chief let go his struggling prize, and turned to receive the attack, flinging off the *frezada*, and drawing a revolver—for this weapon had found its way into the hands of the Italian banditti.

As good luck would have it, the first cap missed fire, and before he could draw a trigger upon a second, the sword of Guardioli, wielded by a more skilful hand, had rendered his arm idle, and the revolver dropped to the ground.

Alas, it was to no purpose !

Before Henry Harding could follow up the thrust with one more deadly, he was assailed from behind by four fresh adversaries, for the two that guarded Guardioli had let him loose, and the captain-count was now running down the slope as fast as his scared legs could carry him.

With the young Englishman it was now one against five, or rather, one to four—for the moment the brigand chief saw his four satellites engaged with a single adversary, he flung his left arm around Lucetta, and, raising her aloft, hurried off towards the ravine, up which as a shepherd he had ascended.

CHAPTER XLVIII

HALF frenzied by the sight of the young girl borne off by the brigand, Henry Harding would have rushed instantly after.

But the way was barred by two of the band, while the other two assailed him from behind. He had enough on hand to defend himself from their quadrilateral attacks; and only by the activity of an ape, borrowed from an excellence in athletic sports, oft displayed at Eton and Oxford, was he enabled to show front to all four.

Fortunately they had all emptied their pistols upon him, without doing him any serious injury—fortunately their pistols were not revolvers—their chief alone carrying the repeating arm. They now assailed him with their less dangerous daggers; and, but for their number, he might have fought them with success. He struggled to reduce it, but the bandits were as active as he, and his sword-thrusts and lunges were spent upon the air.

Full five minutes did the desperate strife continue. He was fast losing breath and must in the end have succumbed.

So he was thinking, when his eye fell on the hermit's cave, toward which the strife had been tending.

By an effort he broke through the circle of his assailants, and placed himself in its entrance.

A simultaneous cry of disappointment escaped from the brigands, as they saw the advantage he had thus gained. With his long blade he might now defend himself against a score of stilettos !

As if by an instinct, one and all resheathed their

daggers, and commenced loading their pistols. It was a fearful crisis ; and the young Englishman felt that his time was soon to come.

The four men were in front of him, guarding the only passage by which he might retreat.

It was a narrow gorge leading up to the entrance of the cave. He could not possibly penetrate through the line without encountering their stilettos—ready to be regrasped. Their pistols once charged, and his doom would be sealed, for the cave was a mere alcove in the rock—where he was exposed like a statue in its niche.

He had given himself up for lost, but he would not stand to be slaughtered. He was about to spring forward upon his assailants and run the gauntlet of their daggers, when shots and shouts came ringing from below, accompanied by a shower of bullets that struck spattering against the rocks around him.

Startled by this unexpected volley his four assaulters turned quickly round, and without waiting to complete the loading of their pistols ran like scared fiends from the cave.

The young Englishman saw that he was no longer in danger from their bullets, but from those of the soldiers now seen coming up the slope. Regardless of this, he rushed out and turned after the retreating brigands.

They had already entered the ravine at the back of the mountain, and, far away, scaling the steep on the opposite side, he could see Corvino with a white shape lying over his left arm.

He knew it was Lucetta Torriani—she lay motionless, no longer making any struggle, the skirt of her dress trailing on the loose stones that strewed the mountain-path.

No cry came back.

Was she fainting or dead ?

The soldiers came up with Guardioli at their head. They halted at the head of the pass, reloading and firing at the few retreating brigands—now far beyond the range of their antiquated carbines. Already Corvino was out of sight, carrying his white armful along with him, and the others soon after disappeared among the rocks.

Surely the soldiers would follow them, and recover the captive?

Who thought of asking the question?

It was the young Englishman—wondering at the present halt made at the head of the ravine.

It was protracted, and once more he repeated it.

Still there was no answer, and the pause continued.

For the third time he made the appeal in frenzied tones, addressing himself to Guardioli.

"You are mad, Signor Inglese," replied the captain-count, with a coolness that came only from his cowardice. "I can understand your folly. As a foreigner, you cannot know the ways of these Neapolitan banditti. All you have seen may be an artifice to draw us into a trap. As likely as not, over yonder,"—he pointed to the pass through which the bandits had disappeared,—"there are two hundred of the rascals lying ready to receive us. I am not such a fool as to have my followers sacrificed by such an unequal encounter. We must wait for a reinforcement from the city."

By this time the Sindico had come up, too late to see the shape of his daughter, carried in Corvino's arms over the crest of the opposite hill—fortunate in being spared the sad spectacle.

Not the less was he urgent in the pursuit, joining his voice to the appeal already made by the young Englishman.

Appeals and reproaches were alike uttered in vain.

The cowardly commissary of the Pope—false lover that he had proved—thought more of his own safety than that of the maiden to whom he had dared to address his perjured speeches!

With grief and disappointment the Sindico was beside himself, while those of his acquaintance who had come up along with him engaged themselves in endeavouring to comfort him, and the young Englishman added his words of encouragement, with an appeal to the parties present that sounded strange to their ears. "There were people enough in the town; was there not spirit enough to

pursue the brigands and rescue the daughter of the Sindico ? "

The thought thus plainly expressed was new to them ;
it caught like an electric spark, and was hailed with a
chorus of *evvivas*.

For the first time in their lives were they inspired with
a belief that they might resist the banditti.

" Let the town be consulted," was their rejoinder, " let
them speak to their fellow-citizens ;" and with this intent
they turned down the hill, headed by the Sindico, leaving
Captain Guardioli and his troop to continue gazing at the
rocks and trees that concealed the retiring foe, feared even
in his retreat.

CHAPTER XLIX.

ON returning to the town a surprise awaited the Sindico and his friends.

Men, women, and children were running to and fro—the children screaming, the men and women giving utterance to strange cries and exclamations.

There had been a similar fracas on the first alarm of the brigands, but it had subsided as the soldiers started off to ascend the hill.

What had caused it to break out afresh? This was the question hurriedly exchanged between the returning townsmen.

Could it be the brigands who had entered from the opposite side, and taken possession of the town?

Was the skirmish on the hill only a feint to draw the soldiers out of the place? If so it had succeeded, and the shouts heard, with the rushing to and fro, were the signs of a general pillage.

With hearts full of anxiety they hastened on into the streets.

They came in sight of the piazza.

A crowd was collected in front of the Sindico's house—another by the albergo.

Both were composed of armed men, not in uniform, but in costume of every kind—peasants, proprietors, and men in broadcloth habiliments of city life, all carrying guns, swords, and pistols. They were not citizens of Val-di-Orno—they were strangers—this could be told at a glance.

Neither did they appear banditti, though several of the

soldiers who had lagged in the town were seen standing in the piazza, guarded as prisoners.

What could it mean? Who could the strangers be?

The question was answered as the Sindico and his friends came near enough to distinguish the cries. They were, *Evviva ella Republica! Abasso il tyranni! Abasso il Papa!*"

At the same time a tricoloured flag shot up on its staff, telling the citizens of Val-di-Orno that the town was in possession of the Republicans.

And so too was Rome at that moment. The Pope had fled, and triumvirate Mazzini, Saffo, and Armelli held rule in the Holy City.

A fresh surprise awaited the Sindico as he hurried forward toward his own house; his son Luigi was one of the crowd who stood in front of it—one of those who was vociferating the watchwords of *Liberty*.

A hurried greeting passed between him and his father. With a quick glance he caught the expression on his father's countenance.

"What is wrong, father? There have been brigands on the hill—we've heard that; but—but where is Lucetta?"

A groan was the answer—that and a hand raised in the direction of the hills.

"Oh God!" exclaimed Luigi Torriani, "too late—have I come too late?—speak, father! Tell me where she is—where is my sister?"

"*Poverina!—mia povera figlia*—gone, Luigi! Borne off by the brigands—Corvino!"

The words were gasped out amid an agony of grief: the bereaved parent could say no more. He sank into the arms of his son.

"Friends!" cried Luigi Torriani to those who stood listening around, "comrades I may call you, and but for residing in a foreign land I should have been one of you. I am one of you now and henceforth. This is my father, Francesco Torriani, the Sindico of this town; you hear what he has said—his daughter—my sister carried off by the brigands. And that with a hundred soldiers supposed to be protecting the place—this is the protection we get from the valiant defenders of the Holy Faith!"

"Defenders of the Devil!" came a voice from the crowd.

"Worse than the brigands themselves," added another. "I believe they've been in league with them all along—that's why the scoundrels have so often escaped."

"Quite true," cried a third; "we know it—they're in the pay of the Pope and His Majesty of Naples; that's one of the ways by which our tyrants have controlled us."

"You will stand by me, then?" said the young artist, his face brightening with hope, "you will help me to recover my sister? I know you will."

"We will! we will!" answered a score of earnest voices.

"You may depend upon that, Signor Torriani," said a man of imposing aspect, who was evidently the leader of the Republican troop. "The brigands shall be pursued, and your sister saved if it be in our power; nothing shall be left undone. But first we must dispose of these hirelings; see, they are coming down the hill. Into the houses, *compagnos!* Let us take them by surprise. Here! Stramoni, Giugletta, Paoli, on to the end of the street, and shoot any one who attempts to go out, and give them warning. Inside, *compagnos!* in! in!"

In a score of seconds the piazza was cleared of the crowd—the strangers hurrying inside the houses, forcing along with them the soldier-prisoners whom they had taken.

Half a dozen men hastened toward the outlets to cut off any communication that might be attempted between the citizens and soldiers, now returning *en masse* down the slope of the mountain—their captain at their head.

Such of the townsmen as chose were allowed to remain in the streets, with a warning that any attempts at treason made either by word or sign would bring the fire of the Republicans upon them. Few of them stood in need of it; under the administration of

such a Sindico, there were not many of the inhabitants of
Val-di-Orno who did not secretly rejoice at the new order
of things. They had already hailed with acclamation·
their deliverers from the city, and were joyed at the
prospect of a Republic.

On came Guardioli at the head of his troop; they
were not marching in much order. Their captain was
not himself in the best of spirits; false as his love had
been he yet suffered at the thought of a disappointed
passion, a mistress lost, he might some day have enjoyed.

His own recreance, too—there was something of regret
about that. Now that the excitement was over, he could
not help recalling it.

With soiled shield and trailing pennant he was returning into the town. He cared little for the sentiment of
the citizens, less now that *she* was no longer among them.
But his own followers had been witnesses of his cowardly
conduct — and he would hear of it — perhaps at the
Vatican.

Captain, subalterns, and troop tramped back towards
the town, observing neither order nor caution. Little
did they dream of the trap into which they were advancing.

The measures of the Republican leader had been well
taken.

On each of the four sides of the little piazza he had
placed a portion of his force—distributed into nearly equal
parts. Hidden by the blinds inside they commanded the
whole square, and could take it with their fire through
the windows and doors.

The carabineers would have no chance—once within
the piazza they would be at the mercy of the revolutionists. And into the piazza they came, utterly unconscious of the fate that awaited them.

They had noticed the silence pervading the place, and
wondered that their comrades left behind came not forth
to greet them.

They were reflecting on the strangeness of these things

when a loud voice, issuing from the albergo, summoned them to surrender.

"*Rendate, capitano!* Yield up your sword to the soldiers of the Republic!"

"What's the meaning of this impertinence," cried Guardioli, facing toward the albergo, and endeavouring to discover from whom proceeded the voice. "Sergeant!" he continued, "drag that man out into the street, and see that he has a score of blows upon the back—heavily laid on."

"Ha! ha! ha!" laughed the voice, while the laughter was loudly echoed from the four sides of the square, and again the demand was repeated.

The carabineers unslung their firelocks and faced in different directions, ready to make havoc among the jeering citizens, as they supposed them to be.

They only waited for the word to fire at the windows and doors.

"We don't want to spill your blood," said the same stentorian voice, speaking from the albergo, "but if you insist upon it, we shall. Soldiers of the Pope! you are surrounded by soldiers of a higher power—the Republic—your master is no longer in Rome. He has fled to Gaeta. Mazzini rules in the city, and we mean to rule here. You are completely in our power. The first of you that draws a trigger will be answerable for the sacrifice of your whole troop; for we shall not leave a man of you standing. Be wise, then, and surrender as we tell you. Put down your arms, and we shall treat you as prisoners of war—use them, and you shall have the treatment you better deserve—that accorded to hirelings and brigands!"

Guardioli and his troop were astounded. What could it mean?—this summons so impudently and yet so confidently spoken—they stood amazed and irresolute.

"*Compagnos!*" cried the voice from the albergo, speaking as from the interior of some Delphian shrine, and loud enough to reach the four sides of the square, "these worthy gentlemen seem to hesitate, as if they doubted the truth of my words. Convince them by showing the muzzles of your guns. When they have counted those, perhaps they will be less incredulous."

Quick following upon this speech came the clanking noise of gun-barrels brought into collision ; and to the consternation of Guardioli and his carabineers, a score of windows around the piazza glistened with the iron tubes that could not be mistaken. There appeared to be at least two hundred, but they did not take pains to count them.

One-fourth the number would have been sufficient to subdue them. They saw that they were in an ambuscade ; that the revolution long threatened had at last come, and without waiting for the sanction of Captain Guardioli or his subalterns, they flung their carbines to the ground and declared themselves agreeable to a surrender.

In ten minutes after they were standing under the tri-colour flag, and crying "*Evviva ella Republica !*" while the captain-count, swordless and looking very uncom-fortable, was pacing a chamber in the albergo to which but three days before he had consigned Henry Harding as a prisoner.

He was now himself a prisoner to the soldiers of the Republic.

CHAPTER L.

HALF carrying, half dragging the girl with him, Corvino kept on through the mountain-passes; when he thought himself safe from immediate pursuit he stopped to await the coming up of his comrades.

He had heard shots on the other side of the hill, and knew the soldiers were on the alert. But he had little fear of being overtaken by them.

He calculated the time it would take them to ascend the slope, and before they could reach the summit his men would have secured their captive and retreated down the ravine.

Four to one—for he had witnessed the cowardly abandonment of the officer; he had no thought of their failing. He had himself hurried ahead to gain a good start, knowing that he would be impeded by the transporting of his new-made captive in the event of a pursuit.

Before leaving the ground he had shouted—"*Dagli! Dagli!*" but coupling it with a caution to take the prisoner alive if possible. It was this that at first prevented them from making use of their pistols. By his death they would have sacrificed the rich *riscatta* they had been so long counting upon.

Having given the order, he had hastened down the ravine, taking his captive along with him.

The young girl had made no resistance; she had swooned, and in this unconscious state had been carried along by Corvino.

On recovering her senses she saw that she was no longer on the Hermit's Hill, but in a wild spot surrounded by trees and rocks ; the brigand captain standing close beside her. She neither screamed nor attempted to escape. She saw that it would be idle, and that she was helplessly in the power of her captor.

Her thoughts were still scattering and confused ; she felt as if just waking from some disagreeable dream, with its scenes still vivid before her fancy. She remembered the approach of the shepherds, their rude address, the throwing aside their disguises, the cry "Corvino ! " as it came from the lips of the late captive, the face of the brigand chief suddenly showing from under the *capuce*, and which she herself recognised—the seizure of all three, the struggle, a sword gleaming in the hand of the young Englishman, his rushing upon her captor—a shot fired by Corvino, the angry exclamations of the pseudo-shepherds, the glancing of their stilettos, the scampering of the scared sheep, the quick, confused tinkling of their bells, and Captain Guardioli running away from the spot.

All these she remembered, like the incidents of a disturbed dream.

She remembered Corvino once more coming up to her —once more laying hold, and hurrying her from the spot. After that she became unconscious, her senses returning to tell her that she was alone with the brigand.

On opening her eyes she saw blood on the bandit's dress, and that the skirt of her own robe was sprinkled with it. It appeared to proceed from a wound in his right arm, and she now recalled the sword in the hands of the young Englishman, and the gallant use he was making of it.

What had been the result of the unequal combat ?

Had the stranger succumbed ? Had he been killed, or was he, like herself, a captive ? She had heard the orders for him to be taken *alive* shouted back by Corvino. She hoped they had been obeyed ; she trembled to think he might be dead.

It was her first anxiety after coming to her senses ; she looked around, but there was no one near, only the chief standing by, busied in binding up his wound. He had cut open the sleeve of his velvet coat, and was stanching the blood with strips torn from his shirt.

She made no offer to assist him ; she could only regard him with horror. His savage aspect, heightened to hideousness by the profuse smearing of blood on his hands, arms, and face, was sufficient to inspire both fear and aversion.

She trembled as she lay watching him, for she was still upon the ground, where she had been placed, like a parcel of goods.

" Lie still, signorina ! " said her captor, on perceiving she had come to herself. " Have patience till I get my arm slung, and then I shall take you to a softer couch. *Sangue di Madonna !* The *Inglese* shall pay for this with the loss of his ears, and double the ransom."

" Now," he said, having finished slinging his arm, " *Alza ! Alza !* We mustn't stay, or that valiant captain may come after us with his soldiers. Come along, signorina ; you must walk the rest of the way, *Corpo di Bacco !* I've carried you far enough, *su via !* "

As he said this he stretched out his left hand, seized the young girl by the wrist, raised her on her feet, and was about to proceed along the path, when hearing his four comrades coming up behind, he stayed to wait their approach.

Presently they appeared filing through the rocks, but with no prisoner along with them.

He waited till the last was in sight ; then letting go his hold upon the captive, he rushed back toward the men, fiercely vociferating as he went.

" *Dio Santo !* " he exclaimed, " where is the *Inglese ?* Not with you ? *Maladetto !* What have you done with him—killed ? "

With a palpitating heart Lucetta listened for the reply. The men were slow to make answer, as if unwilling to tell the truth. She did not draw hope from this ; they might be afraid to confess they had killed him. She remembered the command to take him alive. She trembled as she stood listening.

Another string of mingled oaths and interrogations was terminated by the same demand—had they killed the *Inglese?*

"I heard the reports of your pistols, after that the volley by the soldiers. You were firing at him, I suppose?"

"We were, capo," answered one of the men.

"Well?"

"He succeeded in taking shelter under the cave, and we could not get at him. His long blade defended the entrance. Of course we could not surround him. If it had been a question of killing, we could have done that long before, but your orders were against it."

"And you've left him alive—unscratched—free!"

"No, capo; we think he must have fallen at our fire. We could not stay to see, for the bullets were raining round us as thick as sleet. No doubt he's dead by this time."

By the look and tone the young girl could tell they were prevaricating. There was still a hope he might yet be alive.

The chief equally perceived their evasion, and broke out into a paroxysm of fury. Forgetful of his injured arm, and almost wrenching it from its sling, he rushed upon his defeated followers.

"Cowards! imbeciles!" he cried, striking with his left hand now one, now the other, and tearing the hats from their heads, "*Sangue di Bacco!* Four of you conquered by one man—a boy—with the loss of 30,000 scudi! *Vada in Malora!*" he exclaimed in agony, as he felt the pain of his disabled arm. "Take hold of the *giovenetta*, and bring her along. See that *she* does not escape you as well, *su via!*"

And saying this he strode off, leaving his companions to conduct the *giovenetta* after him.

One of them, roughly seizing her by the wrist, and repeating the words *su via!* hurried her off after the chief, the other three following sullenly after. The young girl offered no resistance.

Any attempt to escape would have been hopeless. Her savage captors had freely flashed their daggers before her eyes, threatened to use them if she resisted, and she accompanied them with a sort of mechanical acquiescence springing from despair.

Her thoughts were not with herself, they were behind upon the Hermit's Hill, though she had but little hope of a rescue from that quarter, having witnessed the dastardly desertion by Captain Guardioli. He would be equally backward in the pursuit, and indeed her captors showed scarce any apprehension of it, as they wound their way slowly and deliberately through the defiles of the mountain. It might have quickened their steps had they known of the change that had taken place in the garrison of Valdi-Orno.

CHAPTER LI.

ON THE TRAIL

It is scarce necessary to say that the appeal made by the brothers and father of the abducted girl found a ready response in the hearts of the Republican *volontieri*. It came upon them with the force of a double call, for in addition to the dictates of humanity, these men looked upon brigands as a part of the despotic government they had just overthrown.

The Sindico, too, had claims upon them, for it was well known to their leaders that he had long secretly sympathized with them, his oath of office hindering him from any open demonstration in their favour.

Besides, his son—encountered by mere accident, as they were issuing from the gates of Rome—had declared in their favour, and was now one of themselves; under such circumstances there could be no desire to withhold assistance from their newly enrolled comrade, nor was there any, but, on the contrary, enthusiasm to act in his favour, with an unanimous determination to take steps for the rescue of his sister.

As soon, therefore, as Guardioli and his troop were disposed of by being disarmed and placed in charge of a detailed guard, preparations were entered upon for the pursuit of Corvino and his bandits.

Luigi Torriani, a prey to the agony of a terrible apprehension, would have started off after them at once, and so, too, the young Englishman. But the leader of the Republican battalion—Rossi by name—was a man of more prudent impulses, and saw that such a step would only defeat the purpose they had in view.

He had been himself an officer in the Neapolitan army; had plenty of experience chasing of banditti, Sicilian and Calabrian, and knew that any open pursuit of these watchful outlaws could end only in a ridiculous failure; the brigands themselves often witnessing such a result from the crest of some inaccessible cliff, and hailing it with taunts and scornful laughter.

It is true that in the present case there was an advantage. The rendezvous of the brigands was known. The late captive could guide the pursuing party to the spot, a chance not often obtained.

So far all seemed well, but not to the experienced pursuer of Neapolitan brigands.

" The advantage would be lost," argued Rossi, " if any attempt be made to approach by daylight—the vedettes would see us from afar and give them time to decamp. We must make our march in the night, and now that we know the road there is some chance of our being able to overhaul them."

Some chance ! the phrase fell harshly on the ears of Luigi Torriani, his father, and his friend. It was torture to think of delaying, to contemplate starting only after nightfall, with twenty miles of mountain road between them and the dearest object of their affections perhaps at that moment struggling——

The thought would not bear completion.

To the three individuals most interested the suspense was terrible, it was killing, and, to speak the truth, there were many of the others who showed it, both townsmen and *volontieri*. Could nothing be done in the shape of immediate pursuit ? All knew well enough that to follow the five who had carried off the Sindico's daughter would be an idle chase, for much time had elapsed, and with the knowledge the bandits possessed of the mountain-passes, they would long since have placed themselves in security.

The only hope was finding them at the rendezvous described by the escaped captive.

Was there no way by which this might be clandestinely approached during the daylight ? It would be night before the brigands themselves could reach it—for it was now noon, and the distance was at least twenty miles.

Night would be the time for attack, but it also needed night to cover the approach for this intervening march of twenty miles, else surprise would be impossible ; there would be vedettes along the line, if not brigands themselves in their *mamtergoli*, peasants, shepherds, or *vetturina*.

So said the leader, Rossi, and with reason.

Who could show a way out of the dilemma—a plan by which the brigands could be captured that very night, and before a crime might be committed which, to say truth, was in the minds of all the relatives of the abducted girl not more than those who had volunteered to effect her rescue.

Who could suggest such a scheme ?

"I," said a man, stepping forward into the midst of the council, which was held in the open piazza.

"If you'll follow my advice, and after that my guidance, I shall place you in a position not only to rescue the daughter of our worthy Sindico here, but to capture the whole of Corvino's band, with whom for three years I have been myself compelled to associate."

"Thomasso !" exclaimed the Sindico, recognising his old retainer.

"Thomasso !" cried the leader of the revolutionists, seeing before him a man known as having suffered in the good cause—a victim of the Vatican, who had preferred brigandage to rotting in a Roman prison. "Signor Thomasso, is it you ?"

"It is I, Signor Rossi, thanks to Heaven, no longer compelled to skulk among the hills, to conceal myself from the sight of old friends, to associate as I have done with the vilest scums of mankind. Thank Heaven and Guiseppe Mazzini ! Long live the Republic ! "

A shaking of hands succeeded, a series of grasps between Thomasso and the *rolontiiri*, those of them who were old acquaintances, and had known him in the streets of Rome.

Not less friendly was the grasp he gave to the young

Englishman, who was now made certain that his mysterious correspondent and the donor of the knife was no other than Thomasso.

But there was no time to be wasted in idle congratulations, it was not the occasion for them, with the cloud that still hung over every heart, and Thomasso was not the man to need prompting.

"Follow me," he said, speaking to Rossi, the Sindico, and his son, "I know a way by which we can reach the den without being seen, and before sunset, if need be. But Corvino will not get home until midnight, and by that time we can have him and his in the trap, completely surrounded and without a loophole of escape. But we must start at once, there is no time for lingering, as the path by which we must approach is long, devious, and difficult."

No one hesitated to accept the proposal, or asked further explanations, and in less than ten minutes after the Republican *volontieri*, leaving sufficient of their number to take care of their Papal prisoners, marched out of Val-di-Orno and took their way toward the Neapolitan frontier, under the guidance of a man dressed in the garb of a Neapolitan brigand.

CHAPTER LII.

A SUFFOCATING DRINK

It wanted an hour of midnight, when the brigand vedette stationed at the mountain foot heard the howl of the Apennine wolf, three times repeated.

" *Il capo*, I suppose," muttered he, as he answered the signal and stood up to take note of who was thus making approach.

Himself concealed, he could see who was coming, time enough to sound another signal to the sentry on the summit of the hill. This would communicate the character of the approaching party, whether friendly or hostile, by him above to be telegraphed on to the quarters of the band.

The vedette soon perceived that his conjecture was correct. The chief came up, stopping only to mutter some inquiry, and then passed on.

He was closely followed by a woman, whose fine muslin skirt, seen under the coarse *frezada* that hung down from her shoulders, told that she was richly robed; while her drooping head and slow, unwilling step, proclaimed her a captive. The *capuce* drawn over her head concealed her face from the eyes of the sentinel, who could tell however, by a small white hand grasping the folds of the *frezada*, that the captive was a signorina.

Four other men, bandits in the disguise of shepherds, going in single file, followed after.

The wolf-howl was uttered as they passed; its lugubrious notes preceding them up the gorge and receiving a response from the sentry at the summit; and then silence succeeded, broken only by an occasional rumbling noise as some fragments of rocks, detached by the feet of the ascending bandits, came rolling back down the declivity.

"That's the new wife, I suppose," soliloquized the sentry, as soon as the party had gone past. "I should like a squint at her face. No doubt it's a pretty one, or the Signor Corvino wouldn't have taken all this trouble to secure her. His arm in a sling, too! The bird hasn't been caught without a scuffle. I wonder if it be that Sindico's daughter there's been such talk about. Like enough it is. *Eufedi mia!* our capo strikes at high game. Well, after all, what's better than to be the *cara sposa* of a brigand? plenty of jewellery, rings, chains, buckles, and bracelets; plenty of *confetti* and kisses; what more can a woman want? And plenty of walloping if she don't behave herself. He! he! heio!"

And chuckling at his coarse jest the vedette once more resumed his seat upon the rock, and folding his *frezada* around him, relapsed into silence.

About an hour after, he was again startled from his sedentary attitude on hearing the well-known wolf-howl.

As before, the signal came from the outward side—from the scorza leading toward the Roman frontier.

"*Ecori!*" he exclaimed, "who else is abroad to-night? I only remember the capo and his party. Ah, now I think of it, Thomasso went out in the morning on some fool's errand. I wonder that capo trusts that fellow so, after that ugly disclosure about his Cara Popetta—Poverina! If she were alive to see what's going on wouldn't there be trouble in the camp! *Corpo di Bacco!* There again! Don't be in such an infernal hurry, Signor Thomasso. Let me gather my breath for the answer, ' *Wah-wah-wonagh!* '" he howled out, in response, the lugubrious signal, "now you may come on."

Shortly after a figure was seen stealthily approaching through the darkness, but with a step that showed acquaintance with the way.

"*Chi e' di la?*" hailed the sentry, as if some presentiment had increased his caution.

" *Amico !* " responded the stranger. " Why do you hail—you heard the signal ? "

" Ah, Signor Thomasso ! I had forgotten that you were out, I thought you had gone in with the others."

" What others ? " inquired Thomasso, with an interest he endeavoured to conceal under a pretence of ill-humour.

" What others ! " echoed the unreflecting sentinel. " Why, the capo himself to be sure, and the party of *pastores* that went abroad with him ; you were at the rendezvous when they left ? "

" Ah, true ! " carelessly remarked Thomasso. " I thought they had got back before night. How long since they passed up ? "

" About an hour ago."

" Well, have they made anything by their sheep-driving ? "

" A lamb. A young ewe, I take it, by what I could see of her wool. *Do Santo !* there have been sharp horns in the flock from which they have separated her. Our capo has had one thrust through him. I saw the blood upon his shirt."

" Wounded, you think ? In what part ? "

" In the right wing ; he was nursing it in a sling. There must have been a fight, I suppose. Did you hear nothing of it outside ? "

" How could I ? I've been too busy in a different direction."

" I hope you've not been so busy as to hinder you from filling your flask, Signor Thomasso ? "

" *Por Bacco,* no," answered the latter, evidently more pleased than offended by the reminder. " I always find time for that : you want a pull, I suppose ? "

" You're right, Signor Thomasso. It's a bit chilly upon post to-night, and a cup of rosolio would do me an infinite amount of comfort."

" You shall have it. I can't give it you in a cup : can I trust the bottle in your hands ? "

" *Che dramine !* yes. You don't suppose, signor, I am going to rob you. One pull will content me."

" Here then," said Thomasso, handing over the leather
bottle. " I'll give you a good pull. You can drink while
I am counting twenty—will that do ? "

" *Mille grazzie !* yes. You are very good, Signor
Thomasso."

The man, laying aside his carbine, caught hold of the
proffered flask from which Thomasso had already removed
the stopper, and with the exclamation, *" Oh me felice !"*
inserted the neck between his teeth. Holding his countenance skyward, he commenced swallowing in copious gulps
the delicious liquor.

Thomasso had watched for this opportunity ; and, suddenly stepping forward, he seized hold of the flask with
his right hand, while with his left he grasped the drinker
by the back of the neck ; then, kicking his feet from under
him, he flung the vedette back downward on the grass,
falling purposely on top of him.

The man, taken by surprise, was at first hindered from
calling out through sheer astonishment. He at first supposed it to be a joke, and that Thomasso was very generous
of his liquor ; then he became doubtful about the design
of such rough larking, and then angry. He would have
called out, but the bottle filled the whole cavity of his
mouth, and the rosolio running down his throat put a
stopper to his speech.

A few choking sounds escaped him ; but before .he
could free himself to give a good shout or utter the curses
he intended, three or four other assailants, already summoned by a low whistle from Thomasso, came running
upon the ground. These, flinging themselves upon the
prostrate body of the vedette, soon put an end to the
struggle, securing a gag permanently between his teeth
and pinioning his arms to his side, so that in six seconds
he was not only speechless, but a prisoner, powerless to
stir from the spot.

A long line of men, for whom Thomasso had returned
some distance along the scorza, now came filing past, and
led by the latter, went silently up the gorge, their silence
showing them bent upon an enterprise requiring the utmost
secrecy of approach.

CHAPTER LIII.

COURTSHIP WITH A CAPTIVE

CORVINO, his captive, and four followers, had passed up the gorge, crossed the ridge, and descended into the crater.

On nearing the cluster of houses they had been again challenged, this time by the regular sentinels of the rendezvous, of which there were two, one on each side. There was not much fear of these being found asleep. They had been lately taught a lesson, well calculated to keep them on the alert, having seen two of their comrades summarily shot for neglect of watch duty.

They were the two who had suffered the English captive to escape.

They had been tried, condemned, and shot—all within an hour's time, on the morning upon which he had been missed.

Such is the code of the bandit, its stringency being his best safeguard against surprise and capture.

A member of the band placed over a prisoner answers for the keeping of him with his life.

No wonder the escapes of *rescatattos* are so rare, scarcely ever occurring.

No dog barked at the chief's return, only the wolf-howl of the sentinel three times repeated; no one came forth to welcome him; one of the *pastores* opened the door of the capo's house, entered and struck a light which he left burning in the chamber.

The man then came out and the four scattered off to their respective *pagliattas*.

Corvino was alone with his captive.

" Now, signorina ! " he said, pointing to the house,
" behold your future home. I regret I have not a grander
mansion to receive you, but such as it is you are its
mistress. Allow me to conduct you in."

With an air of assumed courtesy he offered his arm,
which the captive made no movement to take.

" *Eh Cori !* " he exclaimed, taking hold of her wrist
and drawing her up the stone steps. " Don't be so shy,
signorina, come in ! You'll not find it so uncomfortable.
Here's a chamber specially fitted up for you. A sofa—
you must be fatigued after your long march over the
mountains. Be seated while I find something to refresh
you—can you drink rosolio ? Stay, here's better, a bottle
of sparkling capri."

As he was talking, with his back turned to the door, a
third individual entered the room.

It was a woman of considerable beauty, but with that
bold, fierce look that tells a sad tale.

She had stepped into the room without noise, stealthily
and catlike, and still remaining silent she stood just inside
the door; her eyes fixed upon Lucetta Torriani and
scintillating, as though at each moment they emitted
sparks of fire.

It was the woman who had betrayed Popetta, and who
had hoped to become her successor.

At the sight of the new arrival, her hopes became extinguished, and the look of concentrated rage with which she
regarded the young girl was fearful to behold.

It caused the latter to utter a cry of alarm.

" *Che sento ?* " asked the brigand, turning suddenly around,
and for the first time perceiving the intruder. " Ah ! you
here ! *Che tre sia maladetta !* Why are you here ? Off
to your own apartment ! Off, I say ! *Largo ! largo !*
This instant, or you shall feel the weight of my arm."

The woman, awed by the threatening gesture, turned
slowly out of the room ; but as she passed into the shadow
of the corridor the fierce flashing of her eyes, accompanied
by some words low muttered, might have told Corvino that
there was danger in what he was doing.

Perhaps he thought so, but his indignation hindered him from showing it.

"Only one of my domestics, signorina," he said, turning once more toward his victim. "She should have been to bed hours ago. 'Tis for that I have scolded her. Do not let our little troubles make you unhappy. Drink this, it will refresh you."

"I have no need of it," replied the girl, scarce knowing what to say, at the same time putting aside the proffered cup.

"But you have, signorina. Come, my fair girl, drink; and then for some supper—you must be hungry as well as fatigued."

"I cannot drink—I am not hungry—I cannot eat."

"What would you then? To bed? There's a couch in the next room; I am sorry I have no maids to help undress you. She whom you have just seen is not used to that kind of duty. You would prefer going to rest? Is that it, signorina?"

There was no reply. The young girl sat on the sofa with her head dropping down till her chin touched her snow-white breast, bared by the buttons having been torn from her bodice as she was carried in the arms of her captor.

There had been tears upon her cheek, but they were now dried, their traces still remaining. She could not again weep. She had reached that crisis of agony no longer to be relieved by tears.

"Come!" said the brigand, affecting an air of sympathy, like some cunning serpent in the act of fascinating its victim. "Cheer up, signorina, I acknowledge the rude fashion by which I have made you my guest, but who could resist the temptation of having so beauteous a lady under his roof? Ah! signorina, though you know it not, I have been your admirer; long have I been enslaved by your charms—charms celebrated far beyond the mountains of the Romagna, for I've myself heard speak of them in the *salons* of our Holy City. Ah, *miseri me!* Being your captive, can you blame me for making you mine?"

" What would you, sir ? Why have you brought me here ? "

"What would I, signorina ? What but have you love me as I love you. Why have I brought you here ? To make you my wife."

" *Madonna mia*," murmured the girl, without regarding what he had said. " *Madonna santissima.* What have I done to deserve this ? "

"To deserve what ? " asked the bandit, suddenly changing his tone. " To deserve becoming the wife of Corvino ? You speak proudly, signorina. 'Tis true I am no grand Sindico like your father, nor yet a *povero pittore* like the cur from whose company I have snatched you. But I am master of these mountains—ay, and of the plains too. Who dares dispute my will ? You will find it law, signorina, to the very gates of Rome."

After this outburst the brigand paced for some seconds over the floor, proud, strong, exultant.

" I love you, Lucetta Torriani ! " he exclaimed, after a time. " I love you with a passion that does not deserve such cold repulses. You may not like the idea of becoming a bandit's wife, but remember you become also a bandit's queen. There is not a plume in all the Abruzzi that will not bend to you—not a hat that will not be taken off in your presence. Throw aside your shyness, fair signorina. Don't fear you will lose caste by becoming my wife—the wife of the chieftain Corvino."

" Your wife, never ! "

" Call it by another name, then, if you prefer splitting about terms. We don't stick to formalities in our mountain marriages, though we can have a priest when we want one. If you prefer the ceremony in a simple way, I, for my part, shall have no objection to doing without the intervention of the *curita.* You shall have your choice, signorina."

" Death then shall it be ! Death before dishonour to the house of Torriani ! "

" *Eh ginsto.* I like your spirit, signorina. It pleases me almost as much as your personal appearance. Still it

wants training—just a little. Twenty-four hours in
my company will accomplish that—perhaps twelve. But
you still have the allowance of twenty-four. If at the end
of that time you do not consent to have our nuptials
celebrated by the *curita*—there is one convenient—why
then we must get married without him. You understand
that ! "

" *Madonna mia !* "

" No use in calling upon her, she cannot save you, im-
maculate as she is said to have been ; nor any one else. No
rescuing hand can reach you here—not even the hand of
his Holiness. Among these mountains Il Capo Corvino is
master, as Lucetta Torriani shall be mistress."

Before the boast had fairly parted from his lips, a sound
from without caused the brigand to start, changing as if by
electricity his air of triumph to one of alarm. " *Che
sento*," he muttered, gliding toward the door and standing
upon the stoop to listen.

The howling of the Apennine wolf, " *wah-wah-
wonagh !* " responded to by some one coming along the
scorza.

But now it was uttered on the other side by the sentinel
set toward the south, and answered also from that
direction.

What could be the meaning of this? Which of the
band had been abroad ?

He could think only of Thomasso, whom he had that
morning despatched on a particular errand. There could
not be two Thomassos coming home thus simultaneously
from the north and from the south.

He was not given much time for speculation. Almost on
the instant of his taking stand in the doorway a struggle
was heard on both sides, followed by shots and shouts, the
shots from the carbines of the sentries, the shouts from
their throats as they ran in, loudly vociferating the cry :

" *Tradimento !* "

CHAPTER LIV

A TERRIBLE TABLEAU

AND treason it was—treason and surprise, almost instantaneously followed by the capture of the whole band of brigands.

First the *pagliatti* huts were surrounded, and then the house inhabited by the chief encircled by crowds of men, upon whose persons, despite the darkness, could be distinguished the sparkle of arms.

There was light enough from the stars and the chamber lately quitted by Corvino, to show him that his quarters were completely enfiladed by dark, shadowy forms, each holding in his hand a gun, pistol, or sword.

At the same time there was strife going on among the *pagliatte*, stray shots, and groans mingled with ludicrous exclamations proceeding from the mouths of men dragged suddenly out of their beds, and scarce conscious of the cause of their quick awakening. But it was a strife soon brought to its close—even before Corvino could take part in it.

During a long career of crime it was the first time he had ever suffered surprise—the first time for him to feel something like despair. And at the very moment, too, when he was indulging in a dream of luxury and triumph.

Who could have brought this calamity upon him? Who was the traitor?

There must have been treason, else how could his sentinels be cheated? Who could have had acquaintance with the wolf-signal?

But there was no time to think of this. Thoughts of vengeance must needs be postponed to those of self-preservation, and the brigand chief suddenly found himself reduced to this.

His first impulse was to rush outside and take part in the conflict between his band and those who had so mysteriously assailed it.

But the conflict was scarce entered upon until it was over. It was less a strife than a capture, a seizing of men in their shirts who surrendered without striking a blow.

Even the thundering voice of their chief could not have aroused such yawning partisans to the energy required for their protection.

It was but an ordaining instinct that impelled him to shut the door and rush back to the room he had quitted, determined to defend himself to the death.

His first thought was for putting out the light.

He would be safer in the darkness.

And then what would this avail him?

Sooner or later other lights would be procured—candles or torches—or if not, his assailants need only wait till morning, now close at hand.

It could only be a suspension of his fate, at best a respite of two or three hours not worth the struggle.

His next thought—her; in it there was a hope, a chance, not for triumph, but safety.

There was a way by which he might still save his life.

Let the light burn, let his assailants see inside the house, let them look upon the tableau that had suggested itself to his imagination.

Quick as thought that tableau was formed in the centre of the room, already illuminated.

It consisted of two figures — himself and Lucetta Torriani.

The young girl was in front, the brigand as a background behind her.

His left arm encircled her waist with the hand clutching a stiletto, whose point was presented to her heart.

His right arm still rested in the sling, powerless to detain her.

R

But he had contrived a way of keeping her in her place by his teeth, that were closed upon a coil of her hair.

Outside were the spectators of this singular tableau, excited, angry, two of them almost mad.

One was the brother of her who formed the female figure in it, the other Henry Harding.

Either would have dashed through the window, but the bars forbade them; and although both carried guns and pistols they dared not discharge them.

They stood with a score of others almost within touching distance of the outlaw, and yet dared not stretch forth a hand either for his capture or destruction.

They were compelled to listen to the parley which at that moment he commenced making.

" Signori," he said, taking his teeth out of the young girl's hair, but still keeping the coil close to his lips, "I'm not going to make a long speech to you, I see you're impatient, and mightn't care to listen to it—you want my blood—you are thirsting for it—I am in your power, and you can take it. But if I am to die—so shall Lucetta Torriani—yes, the girl dies with me. One of you stir but a finger, either to draw trigger upon me or to enter the house, and that moment my poignard pierces her heart."

The spectators stood silent, with their breathing. suppressed and their eyes angrily gleaming upon the speaker.

" Don't mistake what I've said for an idle threat," he continued; " it's no time for talking nonsense; I know that my life is forfeited to the laws, and that you would show me about as much mercy as you would to a trapped wolf. Be it so, but in killing your wolf you would save your lamb. No! *Sangue di Madonna !* She shall die along with me. If I can't have her company in life I shall have it in death !"

The expression upon the brute's face as he gave utterance to the threat was revolting in its very earnestness.

No one who saw it doubted his intention to do as he said.

In fact, a movement made by him carried a vivid apprehension that he was at that instant about to carry out his threat, and the spectators stood transfixed as if the blood had frozen in their veins.

But no, this was not his intention.

He was only preparing for further parley.

" What do you want us to do ? " inquired Rossi, the leader of the victorious revolutionists. " I suppose you know who we are. You see we are not the soldiers of the Pope."

" Cospetto ! " exclaimed the bandit with a scornful toss of the head. " A child could have told that. I had no fear of seeing the brave *Bersaglieri* of his Holiness here. They don't relish the air of these remote mountains. That's how you've been able to surprise us. *Basta, signor!* I know who you are—and now for my proposal."

" Ah, what is it ? " demanded several of the spectators, chafing with impatience at the continued talk, and indignant at seeing the young lady still trembling in the bandit's embrace. " Let us hear what you have to propose."

" Absolute immunity for myself and such of my men as you have captured. Those you have killed may remain with you, and I hope you will give them Christian burial. And if any have escaped they can take their chances, we don't stipulate for them. For myself and comrades, who are your prisoners, I demand full freedom, and a promise that we shall not be pursued. Do you agree to it ? "

The leaders outside turned to one another, and commenced discussing the question.

It was painful to think of accepting such a proposal and letting these red-handed criminals escape. They had long been the terror of the district, committing outrages of every conceivable kind. Now that they were captured and could be rooted out, it would be a shame—a disgrace to the regenerators, whose natural enemies the bandits had been—to let them go free again only to recommence their depredations.

Thus spoke several of the Republican party.

On the other side, there was the danger in which stood the young girl—the absolute certainty that she would be sacrificed.

It is needless to say that Luigi Torriani, the young Englishman, and several others urged acceptance of the proposal, as also the leader, Rossi.

" And if we comply with your demands, what then ? " asked the latter.

" What then ? Why, the *giovenetta* shall be given up. That is all you want, I suppose ? "

" Are you ready to give her up now ? "

" Oh, no ! " returned the brigand, with a scornful laugh. " That would be delivering the goods before they are paid for. We bandits don't make such loose bargains."

" How then ? What do you propose ? "

" That you withdraw your men to the top of the ridge where the pass leads out northward ; mine, set free, shall go up to that on the south. You can then see one another. You, signor, shall yourself remain here with me, and receive the captive. You have nothing to fear, seeing that I have but one hand, and it the weak one. On your part, I must have a promise that there shall be no treason."

" I am willing to give that," responded Rossi, who felt that he was speaking the sentiment of his followers.

" It must be in the form of an oath."

" Agreed, I am ready to take it. Now ? "

" No ; not till we have daylight. We must postpone it till the morn. It is near now, and you won't have long to wait."

This was time enough ; the scheme could not be carried out in the darkness without risking treason on one side or the other.

Both could perceive it.

" Meanwhile," continued the proposer, " I must put out the light inside here. Else you may be chancing to steal a march on me by trying to get in from behind. I don't intend to let you surround me ; and in the darkness I shall be safe. *Se buono notte, signor !* "

A fresh thrill of apprehension ran through the veins of the spectators, more especially was it felt by Luigi Torriani and the young Englishman.

The thought of the young girl being left alone in the darkness—alone with the brutal brigand, even though they were themselves close by!

It filled them with horrid fears. Once more they were racking their brains for some plan to prevent such a repulsive compromise.

But they could think of none that did not also compromise the safety of Lucetta.

They had their guns cocked, ready to shoot the ruffian down had a chance presented itself. But there was none.

His body was screened by that of the girl—a shot, ill-aimed, and she only might receive it.

Half frantic they saw Corvino stoop down toward the lamp with the intention of extinguishing it.

Before he could succeed a third personage appeared in the room, a dark form that came through the door behind them.

It was a woman of wild aspect, in whose hand something could be seen to glitter in the dim light.

A stiletto!

With a gliding spring, like that of an enraged tigress, she placed herself close behind the bandit, and uttering a quick angry cry, plunged the poignard into his side.

Relaxing his grasp upon Lucetta, he turned suddenly round to defend himself; but almost on the instant staggered back against the wall.

The young girl, finding herself released, glided instinctively toward the window.

But it was not the intention of the murderess that she should escape, and with the bloody stiletto still grasped in her hand, the she-assassin came rushing after.

Fortunately for her intended victim she had reached the bars, and stood protected by a score of gun-barrels and swords thrust through them—among them the sword that had been snatched from Guardioli.

A volley succeeded—an interval of deep silence inside —and soon as the smoke cleared away two dead bodies were seen lying upon the floor, which under the light of the lamp could be distinguished as those of Corvino and his murderess.

Lucetta Torriani was saved!

CHAPTER LV.

"LONG LIVE THE ROMAN REPUBLIC!" Such was the cry that resounded through the streets of Rome in the year 1849; and among the voices vociferating it were those of Luigi Torriani and Henry Harding.

But while the young Englishman was helping the cause of freedom abroad, older Englishmen at home were plotting its destruction.

At that same time a secret convention was sitting in London, composed of representatives from all the crowned heads of Europe—its purpose being to arrange the ways and means by which the spark of liberty should be trodden out wherever it should show itself.

In Hungary it had flared up into a brilliant flame, but by the aid of British diplomacy and Russian bayonets, it had been stifled. The same result had followed in France, the means being slightly different. English diplomacy again had its influence backed by English gold, secretly but profusely supplied to place in the presidential chair a man sworn body and soul to change that chair to a throne. And with this same corrupting metal, and the sinister influence supplied by a great historic name, he had then almost as good as succeeded.

A president in name—an emperor in embryo, assisted by the caucus of crowned heads, as by his billiard-sharping confederates of Leicester Square, he had France at his feet.

It only required the trick—suggested, no doubt, by Lord Palmerston—disfranchise the two million of blouses, and

then the Assembly will be sufficiently conservative to trans-
form the Republic into an Empire.

There was still danger in it. How was this grand dis-
franchisement to be done?

The English Foreign Office supplied the answer : "We
shall snub your minister, De Morny. You can recall
him. Let us pretend an attitude of mutual hostility,
and while that is on, your Assembly can take its
measures."

The counsel was followed. De Morny was "snubbed"
and recalled; and while the British bulldog was barking
at Dover, and the Gallic cock crowing at Calais, the
betrayed "blouses," standing with angry faces towards
England, instead of having their eyes turned—as certainly they otherwise would—upon their own National
Assembly, were by this packed Parliament speedily dis-
franchised.

In Prussia the game was easier, though there, as in
France, liberty fell by the basest of all betrayals, by the
blackest perjuries on record.

And then in Baden and Bavaria that was still easier,
though the secret convention there decided to settle it by
the sword. The perjured King of Prussia was the man
called upon to wield it, and his hireling soldiers proved too
strong for the patriots of the Schwarzwold.

And now, at the eleventh hour, another spark of that
eternal flame of freedom appears in an unexpected quarter
—the very hot-bed of despotism, political and religious—
in the ancient city of Rome.

And again sits the secret convention. The late Lord
Palmerston—the most conspicuous of its members, because
of all others the most successful cajoler of the people—he
whose long career had been a succession of betrayals, and
yet has gone hence without witnessing their exposure.
For all that, history has it in hand.

Once more, then, sat the secret caucus, and once more
went forth the edict for this fresh spasm of liberty
that had sprung up in agonized Italy, to be stifled like
the rest.

There was no use to use artifice ; slight strategy would suffice for an enemy so insignificant.

It was merely a graceful concession to Catholic Christendom—to make it a pretence of restoring the Pope. The Republic would have been crushed all the same if the Pope had gone to purgatory. The sword was again invoked, and it became a question of who was to wield it. English soldiers could not be sent, for England was a Protestant country, and the thing would have looked strange. But English gold was easily converted into French soldiers, whose nation had no such scruples ; and the ex-billiard-sharper was selected to restore the Pope.

By him it was ostensibly done ; but the act was common to the caucus of crowned heads, and its direction special to the English representative—Palmerston. Of this history holds the indisputable proof.

Poor Mazzini, and Laffi, and Armelli ! Deluded triumvirate ! If there had not been a voice in all Rome against you—in all Italy—you could not have triumphed.

The decree had gone forth for your destruction. Your doom had been pre-ordained, and was pronounced in the very hour of your victory—even while the streets of Rome, cleared of the rotten rubbish of despotism, were ringing with that regenerating shout, " Long live the Republic ! "

For three months did it resound through the *stradas* of the classic city—the city of the Cæsars and Columas.

It was heard upon bastion and battlement, from behind battery and barricade, amidst scenes of heroic strife that recalled the days of Horatius. It was heard in the eloquent speeches of Mazzini, in the hoarse war-cry of Garibaldi.

All in vain. Three short months, and it was heard no more. The Republic was overthrown, less by bayonets than by betrayal ; but the rule of the bayonet succeeded, and *Chaesem* and *Gouave Spatine* and *Tuic*—all ruffians of the true French type, from that day to this—have stood guard over the ruins of Roman liberty.

In these troublous times, of three months' duration, Luigi Torriani took part with the Republic. So did his friend, the young Englishman. So too his father; for the Sindico, shortly after the affair with the brigands, had transferred his household gods to the city, which then promised a safe retreat from the insecurity he had long experienced.

But with the Republic at an end, and despotism once more triumphant, Rome itself was only safe for the foes of freedom, and Francesco Torriani was not one of these.

Another move became necessary. In what direction was it to be made?

There was no part of Italy that offered temptation. The Austrians still held Venice. Carlo Alberto had been beaten in the North, and the brigand King ruled the Neapolitans with a rod of iron. Turn which way he would, there was no home on Italian soil for Francesco Torriani.

Like all men similarly situated, his thoughts turned toward the New World; and, not long after, a bark sailed down the Tyrrhennian Sea and through the Straits of Gades, bearing him and his to the shores of a far Western land.

CHAPTER LVI.

GENERAL HARDING was not slow in transacting the business that carried him to London. It was too important to admit of delay. Even the old lawyer acknowledged this, on reading the quaint letter of the brigand, and scrutinizing its still more quaint inclosure.

Mr. Lawson's Italian tour had given him the experience to comprehend the case—peculiar as it was—and at once to recommend the steps necessary to be taken.

Five thousand pounds could not well be intrusted to the post, nor yet the management of such a delicate affair—in reality, not matter of mere fingers and hands, but of life and death. Even a confidential clerk was scarce fit for the occasion, and after a short conference between the lawyer and his client, it was determined that the son of the former —Lawson *fils*—should go to Rome, and place himself *en rapport* with "Signor Jacopi."

Who Signor Jacopi was could only be guessed at. In all likelihood, that strange specimen of humanity who had presented himself at Beechwood Park, with a reckless indifference either to kicking or incarceration.

*   *   *   *   *

The first train for Dover carried young Lawson *en route* for Rome, with a portmanteau containing five thousand pounds in gold coin, stamped with the graceful head of England's queen.

He went fully armed for the interview with Signor Jacopi.

Rome was reached in due course by rail and steam, and inside the ten days stipulated for in the letter of the brigand the Lincoln's Inn lawyer might have been seen with a heavy bag in hand, perambulating the streets of Rome, and inquiring for the Strada Volturno.

He found these streets in some disorder. Instead of the cowled monks and sleek silken-robed cardinals, who usually crowd them ; instead of grand *galantuomos* and most gaily dressed ladies, with here and there a sprinkling of impertinent *sbirri* and *gendarmerie*, he met men of brave bold aspect—honest withal—bearded, belted, in costumes half civic, half military, armed to the teeth, and evidently masters of the situation.

He was not astonished to hear from these men the occasional cry, " Long live the Roman Republic ! " He had been prepared for this before leaving England, and it was only by a well-attested passport that he had been enabled to pass their lines, and set foot upon the streets of the Eternal City—at that moment threatened with siege.

Once in its streets, however, he no longer met any obstruction, and losing no time, he commenced searching for Signor Jacopi.

He had very little difficulty in finding the Strada Volturno, and still less the domicile numbered 9. The men with long beards, and pistols stuck in their belts, were neither morose nor ill disposed to the answering of his questions.

They seemed rather to take a pleasure in directing him —with that hearty readiness that marks the intercourse of those who have been engaged in a successful revolution.

He did not ask for the residence of Signor Jacopi, only for the street and the number.

Once at the door, it would be time enough to pronounce the name of the mysterious individual to whom he was about to deliver a load of golden coins he had been constantly changing from arm to arm, and that had almost dragged both elbows out of joint.

Without further difficulty than this he reached the Strada Volturno—a paltry street it proved—and discovered at No. 9 the residence of Signor Jacopi.

He needed not to inquire—there could be no mistake as to the owner of the domicile.

His name was lettered upon the door, " Signor Jacopi, Solicitario."

The door was closed as if consultation could only be had after knocking.

The London solicitor knocked, and waited for its opening.

He was not without some curiosity to make the acquaintance of a member of the fraternity whose practice was of such a peculiar kind—who could demand payment of five thousand pounds, and get it without any appeal to a court—either to judge or jury—so unlike the practice of Lincoln's Inn !

The door was opened—not till the knock was repeated, and then after considerable delay. A hag, who appeared at least seventy years old, was the tardy janitor. But this need not dismay a solicitor of Lincoln's-Inn-Fields. She was no doubt the housekeeper of the " solicitario ! "

" Does Signor Jacopi live here ? " asked the young Lincoln's Inn lawyer, who having accompaned his father on the Italian tour, was able to make his inquiries comprehensible.

" No ! " replied the septuagenarian housekeeper.

" No ! His name is on the door."

" Ah ! true ! " responded the old woman, with something like a sigh. " They haven't taken it off yet. It's no business of mine—I'm only here to take care of the house."

" Do you mean that the Signor Jacopi does not live here any longer ? "

" *Ecori ?* What a question to ask ! You are joking, signor ! "

" Joking ! No, I am in earnest—never more so in my life. I have important business with him."

" Business with Signor Jacopi ! *Madonna Virgine !* " added the old woman, in a tone of consternation, and making the sign of the cross.

" Certainly I have ; and what is there strange in it ? "

" Business with a dead man !   *Dio mi amiti !*"

" Dead !   You don't mean to say that Signor Jacopi is dead ? "

" Si, signor, surely you know that !   Don't everybody know that he was killed in the outbreak—the very first day—knocked down, and then taken up again, and then hanged upon a lamp because they said he was one of the—— Oh, signor !   I can't tell you what they said about him. I only know they killed him, and he's dead, and I've been put here to keep the house—that's all I know about it."

The young Lincoln's Inn lawyer let his bag of gold drop heavily upon the doorstep.   He felt that he had come to Rome upon an idle errand.

*   *   *   *   *

And an idle errand it proved.   All he could learn of the Signor Jacopi was that the individual was an Algerine Jew, who had settled in the Holy City and embraced the Holy Faith ; that he had practised law—that department of it which in London would have entitled him to the appellation of a " thieves' lawyer "—that furthermore he was accustomed to long and mysterious absences from his office, but where or wherefore there was none to tell, as no one could be found who professed intimacy with him.

In consequence of some unexplained act, he had made himself obnoxious to the mob during the first hours of the revolutionary outbreak, and had fallen a victim to their fury.

These and a few other like facts were all that the London lawyer could learn about his professional brother of Rome ; but not one item to assist him in the errand upon which he had been sent to the Eternal City.

CHAPTER LVII

WHAT was the next thing to be done?

This was the inquiry which Lawson, junior, put to himself as he sat reflecting in his *locanda*.

Should he go back to London, carrying his bag of sovereigns untouched, and along with it the news of the failure of his mission? This course might be terrible in its consequences. The letter of the brigand chief—which of course he had brought along with him—plainly stated the conditions.

After ten days from its date, the hand of Henry Harding would be sent to his father inclosed in a similar fashion.

Nine of these days had already elapsed. Only one intervened, and now that the go-between, Jacopi, was no longer in existence, how was he to communicate with those who had threatened the horrid amputation?

"A band of brigands on the Neapolitan frontier— about fifty miles from Rome." This extract from Henry Harding's first letter was all the clue he had to guide him to the whereabouts of his captors. But the description might apply to the whole frontier from the Terra-ciana to the north-western angle of the Abruzzi—a line that, from all that he could learn, contained as many bands of brigands as there were leagues in its extent.

For the Lincoln's Inn lawyer to make a tour along it, discover the locality of each band, and ascertain which of them held the young Englishman in captivity, might possibly have been done at the daily risk of being made captive himself.

But even if successful in such a search, it could not be

accomplished in time. Such a scheme was not to be thought of—Lawson, junior, felt himself in a dilemma.

Never in his life had his father's firm undertaken such a case. It bristled with difficulties—or, to speak more truly, with impossibilities.

What was he to do?

He bethought him of the application that had been made to the Foreign Office in Downing Street, and the promises there given to communicate with the Papal Government. Had their promises been kept? Had any action been taken in the matter.

He rushed to the Vatican to inquire. But the Vatican was a thing of the past—the *régime* of Rome was now in Republican hands. And to his inquiries made in official quarters he could only obtain the answer that nothing was known of the affair.

Besides, the new rulers were too busy with their own affairs to take an interest in his. What was the liberty of an individual to that of a whole nation—threatened by the approach of the two hireling hosts—Neapolitan and French, now hastening toward Rome for the destruction of the Republic?

Every one was busy upon the barricades. There was no time to spare for the chastisement of a score or two of brigands.

The representative of Lawson & Son was terribly perplexed as to his course of action. It would be no use writing home for instructions. The communication could not reach in time.

Perhaps by the same steamer that would carry his letter, another might be despatched with a packet containing the bloody hand of his client's son. It would be a terrible consummation; but how was it to be shunned?

He could think of no means; and to wait for a return letter of advice from London seemed almost like leaving the prisoner to his fate.

But there was no help for it; and he commenced writing the letter, firmly believing that the return post would bring him the sad news of the brigands having carried out their atrocious threat.

It was less with the hope of hindering this, than that other menace of a still more terrible event, that induced him to indite the letter.

Before he had finished writing it, a new idea came in his mind, causing him to desist. What if his letter should miscarry? In such times, could the post be relied upon? Besides, why write at all? Why not go himself? He would reach London as soon as a letter could; and a matter of such importance should not be intrusted to chance.

Further reflections convinced him that he had best go back; and tearing up the unfinished despatch, he at once started to return to London.

He had some difficulty in getting through the lines, now close guarded against the approach of the hostile forces, that were every day expected to arrive before the gates of Rome. But gold, and a good English passport, smoothed the way; and he at length succeeded in reaching Civita Vecchia, from which the steamer transported him to Marseilles.

$$* \qquad * \qquad * \qquad * \qquad *$$

Not much was gained by the return of the emissary to England.

Fresh inquiries were made at the lodgings formerly occupied by the Italian artist; but no new facts were elicited. Of his haunts there was nothing known.

There could be nothing done but to despatch the junior partner once more to Rome; and to Rome he went.

But not to enter it. The Holy City was now besieged by the hireling hosts of France, acting under Oudinot; and the London lawyer had to stay outside—thus even deprived of the chance of prosecuting his inquiries.

Twice were the invaders repulsed, amidst scenes of carnage in which the streets of Rome ran blood—the blood of the gallant Republican defenders, led by that now well-renowned chief, Garibaldi, who in this struggle first made himself conspicuous on the pages of European history.

But the unequal conflict could not last; the Republicans were defeated by a base betrayal; and when at length the French took possession of the city, the London solicitor became free to renew his researches.

He succeeded in discovering that a young Englishman had been captured by a band of brigands, under a noted chief named Corvino—that he had afterwards made his escape from them—that the band had been nearly annihilated, and its chief killed by a party of Republican *volontieri*—that their late captive, acting along with the latter, had returned with them to the town of Val-di-Orno, and thence proceeded to Rome, in the defence of which city he was supposed to have taken part.

Whether he fell among the slain revolutionists in the carnage that ensued, there was no one could tell.

This appeared to have been his fate, since beyond the fact of his having returned to Rome, along with the *volontieri*, no further news of him could be discovered.

Even thus far, General Harding did not live to learn the history of his son.

From the day on which that epistle had been put into his hands—the one containing the hideous inclosure—his life had been one continuous misery. It became intensified on the return of young Lawson, to announce the failure of his first attempt.

From that hour the General lived in a state of excitement bordering upon insanity. He trembled at each post, expecting by it an epistle with more painful details —with a still more horrible inclosure. He even fancied that the second parcel might have miscarried, and the third would be that containing his son's head.

The ghastly apprehensions acting upon his excited imagination threw him into a brain-fever, from which he only recovered to linger a few days in a state of bodily prostration, and died accusing himself for having killed his son.

With this self-reproach he departed from life; though it could hardly have been a belief, since the last words spoken by him were instructions to his solicitor, Mr. Lawson, that the search was to be continued, regardless of cost, until his son's fate should be ascertained; and if dead, that the body should be brought home and buried beside his own.

What were to be the conditions, if living, no one knew, except, perhaps, Mr. Lawson; but that there were such might well be supposed.

The solicitor faithfully carried out the instructions of the deceased General—spending a large sum that had been left him for prosecuting the search, both by agents and advertisements.

It was all to no purpose.

Beyond what he had already discovered at Rome, he could hear no more of Henry Harding—whether living or dead—and in due time the emissaries were dismissed and the advertising abandoned.

CHAPTER LVIII.

On the death of General Harding, his son Nigel became master of Beechwood, and soon after—almost indecently soon—the husband, though not the master, of Belle Main-waring.

To the former no one thought of questioning his claim.

He was the eldest son, and, as most people now believed, the only one. The report that the other met his death among the revolutionists of Rome soon got abroad, and was generally believed in.

But even had it been supposed that he was living, one-half the world knew no better than that General Harding's estate was entailed, and that therefore Nigel was entitled as the heir. If the other half wanted to know better, and would take the trouble to inquire of Mr. World, the new solicitor to the estate, that gentleman could assure them of the soundness of his client's title, by reference to a document of a certain date, which he kept in a large tin case, conspicuously lettered. The case itself had the honour of the most conspicuous position upon the shelves, so that no client could commune with Mr. World without knowing that he was talking to the solicitor who held in his keeping the title-deeds and other legal documents of NIGEL HARDING, ESQ, OF BEECHWOOD PARK, BUCKS. So said the lettering on the case.

About the ownership of the Beechwood estates there was no question or dispute. In times past there had been a talk about its being divided between the two brothers; but afterward came out a rumour of a will, leaving all to the elder; and now that the younger had disappeared and was deemed dead, the point was no longer mooted.

Indeed, the memory of the latter was almost dead. He had been already more than twelve months out of sight, and with such associates as he used to keep, out of sight is soon out of mind. He was only a generous, somewhat reckless disposition, not likely to make much way in the world, either to fame or fortune.

But he was now dead; that was an end of him, and his brother Nigel was looked upon as one of the luckiest fellows in England, and one of the most prosperous squires in the shire of Buckingham.

He was at all events likely to be one of the most conspicuous, for the husband of Belle Mainwaring could not be hidden under a cloud. If he should choose to lead an unsocial life, she was not the lady to become the companion of his solitude, and he was not long before making this discovery.

The tranquillity of Beechwood Park ceased upon the same day that Miss Belle Mainwaring became the mistress of its mansion, and the drowsy solemnity of the old trees, hitherto disturbed only by the cawing of the rooks or the soft cooing of the pigeons, was now constantly assailed by the sound of human voices, gay and jocund.

Under the rule of its new mistress—for *she* in reality ruled—Beechwood became the centre of festivities, and the *élite* of the neighbourhood were only too happy to accept of its hospitalities as they would those of a retired knacker, provided he can offer them with sufficient profuseness.

But neither in the host nor hostess of the Beechwoods was there any question of retired knacker, and everything was therefore *en règle*. Select parties for outdoor sports— archery in summer—hunting spreads in the winter— dining and dancing at all seasons of the year.

Belle Mainwaring had obtained the reward of her great beauty, and her mother the recompense of her consummate skill; for the widow of the Indian colonel had found a snug corner in the establishment of Beechwood Park. It was not shared either by the sister of its late proprietor. The spinster aunt had disappeared previously to the nuptials of Nigel; and was now knitting that eternal stocking in a humble abode proportioned to the allowance left her by her brother's will. Her chair was now occupied by the widow Mainwaring, though not set so condescendingly in a corner.

And so for several years passed the life at Beechwood Park, and the outside world took part in it, or looked on and admired—not a few feeling envy.

How could it be otherwise where two young people, both gifted with good looks—for Nigel Harding was far from being personally plain—were thus in the enjoyment of so many advantages—property, position—in short, everything that should make life desirable.

The world is not very discriminative—else it might have seen under all this apparent joy something that resembled a sorrow.

I did; though never at Beechwood Park, as after my unfortunate *contretemps* at the county ball I was not likely to have the opportunity. But there were other houses still open to me; and at these I not unfrequently came in contact with the distinguished couple — as also that interesting individual to whom I had been indebted for getting my name scratched upon the dancing card.

And the more I now saw the more felt I thankful for that lucky deliverance.

Perhaps but for it I should have been one of the broken-hearted bees, who with scorched and shrivelled wings still continued to buzz around Belle Mainwaring long after she had become a wife.

It may have been some thought connected with these that caused the cloud I observed on the brow of Nigel Harding, with now and then a fierce flashing in his eyes, that betrayed his semi-Oriental origin. I could not tell, nor did I indeed care. I had never much respect for the man.

I was perhaps more observant of his wife, and speculated a little more profoundly as to the cause of her shadow, which to me was equally apparent. During all her gaiety, I could see traces of abstraction—even when flattery was being poured into her ears.

On her part there appeared to be no jealousy of her husband—on the contrary, his presence only seemed to give disgust to her—his absence relief!

All this I could easily perceive, and as easily tell the reason.

That short conversation I had heard under the Deodora was sufficiently explanatory, and I knew that Nigel Harding had married a woman who, in the true sense of the word, would never be his wife.

Love him she certainly could not and did not; but it was not certain that she could not and did not love another. On the contrary, I was certain that she *did*. Who that other was I could not so confidently say, though I must confess to many surmises. At times I thought it might be the man she had so cruelly jilted. At others I fancied it was one who with less cruelty, but like firmness, would have rejected *her*.

The last time I saw Miss Belle Mainwaring—I forgot she was then Mrs. Nigel Harding—was under circumstances that might be called peculiar.

It was at the close of a quiet dinner-party given by a country squire on the borders of Berks.

I had repossessed myself of my wrapper and wide-awake, and stepped out to await the coming up of the modest fly which was to transport me to the railway-station, and which the squire's brother had pompously summoned as " Captain R——'s carriage!"

As I stood awaiting my train, I saw before me an equi-page of elegant appearance, two splendid horses in front, a splendid coachman on the box, and an equally splendid footman stood by the step. Gold glittered on the liveries of the lackeys; a coat-of-arms glistened on the panel of the door. It was a turn-out in strange contrast to the dingy fly that had driven up behind it.

" Whose carriage ? " was the mental inquiry I was

making, when the stentorian voice of the butler unde-signedly gave me the answer.

It was the carriage of Nigel Harding.

At the same instant he came out, closely followed by his wife.

I stood aside to give them passage.

He entered the carriage first, as if driven in under direction. The lady, resplendent with fur robes—it was winter—placed her foot upon the step to follow.

At that moment, the horses, already pawing the ground with impatience, made a false step forward. They were suddenly checked by the coachman; but the lady, stag-gering, would have gone to the ground but for my person interposed to prevent her. By a mere mechanical act of politeness I had stretched forth my arms, between which sank Mrs. Nigel Harding.

"You, of all men!" muttered she, in a tone I could not easily forget, and which conveyed to my ear less of gratitude than reproach. Then breaking off, and trans-ferring her spleen to the peccant coachman, she flounced into the carriage, and was whirled off out of my sight.

What astonished me still more was the behaviour of her husband. I saw his face as the carriage drove off projected out of the open window. By the light of the lamp I could perceive that there was a black look upon it; but instead of the coachman it appeared to be directed toward me, as if he, too, had been angered by my invo-luntary act of politeness.

It was five years before I saw either again. I had almost, if not altogether, forgotten them; when a cir-cumstance occurring, many thousand miles away, restored to my recollection the young squire of Beechwood Park, and of course, along with him, his interesting wife.

The circumstance to which I allude was not only strange, but of serious consequence to several of the characters who have figured in this tale. Among others, to the squire of Beechwood and his lady.

Perhaps better for them had it never occurred—but I anticipate details which must be given.

CHAPTER LIX.

ON THE PAMPAS

FIVE years spent in foreign travel—confined to the continent of America—found me in the southern division of it, on the banks of the river La Platte.

Choice and chance—combining a little business with the prospect of a large amount of pleasure—had conducted me into the Argentine Republic, and the same had carried me into one of its upper provinces bordering upon the Pàrana.

I was journeying through the *campo*, about twenty miles north of Rosario, from which place I had taken my departure.

My object was to reach the *estancia* of an English colonist—an old college friend—who had established himself as a cattle breeder and wool grower, some fifty miles to the north of Rosario.

I was on horseback, and alone. I had failed in engaging a guide; but knowing that my friend's house stood near the banks of the river, I fancied there would be no difficulty in finding it.

There were other *estancias* along the route, sparsely scattered it is true, but thick enough to give me a chance of inquiring my way.

Besides, the river itself would guide me to a certain extent; at all events, it would keep me from going many miles astray.

My horse was an excellent animal, and I was expecting to do the fifty miles—a mere bagatelle to a South American steed—before sunset.

And in all likelihood I should have succeeded, if in the kingdom of animated nature there had been no such animal as a *biscacho*.

But there is such a creature, whose habit it is to honeycomb the *campo* with his burrows, in some places forming most treacherous traps for the traveller's horse.

On one of these, while traversing a stretch of *pampa*, my steed was imprudent enough to plant his hoof, and first sinking and then stumbling, he came down upon the plain, and of course his rider along with him.

The rider was but slightly injured, but the horse was seriously.

On getting him upon his feet, I found he could scarce stand, much less carry me the thirty miles that still separated me from my friend's *estancia*. He had strained one of his fore pasterns, and was just able to limp after me as I led him from the spot.

I felt that I had got into a dilemma; and would have to walk the rest of the way, besides making a second day of it.

" Perhaps not," I reflected, on seeing before me at no great distance some tokens of an *estancia*.

There was a clump of trees, most of which appeared to be peaches. This of itself would not have proved the proximity of a dwelling; for on many parts of the Argentine territory the peach-tree has been wild. But I saw something more, a bit of white wall gleaming through the green foliage, and around it a stretch of stockade fence, indicating an inclosure.

Turning directly toward it, I led on my lame horse, in the hope of being able to exchange him for one better able to bear me to the end of my journey.

Even if I could not make such an exchange, it would be better to leave him and proceed onward afoot.

On approaching the place I could see that it promised at least a shelter for my crippled quadruped, and getting still nearer, I indulged in sanguine hopes of being able to obtain a remount.

The house, gradually becoming disclosed through the shrubbery by which it was beset, if not a grand mansion, had all the air of a well-to-do *estancia*.

There was a comfortable dwelling with verandah in front —in style not unlike an Italian villa; and at the back out-buildings, apparently in good repair, and standing singly inside an inclosure.

There were enough of them for me to predicate a stable containing a spare horse.

With the one I could well spare, I was soon standing before the gate. It was that of the little inclosure that fronted the dwelling. I made my presence known by striking the butt-end of my whip against the paling.

Whilst waiting for an answer to my summons, I took a survey of the place. It did not exactly resemble the dwelling of a "criolto," there was evidence of care about the garden—and especially the rose-trellised verandah, that bespoke the European. The owner of the house might be English, French, German, or Italian—for all these are allowed to colonize without prejudice—without distinction.

Which of the four would respond to my summons?

With a curious interest, I awaited the answer.

I was not long in having it. A man, who appeared to issue from behind the house, came forward to the gate. His thick black beard and eagle glance, his white teeth, and nose prominently aquiline, were all Italian. An organ upon his abdomen and a monkey upon his shoulder would not more unquestionably have declared his nationality.

I knew it before he opened his lips to put the interrogatory,

"*Che c signor ?*"

Despite the man's blackness, there was nothing forbidding in his aspect.

On the contrary, the impression made upon me was that I had fallen among good Samaritans.

As good luck would have it, I could talk Italian, or at least "smatter" it so as to be understood.

" My horse," I said, pointing to the quadruped, who stood with a forefoot suspended six inches from the ground, " has met with an accident, as you see. He can carry me no farther ; I've brought him here to leave him in your care till I can send for him ; I shall pay you for the trouble, and perhaps," I continued, nodding toward the buildings at the back, " you might have no objection to lend me a nag in his place—anything that could carry me to the house of a friend I am on the way to visit, about thirty miles farther on ? "

The man looked at me for a moment with a puzzled air —then to my horse—then back to myself—and at length turned his eyes toward the house, as if from it he designed drawing the inspiration of his answer.

He could scarce have sought it at a shrine more like to celestial.

As I stood to catch his reply, the door of the dwelling was opened from within, and a woman stepped forth into the verandah—a woman who might have been mistaken for an angel, but for that maternity that in my eyes made her more beautiful !

Stepping forward upon the verandah, and looking through the roses that appeared to form a chaplet around her brow, she repeated the question already asked by the man, adding to it his own name, for to him was the interrogatory directed,

" *Che e Thomasso !* "

Thomasso made answer—a literal transferrence of the explanation he had himself received, and then waited for instructions.

" Tell the stranger," came the sweet voice from the verandah, " he can leave his horse here and have another to continue his journey. But if he will step inside and wait till my husband comes home, he will be welcome, Thomasso."

Thomasso thought I would, and I need scarce say I quite agreed with him.

He took the horse out of my hand, and led him round toward the stable.

I was left free to enter the house, and availing myself of the gracious invitation, I stepped across the threshold, and was soon seated and conversing with one of the most charming women it had ever been my privilege to meet!

CHAPTER LX.

I SAT enraptured with my fair hostess. I rejoiced at the accident that had thrown me into such pleasant company.

Who was she? Who could she be? An Italian, she had told me at first, and in this language we conversed.

But she could also speak English—about as well as I could speak Italian—and I soon learned from her that her husband was an *Inglese*.

"He will be so glad to see you," she said, "for it is not often he meets any of his own countrymen, for most of the *Ingleses* live further down. He will soon be home. He can't be long now. He only went over to the other *estancia* —I mean papa's—and, I think, he and dear brother Luigi went hunting ostriches. But that must be over now, as they don't chase the bird after midday, on account of their shadows. I am sure he will soon be back. Meanwhile, how are you to be amused? Perhaps you will look at these pictures? They are scenes taken from the country here. Some of them are by my husband—some by brother Luigi. Try it; you can kill a little time over them, while I go looking for something for you to eat."

"Pray don't think of it. I am not at all hungry."

"That may be, signor. But then, there are the ostrich-hunters. Likely enough, Luigi will come home with my husband—and won't they have an appetite ! I must go and get dinner prepared for them."

So saying, my fair hostess glided out of the room, leaving me to an impatience that had little to do with the return either of her husband, or her dear brother Luigi.

CHAPTER LXI.

HAPPY COLONISTS

To "kill time," as I had been requested, I commenced an inspection of the pictures. There were about a dozen of them, lying against the walls of the apartment, otherwise but sparsely furnished, as might be expected of a country house in the remote province of Santa Fé. As the lady had said, they were all scenes of the country, and for this very reason interesting.

The subjects related either to the chase or native industry. These were of ostrich or jaguar hunting, flamingo shooting, running wild horses and cattle, and capturing them with the *bolas* and *lazo*.

I was at first only struck with the remarkable truthfulness of these pictures—the faithfulness displayed in the details of the scenery and costumes. How like true reality were the gigantic thistles, the omba-trees, the wide-stretching pampas, the ostriches, the wild cattle and other animals, the *gauchos* and their costumes—in short, everything delineated. This was all evident at a glance. But I was not prepared for what I discovered on closer examination —that the pictures, at least a large number of them, were paintings of high art, fit for any exhibition in the world.

It would have been a surprise to me to meet with such pictures upon the remote plains of the Pàrana, but it was something more to know that they had been painted there.

Before I had ceased wondering at this unexpected discovery, voices coming from without caused me to suspend the examination and repair to the window.

On looking forth, I had before me a scene very similar to those from which I had just taken my eyes.

Under the shadow of a gigantic omba-tree, which grew in front of the dwelling, a party of men had made halt, and were in the act of dismounting from their horses.

I had a conjecture as to who they were—clearly the ostrich-hunters, as a large cock *rhea* appeared upon the croup of one of their saddles, and a hen bird at the other.

A third spoil of the chase was seen in the spotted skin of a jaguar, strapped behind one of the horsemen, who still kept his saddle.

Two of the new-comers were *gauchos* or herdsmen—the other two could only be the "husband Henry and dear brother Luigi."

Luigi—I could tell it was he by his Italian face—seemed undecided about dismounting, as if half inclined to go further; while the young Englishman, who spoke also in Italian, was urging him to stay.

At that moment my fair hostess stepped out into the verandah, and gliding on to the gate, added her solicitations—perhaps, also, intimating that there was a stranger in the house. Yielding to these, Luigi sprang out of the stirrup, surrendering his rein to Thomasso, who had come out from the stables, and who, with the two *gauchos*, commenced leading the horses away.

The two men entered, and I was introduced. "My husband Henry, and my brother Luigi."

Beyond this, no name was pronounced; and before I could give my own, the lady proceeded to explain my presence, and the nature of the request I had made to her.

"Oh, yes," said the young Englishman, as soon as he had listened to the explanation, "we can lend you a horse, sir—and welcome. But why not stay with us a day or two? Perhaps, by that time, your own will have recovered sufficiently to carry you out to the house of your friend."

"It is very kind of you," I answered, feeling very much inclined to accept the invitation. On second thought, however, it occurred to me that the hospitality proffered might be of the character common in South American countries, "*mia casa a sa disposacion, Senor*," a mere expression of courtesy ; and I was about declining it under some colourable excuses, when a second solicitation from my host, in which the fair hostess joined, and also Luigi, convinced me of its sincerity.

I could hold out no longer, and declared my willingness to remain a " day or two."

I made it three—three of the pleasantest days I ever spent in my life. They were not all passed under the roof of " my husband Henry," for " brother Luigi " had a house of his own—an *estancia* on a still larger scale—of which that of his sister and her husband was only an off-shoot. Into this I was also introduced, finding in it another fair hostess—a young South American lady who had lately become its mistress—as also Luigi's own father —a venerable Italian gentleman who was, in reality, the head of the whole circle.

The two establishments were but a half-mile apart, and what between passing from one to the other, and dining alternately at both, and chasing ostriches or shooting *biscachos* between times, the three days passed so quickly that I could scarcely believe them to have been twenty-four hours in length. I was rather dispirited at the skill of the groom Thomasso for having so speedily cured my horse.

An odd-looking creature this same domestic appeared to me. Had I met him on the mountains of the Romagna instead of on the banks of the Pàrana, I should certainly have taken him for a brigand—not that the resemblance went beyond mere personal appearance—that picturesque-ness we attach to the Italian bandit. Otherwise Thomasso looked honest—was certainly cheerful ; and above all, faithfully devoted to the Signor and Signora, in whose service he lived.

Yes ; I was rather chagrined, when at the end of the third day Thomasso pronounced my steed once more sound. But there was no concealing the fact, and although

I was urged both by host and hostess to prolong my stay, I felt that there should be a limit to such trusting hospitality, and prepared to continue my journey.

I was the less loth at leaving these new friends, from the knowledge that on my return to Rosario I was to take their *estancia* on the way. Only on this promise did they consent to my going so soon.

I need scarcely say that the prospect of renewing such a pleasant intercourse rendered it less painful to take my departure.

CHAPTER LXII.

AN UNKNOWN HOST

Up to the hour of leaving I had never once heard the name of my host.

That of his father-in-law was often mentioned. He was the Signor Francesco Torriani—a native of the Romagna, who some years before had come to the Argentine Republic—as many others of his countrymen—to better his condition.

This only, and not much more, had I learned; for, to say the truth, our daily life during my short stay, filled up with the pleasures of the present, I did not care to dwell upon the past.

In my case it was certainly so, and appeared to be the same in that of my new acquaintances.

Who, breathing the free, fresh atmosphere of the Pampas, or bounding over them on the back of a half-wild horse, would care to remember the petty joys and sorrows of a corrupted civilization—rather does one wish to forget them.

So was it with me; and so, too, I thought with my new-made Italian friends—the Torrianis.

I cared not to know the history of their past—why should they have any interest in communicating it?

They did not, any more than the few facts already stated, and these were revealed only by the accidents of conversation. Little, however, as I had learnt of the Torrianis, still less was I informed of the antecedents of my own countryman—my host.

As I have said, I stood upon the threshold of his house about to bid him adieu without even knowing his name!

It may appear strange, and require explanation. Not much either.

Among the southern nations of Europe—among their offshoots in Spanish America—the surname is but seldom heard ; only the cognomen, or *apellido.*

It is true this need not have been the case as regarded my English host, except from his Italian surroundings.

But for some reason, into which I had no right to inquire, I found him to retreat whenever chance led us to converse upon English affairs ; and though he showed no prejudice against his native country, he appeared to take little interest in it—at times, as I thought, rather shunning the subject.

In my own mind I had shaped out a theory to account for his indifference. Want of success in early life—perhaps something of social exclusion—though I could not so easily account for this. His manners and accomplishments proved, if not high birth, at least the training that appertains to it ; and in our intercourse there had more than once cropped out the masonic sign of Eton and Oxford. I wondered who he could be, or whence he had sprung ; but fearing it might not be relished, had forbore to ask the question.

It was only in the last moment, when I stood upon his doorstep—about bidding him adieu—that the thought came, with the resolution to carry it out.

" You will excuse me," I said, " if, after having been for three days the recipient of a very pleasant and very undeserved hospitality, I am somewhat desirous to have the name of my host. It is not a matter of mere curiosity, but only that I may know to whom I am so largely indebted."

" How very odd !" he said, answering me with a peal of laughter. " But is it a fact, Captain ——, that you have not yet learnt my name ? I took it, as a matter of course ; but now that I remember it, I have never heard you call me, except by my grand Italian title of ' Signor.' What a strange bit of negligence ! Three days in a man's house without knowing his name ! How very amusing, is it not ? Altogether un-English. To make the best amends in my power, I shall adopt the English fashion of giving you my card. I think I have some left in an old case. Let me see if there are."

My host turned back into the house, leaving me to laugh over the circumstance with his sweet wife, Lucetta.

Presently he came out again, with the case in his hand, as he did so drawing out of it several of the enamelled pieces of cardboard that appeared mouldy with long neglect. Selecting one, he placed it in my hand.

I felt a delicacy about scrutinizing it in his presence; and merely glancing at the card, without staying to decipher the name, I bade a final adieu to my host—I had already made my adieus to his lady—mounted my horse, and rode off.

I had not gone far before curiosity prompted me to make acquaintance with the name of the hospitable gentleman from whom I had just parted; and taking out the card, I read—

"MR. HENRY HARDING."

A very good English name, thought I, and one I had reason to remember; though it never occurred to me that the young *estanciero* of the Pampas could be any connection of the same of Beechwood Park, in the county of Bucks, and without making any further reflection I returned the card to my case, and continued my long-delayed journey.

CHAPTER LXIII.

A LOST LEGATEE

THE reader will be wondering at my want of intelligence in not recognising Mr. Henry Harding as an old acquaintance. But in reality he was not so.

I had seen him only once, when a beardless youth, home from a college vacation; and even had I known him more intimately, it is not likely that, sun-browned and bearded as he now was—speaking and looking Italian much better than he either spoke or looked English—I should have remembered the young collegian, unless some circumstance had occurred to awake the recollection.

Perhaps had I learnt the name sooner such might have been the case.

As it was, I went my way simply reflecting what a fine young fellow was my countryman-colonist, and how fortunate, too, in possessing such a treasure of a wife.

As to the others of my late entertainers, the reader must remember that he is already acquainted with much more of their history than I was then.

All I knew of them was what I had learnt during the three days' intercourse just passed; and in this nothing had occurred in any way to connect them with my old acquaintances of the county of Bucks.

This, therefore, will explain why, on reading the name of Mr. Henry Harding on his card, I restored the piece of pasteboard to my pocket, and continued on without any other reflection than that above detailed.

On reaching the *estancia* of my friend, I found him somewhat anxious about my tardy arrival.

He had, of course, expected me three days sooner; and

but that the " thistles " were not yet sufficiently advanced
in growth, he would have supposed that I had either lost
my way among those gigantic weeds, or fallen into the
hands of robbers, who are to be apprehended only after
the thistles have reached their full height.

On explaining the cause of my delay, and telling him .
where I had spent the intervening time, and how pleasantly
I had spent it, my friend suddenly interrupted me with
the question :

" Did you ever know a General Harding, of Bucks ? "

" A General Harding, of Bucks ? "

" Yes; I know you've been a good deal down in that
county.　The General Harding I speak of died some five
or six years ago."

" I knew a General Harding, of Beechwood Park, in
Buckinghamshire.　I had only a slight acquaintance with
him.　He died about the time you say..　Would it be the
same ? "

" By Jove! the very same.　Beechwood—that, I think,
is the name ; but we shall soon see.　It's very odd,"
continued my friend, rising from his seat, and going
toward a secretary that stood in a corner of the room—
" very odd, indeed; but I was half in the mind myself of
riding over to the *estancia* where you have been so well
entertained.　I should have done so this very day, but
that I was waiting for you.　But it was while waiting for
you that I discovered that which would have been my
errand.　I know very little of my English neighbour, Mr.
Harding.　His connection is mostly among Italians and
Argentines ; and we English don't see much of it.　He's
said to be a first-rate fellow, for all that."

" I'm glad to hear him so spoken of.　It's just the impression he has made upon me.　But what has this to do
with your question about General Harding ? "

I need hardly say that by this time my own curiosity
was aroused—so much so, that I had once more taken
the card out of my case, and submitted it to a fresh examination.

" Well," said my friend, returning to the original subject
of his discourse, " while looking out for you, I could not

well leave the house ; and having no other way of amusing
myself, I took to reading some old English newspapers.
We don't have them very new here at any time; but
these were dated several years ago. One of them was a
Times ; and if you'd lived as long upon the Pampas as I
have, you'd not turn up your nose at a *Times*, however
ancient its date, nor would you leave a paragraph unread
—even to the advertisements. I was poring over these,
when my eye fell upon one, which I leave you to read for
yourself."

I took the paper handed me by my friend, and read the
advertisement pointed out. It ran thus :

" HENRY HARDING.—If Mr. Henry Harding, son of the
late General Harding, of Beechwood Park, in the county
of Buckingham, will apply to Messrs. Lawson & Sons,
solicitors, of Lincoln's-Inn-Fields, he will hear of SOME-
THING TO HIS ADVANTAGE. Mr. Harding was last heard
of in Rome at the time of the revolutionary struggle,
and is supposed to have taken part in the defence of
that city. Any one giving information of his present
address, or, if dead, stating the time and circumstances of
his death, will be handsomely rewarded."

" What do you think of it ? " asked my friend, seeing
that I had finished reading the advertisement.

" I remember having seen it before," was my reply. " It
was inserted in the papers repeatedly—several years ago,
and at the time caused much talk. Of course everybody
knew that young Harding had gone away from home—no
one knowing where. That was some time before the
father's death. There were some queer stories afloat about
his having been jilted by a girl. I knew something of her
myself. Then of his having gone to Italy, and got into the
hands of brigands, or joined the partisans of Mazzini and
Garibaldi. No one knew the truth, as General Harding was
a man in the habit of keeping his family secrets to himself.
It was after his death that the talk was—when these
advertisements appeared—and then the young fellow had
been a good while out of sight, and the thing attracted less

attention. It was said that the father had left him a legacy, and that was why the solicitor advertised for him."

" Just what I thought. But do you think he ever turned up ? "

"That I can't tell ; I never heard the result, as about that time I left England myself, and have been abroad ever since."

" Does it not occur to you ? " continued my friend, " that this Henry Harding of the *Times* advertisement and the young *estanciero* who has been entertaining you, might be one and the same man."

" It is quite possible—indeed, it seems probable. This states that he was last heard of at Rome ; and the family into which he is married came from Rome. That much they told me during my stay. It may be the same, and he may have answered the advertisement too, and got the something to his advantage, whatever it was ; though I am under the impression it was not much ; it was generally known that the bulk of General Harding's property was willed to his eldest son ; and that Henry, who was the younger, was left a bare thousand pounds. If my late host be he, in all likelihood he has had the money before now. Might it not have been with this he has here so snugly established himself ? "

" No, I can answer for that," said my friend. " He had settled here long before the date of this advertisement, and has never been out of the country since—certainly never so far as England."

" It would not be necessary for him to go to England for his light legacy of a thousand pounds. All that might have been transacted by letter of attorney."

" True—but I have good reason to know that he is only a tenant of the *estancia* you found him in. His Italian father-in-law is the real owner of both properties ; and this was the state of affairs from the first—long before the advertisement could have appeared. In my opinion, he has never seen it ; and if he be the individual referred to, it might be worth his while knowing it. As I've told you, I had thoughts of riding over, and asking him myself ; for although we've had very little intercourse, I've heard

a very good account of him, though not as a successful
sheep-keeper. He's too fond of hunting for that, and
I fancy he hasn't added much to his wife's dowry or
his father-in-law's fortune. Indeed, I've heard say that he
is himself a little sore about this; and if there should be
a legacy for him, still unlifted, it might come at this time
very convenient for him. One thousand pounds isn't much
in London ; but it would go a wide way upon the Pampas,
here.''

'' Quite true,'' I replied mechanically, thinking whether
it could be possible that the rejected lover of Miss Belle
Mainwaring was the man I had seen, married to a wife
worth ten thousand of her sort.

'' I'll tell you what you can do,'' said my host. '' You
say they've invited you to stop there on your way back to
Rosario.''

'' I am under a promise to do so.''

'' Lucky fellow, to have made such a brace of beautiful
acquaintances ! for the Argentine lady is not thought so far
behind her Italian sister-in-law. All by the stumbling of
a horse, too ! By Jove ! I'd risk the breaking of my neck
every day in the year for such a chance ! You were always
fortunate in that sort of favour.''

It was rather amusing to hear my friend talk in such
fashion. A confirmed old bachelor, who, I verily believe,
would not have surrendered even to the charms of the
lovely Lucetta—such was the name I had heard given to
Mrs. Harding.

'' What were you going to propose ? '' I asked, to escape
from my friend's bantering.

'' That you take back with you this old *Times*, and show
the advertisement to Mr. Harding himself. I'll ride. that
far with you, if you wish; but as you have made
acquaintance, and can know more about this matter than
I, it will be better for you to introduce it. What say
you ? ''

'' I can have no objection.''

'' All right, then. And now to see how I can entertain
you. No doubt, my bachelor quarters will be dull enough

to you, coming from such company.   A dose of purgatory
after paradise !   Ha ! ha ! ha ! "

I could not help thinking there was some truth in what
my friend said, though I did all I could to conceal my
thoughts by joining heartily in his laugh.

CHAPTER LXIV

THE entertainments provided for me by my old college acquaintance were far from being dull, and I enjoyed his company for a whole week.

At the end of that time I was on my way back to Rosario, intending to stop, as promised, at the *estancia* of Mr. Henry Harding, who, if he should prove to be the son of the old Indian General, I could no longer look upon in the light of a stranger.

So far my bachelor friend accompanied me, and I had the pleasure of promoting an intimacy between two of my countrymen who were worthy to know one another better than they had hitherto done.

The Signora Lucetta was beautiful and amiable as ever, and we had soon assembled under one roof the two families to entertain us.

And for several days we were entertained with hospitality that became very irksome for me to escape from, as also my bachelor friend, who, I believe, went back to his solitary *estancia* with strong resolutions of becoming a Benedict.

For my part, I was no longer treated as a stranger. My South American host *was* the son of General Harding, of Beechwood Park—the very man who had been advertised for, and up to that hour in vain.

In a conversation that occurred between us, shortly after my arrival, I was made acquainted with his whole history, as given in these pages.

" And this ? " I said, pointing to the advertisement in the paper that lay on the table before us.

" Never saw it—never heard of it till now," was his reply.

"You heard of your father's death, I suppose?"

"Oh, yes. I saw that in the papers, shortly after it occurred. My poor father! Perhaps I acted rashly and wrongly, but it is too late to talk of it now."

I saw that it pained him to speak of his father, and I passed on to another subject.

"Your brother's marriage—you heard also of that, I suppose?"

"No," he answered, to my surprise. "Is he married?"

"Long since. It was also in the papers, and somewhat conspicuously. Strange, you didn't see it!"

"Ah, the papers! I never looked at an English newspaper since that containing the account of my father's death. I hated the sight of them, and everything else that was English. I have not even associated with my own countrymen here, as you may have learned. And who did Mr. Nigel Harding condescend to make happy? You know the lady, I suppose?"

"He married a Miss Belle Mainwaring," I answered, with a counterfeit air of innocence, but not without some fear that the communication might give pain.

I watched his countenance for the effect, but could discover no indication of the sort.

"I knew something of the lady," he said, with just the shadow of a sneer. "She and my brother ought to make each other very happy. Their dispositions, I think, were suitable."

I didn't tell him how thoroughly I understood the meaning of the remark.

"But," I said, returning to the subject of the advertisement, "what do you intend doing with this? You see it speaks of something to your advantage."

"Not much, I fancy. I think I know all about it. It is a question of a thousand pounds, which my father promised to leave me at his death. It was so stated in his will—that will——" here a bitter expression came suddenly over his features. "Well," he continued, his countenance as suddenly clearing again, "I ought rather to rejoice at it, though it did disinherit me. But for that, signor," he said, forgetting that he was talking to a countryman, "I might never have seen my dear Lucetta, and I think you will say that never to have seen her would be the greatest misfortune a man could have in his life."

It was an odd appeal, to me strange, but I could not help responding to it.

He would have gone on conversing upon this pleasant theme; but the time was drawing nigh for us to join the ladies—Lucetta herself being one; and I redirected his attention to the subject that had taken us apart.

"Even a thousand pounds," I said, "is worth looking after."

"Quite true," he replied, "and I had several times thought of doing so—that is, lately. At first I was too angry with all that had happened at home, and had made up my mind to refuse even the paltry pittance that had been left me. But, to tell the truth, I have not made much money here ; and I begin to feel myself rather a pensioner upon my worthy father-in-law. With a thousand pounds of my own money I think I should stand a little higher in my own estimation."

"What would you do then ? come with me to England and get it ? "

"Not for ten thousand ! No. I wouldn't leave this happy home and forsake this sweet South American life for ten times the amount. It will not be necessary to go to England. If there be a thousand pounds lying for me in the hands of Messrs. Lawson & Son—which I suppose there is, I must extract it from them by a lawyer's letter —by power of attorney. By the way, you are going there, are you not ? "

"I intend taking the next steamer to England."

"Well then, why—but I am asking too much ? You have your own affairs to attend to ? "

"My affairs are not so onerous but I can find time to attend to any business you may choose to entrust me with, if you will only allow me to consider as my commission the hospitality for which I feel myself your debtor."

"Oh, don't talk of hospitality. Besides, it is not mine.

It was Lucetta who first received you. If I'd been at home myself, seeing you were an Englishman, I should, perhaps, have lent you a horse and let you ride on; and being myself an Englishman, in all likelihood should have jockied you out of that fine steed of yours, and given you a screw in exchange. Ha! ha! ha!"

I joined him in the laugh, well knowing that his sardonicism was but a jest.

"But to be serious," he continued, "you can do me this service better than any scamp of a lawyer. Go to this Lawson, of Lincoln's-Inn-Field. I know something of the old fellow, and his son too. They are not a bad sort—that is, for solicitors. If there be money left me in their hands, I shall be likely to get it. I shall give you a letter to receive it, and you can send it to some bank in Buenos Ayres, so that it may reach me through their agents in Rosario. You can do that for me, and will?"

"With pleasure!"

"Enough! the ladies are longing for us to rejoin them. You are fond of the guitar, I believe. I hear Lucetta tuning the strings. Luigi can sing like a second Mario; and the *senorita*, as he calls his South American wife, is a perfect nightingale. Hear! They are calling for us. Come, captain!"

It needed no pressing on the part of my host to yield obedience to those silvery voices commanding our presence in the adjoining apartment.

CHAPTER LXV

THE LAST WILL AND TESTAMENT

Two months after that day I was under a sky unlike to that which canopies the region of the Pàrana, as lead to shining sapphire, in a room as different to that pleasant *cuarto* in the South American *estancia* as a Newgate cell to an apartment in Buckingham Palace. I stood in the dingy office of a Lincoln's Inn lawyer, by name Lawson.

It was the senior partner who received me, a gentleman with all the appearance, and, as I afterwards discovered, all the claims to respectability in his possession.

"May I inquire your business, captain?" he politely asked, after examining the card which had been sent in to introduce me.

"You will find it here," I answered, placing before him an old *Times* newspaper, and pointing to an advertisement, marked with an asterisk in pencil. "I presume it is your firm to which the application is to be made?"

"It is," he said, starting up from his office-chair, as if I had presented a pistol at his head. "It is very long ago, but no matter for that. Do you know anything of the gentleman to whom it refers?"

"Yes, something," I replied, cautiously, not knowing how far I might be committing the interests of my *client*.

"He is still alive, then? I mean Mr. Henry Harding."

"I have reason to think so. He was two months ago."

"By ——," exclaimed the lawyer, evidently using a phrase forced from him by the importance of the occasion.

U

"This is serious, something very serious—very serious, indeed. But, sir—captain, I beg your pardon—you will excuse me if I ask on which side you came. I know your name, sir. I believe I can trust you to speak candidly. Are you here as a friend of Mr. Nigel Harding?"

"If I had been, Mr. Lawson, it is not likely I should have given you the information which it has been my pleasure to impart. From all that I hear, Mr. Nigel Harding would be the last man to be pleased with hearing that his brother is alive."

My speech acted like electricity on the solicitor. I could tell at once he was upon *our* side, as he saw I was upon his. Out of doors I had already heard that he was no longer the trusted attorney of the Beechwood estate.

"And you tell me he *is* alive?" was the question next put, with an emphasis that showed its importance.

"The best proof I can give you is this——"

I handed over the letter written by Henry Harding, containing the requisition for the presumptive legacy of a thousand pounds.

"A thousand pounds!" exclaimed the lawyer as soon as had read, "a thousand pounds! A hundred thousand, every shilling of it! Ah! and the accumulated interest, and the mortgages already obtained, and the waste of that scoundrel Woolet. Whew! here's a penalty for Mr. Nigel Harding and his sweet spendthrift of a wife!"

I was not prepared for this explosion, and as soon as it had to some extent subsided I asked Mr. Lawson to explain.

"Explain!" he said, putting on his spectacles, and turning toward me with a business-like air. "To you, sir, I shall have much pleasure in explaining. This letter tells me I can trust you—thank God, the lad still lives— the true son of my old friend Harding, as he told me on his dying bed, and with his last breath. Thank God, he is still alive, and we shall yet be able to punish the usurper, and the pettifogger, Woolet, as well. Oh! this is good news, a glorious revelation, a resurrection I may call it."

"But what does it all mean, Mr. Lawson? I came to

you at the request of my friend, **Mr.** Henry Harding, whom by chance I met while travelling in South America on the Paranà, as you will see by his letter. He has commissioned me, as you will perceive by his letter, to call upon you, and make an inquiry. He is under impression that you hold in hand a legacy of £1,000 left him by his father, and if so, has given me the authority to receive it."

" A thousand pounds! A thousand pence! Is Beechwood estate worth only a thousand pounds? Read this. I know that I can trust you, captain. Run your eye over that!"

A grand sheet of parchment, pulled from out a tin case, was flung before me. I saw it was lettered as a will. I took it up, and spreading it upon the table, read what was written. I need not give its contents in detail.

By this document General Harding revoked the terms of a former will, which left the whole of his estate to his eldest son, Nigel, and a legacy of *one thousand pounds* to his youngest son, Henry; the present will exactly transposed the condition—devising the estate to Henry and the thousand pounds legacy to Nigel!

The will contained ample instructions for its administration: Mr. Lawson and his son being the appointed administrators. It was not to be made known to Nigel Harding himself until it should be ascertained that Henry was still alive; and for this purpose, all due diligence was to be used by advertisement in the papers, and such other means as the administrators should see fit. Meanwhile Nigel was to retain possession of the estate, as by the terms of the former testament, and in the event of Henry's death being proved he was not only to be left undisturbed, but also ignorant of the existence of the second will, which was then to be null and void.

There was a codicil, citing and comprising a similar addition in the former will, by which the General's sister was to have a life interest out of the estate amounting to £200 per annum.

Such were the terms of the singular testament which the solicitor placed before me.

It is scarce necessary for me to say that I perused the "last will and testament" of the deceased General with no slight astonishment, and certainly with a feeling of gratification.

My hospitable host—the young *estanciero* on the Pàrana —need no longer feel under any obligation to his worthy father-in-law ; and little as he professed to love England, I could not help thinking that the possession of the paternal estates would do much to modify his prejudice against his native land.

"By this," I said, addressing myself to the solicitor, "it appears that Mr. Henry Harding becomes the sole proprietor of the Beechwood estate ? "

"It is certain," answered he, "all but the £1,000 legacy and the life annuity."

"It will be a surprise for Mr. Nigel."

"Ah! and Mr. Woolet, too. They did all they could to keep me from advertising for the lost legatee. Of course they supposed I did so in order to pay him the paltry £1,000. Mr. Nigel may now have that, and see how far it will cover World's costs. My word ! it will be an explosion ! And now for the first steps toward bringing it about."

"How do you intend to proceed ? "

The lawyer looked at me as if hesitating to answer the question.

"Excuse me," I said, "I asked rather out of curiosity than otherwise. It is, after all, no affair of mine."

"There you are wrong, captain. Pardon me for being plain with you. It is an affair of yours, in so far that Mr. Henry Harding has given you the legal authority to act for him."

"That," I said, "was only under the supposition that he was to receive a legacy of £1,000. With an estate, as you say, worth £100,000, the affair takes a different shape and clearly goes beyond my discretionary powers.

"Though I cannot act as a principal in the matter, I am willing to help you every way in my power. I feel sufficiently indebted to your client to do that."

"And that is just what I intended asking you ; hence

my hesitation in replying to your question. I am glad to know that we can count on your assistance. No doubt we shall need it. Men don't yield up possession of a property like this without showing fight. We may expect all that, and some questionable strategy in conducting it, from such a fellow as Woolet—a thorough pettifogger, without one iota of principle."

"But how can they dispute this will?" I asked. "It seems clear enough, and of course you know it to have been the latest and last."

"Signed by General Harding the day before he died, regularly and carefully attested. You see the names upon it. They cannot dispute the document."

"What then?"

"Ah! what then. That is just the point, and I think it will be the *identity* of our claimant. By the way, what does the young fellow look like? Is he much altered in appearance since he left England?"

"That question I cannot answer."

"Indeed! It is but two months since you have seen him?"

"True, but then I may almost say I saw him for the first time. I had met him six years before, but only on one occasion, and I had lost all remembrance of him."

"He was very young," pursued the solicitor, in soliloquy, "a mere boy when that unfortunate affair occurred—after all, perhaps, not so unfortunate. No doubt, he will be much changed. A captivity among brigands, fighting on barricades, a beard, the tan of a South American sun, to say nothing of being a Benedict, no doubt the Henry Harding of to-day is entirely unlike the Henry Harding who left his home six years ago. My word, there would be a difficulty in identifying him, and we might dread the worst. People nowadays can be got to swear anything—that black's blue, or even white—if it's wanted, and there be money enough to pay for it. In this case there will be both money and the determination to use it. World won't stick at anything, nor would Mr. Nigel Harding either, to say nothing of Mrs. Nigel and her amiable mother. We're sure to have a fight, captain, sure of it."

" You don't appear to have much fear about the result? " I said this, noticing the old lawyer talked with an air of triumphant confidence, besides having used the conditional tense when speaking of the chances of his client being identified.

" Not the slightest, not the slightest. I don't apprehend any difficulty. There might have been, but—but I fancy I have a scheme to set all right. Never mind, captain, you shall be told of it in good time. And now for citing all parties into court."

" But do you mean to do that now? "

" Of course not, captain. I was only speaking figuratively. The first thing is to get Mr. Henry Harding here. He must be sent for immediately. Let me see. *Estancia Torriani Rosario.* Up the Parana River, you say. With your kind directions, captain, my son will start for South America at once. It's a long way, but no matter for that. A hundred thousand pounds is worth going round the world for more than once. And now, captain, I will ask you for two favours: one, that you will write to your friend, Mr. Henry Harding, telling him what you have learned. My son can carry your letter along with our instructions. The other favour I speak of is that you will give your word to keep the affair secret until— well, until Mr. Henry Harding himself appears upon the ground."

Of course the promise was given, as also the directions to serve Lawson, junior, on his Transatlantic itinerary ; and leaving my address, so that Lawson, senior, could at any time communicate with me, I took my departure from Lincoln's-Inn-Fields, rejoiced as well as surprised by the discovery I had made.

CHAPTER LXVI.

THE FINGER OF FATE

IN less than six months from the date of my interview with the Lincoln's Inn lawyer I was witness on a trial of more than the usual interest.

It was a case of contested will—no very uncommon thing.

But in that to which I refer there were circumstances of a peculiar, I might say curious, kind, and these, with the position of the parties concerned, rendered the suit worthy of being placed among the record of *causes célèbres.*

It was the case of Harding *v.* Harding, the defendant being Nigel Harding, Esq., of Beechwood Park, Buckinghamshire; the plaintiff, a Mr. Henry Harding, who claimed to be his half-brother.

The matter in dispute was an estate, valued at £100,000, of which defendant was in possession. He held it by a will, made by General Harding, his father, and former owner of the property, prepared some twelve months before the General's death, and at the same time duly signed and attested.

It had been made by a county attorney named Woolet, and signed by himself and his clerk, acting as witnesses to the testator.

It gave the whole of General Harding's estate to his eldest son, Nigel, with the exception of £1,000 to be paid out of it to his other and younger son, Henry.

So far the document seemed quite correct, except in the strangeness of the unequal distribution. But there were reasons for that, and no one disputed the genuineness of the instrument.

The question was one of an alleged later testament, which, if also proved genuine, would have the effect to set aside Woolet's will by a transversion of its terms.

By it the estate was bestowed on the younger son, and the £1,000 given to his brother.

The strange transfer was, however, coupled with the condition also strange. It appeared by the citing of the second will, that the younger brother was abroad when it was made; not only abroad, but supposed to be dead.

A doubt of his death must have been in the testator's mind, leading him to insert the condition, which was to the effect, that in the event of his return he was to enter upon quiet possession of the property, all of it excepting the aforesaid legacy of £1,000.

He had returned, at least so alleged the plaintiff, who claimed to be Henry Harding, the legatee of the second will.

But he was not admitted into "quiet possession," according to the words of the will.

On the contrary, the case was going to be contested with all the legal strength, and cunning too, that on both sides could be brought to bear upon it.

On the part of the defence there was no attempt to disprove the genuineness of the second will. It had been made by a lawyer of the highest respectability, who was ready to prove it.

The point turned upon a question of identity, the defendant denying that the plaintiff was his half-brother, or in any way entitled to relationship.

There was no proof that Henry Harding was dead, only the presumption, and to strengthen this the defendant's counsel—impudently, as it afterwards proved—put in certain letters written by the plaintiff, that is by Henry Harding, showing that he had been captive to a band of Italian brigands, who threatened to take his life unless a certain ransom was paid for him.

It was proved that this ransom was *not* paid. That it had been sent, but, as the defence alleged, too late.

The plaintiff's own witnesses were compelled to testify to this.

The presumption therefore was that the bandits, speaking through their chief Corvino, had carried out their threat.

This was the impression produced upon "twelve men good and true," by an eloquent speech made by an eminent counsel to whom Mr. Woolet had committed the briefs for the defence.

On the plaintiff's side, a story had been told that appeared altogether incredible.

It was preposterous to suppose—so thought twelve English tradesmen—that the son of an English gentleman, one of wealth and standing, should voluntarily take to the poor profession of painting pictures, and afterward exile himself to such a country as South America, there to stay, forgetting his fine chances at home, till the merest accident gave him cause to remember them.

They could have believed in such self-banishment in one of their own sons, but the son of a general, or county squire, the owner of a large landed estate—the thing was not to be credited.

They could give credence to the brigand part of the tale, though that was a little queer to them.

But the story of the banishment—the plaintiff's counsel might tell that to the Marines.

So stood the case after several days spent in the examination and cross-questioning of witnesses, and the trial approached its termination.

All the testimony which the plaintiff's counsel could produce was not sufficient to establish an identity. It could not convince a British jury that the sun-embrowned and bearded young man, set forth as the claimant of Beechwood Park, was the son of its former proprietor, while the pale silent gentleman who now held possession of it undoubtedly was.

"Possession" has been said to be nine points of the law. Coupled with wealth it is certainly so in the eyes of a jury of British tradesmen.

The plaintiff's case appeared hopeless. Notwithstanding all that is known to the reader, it trembled on the edge of being decreed an attempt at usurpation—he himself declared an attempted defrauder.

The trial had reached its course, and would soon come to an end.

But before the end came the plaintiff's counsel begged leave to call a witness, who had already stood upon the stand, but on the side of the defendant. Then he had been a witness against his will to give testimony that seemed favourable to the plaintiff's opponent.

The witness was **Mr. Lawson**, of the firm of **Lawson &** Son, solicitors, of Lincoln's Inn. It was the senior **partner, old Lawson himself, who was called.**

As he took his stand in the box, there was a twinkle in the old lawyer's eye that, although something comical, seemed to have mischief in it. The "twelve good men and true" could not understand what it meant, though they came to comprehend it before his counsel had done with him.

"You say General Harding received another letter from Italy," questioned the latter, after Lawson, senior, had kissed the book, and been put through the usual preliminaries of examination.

"I do."

"I don't mean either of those already submitted to the jury. The letter I refer to is one written, not by his son, but by the bandit chief, Corvino. Did General Harding receive such a letter?"

"He did."

"You can prove that?"

"I can prove it by his having told me he did, and placed it in my hands for safe keeping."

"When did this occur?"

"Shortly before the General's death. In fact, on the same day he made the will."

"Which will?"

"The one under which the plaintiff claims."

"You mean that was the date when he placed the letter in your hands?"

"Yes."

"Can you tell when the General received it?"

"I can. The postmark will show that, as also whence it came."

"Can you produce this letter?"

"It is here."

The witness took an epistle out of his pocket, and handed it to the questioning counsel, who in turn passed it up to the judge.

It was a dingy-looking document blotched over with postmarks stained by travel, and a good deal embrowned by being kept several years in the atmosphere of a London law office.

"Your honour," said the plaintiff's counsel, "I have to request that the letter be read to the gentlemen of the jury."

"Certainly, let it be read," was the response of his honour.

It was read, and proved to be the letter of Corvino, addressed to the father of his captive, conveying a terrible threat, and a still more terrible inclosure.

The reading caused "sensation in the court."

"Mr. Lawson," pursued the same questioner, after the excitement had a little subdued, "may I ask you to state to the jury what you know about the inclosure, spoken of as contained in this letter?"

"I know what General Harding told me of it. He said he received in it a finger, which was that of his son. He recognised it by a scar well known to him. It was the scar of a cut given him by his elder brother when they were boys together out shooting."

"Can you tell what became of that finger?"

"I can: it is here. General Harding placed it in my hands along with the letter that had inclosed it."

The witness here handed over the finger spoken of.

It was a ghastly conjunction to his testimony, and produced a tremendous sensation in court, which continued long after Mr. Lawson had been noticed to leave the witness-box and returned to his seat.

"Your honour," said the plaintiff's counsel, "we have one more witness to call, and then we shall be done. I want to examine Mr. Henry Harding."

"The gentleman who so calls himself," interposed one of the barristers who had been briefed by Mr. Woolet.

"And who will so prove himself," confidently retorted the plaintiff's counsel.

By consent of the judge the plaintiff was put upon the stand, and became, emphatically, "the cynosure of every eye" in the crowded court.

He was elegantly, though not foppishly, dressed, and wore upon his hands a pair of stout dogskin gloves.

"May I ask you, sir," said his counsel, "to draw off your glove, I mean the left-hand one?"

The request was complied with; the witness making no other answer.

"Now, sir, have the goodness to hold up your hand, so that the jury may see it."

The hand was stretched forth. It wanted the little finger.

Increased sensation in the court.

"Your honour, and gentlemen of the jury, you perceive there is a finger missing. It is here."

As the counsel said this he stepped towards the witness-box, still holding the strange object in his hand. Then gently raising the hand of his client, he placed the missing finger in juxtaposition with the stump, from which it had long ago been so cruelly severed.

There could be no doubt about the correspondence. The white cartilaginous seam that indicated the scar, starting upon the back of the hand and running longitudinally, was continued to the tip of the finger. Even a bribed jury would have given in to its belonging to the hand.

The sensation in court had now come to its climax.

And so had the trial to its end.

The counsel for the defendant threw up his brief, and stepped hastily out of the room, his attorney sneaking shortly after him.

The jury did not remain longer in deliberation.

The case of Harding *v.* Harding was, by an unanimous verdict, decided in plaintiff's favour, defendant to pay costs in the suit.

CHAPTER LXVII.

WHAT BECAME OF THEM

Six months after the trial I received an invitation to spend a week at Beechwood Park, and take a share in its shooting.

Start not, readers, my host was not Nigel Harding, nor my hostess his wife, née Belle Mainwaring.

The new master and mistress of the mansion were both better people, and both old acquaintances, whom I had encountered in the *campo* of the Pàrana.

They were Henry Harding and his fair Italian *sposa*, now fully installed in their estate.

I was not the only guest they were entertaining. The house was full of company, among whom were the *ci-devant* Sindico of Val-di-Orno, Luigi Torriani and his beautiful bride from the banks of the Pàrana.

If Henry Harding had lost one of his fingers, he had recovered his old friends and added a host of others, while Lucetta was surrounded by hers.

In the mansion of Beechwood Park there was as much cheer, and perhaps more contentment, than when the un-amiable Nigel, and his not less unamiable wife, had the ordering of its entertainments.

I never met either of them again, nor were they ever seen in that neighbourhood. But I have heard of them; and their life since then, though dark compared with the splendour that had for a time surrounded it, has not been one to be deemed unendurable.

The generous Henry did not prove resentful for the wrong his half-brother had done him.

Though of different mothers they were sons of the same father, and for that father's sake he kept himself free from all thoughts of revenge. Not only this, but he acted towards Nigel with a noble generosity. To the thousand pounds left in the deceased's will he added nine thousand, giving Nigel enough to keep him and his wife from want, even in England.

But England was no longer a land to Nigel's liking. No more did it suit the taste of Belle Mainwaring, no more that of Belle Mainwaring's melancholy mother, who had ignally failed in her scheme.

India was the country for them, and to India they went. Nigel to become a resident magistrate, and perhaps deal out injustice to the talookdars—his wife, perhaps, to distribute bewitching smiles to subalterns, captains, and colonels, while her mother found solace in "tiffin" and scandal.

Of most of the other characters who have been companions in our tale I am able to say something of later record.

Mr. Woolet is still pettifogging, still swindling his poor *clientelle*, sufficient to keep a carriage at their expense, and a clerk to play spy on them, but not enough to tempt employment from the rich. Of these General Harding was his first client, Nigel the next.

Doggy Dick in due time gave up being a bandit, not from any repentance, but because the life was to him a hard one. He had found brigandsge in Italy not quite so safe, not even so pleasant, as poaching in England.

He was satisfied enough to return to this practice, now and then varying it with a job of burglary or garroting.

The consequence was, that about a year after his return he got his own neck into a noose tight as ever he had turned for one of his victims. It was a halter he had earned by the deed of blood done before going abroad.

From the contemplation of such a dark character it is pleasant to turn to those of lighter shade.

Thomasso, the wronged, misguided Thomasso, is no more either wronged or misguided. As head groom at Beechwood he may be seen any day about the yard or the stables of that splendid establishment, faithful as ever to him he rescued from captivity, and her he was instrumental in saving from dishonour.

To him is the writer of this tale indebted for a knowledge of much of the brigand life therein depicted.

Through the influence of his new client, the squire of Beechwood Park, Lawson, *père*, has succeeded in obtaining a seat in Parliament, and Lawson, *fils*, expects some day to trend into the property of his father.

A still more agreeable task to record, the after fate of those who have more agreeably interested us, especially since the record is one of prosperity.

It is so in the case of all: Luigi Torriani, his pretty wife, and his noble father.

The three, after a prolonged sojourn among the Chiltern Hills, returned once more to their home upon the Pàrana—their home not only by adoption but choice.

They are still residing, the *ci-devant* Sindico playing patriarch on his vast *estancia*, his son, part planter, part painter, and his daughter-in-law keeping house for both.

It is not improbable that some day his son-in-law and daughter may join them there, for more than once has Henry Harding been heard to say—Lucetta repeating it—that he was never so happy as in his South American home.

And this, too, in the middle of wealth, power, and splendour.

To the true heart there is no wealth to compare with contentment, no power so enjoyable as that of free physical strength, no splendour of European country, when compared to the savage charms of an American primeval scene, be it forest, prairie, or pampa.

There lies the future of Freedom.

THE END.

Ba.—162—12-85—*P*.84.